The Reverse Healer Case Files

HIYODORI

Copyright © 2023 Hiyodori

For permissions contact: hiyodori.publishing@gmail.com

Cover art by Tithi Luadthong / Shutterstock.com

Contents

Part Three: Vorpal Rabies

Part Four: Healer Versus Healer

PART ONE

The Vigilante

1

I WAS WALKING HOME from the corner store when I saw a mage start to go berserk.

It was February, still chilly enough to wear gloves out. I had an eight-pack of toilet paper dangling from my right hand and a small brown paper sack of roasted sweet potatoes in my left. In less than five minutes from now, those poor sweet potatoes would meet a cruel fate. Alas—they were supposed to have been my lunch.

Lately I'd stopped wearing my scarlet parole thread on my wrist. I wrapped it around an ankle instead, tucked discreetly under my sock. It still did its job of magically restricting my movements. I could only wander freely in Osmanthus City and a few other select locations. But at least this way I ran less risk of advertising my ex-con status to total strangers.

No one in the convenience store knew that I'd gotten convicted for treason against Osmanthus.

Or that I'd pounced on a once-in-a-lifetime chance for parole after serving only seven years of my original sentence.

Who could've guessed that one day I'd find myself sheepishly grateful to be living in such a censor-happy country? My past self would've been horrified, that's for sure. No such thing as freedom of the press in Osmanthus. Which was probably part of why no one in my neighborhood had any idea who I really was. All they saw was a diminutive woman in her thirties with boyish taste in clothes and curious white hair.

So that was me, Asa Clematis. Your lovely heroine. There I went, swinging my bale of toilet paper as I sauntered down the brown brick path. I thought of nothing except getting back to my apartment and shoving my face into those sweet potatoes.

There were only three of us on this segment of sidewalk, which ran past a few sets of six-story apartments (all much ritzier than mine). Up far ahead: a woman pushing a stroller. From behind there was no way to tell whether it contained children or tiny dogs. Shambling along right in front of me: a man in dark coveralls with thinning hair.

Magic perception is a type of sense. You can try to block it—like closing your eyes to stop seeing, or covering your ears to stop hearing, or pinching your nose to stop smelling. But unless you make that extra effort in advance, you'll observe magic constantly, just as part of navigating your way around the world.

Of course, sensitivity varies hugely from person to person. I happen to be very, very perceptive.

Which was how, without devoting much conscious attention to it, I noticed that the man with the thinning hair was a mage.

He almost certainly didn't make a living as one, though. Simply being able to wield a couple of magic skills doesn't guarantee you a career in magic. Plenty of mages end up as salespeople or accountants or landscapers.

Anyway, this older man could at most use one lonely skill. I saw only a single magic branch unfurling from the magical core in his torso, a radiant lump nestled right by the small of his back.

Well, Class 1-1 mages were nothing unusual. I started to pass him.

My foot refused to lift off the sidewalk. My arms flailed. My bag of sweet potatoes went flying. I almost fell splat on my face. The stack of toilet paper hit the ground first—a terrible substitute for a walker, but at least it helped me catch my balance.

The entire time, the soles of my boots stayed glued in place.

Magic shimmered like an oily puddle on the ground below me. It trickled feebly from the mage, blood from an old wound. He regarded me with something akin to confusion.

He wasn't trapping me here on purpose, I realized.

He had no idea what he was doing.

The solitary thread of magic that branched from his core grew more tangled as I watched—curling in on itself, knotting painfully.

It only took milliseconds, less than the space of a breath. It felt like a sped-up recording of flowers blooming, worms writhing, compost decomposing. That's how unnaturally fast the tangling of his magic seemed to me. Faster than I'd ever seen it happen in real life, and without any particular provocation.

When I looked at that haggard face again, there was a deep red sheen to his eyes.

My brain went into overdrive. My heart seemed to slow as the tangling of his magic accelerated. I stopped seeing my sweet potatoes lying abandoned on the sidewalk, stopped hearing the occasional whoosh of people on skimmers gliding down the higher-speed street off to our right.

All I saw was the distance between the mage and the woman with the stroller. Far too short. He could kill her from here on a whim, just as easily as he might kill me. How could she be so incredibly slow?

No, that wasn't fair. Hardly any time had passed since I'd found myself frozen in place.

The man's face shifted, relaxed.

Not every berserk mage immediately resorts to violence, I rationalized. The nearest Mage Police box was on the other side of the street. Maybe I could just, you know, convince him to let me take a few steps away from the puddle of magic locking me in place.

I had no obligation to try to neutralize him. And it's not like anyone would pay me for it even if I succeeded. Let the professionals take care of it.

The tasteful stone wall around the apartment behind the mage was beginning to subtly bubble and melt. It stank like burnt sugar. Meanwhile, the back of my mouth had gone unbearably dry. I couldn't remember how to force it to wet itself, how to swallow.

When mages go berserk, all kinds of wild magic phenomena start to swirl around them. But that alone isn't what makes berserk mages so dangerous.

Clem? said a low voice in my head.

Wist. Of course she would notice. I'd been too busy standing stuck here to the brick sidewalk like a fly on flypaper. I hadn't devoted so much as a speck of effort to controlling—to concealing—my internal reaction.

Again: *Clem?*

Not now, I thought back at her, albeit more in a rush of pure intention than actual words. *Nothing to worry about.*

I could handle this on my own. As long as I didn't have to carry on an inner conversation at the same time that I dealt with the red-eyed mage right in front of me. I gave Wist another quick mental shove, one firm enough to keep her from immediately rounding back with follow-up questions.

The male mage hit me with a smile. It looked deeply unfamiliar on his face, as if all the wrinkles had been carved in by different (and far less chipper) expressions.

That look alone was enough to tell me that I'd better abandon the idea of negotiation.

The stone wall collapsed into a tide of caramel. Not quite boiling, but close to it. It surged past our feet like the last remnants of a wave sloshing up a beach. I was very glad to be wearing thick-soled boots.

The mage's smile seemed clenched somehow, as if he'd forgotten how to pry it off his mouth. He reached for me.

I thought I heard Wist trying to say something, far in the back of my head. I blocked her out. Sorry, Wist. Gotta focus.

If you're a healer like me, possessing neither the ability to use magic nor any sort of defense against it, the best way to deal with a berserk mage is to run as far and fast as you can.

But if that's not possible—if neutralizing them is the only option left—you can't afford to fail. You can't afford to falter. You just have to throw yourself in there, like jumping off a cliff into the sea, and hope for the best.

To neutralize a powerful mage, I'd need to get closer to the magic core at the small of their back. If I were a weaker healer, I'd need to take off my gloves first, too. Skin-to-skin contact always makes healing work easier.

But this man was the lowest possible class of mage that can actually use any sort of magic. And I, as you ought to know, am an extremely capable healer.

The moment the mage reached for me, I grabbed his hand. I'd kept my gloves on. But I could still touch the thread of magic running like an artery through his arm.

I gave his magic a sharp twist. The motion snaked through the wild tangles of his lone magic branch, snaked all the way down to his core. He started to sag as if fainting. Oh, damn.

My feet came free. I fought to heave him further down the sidewalk, outside the range of the seething mass of stone-wall-turned-sugar. For some reason it was extraordinarily difficult. Even though he wasn't completely dead weight, and even though I could move now.

I heard screaming. Presumably the woman with the baby stroller. The stench of burnt rubber mingled with the stench of cooked sugar. My shoes weren't that hardy, after all. And who knew about his?

But in the end, between his thick coveralls and my clumsy efforts, the mage was most likely spared from getting more than a few second-degree burns. Could've been worse.

I sat down hard on the sidewalk once we'd reached relative safety. Eyes shut, the mage slumped against an undamaged section of the decorative stone wall. A few feet away, butterscotch-colored gel oozed over the curb and into the gutter.

Finally I realized why it had been such a struggle to haul him over here. My right arm—the one I'd touched him with, the one I'd stretched out to neutralize him—had bones protruding. In about three or four different places.

His magic had struck my arm with some kind of shattering torque—even as I gripped him with my gloved hand, even as I focused my entire being on neutralizing him out of berserker mode.

Funnily enough, I felt nothing until I had a moment to actually look at it. Even more so than pain, the first thing that struck me was an overwhelming urge to vomit. The second thing that struck me was an overwhelming urge to call out to Wist.

But I wasn't dying. I wasn't even that bad off. I'd been half-prepared for him to stick his hand straight through my torso.

There's no telling what a berserk mage will do, but it quite frequently involves blood, guts, and murder. I needed someone to fix my arm, yes, but that didn't mean I needed Wist.

I kept telling myself that as the magical melted sugar simmering on the sidewalk spread thinner and wider, inching ever closer and closer. I kept telling myself that as the MPs started to arrive, and I see-sawed between violent highs of pain and equally violent highs of nausea. I kept telling myself that when one of them found the red parole thread on my ankle.

I wasn't exactly in peak form, mentally or physically. It took me longer than it should have to understand that I was most definitely getting arrested.

I realized something else in the same moment, too: at this point there was no way to stop Wist from intervening. In fact, I'd better hope she intervened if I didn't want to spend the next few days in custody. I could only pray they patched my arm up before Wist arrived on the scene. I really didn't want to know how she'd react to seeing bones sticking out of me.

2

THE INTERROGATION ROOM rather resembled the inside of a tin can. No windows. No corners. Dull metallic walls undulating with mysterious ridges. A mode of interior design that would be quite intimidating to those seeing it for the first time.

I was pretty sure I'd never been to this particular room before. But I was very familiar with the style. Chairs sprouted seamlessly out of the floor like metal shrubbery—rooted implacably in place, though no visible bolts held them down.

Before you get confused, I should clarify that I'm a healer of magic. I can cure mages' metaphysical aches and pains. As a general rule, the more magic you have, the more it hurts. That's where we healers come in.

Unfortunately, this meant that despite being a so-called healer, I couldn't do a thing to repair my own broken bones. That'd be a job for a medical doctor, or perhaps for a mage with a relevant skill set.

To their credit, the Mage Police used a variant of ultra-basic First Aid magic on my arm before they started questioning me. It still felt far from normal, but I could bend it a little upon request. I declined their offer of painkillers.

One of the MPs asked me to state my name.

"You just took my ID," I said.

They asked me to please just state my name. Please. For the record.

"How about you read it off to me," I suggested. "You can read, can't you?"

This continued for a while. I'll spare you the details.

Those who know me might beg to disagree, but I swear I don't have a problem with authority per se.

Do I have any love for the mageocracy that rules over our fair nation of Osmanthus? Well, no. Do I have a permanent grudge against the supreme Board of Magi? Well, yes. Do I find myself overcome with the irresistible urge to act obnoxious when in the custody of mages?

I'd say yes, but that's hardly the only time I excel at irritating anyone and everyone in earshot.

Don't forget, I spent seven years in a government prison. In a wretched sort of way, this interrogation room felt like home. It was reminiscent of visiting my parents' house in my late teens and early twenties, shortly after I'd moved out for good. The old familiarity of the environment made me lapse into a kind of childish rebellion.

Partway through the interrogation, it honestly began to seem more as if I were torturing them than anything else.

It's not that I never answered their questions. But I figured I'd better answer strictly as my cover identity, the boring one Public Security had given me after I won parole and moved back to the city.

I began taking mental bets on what would happen first: the MPs discovering who I really was—a notorious traitor—or Wist barging in to interrupt.

The Mage Police fell under the umbrella of Public Security, which fell under the Ministry of Justice, which reported to the Board of Magi. They'd have to inquire pretty high up in PubSec to reach someone who knew how I'd ended up in witness protection.

I bet myself a sack of sweet potatoes that Wist would get here first. And guess who won?

About an hour into the interrogation, I had my feet up on the table. The MPs told me to take my feet down.

Let me stand up then, I said. Gotta keep the blood flowing.

They told me no. I put my feet back up. I could just about taste the sweet strain of them fighting not to leap across the table and strangle me. Oh, I could do this all day.

A cold knock sounded through the curved metal wall. I think my interrogators were exceedingly relieved to have received the gift of a distraction. One of them sprang up to answer, though there was no visible door. He touched an earring and muttered to himself.

More muttering. A caught breath, close to a gasp.

Brief silence.

Stifled assent.

The tin-can wall flickered. Its shape mutated. Now it cut itself open, unveiling a tall archway taut with magic.

Wist walked through, followed by another handful of stressed-looking MPs. The wall soon blinked shut behind them.

Appearance-wise, the MPs were all very professional. Both those questioning me, and those escorting Wist. They wore smart black uniforms with dark red and purple accents, colors meant to invoke the Osmanthian flag. They knew how to stand to attention. They knew how to submit to a hierarchy.

And their body language practically quivered with awareness of exactly who Wist was, and exactly where she landed in the hierarchy of mages. Despite the fact that, in typical fashion, she'd drifted in wearing a slouchy hoodie and track shorts over ragged leggings.

I nearly took my feet off the table when Wist looked at me. I didn't, of course. I fisted my hands in my jacket pockets and gave her a most genial smile.

There was nothing particularly intimidating about her expression. A bit blanker than usual, perhaps. Nothing special. But I could detect an unsettling pressure deep in my belly.

"Took you long enough," I said.

Wist ignored me. She ducked her head at the gaggle of MPs. The ones questioning me had leapt out of their chairs as if they couldn't possibly remain seated in the presence of such glory.

Wist was taller than most of them, male and female alike. She shifted from foot to foot as they gawked at her. To be fair, most of them had probably never seen her in person before.

I refused to call her anything other than *Wist*. But her full name was Wisteria Shien. She was a Kraken-class mage—the only one alive today. The single most powerful mage in the world. The most powerful mage to be born in thousands of years.

She had chin-length black hair and a dark dead-eyed stare that would be absolutely paralyzing if you didn't know her well enough to realize it was simply her default expression.

"I'm sorry for the trouble," she said to the MPs. She always sounded like she'd just rolled out of bed.

I, for one, knew she meant it as an apology for any hassle I'd caused them. I'm not sure they took it that way. They nearly fell over each other as they rushed to assure her it was really no problem, no problem at all. Anything for the Kraken.

Wist glanced back at me as she mumbled something or other to calm them.

"Your arm," she said.

Damn. I hadn't thought it would be so noticeable.

"Could be worse," I answered. "They fixed it up for me."

I tried to flex my nonexistent bicep at her. I immediately regretted it.

Wist watched me emotionlessly as I cradled my right elbow, cringing. Barbed pain ping-ponged from my wrist to my shoulder and back again, as if to make up for my having felt nothing when the berserking mage first broke my arm.

"Really," I ground out, once I'd recovered myself enough to cough up something resembling coherent speech. "It really could be worse. A few fractured bones? No big deal. At least I didn't lose an eye."

Wist chose to pretend I hadn't spoken. "Cle—Asa is my employee," she told the MPs. "I'm in need of her services."

"Yeah," I said through clenched teeth. I really should have swallowed my pride and taken those painkillers. "Best boss ever."

Wist made the MPs promise to contact her through Public Security if they had any follow-up questions. Then she took me by the elbow— the uninjured one—and ported me right out of there.

That was how we ended up back at the corner store, buying another case of toilet paper and another sack of roasted sweet potatoes. I whined about my arm until Wist offered to carry all the loot for me.

Just to be clear: Wist was not, in fact, my employer.

At various times in my career as a healer, she'd been my best friend, my nemesis, my (almost) partner in crime, my guilt-ridden savior.

And as of about four months ago, we were officially a bonded pair.

The MPs couldn't possibly have known, of course, not even when gawping at the two of us in the same room together. Very few people have magic perception sharp enough to tell if any given individual is bonded.

On top of that, even if you think someone looks bonded, it's all but impossible to definitively pinpoint their exact bondmate without the full cooperation of both parties.

Besides, we were a most improbable match. Whether she liked it or not, Wist stood at the pinnacle of mage society. I, in turn, was a widely reviled troublemaker fresh out on parole. From a distance, my short stature and artificially whitened hair made me look the splitting image of an eighty-six-year-old. Not quite your typical trophy wife.

I say this not to denigrate myself, but rather as a simple statement of fact. Very few people in the world knew that Wist the Kraken was bonded. Even fewer knew the true identity of her bondmate.

We both preferred it that way. Wist for reasons related to safety and privacy. Me for reasons related to dumb pride and my sense of independence.

Nothing else tied us together: neither engagement nor marriage nor an employment contract. Like it or not, mage-healer bonding was for life. After everything we'd been through, I didn't see the point in tangling that up with other—arguably lesser—commitments.

In keeping with my much-prized spirit of independence, I currently lived alone in a cheap toad-colored apartment. Wist had to bend over to keep from smashing her skull on the door frame.

I could've invited myself to live with Wist in her tower. I spent plenty of time there anyway. It had thousands of rooms, no exaggeration. And I knew for a fact that she'd take me.

Still, right now I liked having my own place far too much to give it up. Especially after seven years as a prisoner.

By the time we got away from the MPs and made it back to my apartment, it was right around noon. I offered Wist one of my beautiful red-skinned sweet potatoes. She turned me down. I shrugged and proceeded to devour all three of them, one after another.

"Thanks again for getting me out of there," I said as I packed the sweet potato skins away in my freezer. "I've got a client stopping by soon. You going to stay or go?"

"I'm free the rest of the day," Wist said.

"All right, then. Bum around if you want."

I straightened up and started tidying the kitchen. I had no office, so I needed to host prospective clients right here in the same space where I sliced bagels and ground coffee and hung my laundry to dry.

Wist helped wipe down the range while I flitted around and complained about how long the MPs had kept me.

To be honest, I'd been a little taken aback by the intensity of their questioning. Sure, they could see from my parole thread that I had some kind of criminal record, even if they hadn't realized I was an infamous traitor. But in terms of that random mage on the street suddenly going berserk, I was—above all else—an innocent victim.

If anything, I was a hero. I'd neutralized him before he did irreversible damage to himself or others. The melted stone wall and my splintered arm were nothing compared to what might've happened if he'd been allowed to continue rampaging unchecked.

There was no other way to interpret the situation. I was a healer, incapable of using magic. I certainly couldn't have framed him.

Yes, okay, I had a personal history of very unhealer-like activities. In prison they used to call me the Magebreaker. But the MPs hadn't known I was *that* Magebreaker.

More to the point, I'd never tried deliberately making a mage go berserk. I suppose it might be possible on a technical level. For a prodigy like me, anyhow, if not for your average healer.

Not that other healers would ever dream of attempting such a thing. To them the mere idea would be deviant—blasphemous—unthinkable.

Now, deviant and blasphemous forms of healing are my specialty.

Yet the thought of attempting to push a mage over the edge had simply never occurred to me, either.

Why would it? Berserk mages were uncontrollable, a menace to everyone and everything around them. Unless you were actively suicidal, there would be zero benefit to making a mage snap on purpose.

Nor had the MPs outright accused me of doing so. Their questioning had nevertheless been laden with peculiar implications. It was all very strange.

"Clematis," Wist said.

Oh, no. That was her attempt at a serious voice. Apparently she'd finished all the scrubbing tasks I'd thrown at her.

"What?" I asked. "Need lunch after all?"

"Lunch? I'm not—"

"You'll have to order delivery or something. All I've got left in stock is rice, ketchup, and peanut butter. If you're really hungry, I guess you could try combining them."

One of Wist's magic branches snaked out and coiled around my still-awkward right arm like an invisible rope. Invisible to the naked eye, anyway. I tracked it with my magic perception.

I flinched, expecting it to hurt, but instead the jagged bone-deep discomfort melted away in an instant.

Wist's magic retreated. I experimented with lifting and lowering my right shoulder, stretching and bending my arm in all sorts of different directions.

Only now did tears sting my eyes. Not from pain, but from its abrupt and overwhelming absence.

Wist padded closer, hands in her hoodie pockets.

"I felt you panicking," she said. "That's why I called to you."

"I was *not* panicking!" I snapped. "When have I ever panicked? Go on, name one time. I am the calmest, most collected—"

"I felt you panicking," Wist repeated. "That's the only reason I spoke to you through the bond. Why didn't you answer?"

I seized on this. "Right." I stooped to furiously dust nonexistent crumbs off my one-person kitchen table. "We've discussed this. We can get along just fine without barging into each other's minds like that.

"In fact, I insist on it. You wouldn't be able to project into my head if we weren't bonded. No reason to rely on it just because we are."

"I don't think I'm overprotective."

Wist's tone was drier than usual. Parched, even.

"Good," I shot back. "Don't be."

"I don't keep tabs on you. I have no idea what you do when we're apart. The only times I've ever jabbed you through the bond are when it feels like something genuinely terrible might be happening."

"This time you were mistaken," I said. "I was in perfect control. In fact, I neutralized that mage so damn well that the MPs somehow seemed to suspect me of engineering the entire situation, Broken arm and all. They didn't spare me an ounce of pity."

Wist looked at the top of my head. She looked at the stubby fridge. She looked at the dingy ceiling.

"Would you call for me if you were truly in danger?" she asked. "Before it became too late?"

"I mean, I like being alive," I said.

She hesitated. She wet her lips.

She looked down at my house slippers.

At last she raised her gaze again.

"Don't put me in the position of having to come collect your corpse," Wist said.

An unnameable feeling—a distant relative of guilt—spread through me in the form of a hot sick infectious flush.

I meant what I said. I very much wanted to live. I had no doubt that if I were truly desperate, I'd scream to her mind-to-mind with every word in my vocabulary.

I don't know how to explain my resistance to communicating like that on an everyday basis. All I can say is that it felt much closer than, say, seeing each other without any clothes on.

I'm not a shy or shame-prone person. Most of my acquaintances might go so far as to call me shameless. Even before going on trial and getting convicted of treason, I'd had a certain immunity to people staring at me, whispering things about me, resenting me, disdaining me, wounding me.

Here's why: they could say whatever they wanted about me. They could turn off the heat in my cell to keep me from sleeping. They could disparage me for my mistakes; they had plenty of material to work with.

Yet their words and the cold and the misery could only get so far inside me. I could always retreat deeper, to places nothing outside me could touch. I could watch distantly as the prosecutors cross-examined me, as the guards mocked me, as the families of those I'd hurt wept and cursed me.

Being bonded was different. When Wist spoke to me through the bond, there was nowhere left to run. She was always already in the deepest place possible. I couldn't retreat any further. I couldn't take a breath and project myself far, far away to collect myself. She'd be right there with me.

That's what made it so much worse than being naked. I didn't care who ogled me naked, really. Their eyes could rake me from head to toe, but all they'd see was my surface. They weren't right there with me, next to me, inside me.

I'm trying not to exaggerate here. I just don't know how else to explain it. It wasn't as if bonding let Wist read my mind in detail. At most she'd sense unusual spikes of emotion, and it went both ways. She almost never used the bond to reach out to me; she respected my request to touch it as little as possible.

As a result, I still wasn't used to it. The slightest nudge threw me off.

People weren't supposed to be connected this deeply, I thought. It made me want to claw myself inside-out. It made me want to run and hide balled-up under a table.

Wist's warmth against the raw peeled-open inner parts of me—not my skin, not my surface, not any aspect of my physical body, but *me*—summoned a kind of instinctual terror that I couldn't even begin to articulate.

I'd done it to myself, of course. I was the one who'd agreed to bond with her.

I put a hand on Wist's side. She blinked down at me.

Her sweatshirt was still quite lopsided. She'd been fairly top-heavy since adolescence, but had recently lost her entire left breast to—well, it's a long story.

Point is, with her nigh-infinite number of magic branches, she could've acquired a magic skill that would work to reconstruct it. So far she simply hadn't bothered. Don't think I hadn't noticed a few of the MPs skating puzzled (if respectfully brief) glances over her asymmetrical chest.

At last I figured out what to tell her.

"You know me," I said lightly. "The last thing I want is to be some kind of damsel in distress. On the one hand, you're the ultimate trump card. On the other hand, I don't want to be constantly beckoning you over to solve my problems."

Wist tilted her head. "Since when did you care about inconveniencing anyone?"

I dug my fingers like claws into her ribs. "Right," I said. "How unlike me. I'd better aim for maximum inconvenience."

"That's my girl."

"I'll make you come twist open a jar for me next time you're in the middle of a dinner with heads of state."

"Yes," Wist said, deadpan. "Do it."

We glared at each other. I was clawing her torso with all my might, but failed to eke out so much as a wince. The hoodie gave her too much protection.

I shot my hand up beneath it. Good—just a thin undershirt below. I clawed her in the side again.

A twinge crossed Wist's face. "Is that fun?" she asked.

"You sure seem to like it."

She leaned toward me.

The doorbell rang.

"Oh, what a shame," I said gaily. I sailed off to welcome my would-be client.

My mood was already a thousand times better. You see, Wist almost never betrayed a hint of anything resembling visible irritation. The whole argument—if one could call it that—had been worth it simply for the look in her eyes when I let go of her and danced cheerfully away out of reach. Sorry, Wist! You can't always win. This one goes to Clematis.

3

MOST OF THE WORK I did for the government involved hobbling convicted mages. I manipulated the threads of their magic so as to render them temporarily incapable of using any magical skills whatsoever.

Once I applied a hobble, they'd remain magically helpless for a specific period of days, weeks, months, or years—for the exact length of their sentence, as defined by the Ministry of Justice.

Hobbling, however, was an art unique to yours truly. I'd essentially invented it, and it had nothing to do with typical mage healing labor. The government gleefully took advantage of my ability to help them control magically gifted criminals. But Osmanthus was nonetheless a mageocracy.

Among the various conditions of my parole: I couldn't tell anyone my real identity. The Board of Magi didn't want common folk knowing that they'd released a healer guilty of high treason. Nor could I hint at being the rumored Magebreaker.

Nor could I attempt to teach any other healers how to hobble.

My cover story depicted me as an ordinary citizen healer—one dealing exclusively in the standard, supportive sort of mage healing.

I knew how to act the part. That could very well have been my life if I'd never met Wist. If I'd never overestimated my political savvy. If I'd never gotten hauled away to prison.

Typical mage healing could be split into two categories. The first was general pain treatment and preventative care. Every mage with at least one magic branch needed to visit a healer every so often.

Some saw healers as frequently as they could afford it, unable to tolerate the chronic pain that tormented all magic-users (albeit to varying degrees). Others just followed the bare-minimum mandatory healing schedule dictated by the government.

Even if the pain didn't bother them, mages needed some form of periodic healing to reduce the chances of their magic getting uncontrollably tangled. Eventually the tangling would drive them berserk.

Higher-level mages, however, expected more than pain relief and berserking prevention. This was where the second category of healing came in: services rendered not merely for the sake of staving off disaster, but rather with the objective of amplifying patients' magical output.

Such mages expected higher caliber treatment. They expected healing to set them up for peak performance—to improve metrics like how many seconds it took them to initiate a magic skill.

If they bonded a healer, they expected a far greater boost in power, and they expected their bondmate to be on-call for healing all day and all night. For the rest of their natural lives.

That was the downside of getting noticed as a capable healer. If a high-status mage wanted to bond you, it didn't matter what sort of plans you had for your own life, your own career. There was almost no way to say no.

I say all this to explain that my government contract work as a mage-hobbler—as the so-called Magebreaker—was nothing like what most healers did day-to-day. Bonded or otherwise.

So when I told my parole officer I wanted permission to take on private clients, she had a *lot* of questions.

She already knew I'd expressed little interest in offering regular healing services. She knew how well the government paid me (nothing extravagant, but let's just say that I had zero competition). She knew I liked to live stingily; I'd picked my apartment mainly for its deliciously cheap rent. I couldn't claim to be hurting for money.

"I'm not opposed to healing on principle," I said. "I have to heal Wist, after all. I'd like to take on the strange edge cases. Stuff no one else knows how to deal with."

One of my best friends was a duelist who'd gotten rather famous in the world of magesports. Something about the shape of his magic made him alarmingly vulnerable to going berserk without warning—far more so than the average mage, at any rate.

When I first met him back in prison, I soon spotted the quirk in his magic branches. The unusual risk factor that no other healer had seen or understood well enough to fix it.

There must be other mages out there like my friend, I figured. Those with persistent magical pain that no amount of healing had been able to mitigate. Those whose magic branches were naturally so twisted that they'd resigned themselves to only using a portion of their full potential.

I abhor the mageocracy. But that didn't mean I'd mentally written off every single individual mage out there. I was bonded to one, after all.

The system was the system, and I found it despicable. People were people, and they came in all sorts of flavors. I didn't mind offering healing services if it meant I'd be helping mages who couldn't get meaningful assistance from anyone else.

At last I received permission to start taking private clients. Not long before the berserking scare near my city apartment, actually. Yet the first person who came to see me wasn't any kind of mage.

Wist was still in the kitchen when I opened the front door of my apartment. A mousy woman in a long pleated skirt stood on the other side, clutching her purse in front of her like a shield.

She had ash brown hair. Definitely colored. Her natural hair had probably been almost as black as Wist's. No magic branches curled like veins through her body. No magic core shone deep in her torso.

Several questions came to my lips, but I restrained myself. If anything, the fact that she wasn't a mage automatically made me more interested.

I'd wanted unusual cases, after all. I'd welcome the unexpected.

"Come on in," I said.

She thanked me in a tiny voice as she slipped off dainty heeled boots just inside the entrance. I ushered her to a chair (the only spare seat I had) in the kitchen. Her eyes flicked over the garage-sale amateur art on the walls. She looked straight across the room at Wist but showed no indication of seeing her.

Wist rarely went fully invisible. In public, though, she often used a magic skill that made it borderline impossible for anyone but me to consciously notice her.

She'd used it in the convenience store earlier today, for instance. Now she leaned against the wall on the other side of the kitchen, arms folded. My visitor seemed to have no idea she was there.

"What would you like to drink?" I asked. "I've got coffee, tea, spica, and hard liquor. Oh, and orange juice."

Wist shook her head. She must've finished the last of it.

"Sorry," I amended. "Never mind about the orange juice."

"Tea, please," said my guest.

"Coming right up."

I don't think I'd ever met someone with such a picture-perfect librarian aesthetic. She had the look down from head to toe. Then again, we'd all worn the same clothes in prison, and I'd only been free for a few months now. I was hardly in a position to criticize anyone's choice of fashion.

I introduced myself with the false name PubSec had bestowed on me when I first moved here. Asa Lantana. *Asa* was a common enough family name that they'd said I could keep it. Certainly made it easier for me to remember.

The woman told me I could call her Pine.

"Mori referred you," I said. I offered her sugar and milk to go with her black tea. She declined. "Sounds like he knows you from the National Healing Research Institute."

She had been blowing softly at the steaming surface of her tea. Now she paused to nod.

"Are you a researcher? Some kind of academic?"

"I'm an administrative assistant," said the woman called Pine. Fog from the tea clouded her glasses. "I don't do any healing work—I'm a subliminal."

Ah. Subliminal mages were easy for me to distinguish at a glance, due to their complete lack of magic branches. Subliminal healers were a bit harder to tell apart without actually testing them.

Everyone in the world was either a healer or a mage, but only a minority had enough raw talent to actually use even the tiniest bit of magic, or do even the most basic form of mage healing. All others—in other words, the vast majority of the population—were subliminals.

If you couldn't use magic or heal mages, did it really matter whether some old fart diagnosed you as a subliminal mage or a subliminal healer?

Oddly enough, it did. At least to some people. I'd seen subliminal mages—who themselves would never be considered for government positions of any power—argue passionately about the importance of preserving the mageocracy.

So here I was with a subliminal healer in my apartment-slash-office. I couldn't begin to guess why she'd come.

Pine looked me in the eye. There was a peaky tightness to her face. I'd thought she was around the same age as me, but she might be quite a bit older. Or just very tired.

"Mori said I could trust you to—to keep patient confidentiality."

"I'm not sure if patient is the right word here," I said. "Considering that you've got no magic for me to heal. But you can trust me not to snitch."

She had her bag perched on her lap. She gripped it shut as if she were afraid I'd try to pickpocket her.

"I had a friend," she said. "A healer."

"A subliminal?"

"No. A true healer. Worked at NHRI. That's why I originally started working there, too." She stopped to swallow. "Five years ago, he bonded a mage. She made him quit his job."

I had a friend.

The key word there was *had*. I had a feeling I already knew how this ended. I made a small noise to show her I was still listening.

"He died last summer. His mage bonded a new healer less than a week later."

"A stronger healer?" I asked.

"Stronger and younger."

"Did they rule the death an accident?"

"Suicide."

The apartment felt very quiet.

I watched Pine twist futilely at the beige handles of her purse. "What was your friend's name?"

Not that it made a difference. I just wanted to hear it.

"Luka."

"What about the mage? His bondmate?"

At first she didn't answer. I started to repeat myself, thinking maybe she'd been too lost in memory to hear me.

She pressed her lips inward as if she were trying to eat them. Her fingers stopped fidgeting with her handbag.

She looked up.

"Shien Miyu," she said.

For a single paranoid instant, I was positive that she—this subliminal healer—had somehow seen through Wist's magic. That she knew I had a Shien right here in the room with us, listening to every word she said.

Wisteria Shien. Adopted, with her family name coming last rather than first. Yet undeniably a member of the Shien clan. A sister to the woman named Shien Miyu.

Wist, too, looked a little rigid. But Pine's eyes still passed right over her. No acknowledgment. No reaction.

"You think Shien Miyu killed your friend," I said.

Pine didn't answer.

"You think she killed him so she could turn around and bond a stronger healer."

Bonding was for life. Or at least until one of the bondmates died. Then that supposedly lifelong bond would disappear as if it had never existed.

I sighed. I sat up. I put my hands on the table.

"I'll be straight with you," I told Pine. "You're probably right. I'd bet money on it. Maybe not a lot of money—but sure, I'd put some down. I'm guessing you didn't come to me just to hear that."

"I want proof," she said. Now she stared straight down into the mouth of her bag.

"Mori did warn you that I'm not a private detective or anything, right?"

"He said you were interested in difficult cases."

That almost surprised a laugh out of me. I had to disguise it with a fake-sounding coughing fit.

"Listen." I leaned forward. "Hypothetically, let's say I turn out to be the best PI there ever was. Let's say I find your proof. Great. Good for me.

"Still, proof isn't really all you want, is it? You want justice. But I don't want to get your hopes up. Nothing will come of it. The Shiens have too much influence. No public prosecutor would take up the case."

I felt a spike of annoyance at Mori for sending her here. He was in his early twenties and could be a tad idealistic. All the same, he should've known better.

I understood exactly why he'd referred her, of course. Mori, unlike me, officially worked part-time for the Kraken. For Wist. He knew she was a Shien. He knew Shien Miyu was her sister. He knew Wist and I were bonded.

He knew if we used Wist's connections, we could easily find a way to search the Shien clan manor. Or probe into Shien Miyu's activities. Or do whatever else it was he imagined us doing.

Sure, if Wist threw her weight around, the government might take up the case. The real problem was that even Wist couldn't rewrite Osmanthian law at her whim. And the law was very clear about the rights of bonded healers: they had virtually none.

It didn't matter if Shien Miyu had killed her healer in cold blood, right in front of twenty reliable witnesses. Shien money could buy a good lawyer, and a good lawyer could stretch the truth to concoct a story about healer dereliction of duty.

At most, Miyu might get slapped with a few hefty fines. Fines that would be hefty to me and to Pine, at any rate—but nothing to a wealthy mage clan like the Shiens.

"I know it won't go anywhere," Pine said. There was a tension to her voice, as if she had to fight to keep it from trembling. "I know she'll never undergo any real punishment. Does that mean—does that mean no one should even try?"

I didn't know what to tell her.

For some reason, apropos of nothing, I kept thinking of the mage from this morning.

He was no Shien, that's for sure. He probably didn't have much money to his name. And for whatever reason, he probably hadn't been receiving adequate healing. Why else would he snap like that?

Now he was probably languishing in a jail cell, waiting to be sentenced for his sudden loss of control. That was just a guess, though. None of the MPs had told me what they did with him afterward. None of them had mentioned his name.

"I can try to find out what happened to your friend," I said to Pine. "I can't promise you any more than that."

She claimed she understood. I told her she didn't have to pay me anything unless I delivered actual results.

I hope I didn't treat her too rudely as I saw her off to the door. My head was in a completely different space now, batting around a surge of malformed ideas.

I recalled the MPs demanding that I explain to them what I'd done to the berserking mage. "Nothing," I'd retorted, utterly indignant. "I neutralized him. And I did a damn good job of it. Saved you lot a whole bunch of work. You should be thanking me!"

But what if—

"Want me to take you there?" said Wist.

I turned, startled. I hadn't even registered the sound of the door clicking shut behind Pine, much less the sound of Wist following us over to the entrance.

"Where?" I asked. Just to be sure.

"The Shien family home."

"When was the last time you even spoke to any of them?"

Wist glanced at a shady corner of the ceiling, up above a decidedly amateur canvas painting of giraffes kissing. "A few years?" She didn't sound terribly certain.

"Think they'll even let you in?"

"I'm the Kraken," she said.

That absolute confidence made me want to kick her in the shin.

I had to admit Wist was right, though. If there was one thing these stuck-up old mage clans respected, it was raw magical power. It didn't matter how long Wist had been estranged from them. They'd probably fling the mansion gates open and throw a massive welcome-home banquet. If she let them.

"Yeah, they'll let you in, all right," I conceded. "But what about me?"

"I'll refuse to visit without you."

Oh, boy. A visit to the Shien clan with Wist. It'd be just like old times. When we were teenagers, her whole adoptive family had hated my guts (and made no secret of it). I could only imagine what they'd think of me now.

4

As EXPECTED, Wist had little difficulty wrangling an appointment at the Shien manor. The difficult part would be deciding what to do about me.

Granted, I'd only ever visited her family once, during a school break over sixteen years ago. But I'd stayed with them for almost two full weeks. I met quite a few members of the clan in person.

Obviously now I looked older. For instance, when I was a teenager my hair had been almost pure black, minus a single silver streak. More white chunks started appearing in prison. After getting parole, I turned my whole head pure white (as a half-assed form of disguise).

Still, when faced with the Shiens, I didn't think I could successfully pass as anyone other than myself. Unless I got some last-minute plastic surgery or asked Wist to use magic to fully disguise me.

Then again, both my true identity and the fact that Wist and I had bonded were classified information. Technically speaking, anyway.

The main idea behind hiding our bond was to keep Wist's enemies from targeting me. Which made it the perfect pretext for organizing a very hush-hush visit to the manor.

Many Shien family members had some form of security clearance, so that alone wouldn't thin the crowds very much. Wist took great pains to arrange for us to come at a time when almost no one aside from Shien Miyu and the head of the clan—their grandmother—would be there.

Plus all the NDA-bound household staff, naturally. No point in chasing the servants away. For one thing, I wanted to pick their brains about Luka. Besides, the Shiens would be utterly helpless without them. Probably wouldn't even know how to replace rolls of toilet paper in the powder room.

This would be Wist's first contact with her adoptive family in years. As self-styled high-class people, I suppose they liked to pretend they understood the need for subtlety and discretion. I could imagine them pacing and muttering to each other as they prepared for our visit, working out intricate strategies with the single-minded goal of convincing Wist to return to the fold.

All in all, it was almost March by the time we found ourselves standing outside the manor gates.

Wist, the prodigal daughter, wore a full suit. Vest, tie, and all. She'd compressed her right breast quite a bit, presumably for a smoother silhouette.

It had definitely been well over a decade since I'd seen her in anything but baggy sweatshirts. Part of that was because I hadn't seen her, period, during the seven years I'd spent in prison.

She had her hair slicked back, revealing black stud earrings. An old gift from Grandmother Shien, apparently. I'd gotten dressed up, too, in my own way, with brisk suspenders and a new white blouse. I cradled a garish bouquet in both arms.

It was mid-afternoon. One of those days where the entire sky was boarded up with thick pale clouds. Somehow it still felt uncomfortably bright out.

Wist looked askance at me. "Yeah, yeah, all ready," I said.

There was no one manning the tall black gate. Wist put an arm around my waist and touched one of the many iron leaves of ivy that wound through the forbidding vertical bars. I felt a slight tugging at my spine, the horizontal version of dropping in an elevator.

Then we were inside the mansion proper, having magically skipped past acres of gardens and woodland.

The first thing I saw was a huge water sculpture undulating in the entrance hallway. It floated midair, uncontained and unsupported, clear torrents of liquid winding in and out of each other like a vast tangle of chains.

The jets of water came from nowhere and went nowhere. They curved ever inward, forming infinite pretzel shapes, feeding each other without splashing a single stray drop down on those of us wandering below.

I'd never really understood magical art. It struck me as pretty but frivolous, a complete waste of talent. I'm sure the Shiens thought I had hopelessly plebeian tastes.

As promised, they'd practically cleared the mansion in anticipation of us. I glimpsed servants, but only two actual family members appeared to be present. Wist's grandmother, head of the clan. And Shien Miyu, the oldest of Wist's adoptive sisters. There'd have been no point in coming if Miyu wasn't going to be there.

Wist's grandmother was intimidating, but in some ways easy enough to deal with. I'd had little direct contact with her in the past. That said, I'm sure Wist's adoptive parents and siblings (all six of them) had previously shared plenty of complaints about my lack of manners, my audacity in glomming onto Wist at the academy, and so on.

Either way, I don't think she quite saw healers as people. Once I presented my bouquet to her, she waited in silence for me to bow and scrape my way out of the drawing room.

Maybe she'd failed to recognize me. Or maybe she knew exactly who I was, but had deemed it beneath her to offer any sign of acknowledgment.

On my way out, I saw attendants hustling over to liberate the bouquet from Grandmother's skinny arms. They arranged the flowers in a crystal vase carved from top to bottom with deep interlacing patterns. The cuts in the vase looked to me like fancy scars.

So far, just as planned. I left the three Shiens together to have their private Shien talks. Presumably Grandmother and Miyu would attempt to persuade Wist to contribute more to—or at least not completely ignore—the prestigious family that had bought and raised her.

Just to be clear, I'm no detective. Sorry to disappoint. And even if I were the best detective in Osmanthus City, there's no way I'd find convenient bits of evidence lying around here half a year after Miyu's healer died. Or got murdered.

I wasn't planning on trying to figure out exactly what had happened. Again, I'm not a detective. But I did have a plan.

The mansion staff were mostly a mix of mages and subliminals. I didn't spot any free-range healers, so to speak. All the adult mages in the family already had bonded healers to take care of their needs.

A bonded mage can only be healed by their bondmate, but bonded healers can still heal anyone they want. Guess this meant that between all their bonded healers, the Shiens had plenty of people available to treat the unbonded children of the clan, as well as any unbonded mages on the payroll.

I wandered the open areas of the mansion, dodging servant mages as I went. I passed chandeliers that shed an endless stream of illusory snowflakes. I passed silent picture windows that transformed each time I turned my back on them, like lonely children putting on a colorful show to try to catch my attention.

It was more luxurious than the Palace of Magi, and as quiet and stifled as a mausoleum.

I'd told Wist to drag out her talks with Grandmother Shien and Miyu for as long as she could. I'd let her know when it was time to move on to the next step.

Eventually I managed to chat up a few of the subliminals on staff. I spoke to a gaggle of groundskeepers taking a rowdy tea break, to an assistant sommelier performing some kind of inventory count in a spooky wine cellar. They were courteous but guarded. They claimed they'd had little interaction with Luka the healer, Pine's departed friend.

One reason I'd asked Wist to schedule this visit well in advance was to give the clan plenty of time to make a big deal of it. By the time we showed up, I wanted every single person on staff to have been warned that we were coming.

You might think this would give their bosses more opportunities to instruct them to stay out of the way and keep their mouths shut. And to watch out for me, a known troublemaker. I'm sure they received plenty of lectures about the importance of facilitating a smooth reconciliation with Wist, the most honorable Kraken.

But there was another dynamic at play, one that might very well supersede any personal loyalty or fear the Shiens inspired in their employees.

Our fair nation of Osmanthus was the most hardcore mageocracy on the continent, and had been that way for centuries.

If there was one thing your average Osmanthian reflexively knew to respect, it was pure magical power.

The Shien household staff worked for one of the haughtiest families in Osmanthus. Every day they would feel the pressure of that hierarchy. Whether or not they bought into it, they would understand that Wist unofficially stood at the top.

It didn't matter that Wist no longer held any government positions, that she'd kept her distance from the Shiens for years now. Wist was irreplaceable. She was the one and only Kraken-class mage in the world.

Finally I padded my way up to a gym on one of the higher floors: my last destination in the building. Glass walls gazed out on a huge field of elaborately sculpted rosebushes.

It was a breathtaking showcase of gardening finesse, but the bushes looked unsettlingly like people. No symmetrical layout here. They strained and grappled, reached out to clutch at each other with powerful limbs, far larger than life. Larger than regular humans, at least.

Looking down on the clashing rosebushes felt very much like looking down on a battlefield, a hellscape of muscular hand-to-hand combat frozen in time.

There was only one other person in the gym: a trainer in the sort of tight, practical athletic gear I'd have loved to see on Wist. Maybe I ought to ask if I could join Wist's workouts.

For now, I focused my magic perception on the trainer. No light from a magic core welled in her torso (although her abs were quite dazzling in their own right). A subliminal, then, or perhaps a very feeble healer—one weak enough to be permitted to make a career out of something other than mage healing.

She seemed to be taking her time cleaning the equipment. I sidled over and introduced myself, emphasizing the fact that I'd come as the Kraken's guest.

The trainer was a middle-aged woman with a thick head of finger coils. As I spoke, she kept running a cloth over a bench—the simplest part of some kind of complex machine. I had no idea what it was called.

I paused to gauge her reaction.

She shook the cloth out, folded it, then folded it again. All seemed quite unnecessary.

At last she looked at me.

"You're saying the Kraken … isn't the same as the rest of them."

"It's common knowledge that she's had little contact with the clan for years," I answered smoothly. "She's never come out and said why, of course. But I can tell you it's at least in part because she has more scruples."

"Then why did the Kraken decide to come visit? After all this time?"

I spread my hands. "They've been very persistent. They've done everything short of publicly begging her to come back. The Kraken isn't made of stone. She has a heart. She came to speak with her elderly grandmother. But she still has concerns about the rest of the family.

"That's why she brought me along. That's why I'm here poking my nose around. Asking about Luka."

The trainer pressed her lips together. She glanced around for another machine to wipe. I trailed after her as she homed in on her next target.

"So that's why you're *here*," she said. She used her cloth-holding hand to gesture at the rest of the gym. It made her look as if she were waving a white flag of surrender. "You know he died here?"

"Yeah. I did my research."

She stilled. "You know how he did it?"

"Not in detail."

"He left a note outside the gym," she said. "Addressed to me. He knew I was the first one here in the morning and the last one to leave at night. He knew I'd find him.

"The note told me not to go inside, no matter what. It said to summon law enforcement. Make them go in first. As soon as I read it—I knew he was gone. I just knew it."

"You were close?" I asked.

The trainer shook her head. "We talked some. Not quite friends. The last few months before he passed, he started coming here more and more often.

"At first he almost never actually did anything. He'd just sit in a corner and look down at the roses. Sometimes he'd give me a little wink. 'If she asks, tell her I was here to work out,' he'd say."

"Shien Miyu," I said. "Think he was hiding from her?"

She didn't answer directly. Instead she went back to fussing with the equipment. I really couldn't name a single piece of it. I'd have believed her if she told me these were torture devices.

"He'd watch me clean the machinery," said the trainer. "Just like you're watching now. After a while he started asking all kinds of questions. He didn't seem interested in using the machines—just wanted to know how they worked. How they fit together. How you could customize them. He was very mechanically minded."

A pause. Then: "I'm only telling you this because no one else wanted to know," she said, very low and quiet. "The coroner barely gave me five minutes."

"I'm listening."

"Luka used the machines to kill himself. He rigged them together to—"

She made a telling gesture. I felt myself flinch.

"Really?" I said. "With—with these? Don't they have all kinds of safety locks?"

"I told him too much," she said bitterly. "He should've been an engineer, not a healer."

"No one else could have set it up? Or forced him to do it?"

"Funny you say that."

The trainer was wiping rather harder than before.

The machines clanked reproachfully. The harsh metal noise made me jumpy.

"No," she said, "it was definitely Luka. No one else in the entire household could've thought of something like that, much less actually made it work.

"I'm sure that's why he did it. He didn't want suspicion falling on any of us. He wanted to make it very clear that he was the one who killed himself."

She sat back on her heels. Her hands rolled the gray-streaked cloth into a tiny ball. "He mentioned once that there was a woman he wanted to marry. A no-name subliminal. When he asked Lady Miyu for permission, she went ballistic."

Bonding didn't need to be romantic in nature. Plenty of healers and mages bonded solely for business. They could still have loving relationships elsewhere.

But I could imagine the Shiens demanding that their bonded healers adhere to a stricter standard. Go home to a different family? Heaven forbid. What if your mage needed you in the middle of the night?

"Did they get along better before that?"

"Not at all," said the trainer. "Every single thing that went wrong for Lady Miyu, she took it out on him. We all heard it. Up the stairs, down the stairs. Morning, midday, night. Lady Miyu made sure he knew he was a useless piece of trash. Everything he did was wrong. The way he tied his shoes. The way he stood. The way he looked her in the eye or didn't look her in the eye."

She wrung at the cleaning cloth. I didn't think she knew she was doing it. "We all heard her telling him to go die. She said it so much, we almost stopped hearing it. When I tried to ask him about it, he sort of laughed it off. He said Lady Miyu was all words. He said all that shrieking was just noise to him. It didn't get inside him.

"But after he asked permission to marry, she started bringing up stuff about his intended. Now Lady Miyu's noise wasn't just about him. He talked back more. She got worse. He got quieter. She still got worse."

The trainer looked up at me again, her face taut. "Explain that to the Kraken. That's what passed for normal here. Maybe Lady Miyu wasn't standing there ordering him to put his head under the machines. But you can't tell me she didn't kill him."

5

I spoke to a few other workers who corroborated the trainer's story. One-sided arguments ringing through the halls. Shien Miyu demanding that Luka apologize for smiling the wrong way, for being a failure of a healer, for being born.

Then she'd turn around and upbraid him for having the temerity to say he was sorry. As if apologizing would make it better. If he said nothing, she'd berate him for his callow rudeness, his stupidity, his laziness, his lack of caring.

All the household staff seemed to have overheard it at one point or another. But no one mentioned ever attempting to step in. Not even once. It was background noise to them, unstoppable, a force of nature like some kind of hideous waterfall.

She told Luka he was worthless, a burden. She told him no one else would ever want him. She told him she was doing his girlfriend a favor by blocking their marriage. She said anyone would be grateful to have an excuse not to be tied to him. She said he'd ruined the lives of everyone who knew him—Miyu herself most of all.

Luka had said the abuse was just words to him. Just noise. And maybe he'd meant it.

But they were bondmates. She could've been force-feeding twice as much poison to him on the inside. She could've ranted at him all night, every night, without anyone else to hear it, without any way for him to permanently shut her off. Covering his ears wouldn't have done a thing.

Bonding brought with it an inconceivable closeness. Look at me—I got all shy and itchy whenever I had to face head-on the fact of being so inextricably woven together with someone who loved me.

It was unfathomable to think of enduring that same naked forced exposure to someone who actively hated me. *Unbearable* wasn't nearly enough of a word for it.

It must have been torture. Constant, silent, so many times worse than everything the staff overheard her hissing at him, and impossible to explain to anyone outside the bond.

No wonder Luka had laughed off her voiced invective. Perhaps it really had felt like nothing to him. Nothing in comparison to what came at him straight through the bond, unstoppable. An endless supply of blades stabbed so deep that no one else could see them, much less extract them.

Her tirades hadn't ended after Luka died, either. Miyu's new bonded healer was a much younger woman, timider and less outwardly cheerful than Luka. The new healer was sick all the time now, said the staff. They barely saw her anymore.

Most thought she was making herself sick on purpose. They themselves looked sick to their stomachs when they spoke of how Miyu treated her.

I understood their disgust. Based on what I knew of the Shiens, however, none of this surprised me.

Wist was the only one of her siblings who'd been adopted into the Shien clan. She looked nothing like the rest of them, with their delicate builds and fine hair and fine features.

The other six siblings were all blood relatives, which was why they (unlike Wist) had the privilege of putting their family name first. Wisteria Shien. Shien Miyu.

I'd met most of Wist's Shien siblings during my previous stay at the manor. She had three brothers and three sisters, all older than her. Right now they'd range in age from their mid-thirties to mid-forties. Miyu, at around forty, fell smack in the middle.

To be frank, I had little memory of them as individuals. They'd openly loathed me, after all, for getting my hooks in Wist. For having more influence over her than all the rest of them put together. I was just some random low-born healer classmate.

If I recalled them at all, it was as a hostile monolith. A bunch of interchangeable pieces who rolled their eyes the same way, made the same sorts of oh-so-cutting comments.

But they weren't really all the same. Wist had given me a refresher course when we went to buy flowers for her grandmother.

Miyu, for instance, was by far the weakest mage among them—a Class 3-1 before bonding. She could only learn up to three individual magic skills, and could only use them one at a time.

Mages from less prestigious families would have been quite satisfied at placing in Class 3. It was more than enough to make a career in magic. For the Shien clan, though, Class 3 was almost embarrassing.

Usually the mere act of bonding with a healer would boost a mage's power by at least one full class. Bonding was, in fact, the only way for a mage to level up. No amount of solitary practice or studying could make you miraculously grow extra magic branches all on your own.

After bonding Luka, Miyu had gone from Class 3-1 to Class 3-2. An improvement, yes. But it must have been far less than what she'd hoped for. And bonding was for life.

Once I'd heard enough, I stopped by the gym one last time to thank the trainer on duty. Then I gave Wist a little mental nudge through our bond.

After a few moments of waiting outside Grandmother's drawing room, the ostentatiously gilded door swung open. An attendant saw Wist out.

Wist paused before the door could close on her. "Miyu," she called over her shoulder. "Can I have a moment?"

Shien Miyu came hustling out of the room, a pinched look on her face. She had wan blond hair scraped back into a tight bun and wore a heavy bib necklace with jewels so large they looked fake.

"I'd like to see the gardens," Wist said. "It's been so long."

Miyu stared up at Wist as if she'd started babbling in one of the lost ancient languages. She twisted the stacks of bracelets on her wrists. After another moment she said crisply, "Yes. Of course."

"Thank you."

"Naturally, I have nothing better to do than to play tour guide for the Kraken."

"If you're busy—"

Miyu cut her off. "It would be my *honor*."

She stalked off without another word, and without checking to see if Wist would follow.

They'd grown up together, at least until Wist joined me at boarding school in her early teens. Yet I could hear a clear difference in diction. Miyu had that unplaceable upper-class Osmanthus City accent.

Wist—well, no matter what time of day it was, Wist tended to sound like she'd just woken up.

Miyu led us into the avant-garde rose garden. If you were rich enough, I suppose you could make roses reach full bloom whenever you wanted. Even early March.

I trotted a few paces behind the two mages. It gave me a chance to focus my magic perception on Miyu's core, to count the delicate branches that curled away from it.

Just three branches. I counted several times to be absolutely sure of it. So even though she'd driven Luka to his death last year, and even though she'd immediately bonded a different healer to replace him, she still hadn't managed to leap up even a single full class.

She'd castigated Luka for not trying hard enough, for not being invested enough. For sabotaging her, even. Deliberately dragging her down.

Maybe the problem hadn't been with Luka. Maybe the problem had been with Miyu herself all along.

Walking among the roses really was like touring a parody of a battlefield. Some bushes crawled their branches flat along the ground, clustering into shapes reminiscent of fallen corpses.

In certain places the flowers grew ferociously thick, completely hiding their stems. In others the thorns were as long as woody daggers.

Miyu dutifully rattled off this and that, explaining how the gardens had changed since the last time Wist came to visit. I didn't listen closely. Although I did notice her needling Wist about needing a guide to the grounds of her own childhood home.

I waited until we'd come far from the main cluster of buildings. When I glanced back, it took me a while to spot the seamless glass wall of the Shiens' sumptuous private gym.

At least I thought I could see the gym. It might have been a different room entirely. I'd gotten quite disoriented by the convoluted rows of rosebushes. Regardless, we seemed to have reached a safe distance from the mansion. No landscapers in sight, either.

I'd told Wist I wanted to get Shien Miyu alone in the gardens.

I hadn't told her why.

I'd dropped hints about wanting to see how Miyu behaved when it was just the three of us. About maybe wanting to ask her a few pointed questions myself.

This was all misdirection. Wist didn't need to know the full details of what I was planning in order for my plans to work. All she needed to do was play her part. And she'd done a perfectly adequate job of drawing Miyu out here. Rather deadpan, perhaps, but she always sounded like that.

Besides, if Wist didn't know my exact intentions, she couldn't raise any objections.

I peeled off my gloves as I walked along behind the sisters. I had to admire Miyu's ability to navigate the uneven garden path in those severe-looking dress shoes. She kept pace with long-legged Wist despite not coming up much higher than Wist's shoulder, heels and all.

I sped up a little, side-stepping rosebushes that stretched agonized clawing arms out in front of me. We were almost at the end of the rose garden. I wondered how many workers these bushes had injured to date. Some looked quite deadly.

Beyond the rose garden awaited an open patio laid out around an extravagant circular flowerbed. Miyu's heels clicked briskly on the patio stones. I inched ever closer behind her and Wist.

I pretended to trip.

I fell hard into Miyu. Hard enough for her to stagger. Hard enough that she would've landed flat on her face if Wist hadn't spun to instinctively catch her.

As I knocked into Miyu from behind, I grabbed at her magic and gave it a sharp yank. Smooth as a pickpocket.

Miyu would've felt nothing but the impact of me physically thumping her. As a general rule, most ordinary mages aren't very sensitive to having their magic touched. They could discern the outcome of a healer's work—the pain relief, the long-awaited easing of incorrigible knots—but rarely could they sense the actual process of having their magic manipulated.

"So sorry," I said as Wist helped steady and separate us. "Gosh, I'm so clumsy."

Miyu's nostrils flared. She was still gripping Wist for dear life. "This—this healer of yours is out of control."

"I get that a lot," I confessed.

She didn't acknowledge me.

"You," she said to Wist instead, each word like the thrust of a rapier. "Your sheer gall. You come waltzing back here with a convicted traitor in tow. You expect us to welcome you with open arms."

She flung Wist's arm down and took a few loud steps away. "And we will. Such humiliation."

Her magic branches undulated inside her, braiding together, catching at each other, snarling into a muddled mass as they went. The natural consequences of my one quick, precisely calculated touch.

I'd set her magic in motion. Now the tangling was unstoppable. Every passing second would take her closer to the breaking point.

"You know," I said to her, "I always wondered what was wrong with your magic."

For the first time Miyu stopped pretending not to see me. The expression on her face was pure venom. I let it pass over me. Just like how I'd tolerated her death-stares back when I first visited this estate as a teenager.

"All your biological brothers and sisters are at least Class 5, aren't they?" I asked. Rhetorical question. "Except the ones who don't have any magic at all. But I guess they don't count for anything to you guys."

She started to speak, then caught at her mouth with her hand as if she were about to vomit.

She stopped moving.

Something bordering on confusion came into her eyes.

She'd assumed the hunched posture of someone with stabbing pain in their stomach. I hadn't twisted up her magic simply for the sake of hurting her, but it was an unavoidable side effect.

Wist looked at her sister. She looked at me.

If Shien Miyu had one thing going for her, it was being far more expressive than Wist. Wist's face barely moved. But I knew her well enough to tell that this was her way of asking me what the hell was going on.

"Now I see what's wrong with you," I said to Miyu. I began carefully edging backwards. "There's a fundamental flaw in your magic. No wonder your healers always struggled. It's a miracle that you haven't snapped and gone berserk yet. Speaking of which—"

"How dare you," said Shien Miyu.

She sound like a different person. Clear. Calm. As controlled as the hairsprayed bun on the back of her head.

"How dare you," she said again.

She almost seemed to take pleasure in pronouncing the words, shaping them with that queenly accent. She ran impeccably groomed fingertips over the chunky jewels that swarmed like colorful beetles at her throat.

I scooted over behind Wist, tugged at the back of her suit jacket.

"Wist," I said under my breath. "Watch out. She's losing it."

Miyu's eyes slid over to us. Her left iris was still the same washed-out hue as before, not quite gray and not quite blue. Her right iris was a muddy pink. Deepening rapidly to red.

"You're dead," she said.

It could have been to me, or to both of us. Not a trace of anger remained in her voice. It came out as an unadulterated statement of fact.

She reached an arm towards us.

In the next second, magic splashed from her like a dam breaking. Almost blinding. Still just three branches. But they may as well have been three tornadoes. Mages are capable of incredible feats when they go berserk.

Miyu's arm lengthened, split, shot through the air at us with the speed of a whip. I cringed, my fist sweaty on the back of Wist's jacket. It's hard not to react when someone makes a good-faith effort to kill you.

Wist didn't move a muscle. But the thing lashing out of the end of Miyu's arm hit the air around us with a deafening screech. It stopped in the middle of nowhere as if we were surrounded by a bubble-shaped invisible shield.

I gulped in a breath. My ears were still ringing. Wist reached out absentmindedly and put an arm around me, tugging me in about as close as it was possible to get.

I'd told her I didn't like being a damsel in distress. Then again, I liked the idea of dying far less.

Now I could see what had become of Miyu's arm. It split apart into countless ashen woody growths like some kind of malevolent birch. The wooden growths whined and creaked and lengthened, stabbed incessantly at the hardened field of air protecting us.

With her other hand Miyu scratched at the skin around her bib necklace. She scratched and scratched until I thought she'd draw blood.

Suddenly the jewels fell out, in much the same way as teeth in an archetypal bad dream. They showered prettily to the ground.

Then the jewels began rising. They buzzed into flight like the fat beetles I'd thought they resembled. They ricocheted toward us. My poor battered ears heard a sound like time itself cracking to pieces.

Wist's magic jerked at me.

I blinked, and we were in the air high over the patio. We hovered at our leisure, weightless. Much higher up than the view from the glass-walled gymnasium. The carnage of roses to our left seemed to go on forever.

Jewel-beetles rocketed up toward us. Far below, the gnarled wooden ends of Miyu's arm plunged into the ground as if planting themselves. Wist ported us again—higher, lower, in every direction imaginable. The flying beetles never took more than a second to get reoriented.

"Can you—?" Wist asked.

"Can I what?"

"Neutralize her?"

There was so much happening that she had to bend close and nearly bite me on the ear to be heard.

"Nope," I said at once.

"...Why not?"

"Miyu's bonded," I said. "Wasn't that the whole story? She bonded another healer right after Luka died. Neutralizing berserk mages is still a form of healing. Only her bondmate can properly heal her."

"Ah." I felt Wist sigh. "Can you hobble her, then?"

"Not if you make me motion sick first."

We were still standing on thin air. Hopping, rather, from spot to spot in the sky. I could feel the dry-heaves getting ready for their grand debut.

"All right," she said. "I'll get you down there."

Bird-like wisps of shadow flew from her lips and started circling us.

As the jewel-beetles hurtled closer, Wist's little flock of shadows formed sharp shapes like flying knives and plunged to intercept them.

One more gut-wrenching port later, and we were on the ground again, less than a foot away from Shien Miyu. Wooden shapes—an entire forest of naked birch trees—had erupted from the patio all around her, shattering hard stone, ravaging the flowerbed.

I lunged for the magic core hidden deep in Miyu's back. The wooden monstrosity of her right arm, burrowing deep into the soil below the patio, still rooted her in place. She wouldn't be able to dodge me.

My fingers just barely brushed the edge of the belt around her dress.

A new birch trunk burst from the flagstone between us, knocking my hand away, knocking me back off my feet. I landed hard on my tailbone.

I'd jabbed at Miyu's magic. Not at the exact perfect angle I'd aimed for, but good enough. Well, maybe. Better pray that the hobble would take hold quick.

Her half-tangled magic branches floundered inside her. They whirled tighter and tighter together, started to tie themselves off like a tourniquet.

I heard an awful strained noise and looked back. The birch-tree growths gripped at Wist as if trying to rend her limb from limb. The tall swarming mass of trunks cast a deep shadow over all three of us.

Wist's head hung limp. I felt myself freeze as if a tiny little vorpal hole had formed right inside my skull, right where my brain was supposed to be, leaving nothing useful behind in its wake.

Then—

Another Wist crouched beside me, untouched. "Body Double," she said.

What a supremely annoying skill.

Wist observed me for a moment as if waiting to see whether I would stand up on my own.

I didn't. Wist shrugged and pulled me to my feet.

We regarded Miyu, now slumped on her knees, bark-covered arm anchored to the ground beneath the broken-up patio. Malignant birch trees reared up around her like a cage.

Some kind of cracking, squishing, slurping sound squelched out of the cluster of trees at our back. The ones clutching Wist's effigy. I decided it would be a very bad idea to turn around and look again.

"I don't think she's fully hobbled," Wist said mildly.

"Can't always get it right on the first try."

Wist flicked her hand as if shooing away a pesky fly. The fresh-grown birch trees that had shot up to shield Miyu now dissolved into clouds of purple-white smoke, opening a path for me.

I quickly stooped to give Miyu's magic another sharp turn, as if rattling at a stuck doorknob.

Then I circled in front of Miyu to see her face. Her bib necklace hung empty of its jewels, a sad golden latticework. Her eyes were vacant. Both the same cloudy dark pink. She muttered something to herself with dry lips.

I only caught bits and pieces of it.

"You ruined me.

"You did it on purpose.

"How could you.

"How could you treat me like that.

"How could you do that to me. You're not even human. You're a parasite. A sewer-sucking maggot.

"How could you stand to breathe the same air as me. How could you rip my heart out. How could you stand to keep living for another second. How could you be so cruel. How could you make me suffer like this. You're killing me. You're still killing me. It's all your fault. It's all your—"

She wasn't speaking to me. Nor was she speaking to Wist.

Really, I thought, as bile from belated motion sickness licked its acid up the back of my throat. How could you be so cruel.

Soon Miyu's three magic branches finished knotting together. They tangled themselves up into a finely calculated shape that rendered each and every one of them utterly useless.

All my work—the result of my few quick jabs at the root of her magic.

The hobble would come undone of its own accord in about a week. Before that happened, before she became capable of using magic again, someone had better find her bonded healer and make them neutralize her out of berserk mode.

In the meantime, the flying jewels—still pinned down by Wist's shadow-birds, insects stuck to a decorative board—ceased their struggling. The remaining host of birch trees started crumbling, their white powder choking the air like baker's flour.

Something the size of a human body crashed wetly to the ground close behind me.

I clung to my determination not to look back. But that very determination was what stopped me from stepping away in time. Blood from Wist's mangled magical body double seeped across the equally mangled flagstones. It surrounded my shoes before I knew it.

The living Wist had already taken a graceful step out of reach. I skittered over to join her, tracking brown-red footprints across the pavement as I went.

6

It was still the middle of the day, but I already wanted to go home and sleep. Unfortunately, Wist and I ended up being stuck at the Shien estate for hours to come.

At first I thought maybe we could say our farewells and slink away soon after the MPs arrived. This time, at least, there were no suspicions cast on me, and certainly no threat of arresting me.

I let Wist do the talking. They all spoke directly to her, anyhow, looking straight past me as if I appeared no more potentially informative than one of the twisted-up rosebushes in the background.

Then I saw them bring over Miyu's current bonded healer.

She looked even worse than I'd imagined, based on what I'd heard from the household staff. Very thin. The type of thinness that makes you constantly shiver, no matter what you're wearing.

A pair of MPs tugged her closer and closer to Miyu's hunched form. She appeared to resist without strength, without words.

They probably didn't even notice her attempting to pull back.

I plucked at Wist's jacket and asked her to back me up on what I was about to do next.

I marched over to the MPs and told them they'd better not let Shien Miyu breathe a single word to her healer. "She can't actively use magic right now—thanks to me, by the way—but she's still fully berserk," I warned. "She's still dangerous."

Miyu's right arm still looked rather wooden, but it had come uprooted from the ground and was now more or less in the shape of a human limb. Close enough for them to have successfully handcuffed her, at any rate. Good.

"Cover her mouth if you have to," I said. "I don't care how you do it. But I don't want to hear another word out of her. Neutralizing is difficult even without someone spitting venom in your ears."

Nothing happened until Wist paraphrased my demands. But that did the trick, at least. One of the MPs used gag magic on Miyu.

I turned to the skinny healer and told her I may not look like much, but I was secretly one of the best healers in the nation. If I did say so myself. Maybe not the best in terms of my criminal record or my understanding of ethics. In terms of pure skill, however, I was way up there.

Anyway, at the risk of repeating myself, I told her I'd bet anything that I was one of the most talented healers she'd ever meet. I'd neutralized more than my fair share of berserk mages.

This her first time? Nothing to worry about. I'd stay here with her no matter how long it took. I'd coach her through it.

And I did.

It took over an hour of constant work to finish neutralizing Shien Miyu. Her healer barely said a word. The whole time, she looked like she was about to faint.

But the MPs kept their promise to Wist. They kept Miyu quiet, kept her from struggling or interfering. And the thin healer listened to me. In the end, she got it done.

Afterward, I saw Grandmother Shien stumping around the broken patio with a deadly-looking cane. I saw Wist stoop to speak to her, gesturing to the damage. An offer to help tidy it up, maybe. Grandmother answered with a curt shake of her buzz-cut head.

Staff members trickled out of (or ported over from) the mansion. They conferred with Grandmother, cast a measuring eye over the devastated flower bed at the center of the patio. The trainer from the upstairs gym spoke quietly with Miyu's healer. Higher-ranking MPs exchanged wary looks with sharply dressed family lawyers.

"Wist." I gestured at the lawyer-MP standoff. "Get in there."

She gave me a look of incomprehension.

"They'll blame Miyu's healer for letting her go berserk," I said. "They'll accuse her of dereliction of duty. Don't you dare let them try it. Put your foot down."

Wist started to open her mouth.

"One, you're the Kraken," I said. "Two, this is *your* family estate. Don't let them even think about hitting that healer with a single charge. She's still stuck being bonded to your sister for the rest of her goddamn life. That's already a worse punishment than any healer could ever deserve."

I watched Wist walk over to the suits.

I watched how all of them—MPs and Shiens and the family's hired goons alike—instantly reoriented themselves toward the woman who they knew, both intellectually and instinctually, was the greatest mage alive.

If I were in a better mood, I might've laughed. They looked like pack animals cowering to appease a superior specimen. Wist didn't need to be particularly eloquent or persuasive. All she needed to do was make her desires as clear as possible.

Correctly or otherwise, most people assumed bonded mages were far less likely to go berserk. After all, a bonded mage could theoretically get bespoke healing whenever they wanted it.

Add that to the fact that everyone knew how Miyu treated her bondmates, and it would be an easy matter for both the Shiens and the police to agree that surely her berserking could have been prevented. Surely it was a sign of inadequate healing. Surely Miyu's healer had deliberately withheld healing as a form of petty revenge.

It wasn't true, of course. But the law demanded absolute devotion from bonded healers, and made it very easy to convict them of negligence on the basis of circumstantial evidence. Or even on the basis of pure nonsense, if you asked me.

When she returned to my side, Wist reported success. At minimum, Miyu's current healer would be spared from criminal charges.

The whole thing left an inerasable bitter taste in my throat all the same.

Sure—I'd managed to make Miyu's life a little worse. I suppose that counted for something. Yet that painfully starved-looking healer still had to live every single second of the rest of her life with Shien Miyu pressed in her flesh like acid in a wound.

"Let's go home," I told Wist, too low for anyone else to hear.

"Home to where?"

"The tower," I said. "You look like you have something to say to me. If we're going to have it out, may as well be in a place where I don't have to worry about what the neighbors think."

The white cloud-pasted sky had dimmed to a sulky purple-grey by the time we extricated ourselves from the Shien estate. Wist asked if I needed anything from my city apartment. I shook my head. In response she hooked a finger around one of my suspenders and ported us straight to her tower.

Wist's tower—the Kraken's tower—reared up out of a prairie of blue-tinted grass. Beyond the prairie lay a national forest permanently closed to the public.

It was about as far as you could get from Osmanthus City, from brightly lit convenience stores and sidewalks where busy pedestrians competed for space with squeaky bicycles.

Wist had crafted the tower herself. She'd made liberal use of magic, ignoring every law of physics I knew and probably quite a few more that I'd never heard of. Multiple rooms and roofs shared the same physical space. Some doors and staircases led to a cornucopia of different locations. Others led nowhere at all.

You stop noticing that sort of thing very quickly, though. Everyday magic disappears into the background as soon as you get used to it. At least, that's how it was for me.

I stretched out on a chaise sofa in what I'd come to think of the cat room, filled with a veritable forest of scratching posts and ceiling-high cat towers.

For all that, only one actual cat lived in the tower. A mostly-black tortoiseshell sprinkled with listless hints of brown. Wist called her Turtle.

I'm not a cat person. That said, my favorite thing about Turtle was how she would look with disdain at the monstrous quantities of cat furniture. Then she'd slink on over to the human couch where I lay now, and start methodically scratching it.

"I want a dog," I said to Wist.

"So get one."

"I want to keep it here."

"There's plenty of space," Wist said.

"I want you to take care of it."

"............"

"See how considerate I am?" I asked. "That's why I haven't gotten a dog yet."

Wist had shed her suit for a set of old lavender sweats as soon as we arrived at the tower. She rolled up frayed sleeves to free her wrists. After all we'd been through, her slicked-back hair was starting to fall apart, damp-looking black tendrils tickling the sides of her face. Grandmother's earrings were nowhere in sight.

When I see a deteriorating situation, sometimes I get this unbearable urge to make it worse. I reached up and mussed Wist's hair until she shrugged me off.

"Are you going to change?" she asked.

She'd brought me a stack of home clothes, too. Currently they rested on the couch cushion next to me, untouched.

"Too lazy," I said. "Help me."

I hadn't thought she actually would.

As I lay there on my back, the very picture of sloth, Wist leaned over me and unclipped my suspenders without another word. She had to wriggle her fingers below the small of my back to reach the opposite ends. She folded the suspenders neatly and set them off to one side.

Next she started unbuttoning my blouse. The ends of her fingers were chilly on the tender skin beneath. Three or four buttons down, I squirmed and sat up. Turtle stopped scratching the sofa.

Wist slowly lowered her hands.

There was a guarded emptiness to the way she watched me now. I was used to it, but that didn't mean I had to like it. It gave me the urge to say I wished she would yell at me. Except I don't think I really wanted that, either.

"It was you," Wist said.

There was no emotion in her voice. Nor even a hint of a question.

I spread my hands. "You'll have to be more specific."

"You made Miyu go berserk."

"That I did," I agreed.

"You planned it from the start."

"Of course. I wouldn't play the odds on a whim."

Wist studied her lap. Turtle the cat sprang up onto the couch, paced in a delicate circle, then sat down pointedly between us. She put herself in just the right place to nuzzle Wist's hands and simultaneously shoot me an overprotective glare.

Sometimes I wondered if this creature knew what we were saying. Even if she didn't, anyone could tell whose side she was on.

See—this was why I needed a dog.

Wist started to reach for my buttons again. She paused before making contact; she gave me a questioning look. I made a gesture that meant *be my guest*.

Turtle lashed her tail, hopped up onto the back of the couch, and marched away in an evident show of disgust.

"Why didn't you tell me?" Wist asked as she continued unbuttoning.

"My master plan? I thought you might stop me."

Wist's fingers paused.

"Go on," I said. "It's just you and me and the cat now. Although the cat seems to be losing interest. No one else around for miles. Except maybe a few guards off in the forest.

"No matter. They can't hear a thing. Tell me exactly what you think."

Wist finished unbuttoning me first. She tugged the diaphanous white sleeves off my hands, one arm at a time. Once she'd freed the whole flimsy blouse, she folded it with surprising skill.

All I had on underneath was a loose camisole, the kind with straps so thin they looked like floss. With my build, there was never really any need to wear a serious bra. Wist, still saying nothing, put my arms through a flannel pajama top. I wasn't quite dead weight, but I only did the bare minimum to help her.

I'd already told her what I'd heard from the Shien manor staff. And she'd seen Miyu's new bonded healer for herself. Something wasn't right there.

Legally speaking, abused healers had little recourse. Osmanthus prioritized making sure mages got their due. In the eyes of the law, mages were owed adequate healing. If they were bonded, such healing could only come from their bondmate.

"You told me you were never close with any of your Shien brothers or sisters," I said. "Last time I stayed at that house, it seemed to me like they tormented you growing up, then started to really regret it once you got labeled as a Kraken-class. Miyu was one of the worst of them, wasn't she?

"Frankly, I don't see any room for mixed feelings here. She's a shitty person. I did the best I could, but at most, she'll only get taken down a notch or two. She's still a Shien. Now she happens to be a Shien who's suffered a mild humiliation. That's hardly enough to make up for what she's done to her healers."

Wist rolled down her sleeves until they were long enough to cover her hands like gloves. The ends were visibly dingier than the rest of them. For a few moments, she pressed the sleeves to her face.

"If you'd told me in advance, it would have sounded like a bad idea," she said, muffled.

"So I was right."

"Right about what?"

"You'd have tried to stop me."

Wist peeked at me over the ends of her sleeves. "Berserk mages are uncontrollable. This time only my body double got hurt.

"But that could have been you," she continued. "It could have been me. Or any number of people around the estate."

"That's why I wanted to take a walk in the gardens," I said. "Get some distance from everyone else first. Anyway, let's be realistic. Your sister's Class 3. You're not back at full power yet, but you're still the Kraken. Even with her in total berserk mode, that's not a very fair match-up."

Berserk mages did have some ability to break the usual rules of magic. They could learn and start using random new magic skills in an instant, though they were still limited by their maximum number of magic branches. And even outside that, their very presence woke up wild magic phenomena, made it strike at unpredictable points like summer lightning.

Wist, as a Kraken-class, had a virtually unlimited number of magic branches to work with. She could store as many skills as she pleased. But last year she'd lost her entire magical skill set in one fell swoop.

That wasn't something that could happen to any ordinary mage. Wist was exceptional in all sorts of ways, good and bad alike.

To this very day, she was still in the process of relearning all her prior skills. She needed to imprint them back on her now-blank magic branches one by one, day after day. The process would take years to complete. And until she finished, she would remain technically weaker than her past self, who'd had a lifetime's worth of magic skills ready to work with.

Even so, there was zero chance that Wist could have been bested by a Class 3 mage like Shien Miyu.

That's why I went ahead and twisted Miyu's magic—made her go berserk. I had Wist there as insurance.

"You want to know what I think," Wist said.

"Have at it." I wiggled out of my dress pants—that, at least, I could do for myself—and pulled on the pajama bottoms she'd provided.

Wist had yet to continue speaking.

"So what is it?" I asked. "Should I have called up the MPs and told them your sister's been very mean to her healers? They'd arrest me again for wasting their time.

"Was it wrong to make her snap? What other alternative would've gotten any sort of results?"

I threw Wist my pants. "Well? Are you judging me?"

Wist folded my pants like a pro. Seemed to me like a waste of effort—they'd get hung up in a closet eventually. Maybe it gave her something to do.

"It felt like old times," she said. She rose and straightened the collar of my pajamas, brushed lint off my sleeves. "Before you—"

"Went to prison for treason?" I suggested.

"Before that. You used to have all these plans. It felt like the time when you talked me into joining the Board of Magi. You told me exactly how I should go about getting a seat.

"Or the way you used to game out who to be friendly with, what to say to them, how to secure votes. Or back in school—your schemes for getting people to leave us alone."

"Schemes," I said. "You make it sound like a bad thing."

I caught at her wrists. Wist was physically stronger than me, so long as she didn't forget to feed herself. She was magically stronger than any mage in the entire world. She had an impeccable poker face, the sort that could make people start babbling helplessly to fill air when all she did was stand there and gaze at them.

She could do anything, really. She could become the greatest hero or the worst villain in history. As an adult in her thirties, though, it seemed like she mostly just strove to stay neutral and not accidentally cause extra harm.

I lowered her arms, made her rest her hands on my sides. I pushed the stray bits of hair behind her ears. Unlike her hands, the edges of her ears were very warm. Almost overheated. So was the back of her neck.

"I get it," I said. "Gave you a real thrill, didn't it?"

"I—"

"You like it when I scheme. You like it when I go a little reckless. You like it when I make the decisions you'd never make, and pull you along with me."

Wist wasn't looking me in the eye. I thought I felt her tremble ever so slightly. I swallowed a laugh.

"You're not wrong," she said eventually. "I just—I'm not sure if it's a good thing. To react this way."

"Why not?" I prodded her in the sternum. "I'm glad I've got it in me to make your heart skip a beat."

Wist let out a breath. "Yes. But it makes me worry about repeating history."

Indeed. My seven years in prison were partly Wist's fault, but mostly a direct result of my own failed scheming. Even before that, Wist had arguably been through much worse. Again, all because of my plans. The grander the plans, the greater the consequences of failure.

"I'm older and wiser now," I said. "No more youthful ambition. This was a small-scale bit of meddling. And no one has to know about it except you and me."

I turned my face up to her with my best grim smile. "Unless you decide to report me again, of course."

Wist's hands tensed on my sides. "Do you expect me to?"

"You know I can't resist the occasional low blow," I said lightly.

"Occasional?" Wist said.

I plowed on. "But you wanted me anyway. Having regrets?"

Wist released me. She turned to scoop up my meticulously folded formal wear. A second later she turned back, my clothes crushed under one arm—all that work for nothing—and caught at the back of my head.

It was at first a startlingly light kiss, given how quickly she'd swooped in. Her nails pricked my scalp. It was hard not to smile, and hard to kiss while smiling. I nibbled at her until she kissed the smile right off me.

The cat yowled from some distant corner, as if ordering us to get a room. I erupted in laughter and told Wist we'd better figure out something for dinner.

7

TRUTH IS, I HADN'T even known if it would be possible for me to deliberately make Shien Miyu go berserk. I couldn't exactly go around experimenting with random mages on the street.

I'd hobbled thousands of convicted mages for the government in my career as the Magebreaker. Hobbling, however, simply meant twisting up their magic in a special way that rendered them temporarily unable to use it.

I thought of it as the reverse of normal mage healing, which involved smoothing out painful magical tangles. Yet hobbling didn't bring my victims any closer to going berserk.

Or think of it this way: imagine a magic branch as a long, long piece of yarn. Over time all mages would undergo natural tangling, their magic threads growing more and more disordered and crumpled, sometimes even knotting.

They needed healers to untangle the threads for them, unravel the knots. If their magic was left alone to devolve into total tangled chaos, sooner or later it would drive them berserk.

When I hobbled mages, I first took those long pieces of yarn-like magic and untangled them. Just like any other healer. Then I prompted their magic branches to wind themselves up into a smooth, neat skein.

It was painless for the mage in question, but would render all their magic branches unusable. Over time, the natural tendency of magic to shift and slither would tug little by little at the ends of the skein I'd created.

Eventually the hobble would undo itself completely, expiring without a trace. Thus leaving the mage with temporarily tangle-free branches that they could once again use to wield their chosen skills.

I conceived of hobbling as reverse healing because it took away mages' power. It cut off access to the very thing that made them a mage. That was also why they called me the Magebreaker.

So far no other healer had been able to imitate me, and the government certainly didn't want to encourage them to try. As long as there was only one of me, they could regard me as a singular freak of nature. Concerning, and potentially a threat to the mageocracy. But also quite useful.

On a purely technical level, hobbling was perhaps better described as a form of lateral healing. Not its exact opposite. It didn't make mages more tangled, after all. It simply smoothed and collected and organized their magic threads in a rather non-standard way.

Long story short: I'd never tried making a mage go berserk before.

For one thing, in the past it would simply not have been a useful strategy. There was nothing to gain from it (except, perhaps, tremendous personal risk of being promptly murdered by my guinea pig).

And for another thing, the process of hobbling a mage was completely different from what I'd need to do to drive them berserk. So it wasn't a slippery slope. Being able to cleverly block mages' magic use didn't take me any closer to being able to force them to lose control.

In fact, the main reason I'd thought of doing it this time was pure coincidence. It was that one random berserking mage I'd met on the way back to my apartment in February.

More specifically, it was how the MPs treated me after I neutralized him.

Granted, I was quite used to being met with suspicion, but even I had never been suspected of deliberately driving a mage over the edge. It felt about as ridiculous as accusing a pet hamster of maliciously poisoning your breakfast cereal.

It made me think, though.

What if I *had* driven him berserk? What would happen if I tried?

I chewed over the idea. Though at first it seemed utterly silly, over time I started to believe I could do it.

Other healers? Nah. Me? Maybe. I'm a bit of a self-proclaimed genius.

If I could invent hobbling, surely I could try my hand at true reverse healing. Who better to experiment on than a certified piece of shit like Shien Miyu?

Instead of neatly gathering magic branches into a tightly controlled skein, all I'd have to do was encourage them to tangle faster. Tangle wilder.

Magic was inherently prone to tangling. If anything, boosting its natural tendencies might turn out to be much easier than standard healing.

As much as this new idea intrigued me, I wouldn't have driven a mage berserk purely to satisfy my scientific curiosity. I'm not that much of a psychopath.

But my would-be client Pine had, without knowing it, given me a reason to try.

The second and last time I met Pine was at her workplace: the National Healing Research Institute.

Though most of the staff were healers or subliminals like Pine, the government-appointed head of NHRI was, of course, a mage.

If life had gone a little differently, if I'd never met Wist, perhaps I myself would've ended up working here. Just like my friend Mori.

Then again, it seemed more likely that I would've ended up the same as Luka: forcibly bonded to a high-born mage who despised me.

I'd never been to NHRI headquarters before, come to think of it. They turned out to be located in a crumbling seaside fortress on the city outskirts, just barely within the range of my parole thread. The building looked like a relic of the ancient Osmanthian monarchy.

It seemed colder and windier here than in the city proper. The air smelled delicious, but everyone wore extra layers of clothes. If I strained my ears, I could just barely make out the distant sound of waves crashing into rock.

I was frankly surprised to be allowed inside the building. Apparently the cafeteria was partly open to the public. The building also housed a training center for certifying healers, along with a specialty clinic that saw some outside traffic from difficult-to-heal mages.

Pine got me a one-day permit for the cafeteria. I'd already told her I couldn't take her money, but she insisted on at least paying for lunch.

Privately, I didn't think the type of conversation we were about to have would go particularly well with a meal.

Perhaps Pine thought the same. I'd thought she would be a wishy-washy sort of eater, but she devoured her salad with startling vigor. Tidy, multicolored forkfuls disappeared into her mouth so swiftly that I sat there staring for a while before recalling that I too needed to eat.

We'd avoided the noon rush. It was well after two, and we had a good quarter of the dining hall all to ourselves.

Pine had picked a table by the window. A petite vase of snowdrops sat in the middle. The architecture around us was a peculiar mish-mash of the old stone fortress and brand new additions, with plenty of hygienic-looking white paint.

Pine set down her fork for the last time.

"I'd like to thank you," she said.

I held up a hand. "Please don't. I mean, I love taking credit for anything and everything, but in this case it's a bit too much.

"All I did was have the good luck—or bad luck—to be there on the premises right when Shien Miyu went berserk."

"I understand," she said. "I know it's a coincidence. But I can't help thinking it's thanks to you, somehow, that things turned out the way they did. Mori was right to send me to you."

I relented. "You can feel however you like about it. I guess I have a gift for being in the right place at the right time. Still, you asked for evidence of what happened to Luka. I heard some stories. But I don't have any new concrete proof to give you. I failed on that count."

Pine stirred her drink, though she didn't seem particularly interested in finishing it. I told her the rough outlines of what I'd heard from various workers at the Shien manor. Nothing too direct.

I did make it clear that Luka, and Luka alone, had killed himself.

"Now personally," I said, "I'd call it a form of manslaughter. Based on how she treated him. Her current healer already seems like a wreck, too. But you know the law won't agree with that."

Pine reached over and pushed the little glass vase of snowdrops out of direct sunlight. It was as if the brightness hurt her eyes.

"Shien Miyu will lose her job," she said.

"Will she?"

"Do you know what she does?"

I didn't, actually.

"She works at the Ministry of Justice," said Pine. "She's a civilian defense official. That department has the strictest security requirements. They don't take any mage who's ever gone berserk."

Huh. That would make for slightly more meaningful consequences than I'd expected.

At minimum, a single episode of going berserk would normally result in fines and a mandatory examination. Plus imprisonment and—at the end of it all—hobbling.

I'd looked forward to being called in to hobble Shien Miyu for the length of her sentence. Still, I figured the family lawyers would be able to get her out of serving any actual jail time. Surely they'd also whittle down her sentence—the extent of her mandatory hobble—to a scant few months. Or even just a few weeks.

There would be societal ramifications, too. Mages of such high birth almost never went berserk. Grandmother certainly wouldn't be pleased with how she'd humiliated the clan.

I just hadn't imagined Miyu getting fired over it.

It was nothing resembling justice. But perhaps it was better than nothing.

Pine asked again if she could pay me. I refused. I had no good words of comfort to offer her, and I don't think she wanted any.

Afterward, I handed my visitor badge back to Pine outside the fortress. The cold sea breeze rippled her long skirt.

I recalled the trainer at the Shien manor talking about how Luka had sought permission to marry a woman, a no-name subliminal. I recalled her gestures illustrating how he'd jury-rigged the equipment all alone, after hours.

There wasn't anything particularly special about Shien Miyu's healers. Plenty of other healers in Osmanthus suffered the same way. It wouldn't make the news. It might barely become a local rumor. Report a mage for it, and at most, the nearest MPs might give them a stern talking-to. Nothing would change.

When I was much younger, I'd fantasized about becoming a savior for other healers. And if not a savior, at least a cornerstone of future revolutions.

How could I not let my imagination run wild? I had Wist with me, after all. Wist possessed infinite magic, or at least near-infinite magic branches. You could get anything done with enough magic. Couldn't you?

The problem was that I'd tried to have it both ways—to get a new era started, and to keep my hands relatively clean in the process.

I should've been more committed, one way or another. If I were going to do things by the book, I should've been more patient. If I were going to play dirty, I should've waded deeper in the mud from the start.

I wavered, and it got me seven years in prison. It was supposed to have been far longer—it was supposed to have been a life sentence. As a matter of fact, I should've been slated for execution. My life sentence (as I'd learned quite recently) was a compromise eked out solely thanks to Wist's intervention.

I knew now that I lacked the stomach to use Wist to overthrow the current government. Copious blood would be shed, but it would've been doable. At one point in our lives, she might even have gone along with it.

I'd also failed in my past efforts to change Osmanthus through all the proper legislative channels. Doing something about this country as a whole was beyond me.

And if I went full vigilante, seeking out healers who needed help, delivering whatever punishment I could to the mages who hurt them—well, it wouldn't take Public Security very long to notice and crack down on me.

I couldn't save every healer in Osmanthus. Worse than that, I'd settled for leeching off the government. I lived off the money I got whenever they hired me to hobble allegedly criminal mages. I'd sold out, essentially, in exchange for parole.

Even so. If a case fell right into my lap like this, I couldn't just throw up my hands and ignore it.

When I walked all the way to the fortress gate and glanced back, Pine was still standing there, skirt flapping like a sail in the wind, one hand raised to hold down her hair.

I didn't know what to feel.

What had I actually accomplished here?

I could hobble mages. Apparently I could even drive them berserk.

But I couldn't bring back Luka. I couldn't sever or silence the bond permanently tying Shien Miyu to her latest healer, that hollow-cheeked girl with the whispery voice.

Not even Wist could think of any way to break apart a bonded mage-healer pair. Trust me—I'd asked. Multiple times.

Knowing it was impossible did nothing to put my mind at ease. It just made the frustration worse. And it wasn't like I could turn around and take it out on Pine, my would-be client.

My stomach hurt as I walked onward to the desolate outdoor train station; I lacked the security clearances needed to pass through the magical port gate designated for use by commuters. It kept hurting for the entire ride back to the heart of the city.

PART TWO

The Church of the Kraken

8

I REMEMBERED every mage I'd ever hobbled (and every mage I'd ever healed, too). Though I rarely knew their names or faces, I could recall the exact configuration of their magic cores and branches.

The ends of the magic branches moved incessantly, tangling and untangling. But there was something unique in how the branches grew rooted to each mage's personal core. A sort of indelible fingerprint.

In every other area of life, my memory was nothing special to boast about. Mages were different—I couldn't forget them if I tried.

That was how, during one long day of hobbling sentenced mages for Public Security, I recognized the man who had gone berserk on the sidewalk in February.

He couldn't see me. He had no idea who I was. They kept him in a magically generated column of light, one designed to have much the same effect as a one-way mirror.

I, in turn, could see everything but his face, which to me looked like a mosaic blur of featureless skin. But I still knew it was him. I knew it as soon as my magic perception glimpsed the feeble light of his core.

He thanked me hoarsely after I hobbled him. That probably meant he'd be allowed back into society on condition of being deprived of his magic. In his case, the hobble would last for the next six months.

Low-level offenders were generally allowed to talk to me, and I to them. The pillar of light warped our voices to keep us from recognizing each other on the outside.

Whoever designed this system clearly had no idea that I had a photographic memory for magic cores and branches. Of course, I hadn't gone out of my way to volunteer that information, either.

Anyway, I hobbled mages for the money, and to stay in the government's good graces. I didn't do it as an act of kindness.

I'm only human, though. I can't say I mind being thanked.

On a different day, at a different mage prison, I hobbled Shien Miyu. Her face, too, was an anonymous blob. I knew her from her magic alone. She remained silent the whole time.

Miyu's sentence would last a mere three months. It must have helped that she went berserk on her own family's private property. Grandmother Shien certainly wouldn't press charges for damage. And thanks to Wist's quick intervention, Miyu hadn't directly hurt anyone.

The man on the street had ruined an apartment wall and done some rather nasty things to my arm. I could grasp the logic behind him receiving a longer hobble. But Shien Miyu getting off so lightly still irked me. I hoped Pine was right about Miyu losing her job. I hoped Miyu's current healer was doing—if not well, then as well as could be expected. No one had ever told me her name.

I'd gotten a very early start that day. It was around four in the afternoon by the time I hobbled all the mages waiting for me in detention at the same facility as Shien Miyu.

After I clocked out, my PubSec escort saw me home to my city apartment. I did some brisk grocery shopping, then cooked down a week's worth of crinkly spinach, humming all the while.

I was about to get started on my next task—preparing a huge new batch of refrigerator pickles—when I felt a sudden spike of shock from Wist.

It was over almost as soon as it sliced through me, a cold sickening burn. A sensation like swigging a shot in reverse. It ended with artificial abruptness, as if Wist had clamped down on herself to keep any further emotion from spilling over to me. Hands pressing a wound closed.

Or—or as if something had happened to stop her from feeling it.

I was surprised to find myself still on my feet. I stood there hunched over my stainless steel kitchen counter. It was the sort of pose you would assume when vomiting. I had no lights on in here: the windows were all wide open, and it was only just starting to get dark out.

I didn't give myself any more time to think about it. I touched Wist through the bond. Tentatively, as if tugging ever so lightly at her sleeve.

No reaction.

I forced myself to straighten up. To leave the kitchen area. To think. I started to pace toward the front entrance, then reversed my steps.

Where the hell was I going?

A steady breeze pushed in through my open windows, puffing out gauzy sheer curtains. I drank the outside air as if I were starved of it.

Better not keep bugging Wist, I told myself. Better not call out to her with words.

Wist was the Kraken. Less powerful than she used to be, with the full glory of her former skill set, but still a Kraken-class. She ought to be able to get herself out of any kind of trouble. And if she were in genuine danger, my screeching at her from afar might end up being a risky distraction.

I went to my dresser and fumbled for a slender silver ear cuff, the kind that slips on without piercings. Who to contact, if not Wist?

The first person who came to mind was Manatree, my de facto parole officer. She was very well-connected within PubSec and acted as one of their primary liaisons with Wist.

I put on the enchanted ear cuff with clumsy hands. I touched one fingertip to it and muttered Manatree's name under my breath.

No response. I almost cursed.

No—this meant little. Manatree was an extremely busy woman.

I touched the ear cuff again. "Kuga Mori," I said.

Mori was Wist's assistant, as well as a doctoral student affiliated with NHRI. Lately Wist had cut his hours to almost nothing—she'd told him to focus on preparing for his dissertation defense. But he still seemed to have a way of knowing far more about her schedule than I did.

"Clematis?" Mori said through the ear cuff.

He could be something of a worrywart. Best not alarm him for no reason.

"Hey, kiddo," I said by way of greeting. "Thanks for the referral last month."

"The what? Oh! You mean Pine. She told me what happened. I hope—" He lowered his voice. "I hope it didn't cause you any trouble."

"No trouble at all," I assured him. "Just wish I could've done more to help. If you know anyone else with a problem like that, you send them right to me. May not be much, but I'll do what I can."

It was incredible, really, that my voice could come out sounding so calm while my insides roiled. Maybe I could've been a famous actress in another life.

"Just wondering," I said, lighter than ever. "Did you know what Wist was up to today? Or what she was going to be doing the rest of the week. Just in general."

Thankfully, Mori didn't seem to find it strange that I'd asked him rather than going directly to Wist herself. He knew we could be a little weird sometimes. Anyhow, Wist wasn't always the best expert on her own work schedule.

"Today…" He repeated. "She had a VorDef meeting a few days ago. But today she was just going to focus on relearning a few of the more complex skills from her old skill list."

"No government requests to take care of?"

"I don't think so. Most bureaus are closed tomorrow for the long weekend. That's probably why it's been a little quiet."

"Just another day of Wist mucking around at the tower, then," I said. "Got it."

I don't remember what else we talked about. I thanked him and wrapped up the conversation.

The bond lay deep and silent inside me, still as dark water. It almost made me wonder if I'd imagined the sensation of sheer horror that had torn through it—torn through Wist?—and then vanished.

Maybe it really was just my imagination. A physiological phenomenon. Like lying in bed half-asleep, not sure if you're dreaming or feeling a faint earthquake.

Maybe I'd made the whole thing up.

I forced myself to go through the motions of making those refrigerator pickles. I scarcely saw what I was doing. I almost added baking soda to the brining liquid instead of salt.

After I finished, I folded up my floor bed and stuffed it in a closet. I cleaned the entire apartment floor. I used toothpaste to scrub at grimy spots on the waffle-textured white walls. I wiped every mirror.

The sunset outside was a broad orange glow that seemed to die out to nothing with ominous speed.

Finally I grabbed a jacket. Better than bustling around here numbly.

I retrieved the container of spinach I'd made earlier and stuffed it in a bag.

For all I knew, Mori was right. Wist might've been lounging around at home barefoot the entire time. Maybe that shock I'd felt had simply been from Wist stubbing the heck out of her toe.

The cherry tree at the center of the park around the corner had just reached full bloom. During daylight small birds would spend hours sticking their heads in the pinkish-white clusters of blossoms, feeding on nectar.

I couldn't see any birds now. The dim air thickened with a growing twilight chill.

A hefty stone under the cherry tree glistened with magic cuttings: a permanent portal keyed to work only for me. A shortcut to Wist's tower.

I planted my butt on the boulder.

When I stood up, I was no longer in my neighborhood park, shadowed by the frilly cherry blossoms that sprouted as densely as hungry pink sea anemones. When I stood up, I was on one of the myriad roofs of Wist's tower. The Kraken's tower.

The darkening sky above the tower had crusted over with a mottled pattern of clouds. It seemed flustered, undecided about whether to whip itself up into a full-blown storm.

As I headed for the door into the tower proper, my ear cuff pinched me. My heart squeezed as if it were crammed down into a too-small jar.

"Hi, Manatree," I said.

I hadn't seen my parole officer in person for a while, but it was easy enough to picture the grumpy set of her brow.

"You tried to reach me," she said. "I suspect I know why. The Kraken is fine."

"That's it?" I asked. "I don't get any context?"

"Ask her yourself." A pause. "I have a suggestion for you, Magebreaker. Tomorrow is a holiday."

"So I hear," I said, perplexed.

"Take the Kraken on a vacation."

"A vacation," I parroted—truly a shining beacon of intelligent conversation. "To where? Why?"

"Anywhere," said Manatree. "Take her out of the city. Distract her. Force some rest on her. Make yourself useful for once."

Only that last part convinced me this was truly Manatree, not some kind of sinister impostor. To most people she'd come across as an unflappable older lady. An accomplished mage with long magnificent locs and picture-perfect posture.

I, however, had a special knack for bringing out her petty side.

"Take her out of the city?" I repeated. "The only place outside city borders covered by my parole thread is Wist's tower. Oh—plus a couple of mage prisons.

"I mean, I'd be happy to take her on a tour of the Osmanthian penal system, if you think that'd be restful. I daresay I'm something of an expert."

Manatree said absolutely nothing.

"I'll think about it," I continued, after letting the silence gel for a bit. "I assume this means it's okay to have Wist expand the range of my parole thread. How about giving me all of Osmanthus?"

"That's acceptable. Just don't attempt to leave the country."

"Well, I'm grateful," I said. "But I gotta wonder."

"No, you don't."

"This some kind of political ploy? Does the Board of Magi want Wist out of the way so they can pull something sneaky over the weekend?"

"Don't be paranoid," Manatree said derisively.

I started to object. I tapped at my ear cuff.

Manatree ignored me. Dammit.

One side effect of being bonded with Wist was that I could tell—in a very general sort of way—how close she was to me physically. This ability didn't make much difference when we were miles apart: me in my apartment and she in her tower, for instance.

Now that I crunched my way across the gravel of the tower's rooftop rock garden, though, I could feel with certainty that Wist was in one of the floors below. Without that little tug in my belly to guide me, it would have been all but impossible to locate a single human being hidden away inside this intricate beehive of capriciously linked magical rooms.

I left my shoes on a rack by the rooftop door and followed our bond like a compass.

It led me to a door still very high up in the tower. A door I'd never seen before, or simply never had reason to notice.

It didn't look like a door at all, really. It looked like an empty expanse of wall in an oversized hallway that was otherwise filled with empty gilt frames.

The frames were all at least twice as tall as me. All looked thick enough to kill a grown adult in one fell swoop if they just so happened to topple down. I picked my way gingerly over to the stretch of bare wall with a tiny seam running through it.

When I pushed at the wall, it folded inward like a tent flap.

I decided not to question it. I set my container of spinach down in the hall, then slipped though to the other side. The bendy wall settled back into place behind me with a soft *whump*.

The room was a planetarium.

Not that I'd ever been to a real-life planetarium before. Still, it was the first thing that came to mind. The ceiling was an enormous night-time dome occluded with startlingly colorful stars.

I took another step before my eyes finished adjusting. My foot sank. I may have squeaked a little.

No theater seating in this room. No chairs whatsoever, in fact. Languid dunes of sand covered the entire floor. A shore without an ocean. Or simply a desert.

I peeled off my socks and jammed them in a pocket. I could see well enough to spot Wist now, a featureless form on the sand at the center of the room. Barefoot, I tromped over to join her. It took a surprisingly long time to get there.

The stars choking up the ceiling shed so much light that—once my eyes got used to it—I felt as if I had supernaturally good sight.

I looked down at Wist lying on her back in a hollow of sand, knees up. Hands resting on her stomach. No blanket. Eyes fixed on the celestial dome overhead.

I sat cross-legged next to her. "Never knew you were into astronomy."

When she spoke, her voice sounded no different than usual. "I don't really know any stars."

"Neither do I," I said. "Who's going to teach us?"

"This isn't our sky," Wist said.

"What is it, then?"

"How the sky looks from a different part of the world."

"Where?"

"Far from the continent. Right now it's very late at night there."

At first I'd been too overwhelmed by the size of the ceiling and the sheer quantity of stars to realize exactly what Wist was looking at.

As I followed her gaze, my eyes stopped on a patch of wrongness in the sky. A rough-edged hole of nothingness—a hole into nothingness?—ripping through the creamy swirl of stars.

Now that I'd noticed it, I couldn't unsee it. But something about it hurt to look at.

I focused on Wist instead. She watched the blank patch as if she were having a staring contest with it.

"How high up is that hole?" I asked. "Wherever it is in the real world, I mean."

"Much lower than the stars," said Wist. "Lower than some layers of clouds. They don't often have clouds, though."

"I've heard of this," I said. "Over there they worship it, don't they? What's it called again?"

"The Eye of the Devil."

A huge and ancient vorpal hole. It had formed high in the sky over distant lands, hundreds or even thousands of years ago.

For the most part it seemed to be static, but every few decades it would show signs of sudden expansion, or perhaps spit out waves of vorpal beasts to ravage the towns down below. To those nearby, I suppose it felt something like living near an active volcano.

"You ever been there?" I asked.

"Only like this," Wist said. "Not in person. An Osmanthian delegation offered to have me seal up the hole. They were hoping it'd be a first step toward establishing trade relations. The locals declined. I hear they were pretty offended."

"Guess they want the devil's eye to stay open."

I stretched out next to Wist, propped up on my elbows. She'd have a lot of sand to shake out of her hair whenever she decided to get up. If she ever got up.

"I felt something happen to you," I said. "Earlier today."

"Nothing happened to me."

There was a glassy look to her eyes, still fixed on the faraway devil in the sky.

"All right," I said. "Nothing happened to you. Then what was it?"

First, silence. Then Wist sat up and turned to me.

I felt myself go still. Well, stiller. I was used to seeing her wear a walled-off expression. The surreal starlight turned her usual flat look into something unfamiliar. Almost menacing.

If I could've kept my big mouth shut for just a few more breaths, I'm sure she would've answered me. But the pressure of the cold starry sky and Wist's colder face proved too much for me. Like a fool, I babbled.

"I hobbled your sister today." My voice sounded weirdly high—as uncomfortable as listening to a recording.

"Miyu?"

"Who else? She only got three months, by the way."

Wist scraped together a handful of sand and flung straight up it in the air like confetti. It hung suspended instead of raining down on us. A branch of her magic flared through the floating sand; in this room, it had the glow of an aurora. A variant of the skill commonly known as Zero Gravity.

Her magic pushed the sand into glittering cloud-like shapes, none of them particularly artistic. A donut. A planet with rings. A—

"Is that a chicken?" I said.

"It's a cormorant."

The alleged cormorant flapped its sandy wings to fly a silent circle around the room. Then it glided down to land in the sand below, and promptly collapsed into nothing.

As if to join it, Wist tipped over on her side. She lay curled up with her head resting on my thigh, facing away from me.

"A vorpal hole opened at an elementary school," she said. "A huge one. After hours. But a lot of kids were still there. It swallowed up half a building and the entire playground."

"PubSec called you to seal the hole?"

"Some of the parents got there first," Wist said. "They were already coming to pick up their kids."

For a time, she stopped speaking. I slipped my hand under the hem of her sweatshirt. Wist lying bunched up like this made it easy for me to reach the small of her back, the closest part of her body to her magical core.

The skin there was startlingly cold now. If I focused less with my eyes and more with my magic perception, I could detect countless intricate magic branches winding restlessly through her body like thin bright veins of lava.

"The second I got there—" she stopped.

"Wist?"

"When the vorpal hole manifested, one of the teachers was taking a few of the kids to the bathroom. That one bathroom ended up being just outside the edge of the hole. They got stranded there till I closed the hole. They were the only ones who survived."

Her body was quite motionless, her head a defeated weight on my leg. But the complex light of her magic clenched fitfully, in the way of a spasming muscle.

"What happened when you first got there?" I asked. "Is that when I felt you through the bond?"

"The kids and the teacher trapped in the bathroom were crying. More and more parents kept arriving. The MPs on the scene couldn't explain it, couldn't control them.

"There were parents screaming at each other, screaming at the MPs. A mother heard what had happened and threw herself into the vorpal hole.

"The moment I ported in, I saw her falling. The hole swallowed her. No sound. Nothing left. Then other parents started pushing at the MPs. Almost shoved them in, too."

Wist opened and closed her left hand, as if to make sure it was still there.

"I sealed the vorpal hole," she said. "Everyone on the playground, everyone in the classrooms in the moment it formed—they were already gone. The woman who dove in after them—gone."

She turned a bit, glancing up at me at a slant.

"That's it," she said. "That's the whole story. I felt something when I saw that woman fling herself in. Now? It feels like a dream.

"I've seen a lot of vorpal holes. I've sealed a lot of vorpal holes. I've heard a lot of the same screaming. The similar moments stack up on top of each other like plates. It starts to all feel the same."

Okay. I could see why even matter-of-fact Manatree would all but order me to make Wist take a vacation.

My hand warmed the chilly skin of her back. I pushed at her core with slight—physically almost imperceptible—motions, motions that rippled down through her myriad magic branches with much the same effect as running fingers through hair. It took little conscious effort. It was a way of buying myself time to think.

I've never been any good with comforting words. What sort of comfort could you give in answer to this, anyway? Gee, Wist, sorry to hear that. At least a few children lived. At least not all the parents threw themselves into the vorpal hole in some kind of horrendous stampede of grief.

Obviously I said nothing of the sort. I wallowed briefly in my own inadequacy.

I sensed the weight of the bond resting inside me. I sensed Wist on the other end of it, a seemingly serene presence, stolid as a cliff in the face of raging waves.

I felt not even a hint of that lightning shock that had lanced through her—then through the bond, then through me—a few hours earlier. Yet her thousand-plus threads of magic shivered faintly at my touch.

"You asked me something a little while ago," I said. "Last year, was it?

You told me you knew where my mother and father live now. You asked if I wanted to see them."

Wist rolled onto her back, still using my leg as a pillow. The ceiling of stars above us shed startling amounts of light. Wist studied me with dark impenetrable eyes.

"Manatree says you should be free this weekend," I went on. "I'm calling in that favor. My parents are somewhere in the countryside now, aren't they?"

"You want to visit them?"

"Not visit," I said. "Not show my face or anything. Just spy a little. See how they're doing."

I slid my hand out from under her sweatshirt and started trying to dust the sand from her hair.

"I can only go if I'm with you," I said. "And you'll have to expand the range of my parole thread. Which Manatree says is okay, by the way. So do it. Take me there."

"You sound like a king giving commands," Wist said blandly.

"Would you rather have me ask nicely?"

"Strangely enough," Wist answered, "I wouldn't."

I asked her if she was done looking up at the Eye of the Devil. She got up and shook more sand out of her hair like a dog.

On the way out of the planetarium, I tripped over my own abandoned container of spinach and nearly broke my nose in the process. On the bright side, this saved me from forgetting to retrieve it.

That evening we dined on a fine spread of crackers, my salty spinach, and a variety of canned fish (Wist's favorite food, for some reason). Turtle the cat made jealous noises when she found us hunched like gargoyles over our makeshift meal.

I understood Manatree's thought process. That said, I wasn't entirely sure I agreed with her.

Whatever burdens Wist bore were an inextricable part of being the only living Kraken-class mage in Osmanthus. On the continent. In the world.

A little weekend getaway could take Wist out of the city, but it couldn't take her out of herself. Of course, that didn't mean we couldn't try to enjoy it.

9

THIS WAS TIME OFF, I told Wist. For both of us. That meant no using magic, and no healing. I wanted to make a good-faith effort not to bring work with us on vacation. Unless an emergency happened, of course.

I found myself forced to make an exception as soon as we left the tower.

"Come to think of it," I said, "how do we get from here to the train station?"

Wist looked at the vast sweep of shimmering blue-tinted grass. She looked back at the crooked sky-piercing tower. She looked at me.

"You don't have a skimmer, do you," I said.

"We could walk," she said.

"To the city? It'll take us all weekend. Longer, probably."

"To the outpost in the forest," Wist clarified. "We could ask the guards there to port us."

I cringed to picture it. She was the most powerful mage in the world, and perfectly capable of porting herself anywhere she wanted. The poor guards would think she was hazing them.

"That's not their job," I said. "Let's go through the portal from the tower roof to my neighborhood park. I can get us to the station from there."

"That portal only works for you. It won't take me."

"You're the Kraken. Surely you can tweak it a bit."

"Modifying it would involve using new magic."

Wist flexed her hand. I began to suspect she was enjoying this.

"Oh, forget it," I snarled. "Port us to the station. But that's the last time, okay? Afterward, we relax and savor our trip the slow way."

That was how we found ourselves at Anthum Station early on Friday morning. Our weekend prohibition on magic was more of a private game than anything else. Wist seemed to be taking it seriously enough after porting us to the station, though.

I wore comfy overalls and a windbreaker. Plus my ear cuff, in case someone needed to reach us. Wist looked aloof in tinted glasses, a black cloth mask, and a white bucket hat.

She usually relied on her Disappearance skill to skulk around public areas unnoticed. In lieu of Disappearance, she'd turned to fashion to disguise herself. I didn't spot any paparazzi, so I suppose it worked well enough.

Anthum Station was one of the largest in Osmanthus City, with architecture reminiscent of a colossal animal's fossilized ribcage. A grand hall outside the ticket office held humongous arching portals that led to five or six other major stations throughout the city.

Foot traffic in and out of the portals trickled noticeably lighter than the streams of people pushing through the train turnstiles. Only the very rich—or those whose jobs covered commuting costs—would pay the fees needed to stroll through public portals so casually.

Not all mages chose to devote one of their precious magic branches to a personal porting skill. As a result, Wist's Shien clan relatives very well might be among the sharply dressed women and men savoring the spaciousness of the public portal hall, stopping in to dally at the high-end perfumeries and posh tea lounges and elite designer boutiques that lined the walls.

Luckily for me and Wist, we were at zero risk of encountering any stray Shiens here in the plebeian part of the station. Here was where people lined up to ride ordinary clanking trains.

As we waited, I noticed a large taped-off area across from us. The entire facing platform appeared to be closed to passengers.

We still had time to kill. I meandered over to a station attendant and asked what had happened over yonder.

It was from last night, he told me. A mage had gone berserk during rush hour.

Under normal circumstances, most people could go their entire lives without ever encountering a berserk mage in person. I'd met one on the street by my own apartment last month. Here lingered still-fresh traces of another. (Miyu didn't really count, given that I'd pushed her over the edge with my own two hands.)

Clearly a coincidence. But maybe not the most auspicious way to kick off our mini-vacation.

Our destination was a tiny little town called Sweet Olive. Getting there would require a two-hour train ride to a juncture at Philomena, a mid-size regional city. Then another hour on an ultra-local line.

On our first train, I took the window seat. Bare March fields and worn-down mountains whizzed by outside.

I'd thought Wist might conk out right away, but she kept tilting her head to look out the window.

"When was the last time you took the train?" I asked.

"...When we were students?" Her tone suggested that she couldn't remember.

I leaned on Wist when I got sleepy, which didn't take long. There was something hypnotic about the constant rumble and irregular clanking of the train chassis beneath us.

"Miyu was fired," Wist said just as I'd started to doze off.

I lifted my head a little. "Good. When did you find out?"

"Last night. When I told Manatree about our itinerary."

Wist had mentioned only that we were headed for the southeastern countryside. As long as she didn't bring up the exact town name, I remained hopeful that Manatree might not realize I was going to check in on my parents.

After I got parole, PubSec had handed me a new identity—a crucial prerequisite for my rejoining society. They hadn't expressly forbidden me from seeing my family. Then again, I'd never really inquired if I could, now had I?

"Was she always like that?" I asked.

"Who?"

"Your sister."

Wist appeared to lapse into thought. I could feel the dull growl of the train reverberating through the seat cushions. Past the window, countryside houses stippled half-wild hillsides. I suppressed a jaw-aching yawn.

"She's the lowest-level mage among all my remaining siblings," Wist said. "Ever since we were children, the others always made sure she knew it."

"Remaining siblings?"

"There were a few subliminals. They got sent to live with far-off branches of the family long before the Shiens adopted me. I never met them. Growing up, I hardly had any idea they existed."

"Your family is a real-life horror story, you know."

"They don't see it that way."

"They sure don't, huh." Another yawn escaped me. "Guess that's the problem."

"The six siblings I knew were all mages. Most at least a few classes higher than Miyu. Three sisters and three brothers."

A pause. "Miyu was never a sweetheart. She followed the others' lead. Speaking for myself as a child, though, my brothers were much worse."

Wist had told me once about an old well. It lay dry and abandoned, hidden in one of the wilder sections of the Shien estate.

When she was around six—shortly after being forcibly taken in by the Shien clan—her adoptive siblings were mostly in their teens, with only one other still under ten.

Wist's older brothers took her to the abandoned well. They told her it was time for an adventure. They lowered her to the bottom.

Then they left her.

She hadn't yet learned a single magic skill. She'd been diagnosed as a potential S-class, but at the time she couldn't do anything practical with her plethora of magic branches.

Without any skills imprinted on them, her branches were a useless treasure. Like holding a pile of gold coins in your lap as a mountaintop blizzard froze you to death.

Indeed, she should have died there. Days passed. Her brothers never came back for her. When she grew older and thought back on it, she suspected them of deflecting the search parties.

But this is what happened: six-year-old Wist, with only herself to rely on, invented a new magic skill without anyone there to teach her. She imprinted it on one of her branches without any prior knowledge of how skill acquisition was supposed to work.

It was nothing revolutionary. A weak, malformed variant of Zero

Gravity. It lightened her just enough that she could scrabble her way up the rough stone walls to the top of the well.

She walked part of the way back to the mansion with bleeding feet and fingertips, then passed out near the edge of the rose garden. A landscaper found her.

At the time she hadn't fully comprehended that her brothers—seeing her as a low-bred usurper—had made a sincere effort to murder her. When her Shien parents asked her what had happened, she said she fell in the well by herself.

Maybe she'd thought that would be the best way to end it. Or maybe she'd sensed that telling the truth would lead to further retaliation.

Wist had many stories like this. The well was just the start of it.

On our way to Sweet Olive, we stopped at the city of Philomena to scrounge up some lunch between trains.

The next train we had to take only ran once every two hours. While waiting, we left the mid-size transfer station and wandered into a dimly lit cafe, the sort that transforms into a bar in the evening.

After we finished eating, Wist kept mum while I chatted with the cafe owner. She was probably doing her best to be inconspicuous.

An older man at the far end of the bar turned to stare at her without blinking. He had a younger companion tending to him. Grandfather and grandchild, perhaps.

"Is your friend a mage?" the owner asked quietly.

"Mm," I said. Wist was a mage, all right.

"Don't mind him." The owner tipped his head a bit in the old man's direction. His voice dropped further. "He's not all there, but he has excellent magic perception. He's just looking at your friend's magic."

Wist could hide her face with her hat and glasses and mask. Yet no amount of ordinary clothing could conceal the magic threads that crawled inside her, as bountiful as capillaries.

Of course, the vast majority of people out there could perceive little magic. Even those with sharper magic perception were rarely gifted enough to make out the intricate shape of Wist's branches at a glance.

At most they might sense that she was a higher-level mage of some sort. As long as she didn't go out of her way to look the part, they would hardly guess she was the Kraken herself.

"He a regular?" I asked the owner, dropping my voice to match his.

"He's always here," the owner said. "Rain or shine. The woman with him is his caretaker."

The owner stopped wiping dishes and leaned closer across the counter.

"Terrible story," he said, almost whispering now. "He fought in the Jacian Wars of forty years ago. Got hit by a psychobomb."

I stole another look at the old man. He was still gaping openly at Wist's magic core. His eyes were glassy. His companion gently dabbed bits of spittle from the corner of his mouth.

History had never really been my forte. Even I remembered learning a thing or two about psychobombs, though. They were Jacian technology, an extremely complex amalgam of offensive magic. They could only be formed by weaving together a variety of skill cuttings taken from multiple mages.

And they'd been banned by the International Vorpal Defense Council for decades now. It hadn't occurred to me that there might still be living survivors right here in Osmanthus.

Wist said little as we headed over to catch our next (and hopefully final) train. "Didn't like being gawked at?" I asked.

She adjusted her mask. "Should I have approached him?"

"What for? He seemed content to look from afar."

"Maybe I could have done something for him."

"There's no curing the effects of a psychobomb. Unless you secretly developed a new skill for it without telling me."

Wist shook her head. "No. It's just that I thought psychobomb victims were supposed to be catatonic. But it felt like he could really see me."

"Want to go back?"

Half of me hoped she would say yes. I was starting to get antsy about the prospect of hunting down my parents.

Wist saw right through me. "Not now. Maybe on the way home."

An hour later, we disembarked from a dinky two-car train. We were the only passengers to get off at Sweet Olive. We were just about the only passengers on the tiny local line, period.

Sweet Olive Station wasn't much larger than my Osmanthus City apartment. It was also utterly empty. It would have felt downright apocalyptic if it hadn't been so neatly groomed.

I'd heard of these tiny unmanned train stations out in the countryside, but I'd never actually seen one before. I suppose it operated on the honor system.

We discarded our tickets in the designated box. I put on a large pair of sunglasses and scanned the bulletin board on the wall with interest. Many of the papers tacked up there appeared to be advertising local festivals in neighboring towns. Some were from last summer. Some were from five or ten years in the past.

Wist had said my parents' place was a few miles from the station. We'd planned on renting bicycles. But it soon became evident that there was no sort of bicycle-renting system around here.

I had a feeling this was the sort of village where the locals would be happy to lend us a squeaky old bike or two if we asked.

We didn't ask a soul. We opted to walk.

We were already unusual—downright eccentric, actually—simply by virtue of being strangers here in Sweet Olive. I didn't want to do anything to make our presence even more memorable.

What little town there was soon gave way to empty rice fields. At this time of year they were uniformly bare and dark brown, not yet filled with water. Large birds whose names I'd never learned circled lazily overhead. The sky seemed very tall and remote.

I wondered why my parents had chosen Sweet Olive. I'd never heard of it before. I'd certainly never been here. We had no roots in this part of the country.

Maybe that was precisely what had drawn them. A sleepy town far from the political heart of Osmanthus. A place where no one knew them. A place where no one knew their only daughter.

"There," Wist said.

We stopped in the shadow of a very thick tree, one only just starting to erupt full of bright spring leaves.

Further down the road squatted a run-down house with a brilliant blue tile roof. The garden jostled with late-blooming plum trees and early-blooming cherry trees in every shade of red and pink and white. I spotted bushes dotted with grape-sized citrus fruit. I spotted wayward spikes of incongruous cacti and succulents.

And I saw my father crouched among flower beds, fussing with something. Planting annuals, probably.

The thought floated up to me out of nowhere. I hadn't contemplated my parents' gardening calendar in years and years.

A lump lodged in my throat. All was well if my father still had enough energy and motivation to mess around with planting flowers. But his hair seemed lighter and thinner than I remembered. His whole form seemed smaller, and not just because he was down on his knees.

The front door swung open. I tensed like a rabbit. My mother stuck her head out for a moment, then ducked back inside again.

I wanted so badly to hear what they'd said to each other, even though it was clearly nothing important.

I felt Wist looking at me.

"You know you can approach them," she said.

Again—I'd never specifically asked PubSec if I were allowed to make contact. I suppose I'd been too much of a coward to want to hear the answer.

I feared it might be no. I also feared it might be yes.

"Don't want to cause any trouble," I demurred.

"What sort of trouble?"

"I got parole on a—I mean, it was close to a technicality. I'm still a traitor."

"You're still their daughter."

I turned to Wist. What a suspicious-looking pair we made, with our dark glasses and stylish hats.

"Look," I said. "I can and will live with my mistakes. I like myself just fine."

"You certainly do."

"Yeah. I can live with disappointing myself. But I don't want to force it on them. They must've been so disappointed—hurt, devastated— that I got a Board member murdered. That I got myself locked up for treason. And it wasn't even a false accusation! I really did it. I did everything the government accused me of.

"They've got a nice enough life here. That's all I wanted to see. I don't want to pop up out of nowhere and rip open old wounds again.

"Look—they're doing perfectly fine without me. They always said they wanted a roof like that. Look at those tiles. Perfect. Bluer than anything."

Wist studied my father. Then me. Then the cerulean tiles.

"Maybe," she said in her expressionless way, "they would be more hurt to know that you could have visited but didn't. That you chose not to."

"They don't have to know that, now do they?"

"No," Wist said. "But—"

I cut her off. "The fact is, they never contacted me in prison."

"To be fair, neither did I."

"Very funny. I don't know if they stayed away of their own accord—yeah, like you—or if the government interfered. At this point, it doesn't really matter. I don't want to bother them."

Wist's head perked up. A second later, she put a hand between my shoulders. She started steering me back the way we'd come.

"We're drawing attention," she said under her breath.

Now I saw them, too. A few elderly woman at the corner of an empty rice field. They clustered together, wary as scarecrows. All eyes fixed on us.

"Probably think we're criminals from the big city." I took a moment to reflect on this. "Wait, I *am* a criminal from the big city."

"No need to sound so proud of yourself."

Given that we'd already had lunch, there was nothing left to do in Sweet Olive except stare at the houses close up and the mountains far off. The majority of buildings had traditional steep-peaked thatched roofs. Only a few were topped with colorful glazed tiles, like my parents' place. I remarked to Wist that they ought to promote this village as some kind of historical landmark.

Perhaps we could've found a would-be inn here in town, but I figured we'd best try not to stand out any more than we already had. We took the two-car train back to Philomena.

After booking us a hotel room near Philomena Station, I led Wist over to the cafe where we'd had lunch. It was still light out, rather too early for dinner, and a Closed sign hung on the glass panel door.

Yet the door gave way when I pushed it. The clang of the welcome chime made my shoulders jump.

The owner stopped wiping the bar counter. The old man and his companion were still ensconced in a corner, although the caretaker kept patting at her handbag as though preparing to get up and go.

I greeted the owner, apologized for barging in. I regaled him with a few tales of the sights and smells of Sweet Olive.

Meanwhile, we watched askance as Wist went up to the old man with the half-frozen face.

He was definitely looking at her magic, not her lovely dark eyes. He fixed his gaze on her lower abdomen, on the light of her core. I guess there's no accounting for taste.

I asked the cafe owner if psychobomb survivors all had a fascination with magic. "He's the only one I know in person," the owner answered, too soft for the others to hear.

The old man observed Wist's magic as if he were drinking it in with those glistening eyes of his. No blinking.

"Like a moth to a lamp," I said.

"His children are mages," said the owner. "That's probably why it sparks his attention. They haven't visited him in a very long time."

My parents were younger. And as far as I could tell, they were still sound of mind. My father certainly didn't need a caretaker.

But that was what I thought of when I saw the old man staring hungrily at Wist's magic core, staring as if he could never get enough of looking at it. I thought of my father hunched over the flower bed. The chaotic garden like something out of a storybook. The roof a truer blue than the sky above.

A hand squeezed my heart.

Eventually Wist ducked her head at the old man and his caretaker. The woman said something to her, something seemingly warm and friendly. The old man showed no further reaction. His eyes followed Wist while we trailed one after another out the door, thanking the cafe owner as we went.

I wondered if the old man had felt anything, if he'd remembered anything pleasant or painful. Anything at all.

Or perhaps his fixation on Wist had been a mere reflex with no real thought or emotion behind it. No longing for his own children. Just a blank attraction to the brilliant convoluted maze of her uncountable magic branches.

I wondered which was better. To feel something—along with solitude, along with suffering—or to know nothing.

On the way to the hotel, Wist took my hand.

It was one of those times when our fingers immediately laced together as if compelled to join. Like a trap closing. And our hands fit perfectly despite being different sizes. And there was a curious soft look on Wist's normally unchanging face. But it might just have been an illusion wrought by the sinking light of a long tired day.

10

Before you get any ideas, I should mention that it was just a regular room in a regular business hotel. Clean, but less than sparkling. The windows looked straight into a neighboring office building. I promptly whisked the curtains shut.

I wasn't familiar with the finer details of Wist's finances. But no matter what kind of accommodation I put her in, I couldn't imagine her complaining. I'm sure she'd have been just as happy with crashing in a barn.

Which was a good thing, since I, for one, wouldn't have been able to afford a penthouse suite. Assuming such a sumptuous offering even existed here in humble Philomena.

To a resident of Sweet Olive, no doubt Philomena seemed downright metropolitan. But Osmanthus City was the size of dozens and dozens of Philomenas pushed together.

Put another way, Anthum wasn't even the largest train station in

Osmanthus City. It was simply one of many. And the downtown area right around Anthum could've swallowed up all of Philomena, with plenty of room to spare.

People often spoke of the capital and the rest of Osmanthus as if they were two separate regions—separate countries, almost—with different values and different neuroses. Even just a single day of travel was enough to make me start to understand why.

Anyhow, we hadn't come here in search of luxury. Besides, Wist's tower was more spacious (and had more in the way of visual interest) than any standard city building. A regional hotel chain could hardly hope to compete.

Despite that, there was still something novel to sprawling out in a space not our own. I bought beers from the vending machine down the hall, then recalled after a few bitter sips that I didn't particularly care for lager. Wist dutifully downed both tall cans.

Soulful, somewhat tinny music streamed from the hotel room's melodium. I turned up the volume so we could hear it in the bath.

We quickly abandoned the idea of bathing together, though. The tub was far too small, leaving us a bruised pile of slippery limbs. Fun in its own way, but not exactly conducive to the business of getting clean.

Afterward we rolled about with damp hair on the stiff white hotel pillows. The melodium cooed at us with songs in a foreign language.

I could tell Wist had something to say. She'd been on the verge of it ever since we left Sweet Olive. Nothing about her looked different from the outside, but I sensed the tension in her humming through the bond.

"Maybe it's about time for you to spill it," I said.

She turned her head. The wetness made her hair blacker than ink.

"Your parents reached out to me," she said slowly.

"What, recently?"

"Many years ago."

"While I was locked up, then?"

"Shortly after your conviction. They asked if I could give you a message."

I felt my breath come up short.

"I told them"—Wist had begun speaking faster—"I told them I couldn't. I told them I was the one who betrayed you, who turned you in. They said they understood. They said I did the right thing."

"So they tried," I said eventually. "But the message could've been anything, huh? Maybe they wanted to tell me to go screw a donkey. Maybe they just wanted to say *thanks for nothing, you ingrate*."

"I should've taken the message," Wist said. "I should've faced you instead of hiding for seven years."

I shot her a glare. "Yeah, I know you had all kinds of reasons. Don't think you can trick me into defending you. You should've done this. I should've done that. No matter. It's all done and over with."

Wist reached over and started to fix my bathrobe. I'd done a rather sloppy job of tying it.

"What I'm trying to say," she continued steadily, "is that I doubt your parents meant to tell you to screw a donkey."

"Sounds to me like you're trying to say a lot more than that."

"It's up to you whether or not to reveal yourself to them. But if you do want to visit them, I won't let PubSec bring up a word of complaint."

"I know what we should do," I said. "Let's make this fair. You go find your birth parents. Then I'll reach out to mine."

Wist's hands stilled. "I have no memory of my birth parents. You know that's a false equivalence."

"And you know I was just trying to stall for time," I said. "Okay, you can win this one. Happy? I'll go see mine. Not right away. Not this weekend. But someday."

"Someday?"

"You can port me right to their doorstop when I decide I'm ready. Look, I've only been on parole for a couple of months. I've got the rest of my life to figure this out."

Wist gave me a slow nod. As far as I could tell, the beer had bestowed exactly zero effect on her demeanor. What a bore.

I exacted my revenge later that night, nibbling at the side of her neck until both of our bathrobes abandoned ship. The room's melodium had switched itself off at some designated hour, leaving only Wist's exquisitely pained breaths in my ear.

I'd never beat her at arm wrestling, but she melted when I did my best to hold her down.

"Hey," I said, during a temporary break in the proceedings. "Maybe this is what a honeymoon would be like."

"In a business hotel?"

"What, are you claiming you have higher standards?"

"We've known each other for—twenty years?" Wist sounded startled. "Has it really been that long?"

I counted off the years on my fingers. "We met at fourteen, right? Yep—almost a full two decades. Feel old yet?"

"Seems a bit late to be at the honeymoon stage."

"Maybe we've come full circle," I said. "All the way back to the goopy schmoopy parts."

Wist looked me in the eye. "Prove it."

I burst out laughing. Then I made her eat her words.

In truth, we weren't used to being tourists. Besides, in visiting Sweet Olive, we'd already checked the main item off our agenda. That left us with another two full days to while away.

We strolled though a few public gardens around Philomena. We ogled dogs of every size and shape and color at the dog park.

We hiked an old mountain—more of an uppity hill, really—just outside the city. When I complained of sore legs, we retired to our room and tumbled back into bed. Wist told me that if I found a few mild walks tiring, I really ought to work out more.

But even if you never believe another word I say, you better believe this: I made damn sure she didn't regret spending just as much time in the cramped hotel room as we did outside.

On Monday morning, we were about to board the train back to Osmanthus when my ear cuff pinched at me hard enough to make me yelp.

"Manatree," I said, irked. "What was that for?"

"You're with the Kraken?" Manatree's voice asked in my ear.

"Getting ready to head home from our mini-vacation. The vacation you specifically recommended taking."

"Good. I'm calling an emergency meeting. Be at the Kraken's tower in ten minutes."

So much for our train tickets. I linked my arm through Wist's and informed her that we had orders to meet Manatree at the tower.

A millisecond later, Wist had ported us to her sun-filled tower bedroom. Ten minutes after that, we converged in a circular conference room about midway up the tower.

Abstract stained glass windows—a kaleidoscopic swirl of jewel-tone colors—surrounded the room on all sides. A slanted mosaic of rainbow light painted the table, the floor, the forbidding faces of far more Public Security officials than I'd expected to show up on such short notice.

One of them might've been Manatree's boss. A few others appeared to be of similar or even higher rank, at least judging by their uniforms and body language.

Just from the way they looked at me—or, rather, strove not to acknowledge my presence—I suppose they all recognized me for who

I really was. The one and only Asa Clematis, now miraculously out on parole. I wondered how many of them had the privilege of knowing that this convicted traitor was bonded for life to their precious Kraken.

"It's the Extinguishers," said Manatree.

You could always trust good old Manatree to get right to the topic at hand.

She looked around the sunlit table. "They're threatening to, and I quote, 'exterminate the Old River district.'"

"I thought the Extinguishers were all about exterminating Wist," I said. "What's Old River got to do with the Kraken?"

Manatree and her entourage contemplated me as if I wore a robe of manure. I tilted my head and blinked right back at them, undeterred. For one thing, I was used to it. For another thing, all I'd done was ask a genuine question.

The Old River district was a ward off to the far east side of Osmanthus City. Nowhere near my apartment. Certainly nowhere near Wist's tower. As far as I knew, it was primarily residential.

The Extinguishers, on the other hand, were a long line of cultists whose sworn purpose was to destroy the Kraken. They blamed Wist for the rapid increase in vorpal holes these past few decades. Apparently they also blamed her for earthquakes, flooding, wildfires, foreign border skirmishes, and bouts of food poisoning.

"The threat was sent directly to Public Security," Manatree said, more to the table as a whole than to me. "They didn't specify why they're choosing to target the Old River district.

"I can think of two possibilities. One: the Kraken's eldest brother owns significant property there. A cluster of riverside apartment buildings."

"Does he actually live there, though?"

Her glare hardened. "No. Would you be so kind as to let me finish?"

"Sure!" I chirped. "I'll try."

"Two," Manatree continued. "The Church of the Kraken recently opened an enormous new shrine in Old River."

"The church of the *what*?" I demanded.

Wist, who'd been slouched next to me with her elbows on the table, showed little sign of surprise as she listened. Clearly it wasn't her first time hearing of this—this church. Whatever it was.

Now she gradually slumped forward and dropped her face into her hands. To anyone else, it might have looked like a pose of the darkest despair. I, for one, suspected that she was simply wracked with embarrassment.

"The Church," Manatree repeated, "of the Kraken."

"You hear that, Wist?" I asked. "You've got a church."

"I'm sure the Kraken knows of them." Manatree cleared her throat. "Our intelligence suggests that the threat may not be a hoax. The Extinguishers have previously destroyed Church facilities in neighboring countries."

I'd never felt such a singular combination of entertainment and horror. "This Church is some kind of international religious organization?"

"The Church has been active for close to a decade," Manatree said frostily. "Like the Extinguishers, they claim much older roots. If you don't know who they are, you have only your own lack of cultural awareness to blame."

"I was in prison for seven years," I said. "Give me a break."

The other PubSec officials stirred in their seats as if they dearly wished to shut me up. But there I was, right beside their idol Wist, speaking about twenty times as much as her. And she seemed perfectly inclined to let me get away with it.

Oh, how I loved watching them squirm.

"Furthermore," Manatree said, enunciating like a knife, "we have evidence that the Extinguishers recently made contact with Jacian elements. Whatever they plan on doing in Old River, there's a very high likelihood that they intend to make use of illicit Jacian technology."

"Like a psychobomb?" I piped up.

The grand meeting room went dead quiet.

Wist slowly lifted her head, colored blue and purple and fiery orange by the light from the stained glass window behind her. Manatree regarded me with an expression I'd never seen on her before. Something close to open consternation.

All the other officials riveted their eyes to me, too. After that one long frigid moment finally snapped to an end, they began furiously muttering amongst themselves.

I caught just enough to realize they suspected me of knowing something I shouldn't. Of being involved with the Extinguishers, even.

"I can't hear," Wist said.

The PubSec crew immediately ceased their babbling. Wist glanced at Manatree and motioned for her to continue.

"A psychobomb … is one possibility." Manatree soon recovered her composure. "Their threats sound dire, but they've kept the details vague. Presumably to make it difficult for us to enact appropriate defenses."

She was focused completely on Wist now. "The Extinguishers have given us a very short deadline. Only two days remain. They demand that you turn yourself in at the appointed time.

"If not," she said, still addressing Wist, "they'll carry out their threat to exterminate Old River. They also claim that they will immediately start extermination procedures if they see signs of the district being evacuated, or notice any other PubSec activity in the area."

Well, that was a little strange.

Even if Wist showed up as planned, what exactly did the Extinguishers plan to do with her?

Their best efforts to murder her had already met with spectacular failure. They might lay all sorts of elaborate traps for her, but it was hard not to imagine that backfiring on them in the end.

Then again, if they were true fanatics, perhaps they didn't mind taking such risks. Perhaps they glorified their past brethren who had rushed forward to assassinate Wist—and simply ended up getting themselves hideously killed in the process.

"So I should turn myself in," Wist said.

Manatree's brow furrowed. "We believe their plan is to execute the threat regardless of whether or not you show up."

"But you don't know that for sure."

"If you do show up, it's a prime opportunity for them to strike at you. It would be uncharacteristic of them not to use all the tools at their disposal. Be it a psychobomb, conventional combat magic, physical weapons, or all of those combined. They won't hesitate to violate the Mage Conventions."

Wist scanned the grim faces around the table. "Are you telling me not to go, then?"

"The risks are extraordinarily high." Manatree seemed to speak with more care than usual. "But—"

"How many people live in Old River?" Wist asked.

Her tone was flat. Nothing had changed about her slouching posture or the set of her face. But I felt something in the neighborhood of fear begin to dilate inside me.

I didn't like it. Wist was Wist. I didn't want to react the same as all those flinty-looking men and women in their starched PubSec uniforms, with their large eyes and the sudden sheen of sickly sweat on their foreheads.

When they gaped at her, they didn't see my Wist. They saw only the Kraken, a fearsome dead-eyed judge of lesser beings.

Wist repeated herself. "How many people live in Old River?"

Manatree was holding up far better than the rest of them. She stood erect, chin high, hands clasped at her back. "Over seventy thousand."

"I see," Wist said. "Have you received any orders from the Board of Magi?"

"We reported to the Board that it seems to be a credible threat."

"And?"

"The Board instructed us to share the details with you. And—to stay out of your way."

"Up to me, then." Wist reached up and stretched. From the corner of my eye, I spotted a few of the PubSec officials flinching. So jumpy.

Wist rose to her feet. She leaned on the back of her chair to work through more stretches—quads, hamstrings—as she spoke to Manatree.

"Do what you can to investigate the Extinguishers. Without entering Old River." She paused, switched to her other leg. "I'll take care of the rest."

"You're going in," Manatree said. It wasn't a question.

"No one else can." There was a faraway look on Wist's face.

I missed the stupid Philomena hotel room and its murky-patterned curtains and the industrial feel of its sheets. I missed the lingering smell of top-strength cleaning supplies. I missed the quirky music that piped out through the melodium at sensual moments, making both of us dissolve in laughter.

Most of all, I missed our world narrowing to only me and Wist. To fresh morning air and tedious train trips. No magic, and therefore no need for healing.

But our home city—and those homicidal Extinguishers—had other plans for us.

11

THE TOWER'S FIRST-FLOOR entrance hall was a dusty wooden space reminiscent of an unfinished barn. Wist's cat crouched on a high shelf full of gardening implements. Her tail switched from side to side as she gazed down upon us with an air of profound condescension.

After ushering the Public Security gang out the front door, Wist turned and looked at me as if she weren't quite sure what she was seeing.

The air felt hushed. Morning sunlight came in sideways through smudged windows.

With a sudden air of decision, Wist stooped. She put her arms around me. Surprised, I caught at her back. She was squeezing me quite hard. But the most surprising part was that it didn't hurt my neck. She'd bent much lower than usual, more than making up for the height difference.

She straightened up and released me. I caught at her sleeve. "Where are you going?" I asked hastily.

Wist blinked. "The Old River district."

"What about me?"

"Don't you have work?"

So she *was* trying to ditch me. "Nothing I can't reschedule," I said.

"What I need to do—" Wist stopped and looked up at the vaulted ceiling as if buying time to puzzle out her phrasing. "It'll go faster if I'm alone."

"No doubt," I agreed. "Take me anyway."

"Why?"

"What, my charming companionship isn't a good enough reason?"

Clearly Wist hadn't expected this much resistance. "You would usually prioritize efficiency," she said. "Why not now?"

"No one knows exactly what the Extinguishers are threatening. But even Manatree was starting to look a little nervous there. In other words," I continued, "whatever it is, the danger is genuine. Even for you."

"If it's dangerous for me, then it's ten thousand times more dangerous for anyone else. All the more reason not to bring you."

"Nuh-uh." I wagged my finger at her. "Quite the opposite. Taking me along will force you to act more cognizant of the risks. It'll force you to play it safe."

"You make it sound as if I would act completely reckless without you tagging along."

"Am I wrong?"

Wist didn't answer.

"That aside," I added, "I'll be honest. Part of me just wants to get a good look at the Church of the Kraken."

Wist turned on her heel. "Bye, Clematis."

I dashed forward to catch at her arm. "Kidding! I was kidding."

Wist gave me a bleak look. "No, you weren't."

"Whatever you're thinking of doing in Old River, would it really go that much more smoothly without me?"

From the outside she appeared utterly unmoved. Our inner bond betrayed her: through it I could sense her starting to waver. I tightened my grip on her arm and snuggled in closer, casting my best mournful eyes up at her.

"Maybe I just don't like the idea of sending you off to face grave danger alone," I said. "Maybe I just want to stay with you longer. Imagine if our positions were reversed."

Wist pondered this notion, then said, "You'd find a way to sneak off and leave me behind without a second thought."

Dang it. "I'm the one with a criminal record," I conceded. "A certified bad person. But *you* wouldn't do that to me, would you?"

She just needed one last push.

"Me, I can keep arguing like this all day and all night," I said. "The people of Old River don't have that kind of time to waste. Try porting over there without me. I'll just keep poking you through the bond till you—"

Wist ported us in the middle of my sentence. I felt no shift in gravity. No gust of wind. No ear-popping release of pressure. Yet now we stood on a residential city street, and a hilly one at that. Houses and apartments jostled for space all the way down to the banks of the eponymous river.

"Thanks," I said to Wist. I squeezed her arm. "If it helps, you can think of this as a date."

She didn't dignify that with a response. Fair enough.

Meanwhile, she'd begun using an extraordinarily strong variant of Disappearance. It wasn't even directed at me, but the effect was nevertheless so powerful that I myself would've lost track of her if I weren't clinging to her like a burr.

The Extinguishers had warned Public Security against taking any defensive action in the Old River district. They hadn't necessarily warned Wist herself not to do anything.

It seemed likely, however, that they would use any excuse they could get to deploy their psychobomb. Or whatever other weapons they happened to have on hand.

And if they couldn't find an excuse, eventually they would concoct one. For the time being, in any case, it would be safest for Wist to creep around unnoticed.

Initially, I was content to let Wist take the lead. She wrapped me in her Disappearance and ported us both from one high place to another. The roof of the luxury apartment towers owned by her brother. The peak of an absolutely monstrous evergreen tree in a swathe of undeveloped forest. A mound of grassy earth at the top of a genteel park; it overlooked the glittering water of the wide, shallow river.

The one thing she didn't do was magically scan the district in search of the Extinguishers' weapons stash. She might've been able to find conventional munitions that way. But a psychobomb—crafted of pure magic—would be another matter.

Jacian technology excelled at concealing magic cuttings. A psychobomb was nothing more than a cleverly crafted ball of magic cuttings.

Put it in a regular bag, and I'd be able to spot it from all the way down the street. Through walls and buildings, even.

Put it in a Jacian briefcase, and I wouldn't notice a hint of suspicious magic leaking out. Not even if you plopped it on a table right in front of me.

So I could understand why Wist hadn't bothered with attempting to hunt down the psychobomb itself. And by now I'd begun to comprehend what she was attempting to do instead.

"Hate to say it," I told her in the riverside park, "but you're going to have to expand your range quite a bit."

Wist gave me a look—a silent request to elaborate.

To our left, children clambered over rocks and poked at dead leaves floating in a pond. Their gleefully incoherent shrieks were almost indistinguishable from the voices of all the squawking morning birds.

To our right, families spread tarps and blankets out on the yellow fields of dormant grass. Some blew soap bubbles. Some swung jump ropes. Some ran in hapless circles with dented paper kites.

"The Extinguishers threatened Old River," I said. "But even if their weapon is something magical, I doubt they have it keyed to stop right at the district's exact geographical borders."

Wist, with all her porting to and fro, had most likely been attempting to scout out the full expanse of the district. To visually assess the area she needed to protect.

But who was to say there wouldn't be any spillover into neighboring districts? Imagine a physical bomb. Just because you chose to detonate it inside Old River didn't mean it would politely cease causing damage right at the edge of the map.

"Then I need to shield more of the city," Wist said. She looked uncharacteristically tired. Tinted with genuine exhaustion, I mean, not just her usual aura of sluggishness.

She rubbed at her face. "The question is—how much to shield. How far."

"Right," I said. "Gotta start somewhere. Seems pretty safe to assume their attack will center on the Church of the Kraken. So make sure you have all of Old River covered. Then add a good sweep of the nearest districts to the east."

I sketched an oblong lump—the rough shape of the Old River district—in the air with my finger. I jabbed at a spot to indicate the approximate location of the Church of the Kraken. I drew a large circle with the Church at its center, one that extended into multiple neighboring districts. Hopefully she'd know what I meant, considering that all I'd done was wave my forefinger around in empty space as I spoke.

Wist nodded slowly. "Okay," she said.

She took a breath. I gave her a bracing thump on the back. She leaned over and pushed her eye socket up against the boniest part of my shoulder. She often did that when she had a headache, though I'd be hard-pressed to explain why.

No one could heal Wist better than me. I say this not to brag, but rather as a plain statement of fact. Anyway, it was a moot point now that we were bonded.

Now no one else could heal Wist, period.

Even with my caliber of healing to support her, using magic wasn't necessarily pleasurable for Wist. It certainly wasn't painless. Knowing this, I kept my usual chatter to a minimum.

At one point, we stopped by Old River Station. I filched a map of the eastern third of the city from a rack of free tourist brochures.

I took notes on the map to help Wist keep track as she jumped us from location to location. The riverside park again. The reed-covered bank of silt that poked up out of the middle of the river itself. The top of the train station.

At each spot, Wist broke off one of her skill-imprinted magic branches and planted it in place like a sapling. Then she broke off a different, second branch—one imprinted with Disappearance—and planted it right next to the first. A form of insurance, I suppose, to keep any stray Extinguishers from catching sight of her transplanted magic and growing suspicious.

Ordinary mages needed at least a few hours to regrow a pruned magic branch. Wist's sprouted back longer and wilder and curlier the second she snapped one off. Theoretically this meant there was never any need to stop and rest.

In reality, the more spots on the map she covered, the more her movements slowed. She carried herself like an achy old woman. The crowded magic branches inside her tangled together in a frenzied battle for dominance. She cricked her neck, stopped to massage the small of her back.

Midway through, I plucked at the hem of Wist's cropped jacket. I made her hold still and wait while I swiftly combed out her magic threads. She let out a long sigh that sounded close to a groan. I don't think she heard herself doing it.

Around noon, I showed Wist my now-crumpled paper map. She'd planted magic cuttings at regular intervals throughout all of Old River, as well as a thick swathe of the neighborhoods further east.

"Good coverage," I told her. "So what's next?"

Wist told me she wanted to find a vorpal hole.

At first I thought that sounded like a tall order. Vorpal holes—even the static sort that wouldn't harm you as long as you gave them a wide berth—were most dangerous in populated areas. I had a hard time imagining Public Security letting one sit around untouched in the middle of the capital city.

Then again, Wist was the only mage capable of permanently closing a vorpal hole. The government needed her to seal up vorpal holes throughout Osmanthus. The International Vorpal Defense Council needed her to seal up vorpal holes all over the continent. New ones were constantly emerging, near and far alike.

Plus, vorpal clean-up was hardly the only demand on her time. If worldwide vorpal hole formation really had accelerated as much as experts claimed, perhaps the government had no choice but to let smaller, lower-priority holes lurk untouched for weeks or months or years.

Wist, unsurprisingly, grasped the whole vorpal hole situation much better than I did. Sure enough, PubSec turned out to have records of five open vorpal holes here in Old River.

One behind a supermarket. One halfway down a narrow alley to nowhere. One in the ramshackle yard of an abandoned house. One in the air several meters above a major bridge across the river.

And one in the middle of the new shrine recently erected by the Church of the Kraken.

Wist ported to check them one by one. I dutifully recorded the results on the map.

The first three had already vanished. Truly minor vorpal holes did sometimes go away on their own. Meanwhile, the hole above the bridge was scarcely the size of a pinprick. Far too small for Wist's purposes.

"Guess we've got to pay the Church a visit," I said.

"No need to sound so happy about it," Wist said sourly.

"Relax," I told her, rubbing my hands together. "You stay hidden. I'll do all the talking."

From the outside, the alleged shrine resembled nothing quite so much as a commercial wedding venue. Frilly bas-relief carvings piped their way around the building's facade like decorations on an unnecessarily expensive cake.

An ornately lettered sign above the grand double doors said *Church of the Kraken* and something to the effect of *All are welcome!*

Wist, still cloaked by Disappearance, lurked gloomily behind me. I opted to take the Church at their word. I pushed the right-hand door open and invited myself inside. Wist slipped in after me with all the vitality of a centuries-old ghost.

Our fair Osmanthus was not a particularly religious country. I'd set foot in old temples and churches before, but all of them had long since been converted to public museums. They presented themselves as historical artifacts, not active houses of worship.

In short, I didn't really know what to expect. I thought I'd walked in there with an open mind.

But the Church of the Kraken still managed to catch me by surprise.

I stopped dead.

The door creaked gently shut at my back.

The shrine was a tall magnificent space, with crystal-clean sunlight gushing down from glorious skylights.

And everywhere I looked, I saw Wist.

Life-sized statues. Miniature figurines. Hundreds of them in all, packed in together like a crowd at a stadium. Behind me, I heard a dull thunk that made me wonder if the real-life Wist had turned to bang her head on the wall.

I drifted forward, reeled in by a combination of titillation and mild terror. This tableau would be a nightmare for someone with a phobia of dolls or mannequins.

At the center of the shrine towered a wooden sculpture at least twice as tall as the human Wist I knew.

I'm no connoisseur, but as a pure piece of art, it seemed rather impressive. She wore traditional mage robes complete with floor-length, many-layered sleeves, the draping fabric carved with a startlingly realistic fluidity and sense of weight, the bright colors and fine embroidery painted with such a sure touch that at first I thought the statue wore real fabric.

Come to think of it, I struggled to remember ever seeing Wist put on this type of classical outfit. Maybe when we graduated from secondary school? Or perhaps the Shiens had occasionally wrestled her into mage robes for family portraits.

Curiously, all the statues and figurines depicted Wist with supernaturally long hair. In most cases, it took the form of a glossy black braid that wound around her body like an anaconda or floated tail-like in the air behind her, defying gravity.

As far as I knew, she'd chopped off all that hair of hers years ago.

Nowadays she kept it quite short. Not as short as mine, but still barely long enough to tickle her jaw. Way back when she first debuted as the Kraken, I suppose the prehensile braid must have made quite an impression on the general populace.

Once I grew somewhat accustomed to the army of Wists staring across the room at me, I realized there were a handful of real flesh-and-blood people here in the shrine as well.

One manned a booth that looked suspiciously like a makeshift gift shop. Others stood near the sculptures with feather dusters, or peeked their heads out from behind small doors labeled *Staff Only*.

They wore neither mage robes nor anything close to my mental picture of stereotypical religious garb. They did seem to have some kind of coordinated uniform, but it wouldn't have looked out of place on attendants at a high-end city hotel.

Now that we'd made eye contact, I braced myself. There were a number of them and only one of me. No one would see Wist. She was probably busy trying to dig herself a hole through the floor, anyhow.

At best, I expected them to start fluttering around me in the manner of salespeople working on commission at a designer boutique. I was mentally prepared for much worse, of course. I might very well get surrounded and tackled like potential fresh meat for a multi-level marketing scheme.

But the Church staff simply smiled and nodded to acknowledge me, then left me to my own devices. It seemed that I would be obligated to approach them instead. How diabolical.

I sidled up to the gift shop window and made a show of eying the wares. It wasn't much. A few coasters and keychains, and a selection of dry-looking history books about the previous Kraken.

The trinkets mostly used the Church logo—none of them depicted Wist's likeness.

What a shame. I'd been all excited to ask them if their merchandise was officially licensed.

"Any of those figurines for sale?" I asked the man in the window, gesturing back at the center of the shrine.

"Not at this time, I'm afraid," he said. "They're quite remarkable, aren't they?"

"Indeed," I agreed. "Very vibrant. Very lifelike."

Given that I seemed to be the only non-staff member in the building, I didn't feel too bad about taking up his time. I figured Wist would need a longer break to recover from the mental shock of people worshiping life-size statues of her, anyhow.

At least the statues were flattering.

I gabbed with the clerk about how new and lovely the building looked. Apparently they'd only unveiled the shrine interior a few weeks ago.

I found myself terribly curious about the sincerity of their believers. And, more to the point, about where they got their funds from. The first thought that leapt to mind (not that I voiced it) was money laundering.

Over the course of the conversation, I gleaned that the Church had a much larger base of support in far-off countries, those clinging to the very edge of the continent.

I suppose Osmanthians tended to embrace the Kraken as a kind of hometown hero. But to people living in distant lands, maybe she really did come off as more of a mysterious guardian angel. She'd flit over every now and then to save them from various types of catastrophes, magical or otherwise.

It kind of made me wonder why the Church had gone to the trouble of establishing a fancy new shrine in Osmanthus City. Urbane Osmanthian city folk didn't strike me as being their primary market.

Perhaps the Kraken's birthplace—birth city, anyhow—was the closest thing they had to hallowed ground. Perhaps they planned for true believers to start making pilgrimages here from abroad.

"So—you think the Kraken is some kind of god?" I asked. "Uh, no offense. I'm quite clueless about religion."

"None taken." The man in the gift shop gave me a genial smile.

If there was one thing I could say in favor of Wist's worshipers, it was that they all seemed like remarkably perky, well-fed, and well-adjusted people. At least from the outside. In any event, I much preferred them to the Extinguishers.

The clerk had neat hair the color of house dust and nice crinkly eyes—friendly, if a bit watery in hue. His sleeves were buttoned primly right at the top of his wrists, but he gestured energetically as he spoke.

No light of a magic core shone in him. A subliminal, then. Or just a plain old healer.

I wondered idly about the demographics of Wist's die-hard fans. Did their proportion of mages, healers, and subliminals match the breakdown in the overall population? Or were certain groups drawn to admire her more strongly?

The clerk explained to me with enviable enthusiasm that there was a long history of Kraken worship on the continent. Dating all the way back to the time of the original Kraken, even. The present-day Church of the Kraken was simply the latest incarnation of an ancient and venerable religious heritage.

"Yeah, I'm sure you're quite right about that," I said. "And the original Kraken is one thing. Certainly the stuff of legend.

"But the current Kraken is just another mage, isn't she? An extremely powerful one indeed. But it sure sounds like she lives and breathes and eats just like the rest of us."

The clerk leaned on the counter, visibly eager.

I began to think that perhaps I'd made a mistake.

"That's the really interesting part," he said. "Why do so many people default to thinking of the Kraken as human?"

"As opposed to what? A literal sea monster?"

His smile never faltered. "Our understanding of magic is at least a little more advanced than it was hundreds or thousands of years ago. We have classification systems, numerical ways to assess and measure power.

"If anything, those modern systems make it obvious that the Kraken is truly unlike any other mage. The difference between her capabilities and those of average mages is like the difference between a house ant and a human being.

"No—the gap is just as staggering even if you compare her to the next-most powerful mages of our time, all the greatest S-class mages. Next to the Kraken, they too seem to have all the power of a mayfly."

"Those poor mages," I remarked.

He was nowhere near done. "There's plenty of historical evidence that the previous Kraken really did live for centuries.

"We don't pretend to have all the answers, but to we of the Church, simple observation of the facts suggests that the Kraken is an utterly different form of existence than the rest of us."

"Still," I said. "She grew up right here in Osmanthus City, didn't she?" Best restrict my arguments to matters of public knowledge. "She went to school and took classes with other children her age. She had a falling-out with her adoptive family. She kept aging. She cut her hair. That all sounds pretty human to me."

I had to give the clerk credit for being a good sport. He probably heard stuff like this day in and day out.

"If only the two of us could live for centuries, too," he said amiably. "If we saw the current Kraken stay with us for another three hundred, four hundred, five hundred years—perhaps that would serve as your answer."

"Oh, of course," I said. "I mean, Kraken aside, I'd be happy to live that long. Just to see what happens."

I felt a tad guilty for debating him. I spun the conversation out a bit longer before turning to my main topic.

"Say," I added, once the time felt right. "Earlier I was looking at the very back of your shrine. Way back behind all the figurines."

"Yes?"

"Is it just me, or do you guys have a vorpal hole sitting back there?" I spoke quieter. "Isn't that risky?"

The clerk's face cleared. "Nothing to worry about," he said kindly. "It's officially registered with the local MPs. It's actually been there since before we bought the lot. It's gated off, but we arranged all the statues in front to reduce the risk of any visitors stumbling into it."

"Is that, uh ... is that considered up to code?"

"We've passed all our inspections with flying colors," he said, beaming. What an inexorably cheerful man.

I felt Wist slip past me, unnoticed by the clerk or any other shrine staff. She padded away toward the formidable troupe of statues. Unless she felt up to the task of silently picking her way between them, she'd have to port herself directly in front of the vorpal hole to examine it close up.

I whiled away some more time with breezy chit-chat. In the process I learned that the Church had chosen this location not in spite of, but rather because of the vorpal hole. It held some kind of spiritual meaning for them that I frankly didn't care to understand.

Once Wist reemerged, I bought two keychains as a souvenir and thanked the clerk with all the grace I could muster.

We grabbed some packaged food from a nearby store and regrouped on the riverbank. Wist ate mechanically from a jar of salmon flakes. No sides. No rice.

I held out one of my Church of the Kraken keychains. "Present for you," I said. "Now we can match."

Wist looked balefully at the dangling logo. She didn't move to take it.

"I feel bullied," she pronounced.

I went ahead and tucked it in her jacket pocket anyway. "When was the last time I gave you a gift that cost money? Consider it a sign of my love."

Wist choked. I let her have some time to recuperate before moving on to the next order of business.

"So," I said. "The vorpal hole in the shrine. Large enough for you?"

She nodded.

"You still haven't explained exactly what you're attempting to do. I can guess, of course."

I considered the magic cuttings she'd transplanted all over the district. Some sort of shield. But more than just a vague enchantment of protection.

"Whatever the Extinguishers set off, whatever weapons they use—are you trying make sure all of it gets sent to that one vorpal hole?"

"Something like that," Wist said.

Put simply, if you yanked the pin from a grenade and flung it down the street, people might very well be grievously wounded. But absolutely no one would be hurt if you threw that same grenade in a vorpal hole. Vorpal holes swallowed up anything and everything that stumbled into them—making it vanish from our world without a trace.

It was a clever solution, albeit one that no other mage could have conceived of as possible. The conditions for making sure this ad hoc defense system of hers activated properly, and solely in response to the

Extinguishers—I couldn't even begin to wrap my head around how complicated the triggers must be. I trusted Wist to get it right, though.

"Just one question," I said. "That's a neat way to dispose of any munitions. But there are other worlds on the other side of every vorpal hole, aren't there? What about all those worlds?"

Wist shook her head. "Vorpal holes aren't portals."

"Meaning?"

"You can't reach those other worlds simply by stepping through one."

"You used to be able to."

"Back when I had the skill for it. I haven't reconstructed that skill yet. In any case, it takes a lot of extra magic and effort."

I thought I saw what she meant. I asked again anyway. "So this isn't just going to result in flinging bombs down on other worlds?"

"Other worlds lie beyond vorpal holes, yes. That doesn't mean the holes function as a doorway. They're more like a maw—chewing up everything that enters, never spitting anything out."

"Vorpal beasts come through them just fine," I pointed out.

"The worlds beyond won't suffer unless the Extinguishers' weaponry is literally made of nothing but vorpal beasts."

"Hm. All right," I said. "Good to know we won't be accidentally inflicting horrible suffering on our vorpal neighbors. Or doing the equivalent of vorpal littering, so to speak.

"Anyhow—the deadline is still two days away. So now we go back and wait?"

"No," Wist said. "I'll make them set it off early."

I'd been watching long-legged white waterbirds pick their way around the river shallows below us. Now my gaze snapped back to Wist. She scraped the bottom of her little glass jar of salmon flakes with a disposable spoon. "Excuse me?" I said. I was hoping I'd misheard her. But the look Wist gave me told me I hadn't.

12

I RETURNED ALONE to the gleaming shrine built by the Church of the Kraken. Once inside, I motioned furtively to the clerk manning the gift shop.

He tilted his head, mouthed a question.

I kept beckoning.

Eventually he came out from behind the shop window and joined me by the shrine doors. His manner was (perhaps understandably) rather warier than before.

"Were there any problems with your purchase?" he asked, all politeness.

"My what? Oh, no," I assured him. "No complaints. Very nice merchandise."

The gazes of all the Wist statues arrayed at the other end of the room weighed down on me. I gave a little fake cough, then used my foot to nudge at the nearest of the double doors. I held it open just a few inches.

"You'll find this hard to believe," I said. The clerk had to edge closer—a question in his eyes—to hear me clearly. "Actually, no. Before I say anything else, just take a peek."

I pushed the door open a bit wider. The man peered out into the quiet street in front of the shrine. No skimmers. Not even any passing pedestrians.

Just one person stood out there: Wisteria Shien, no longer cloaked by Disappearance.

I could've told him, "Surprise! I actually know the Kraken in person. We came here together."

Or I could've cried, "Look! Right out there! It's the Kraken!"

Yet I dithered. I couldn't bring myself to say it. If I were him, at any rate, such declarations would only make me more skeptical. Instead I kept my mouth shut. Hopefully he'd be able to recognize Wist on sight.

I feared the chances were low. The Church's figurines and sculptures—though weirdly beautified, in the way of classical portraits—did get her face right. For the most part.

But she no longer had that iconic long braid. She dressed in shabby streetwear rather than regal silken mage robes. Something about the way she stood always made it look like she was skulking, perhaps because she'd grown so accustomed to sneaking around unnoticed.

I preferred my Wist, with her shorter windblown hair and the deadened set of her eyes and her sack-like tops. I just didn't think the Church staff would be immediately inclined to acknowledge her as the illustrious Kraken they idolized. Not at first glance, anyway.

I looked nervously at the clerk. His mouth hung open. Okay, maybe I'd been overly pessimistic.

He swallowed convulsively. "That's—"

"I'm a, uh, messenger from the Kraken," I said rapidly. "As I'm sure you know well, the Kraken is very shy. Shy and retiring.

"She heard she had some admirers here and came by to take a look.

But she could change her mind at any moment. It's quite possibly a once-in-a-lifetime chance."

I gestured around the shrine. "You can't let your coworkers miss out on this, either."

"No." He sounded dazed. "No—no, of course not."

"Go round them up, then. Make it quick."

I waited with my back to the wall as the Church staff flittered around. There weren't too many of them on the premises right now. Probably less than a dozen in all.

Men and women alike, they all patted neurotically at their hair, brushed feverishly at their clothes. Stop wasting time, I wanted to tell them. Too bad for you. She's taken.

Yeah, yeah, I know. There were far more serious matters at hand right now. No need to feign surprise, though. Pettiness has always been one of my specialties.

I stayed there inside the sanctuary, arms crossed, till the last of them tripped out through the double doors. Only then did I follow suit, bringing up the rear.

Wist raised her hand like a queen to greet her visitors. The Church folk rushed into a semicircle around her, but thankfully kept some distance. No one reached out to grab at her.

And no one paid any attention whatsoever to the likes of me. I backed up to the corner of the building—a safe distance away from the worshipers, but still close enough to hear them speak.

Some of them were trying to invite Wist inside.

"No," she said. "I couldn't. Me, the fleshly Kraken, with my own graven images ... it would be—it would be too much glory in one place. It would blind you.

"But please know, I've seen your statues. I've seen all of them. I see everything."

I had to pinch myself to keep from snort-laughing. She spoke in her usual low, toneless voice, but to them I suppose she sounded ineffable. Mystic. Stately, even.

A crashing noise resounded from inside the now-empty shrine building. The Church people jerked in surprise, looked anxiously over their shoulders.

"My apologies," said Wist. "Thunder and lightning often accompany my presence. Majestic, but sometimes inconvenient."

They accepted this explanation at once, nodding vigorously and cooing in awe. If I'd told her to ask them for money, we'd be rich as the rest of the Shiens by now. Oh, well.

I tried to count the Church staff thronging around Wist. Nine? Eleven? How many of them were there supposed to be again?

The shrine had felt empty enough by the time I turned my back on the troupe of statues and made my own exit. I'd just have to trust that the clerk had succeeded in corralling all his friends.

Someone tapped me on the shoulder.

I turned. Just around the corner of the shrine building, leaning heavily against its embellished outer wall, was another Wist.

A second Wist. An extremely exhausted Wist, with lines around her eyes and chewed-looking lips. From this angle, no one could see her but me.

"Nice Body Double." I inclined my head at the healthier-seeming Wist who continued to hold court in the street outside the shrine entrance.

My Wist—the real Wist—kept lurking in the shadow of the frothily decorated building. She made a grumpy noise, as if she lacked the energy to speak full syllables.

I meant what I said, though. Body Double served as the catch-all name for a variety of magical skills in the same general family. Some variants were more convincing than others. I'd bet my pitiful life savings that no other mage had ever produced doppelgangers capable of carrying on a complete conversation.

On top of that, Wist hadn't crafted just one of them. Every single magic branch she'd planted everywhere in Old River (as well as in a few neighboring districts) would now have sprouted up into more clones of her.

The copies would double—pun intended—as conduits for the protective magic Wist had sought to spread throughout the region.

In other words, there were currently dozens and dozens of Kraken look-alikes strolling out in the open all over Old River. Sunning themselves at the waterside. Admiring the view from one of the many bridges. Pondering local knick-knacks at boutiques outside the train station. Awkwardly turning down free food samples in supermarkets.

The Extinguishers were bound to notice her sooner or later.

Hopefully sooner. The original Wist appeared to be on the verge of keeling over.

Body Doubles grown from magic cuttings would normally operate themselves independently. Once the branch was broken off and the skill activated, they wouldn't demand any special extra effort from their creator.

To strain herself to this extent, Wist must've been doing something highly unconventional. If not directly puppeteering her copies, then at least keeping close tabs on all of them at once.

She pushed her sleeve up with evident difficulty. The action seemed to take as much out of her as doing a pull-up.

She showed me the blue thread she always wore wound around her wrist. An old secret between the two of us.

"If I faint," Wist said, "slip a finger through the thread."

"Any finger?"

"Any finger. There's a magic cutting on it. It'll port both of us back to the tower."

Her eyes were unfocused.

"Want to sit down?" I asked. "Just for now."

"Clematis."

It didn't seem like she'd heard my question. "What?"

She caught at my hand. Her grip had grown frighteningly weak. "If anything happens—"

I didn't like where this was going.

"Anything?" I said sharply. "What's that supposed to mean?"

"Please come find me." Wist shifted away from the wall and flumped forward onto my shoulder. Not quite with all her weight. It still made me stagger.

"If anything happens," she repeated with difficulty, now close by my neck, "please come find me."

The street shook. Rather, the shrine building next to us shook once—twice—violently.

If not for what I'd heard about the threat posed by the Extinguishers, I would've assumed it was a regular earthquake.

I tried to hold Wist away from me so I could get a better look at her face. I tried to ask her what the hell she was talking about.

As I started to form words, magic seared my senses.

Not my physical vision. Nothing changed in my eyesight—not the black blur of Wist's hair, not the carved shadows on the white wall, not the limpid blue spring sky.

Yet at the same time, a world-consuming lightning flash scorched my magic perception, crushed the root of my breath.

Now Wist became true dead weight. I crumpled down on the sidewalk, Wist on top of me. I shook her, fought to turn her over. Her head lolled. Her eyes were still open. Black and staring. Seeing nothing.

Immediately I thought of the staring old man in the Philomena City cafe.

But that couldn't be right. A psychobomb would affect all of us indiscriminately. Wist, me, the Church staff around the corner, any Extinguishers lurking in the area. Everyone.

Besides, if the rattling of the shrine was anything to go by, Wist had already successfully redirected attacks from all sorts of weaponry. She'd routed danger after danger straight into the vorpal hole hiding at the back of the Church's parade of statues.

No. The first step was getting to safety. Then I could analyze all I want. I reached for the blue thread on Wist's wrist.

Something slammed into me before I could touch it. It felt as the air itself had punched me. I took a startled, reflexive gulp.

I heard voices—voices that sounded like Wist's double, and maybe the people from the Church of the Kraken—but they seemed very far away.

The space around me and Wist shimmered with a iridescent film like a soap bubble. Shield magic, I realized at last. My brain seemed to have been squirted full of slow-moving honey.

I raised my gaze and locked eyes with two fat killer hornets caught in the protective film, trembling with rage as they fought to break through to us.

Hornets? Not hornets. Just plain old bullets.

The clerk from the Church stood right there outside our shield. He had a gun in his hands. He had the same kindly look on his face as when he'd sold me two keychains.

I looked at his neatly buttoned long sleeves, fastened all the way up to the base of his hands. I pictured the standard Extinguisher tattoo, the snuffed-out candle with smoke winding its sinuous way up the underside of the forearm.

The Kraken is an utterly different form of existence than the rest of us, he'd said. He'd said it so earnestly.

A high-pitched mosquito whine shrilled through the air inside the magical shield. Wist had to be the one protecting the two of us, albeit weakly and unconsciously.

The frozen bullets still buzzed in place—right in front of my eyes. They sounded furious. Wist's shield seemed liable to crumble any second now.

The Extinguisher opened his mouth to speak.

"Not a word," I said. "No. *No.* No!"

I threw myself down over Wist's unmoving body. I jammed my finger through the bond thread on her wrist. At the same time—or perhaps even before I moved a muscle—I heard her unconscious magical shield shatter like a window in a storm.

13

THE MAGIC CUTTING grafted onto Wist's blue thread ported the two of us straight to the tower, just as she'd said. And not just to any old room in the tower.

It dumped us out right on top of her bed.

Suspicion smoldered somewhere in the back of my head. She'd predicted this would happen. She'd planned from the start on porting us to this exact spot.

Why? So I wouldn't be forced to lay her out on the bare floor, or to drag her limp body from room to room in search of an appropriate resting place. I looked at her inert face, at those still-open eyes, and felt the taut beginnings of a towering rage.

Not now. Not yet. I needed to keep my priorities in order.

I clapped a hand to my ear cuff and told Manatree what had happened. I spoke as quickly and concisely as possible. Afterward, I arranged Wist in a more comfortable position on her bed.

Blood spotted her jacket. For a heart-stopping moment, I thought it was hers. Only then did I feel the wetness all down the side of my face.

I found a mirror in Wist's bathroom. Oh. It looked as if someone had dumped a bucket of tomato sauce on my head. I probed my scalp gingerly till I found the wound. It occurred to me afterward that I ought to have washed my hands first. Too late for that now.

Head wounds always look worse than they are in reality, I reminded myself. Head wounds bleed profusely. One or both of the Extinguisher's bullets must've started moving again just in time to graze me. It was probably no big deal. Right?

I wadded up a washcloth and pressed it to the side of my head. That was how Manatree found me. Perhaps an hour later. Perhaps much less. I wasn't really keeping track of time.

I sat in a chair next to Wist's bed, half-heartedly applying pressure to my bleeding scalp. Wist stared back at me with open eyes that saw nothing. I wondered if I should use my fingers to close her eyelids, or at least force her to blink every so often.

When Manatree entered the room and walked over to us, she sucked in a breath that made it sound like she was the one who'd gotten shot.

Not because of me. I'd warned her about looking bloody. Even if I hadn't, I doubt she'd be particularly distressed about me getting a wound or two.

From the start, her gaze was riveted to Wist. Her gloved hand flew to her mouth, as if she had to fight not to be sick.

I'd never seen Manatree like this. It made my stomach roil. I wanted to snap at her to get a grip. Instead—like the true professional I was—I sat up straight and requested a debriefing.

Manatree told me in clipped tones that there had been no civilian casualties recorded in the Old River district.

Right after Wist and I escaped to the tower, the Extinguisher with the gun had tried to attack the other Church staff. The rest of them were innocent, it seemed. They'd had no idea he wasn't a true believer.

Wist's Body Double protected them by taking bullets, tackling the Extinguisher, pinning him down in the street. Once a squad of MPs arrived on the scene, the Body Double vanished in a gust of windborne ash, its duty complete. All her other clones throughout the district had dissipated as well, one after another.

"So far, we've found the aftermath of two weapon stashes," Manatree said. "One near the Church building. One in a warehouse by the river.

"In total, there must have been far more. From what we can tell, they had magical miasma. Poison gas. Along with enough standard explosives to level the entire district and then some."

"They detonated it, didn't they?" I said. "Everything they had. Everywhere they had it. But Wist had already covered all of Old River with her magic. Her cuttings detected every last threat. As soon as anything started to explode or expand, she scooped it right up and ported it straight into the shrine's vorpal hole."

"Yes," Manatree said, her voice harsh. "But she miscalculated. Or she was foolhardy. They did have a psychobomb.

"And she—"

"A psychobomb isn't a cannonball. It won't obediently fall where you throw it. It veers like a magnet toward human minds. It can't be redirected toward a lifeless object like a vorpal hole."

Manatree looked decades older than I remembered. She reached out and touched her gloved hand to a white empty swathe of Wist's pillow.

"I don't understand," she said heavily. "For this to have happened, the Kraken must have known what was coming. She must have deliberately drawn all the psychobomb's effects to herself alone. Thus no casualties. No *civilian* casualties. But—"

She met my gaze from across Wist's bed. For a single horrifying moment, I thought she might weep.

"Such a fool," Manatree said. "Such an incurable fool. If she weren't already like this, I'd kill her myself."

"There's no cure for the effects of a psychobomb. I hope she went out feeling like a hero, congratulating herself, raising a toast to her own bravery. And now here we are, bereft of the Kraken."

Her eyes hardened. "You," she said to me. "You have a remarkable gift for surviving the most improbable situations. Couldn't you have shared with her the smallest fraction of your talent for self-preservation? After getting off so lightly for betraying your own country, couldn't you have taken a moment to remind the Kraken how much her nation—how much the world—needs her?"

"Wait," I said. "Take that back."

I stopped pressing the wound on my head. I chucked the stained washcloth to the floor.

I wanted to bleed at Manatree. My skull throbbed with indignation.

"Wist is—okay, she's not *not* an idiot. But she isn't as much of an idiot as you claim. This is just another day on the job for her. She wouldn't plan for it to end in some kind of grand self-sacrifice."

"Then she planned wrong." Manatree took another look down at Wist lying unresponsive atop the bedsheets. Her hand tightened into an impotent gloved fist.

"You're talking like she's dead," I said. "Look—she's breathing just fine. The bond is still there in me. I feel it. Why can't that be reason for optimism?"

For the first time, Manatree's gaze flickered. Then she shook her head mutely, her long grey-black locs stirring.

She told me she needed to go. True to her word, she turned sharply on her heel and left.

Alone with Wist in the now-silent bedroom, I reached up to poke at my scalp. Still red. Still sticky and wet.

Next I reached inside myself. Not with physical fingers, but with my own self-essence. With tendrils of mind, or soul, or whatever you want to call it. I touched the thread-like bond that tied me to Wist and Wist to me.

I hadn't been lying. It was still there. Only death could terminate a mage-healer bond, and Wist was by no means dead. Look at how she breathed—just as I'd told Manatree. Slow, nigh-imperceptible breaths, yes. But she kept breathing.

And though the bond lingered there inside me, it hung limp. Nothing responded when I tugged at it.

Wist's final words: *Please come find me.*

Manatree and I were in perfect agreement on one thing. Wisteria Shien was an incurable fool. I felt choked halfway between gut-sucking fear and head-steaming anger.

Even so, I wanted to be the one to grab Wist and give her a piece of my mind. Not Manatree. Not anyone else. I, of all people, had the most right to jab a finger in her chest and tell her exactly what kind of a fool she was.

These were the thoughts that stewed in me as I followed the flaccid thread of our bond.

At first it was akin to a mental exercise, a form of meditation. Like lying in bed and envisioning yourself walking along a sunset beach to fall asleep. I traced the length of our bond with my mind, but I could still feel my butt in the hard bedside chair, the bloody dampness of my hair sticking to the side of my head.

Yet at some point, my sense of my body sank away like a corpse dropping slowly to the bottom of a deep, dark lake. At some point, it started to feel like dreaming.

I wasn't just imagining myself following the bond. I was right there in a dark formless tunnel. I took tentative barefoot steps across a cold squishy ground I couldn't even see.

Back in the physical world, I thought vaguely, I'd probably keeled over onto Wist's bed. Maybe I, too, had begun to stare hollowly into empty space with unblinking eyes. What a perfect couple we'd make.

At last, as if emerging from a lightless tunnel, I crossed an indefinable boundary. I crossed the threshold to another world.

Still an inner world, to be sure, but a different one from mine. The bond thread had done its job. It had led me straight to the heart of my bondmate. To Wist.

I stood still in her world to orient myself. I had on hiking boots now. Convenient. I tilted my head back.

I met the impassive gaze of a gray, featureless sky. Spiky tangled grass spread out around me, far wilder and harsher than the silky blue-toned field by Wist's tower.

Patches of black forest reared up in the distance. Behind me, I glimpsed bits and pieces of some kind of building.

Now that I was here in Wist's world, the bond thread slipped out of my hand and swam away into the shadows, fast as a minnow. As if to declare that it was no longer willing or able to give me a clear direction.

I considered turning around and venturing toward the buildings. Toward civilization. But perhaps there was some sort of meaning to the direction I'd been facing when I first emerged here: pointing out toward the wilderness.

At least this spiritual representation of me wasn't stuck here without shoes on. I waded forward through the bracken.

What would happen if I got lost before locating Wist? What would happen if my physical body suddenly needed to use the bathroom?

For that matter, what about Wist? If I took too long, would she pee herself? What if Manatree came back to the tower and found both of us comatose and covered in urine? I'd never hear the end of it.

Devoid of answers, I forged forward. The air felt misty, pregnant with a threat of unborn rain. When I looked back, I could no longer see the buildings in the distance. I wasn't even sure if I'd managed to keep walking in a straight line. Who was to say that a straight line was the correct way to go, anyhow?

"Wist," I said. "Don't make this so hard for me."

Nothing changed.

At least I'd tried.

I stopped. I attempted once more to glean clues from my surroundings. The underbrush was rife with thistles and other thorny traps.

I told myself to pretend I had all the time in the world. Time very well might pass slower here than in reality. I unanchored my mind and set it adrift.

Then I saw a small red-brown splotch staining some flattened blades of grass. I crouched to look closer. I spotted another.

I was no hunter. I'd never tracked an animal in my life. Much less a human. Yet from the moment I first noticed them, I knew with absolute certainty that these were human footprints. A child's footprints. I had no real basis for it; I just knew.

My heartbeat picked up, as though awakening from a deep sleep. I began to follow what I could make out of the bloody footprints. Not forward, but backward. Back to where they'd come from.

I halted at the stony lip of an overgrown well.

The well had no lid. Or if it did, the lid was discarded somewhere among the teeming weeds and grasses, completely covered up by their venom-green vigor. Absent a lid, the well became an unprotected window into blackness.

I'm not terribly fond of heights. Nor, it seemed, of depths. This well had no helpful rope dangling, no rusty ladder rungs bolted to form a path down its curved stone walls.

I called Wist's name. My voice echoed back at me mockingly.

I was growing impatient.

"Wist," I said, "I'm not going to wait up here. You'd better give me Zero Gravity. I don't want to find out if it's possible to break bones in my own mind. Your mind? Whatever."

I clambered over the edge of the well. At first I clung to the rough stone rim like a drowning monkey.

Oh, god. Why was I doing this again? Why had I thought this made sense?

Why hadn't I just followed the bloody footprints in the other direction—the direction they were actually walking—like a sane and logical person?

I remembered Wist telling me in disinterested tones about her brothers leaving her at the bottom of the well. It had been ages ago when she told me this, way back when we were students.

I remembered her speaking of the cycle of day and night, the rain, the slime, the black moss she tried to eat, the stars too far away to see clearly.

The old rage reignited in my belly. Wist might not think much of it anymore, but I would never forgive the Shiens. I took a greedy breath as if I were about to dive underwater. I forced myself to let go of the edge of the well.

I fell for a very long time.

I didn't break any bones. I landed hard enough to wind myself, but certainly not as hard as I should have. And I didn't land at the bottom of the well.

To be more specific—I found myself in a space that at first glance did resemble the bottom of a well. I could still see the mouth of the well far overhead, a grayish-white circle of sky. It hung in the exact middle of infinite darkness like a makeshift moon.

But down on the ground, I encountered no black moss. No threat of claustrophobia. Instead I encountered a cave system. Yes—here the bottom of the well led into a vast, airy cavern of blue-black stone. I was fairly certain that the real well abandoned on Shien property held nothing of the sort.

I ducked my way out of the well shaft and took a few cautious steps into the greater cavern. A bluish ambient light revealed lumpy stalagmites twice my height. Clustered together mournfully, they looked rather like a parody of the statues amassed in the Church of the Kraken. I couldn't tell where all the light was coming from.

"Don't leave me," said a small voice.

I whirled. I almost smashed my head on stone as I dove back toward the ignominious well shaft.

A child covered in shadow huddled against the wall. She watched me approach with dark eyes.

There was something almost alien about her utter stillness, her air of acceptance. Dirt smudged her face and caked her hands and feet. She wore an eyelet dress—completely ruined now—in some ghostly pastel color.

"What am I supposed to do with you?" I blurted.

Of all the things I could possibly say, that was probably one of the worst. The child looked back at me without answering. I wished I could fling myself down and bang my head on the cave floor.

I swear I'm not that bad at interacting with children. But it was different when we had to meet at the bottom of a metaphysical abandoned well.

It was different when the child was Wist.

"They left me," she said.

She might mean her brothers. She might mean her birth parents. She might mean—unfortunately, I could think of a lot of examples.

Was this child's presence some kind of trick question? Was I supposed to—to hug her or something?

That didn't seem right. She sure didn't look like she wanted a hug, anyway. She went on hunching in her corner, watchful eyes on my face, motionless as a cave cricket.

"Yeah," I muttered by way of answer. "They left you, huh? They sure did."

What was I even saying? I wanted to find myself and give myself a good solid uppercut. I made a pathetic gurgling noise in my throat.

"But listen," I said, attempting to recover my poise. "You've got some stuff to look forward to. Being the Kraken, if that counts. And me, I guess. I won't leave you. I mean—okay, historically speaking, I might. Once or twice. For a few years. But it'll be over before you know it. Now I'm here for good."

These were probably the last words that would make any child happy, much less this bedraggled little Wist. Heaven preserve me—what if I made her cry?

But after a tense moment, she gave me a tiny, solemn nod. She raised her small scraped-up arm. She pointed at the cave entrance as if telling me I were free to go now.

I looked from her finger to the bluish light spilling from the deeper cave. When I glanced back at the shadows coating the darkest parts of the well, she was gone.

I decided to take her (admittedly silent) word for it. I left the well shaft and stepped back into the cavern.

It was no longer empty.

Wist—the thirty-three-year-old Wist I knew—sat on a rock shaped like a beanbag, picking at what appeared to be a patchwork quilt of mammoth proportions. Wrinkled and splotched with dampness, the quilt covered nearly the entire cave floor.

Wist's hair was longer than in real life. As long as the hair of the Church's statues. As long as it'd been when I first met her. Unbound, it fell forward like a thick black mantle over her shoulders.

On second glance, her hair seemed to be helping her fuss with the quilt. The ends twisted themselves together into tiny wiry tufts that moved independently, working their way under one stitch after another.

Her hands paused when she saw me. Her hair kept working diligently.

"What are you doing here?" she asked.

The nerve of this woman. I could hardly believe what I was hearing. I drew myself up. "You told me to come find you. You said *please*."

"No," Wist insisted. "I wouldn't say that."

"It's a little too late to change your mind. I'm already here." I nudged the edge of the quilt with my foot. "Why're you quilting? Trying to make this cave feel more homey?"

She glanced at the heap of fabric in her lap. "Quilting," she repeated. "Is that what this looks like to you? Making a quilt?"

"Are you seeing something else?"

"It's the psychobomb," Wist said. "I trapped it in here with me before it could finish detonating. Now I have it frozen. Now I have to dismantle it."

I closed my eyes. I opened my eyes.

It still looked like a quilt. But all the patches of disparate fabric and all the stitches holding them together were magic cuttings. Cuttings pruned from dozens or even hundreds of different mages. The cuttings were the source of the cavern's chilly blue light.

"So there is no physical bomb at all," I said. "It's just a super knotty enchantment. And, what, you decided the best way to protect the city was by swallowing it whole? What are you, a whale?"

Now all of Wist's busy tendrils of hair stilled, too. I could hear water dripping slowly and irregularly, somewhere deep in the corrugated shadows.

She trained her eyes on those shadows. "You would've been safe if you hadn't come here," she uttered.

Oh, was it time to start exchanging accusations? Bring it on.

"I see your plan," I told her. "Nice cave. A reverse bomb shelter, I guess you could call it. You used magic to build this lovely bunker deep in your mind. Just for you, yourself, and the psychobomb. Even if it fully detonated, no one else would have to get hurt."

I gave the quilt a good kick for emphasis. I marched along its edge until I was standing right over her.

"Guess what," I said. "You don't have to beat yourself up for asking me to come find you. I would've come after you even if you said nothing. Even if you warned me to stay out of it. There's nothing you could've done to stop me. Good news, right? You'd be stuck with me here no matter what."

Wist tilted her face up to give me a searching look. "Did I really ask you to find me?"

"You really don't remember?"

"I was building these walls in my mind all day long." She nodded at the wet-looking blue-black rock of the cave. "By the time I said that—I wasn't fully there with you, perhaps."

I sat next to Wist, forcing her to scoot over and make room for me. She hunched forward over her lap. Her quick fingers and long, flexible hair resumed the work of painstakingly undoing stitches.

"How long is this gonna take you?"

"I've never defused a psychobomb before. How long has it been in the real world?"

"Um," I said. "A few hours?"

She eyed the remainder of the quilt. I felt her sag a bit. "You can try to extrapolate based on my progress so far."

I did some very rough math. Might be a few digits off here and there, but if I was guessing correctly—"You're going to need a feeding tube out there in the physical world. Plus a catheter."

"So will you," Wist said brusquely.

"We can be coma buddies."

I forced myself to stay silent and let her focus for the next few minutes. It was downright agonizing. At last I crumbled. "Anything I can do to help?"

"Can you use magic?" She didn't wait for an answer. "Then no."

"Wow," I said. "Ouch."

I wouldn't be able to resist bugging her if I stayed here. I popped up and started pacing a track all the way around the rim of the quilt. It took quite a while to walk a full circuit. The uncanny light seemed to warp the passage of time.

At least part of Wist had wanted me to follow her. Maybe not the smartest part of her—but part of her nonetheless.

Had it been a moment of weakness? A lapse in judgment? Had she been afraid of getting trapped alone inside her own head for however long it took to deactivate the psychobomb, weeks or months or years of constant work surrounded by silent piles of rock?

What was I good for, I wondered. I could try to heal her from the literal inside, but Wist seemed to be doing the magical equivalent of tedious manual labor. Having silky-smooth magic branches wouldn't necessarily make the work in front of her go any faster.

I'd already healed her a lot today, anyhow.

I crouched with my chin in my hands. I cast a critical eye over the ocean-like waves and bunched-up ridges of the glowing quilt.

Don't leave me, small Wist had said.

At this point, I doubted I could leave her even if I wanted to. Wist had put a lot of effort into making this space secure. I assumed the goal was to prevent any possible ill effects of the psychobomb from spilling over to anyone else.

Meanwhile, I'd taken advantage of our bond to stroll on in as if I had an invitation. If Wist knew how to chase me out without compromising our safety, I'm sure she'd have done so already.

"Manatree thinks the bomb already went off," I said, remembering. "She thinks you martyred your mind for Old River. She seemed quite devastated."

"No one was hurt?" Wist asked.

"No one was hurt. Well, I got shot in the head a bit."

"You *what?*"

"Er, on the head," I corrected. "By the head. Not in the head. It just grazed me. I'll live.

"Anyway, the one person I picked to talk to at the Church of the Kraken turned out to be a full-blooded Extinguisher. Just my luck, right? If only he'd known I was your bondmate. He really missed his chance to make history."

Wist gave me a sidelong look. She didn't seem very appreciative of my sparkling sense of humor.

"By the way," I said, "why didn't you just start here?"

"Where?"

I pointed at the corner nearest me. Wist came over to see what I meant. Her hair picked itself up so as not to drag along the rough dewy ground. It hung quirked in waves near her knees like a long trailing skirt hoisted higher by invisible attendants.

"Here," I said, pointing closer.

It was a patchwork quilt, yes, but crafted from one hundred percent pure magic.

It had features that wouldn't quite make sense with a physical quilt. Unless you were trying to concoct a modern art piece. Some stitches were long and sloppy, so discordant that they looked like vandalism. Some bisected multiple patches of clashing fabric. Some looked like surgical staples.

Wist still seemed not to grasp what I was talking about.

"This thread here," I told her, growing impatient. "Wouldn't the rest go much easier if you picked this one out first?"

"I don't see it as a quilt," Wist said slowly.

"What does it look like to you, then?"

"An archaeological dig." She motioned at the undulating heaps of fabric. "I'm sealed down here with the fossilized bones of a mythological creature."

"What, like a dragon?"

"Something along those lines. The bones are very fragile. I have to excavate them without breaking them. That's what's taking so long."

Both the quilt and the fossilized dragon were merely metaphors. Alternate ways of perceiving the maze-like structure of the same high-level enchantment. That pesky psychobomb.

If I looked away from the psychobomb and relaxed my magic perception, made my senses go all blurry and peripheral, I could start to glimpse how one might interpret the quilt's shape in different ways. It was like switching your view of an optical illusion. A flock of ducks suddenly transforming into a beautiful woman.

"Okay," I said. "It isn't necessarily a row of stitches. But my point stands. The logical approach would be to take care of this part first. Then go over there"—I pointed further away—"next. You've got the order of operations all wrong. You're making it harder on yourself."

Wist was silent.

Would she tell me to shut my trap so she could focus on defusing the psychobomb? Would she tell me to quit my armchair theorizing? I was a healer, after all—and a superbly gifted one at that. But I wasn't a mage.

I couldn't hunker down beside her and and offer any practical help. I couldn't use whatever esoteric selection of magic skills she now wielded to disassemble the psychobomb bit by bit. I couldn't do anything except run my mouth and heckle her, really.

"I believe you," Wist said.

Oh. Well, then.

"I believe you," Wist said again, "but I truly can't see it for myself. I'm sorry."

"No one asked you to apologize," I retorted. "Don't make it all weird."

"It must be frustrating for you."

"You're the one who has to do all the grubby work."

I squatted and plucked idly at the quilt. It felt moist to the touch. A perfect breeding ground for mildew, if this were the real physical world.

"I have an idea." Better say it fast. Before I could chicken out. "We're hanging out in the depths of your soul right now."

"Not sure if I would call it that myself."

"C'mon. You know what I mean. This is your mind. Your world. I'm right here with you. We're bonded. Can't there be a way for you to see through my eyes?"

I peeked up at her. Wist didn't move. I wasn't even sure if she was breathing. Then again, we were inside her head right now. If she preferred not to breathe, nothing would force her to.

"I thought ... I thought you didn't like using the bond that way," she said at last.

"What way?" I snapped. "Be specific."

"Reaching across the bond to bridge the gulf between us," she said. "The normal gulf between any two individuals. Using the bond to go inside each other. Using the bond to get closer than it's possible to get with human words or human bodies."

"Right," I said, hot in the face. "If nothing else, prison made me value my—my privacy. My autonomy. But I invaded your inner world first. Fair's fair."

Wist got down on her knees beside me. She wore some kind of long summer dress, with fabric that could just as easily have been fashioned into nice breezy curtains. Certainly not the sort of garment I'd choose for spelunking. Her hair whisked itself out of the way, twirled itself up into a series of heavy sailor's knots hanging down her back.

She leaned in to look me in the eye. "You really don't mind?"

"It's not that I don't *mind*," I said. "We don't have much choice, now do we? Unless you really want to be stuck here defusing your bomb the slow way. For the next couple of real-time years."

Wist studied me for a moment, her face unchanging, then commented: "How come you never act this virginal in—"

"That's different!" I yelped. "Completely different. Hurry up and get it over with, would you?"

It didn't matter how much I told myself that this was not my real body, that I had no real body here, that everything was imaginary.

I still felt like me. I still felt the uneven rock underfoot, the cool stagnant humidity of the cave air, the skittish anticipation in my gut.

I still felt Wist's hand glide down to the small of my back. To the place where my magic core would be, if I were a mage. I felt her fingers sink straight through my skin and spine as if I were nothing more than a hunk of the very softest clay. It tickled horribly. But it was still bearable.

What bordered on being intolerable was the sense that I no longer knew where Wist ended and I began. The sense that I had started consuming her. Or that she had started eating into me. Or both at the same time.

It made me want to finish the job. It made me want to pack her away safely inside me. No embrace could ever seem tight enough after you felt someone starting to meld with the very fabric of your secret self.

The cavern floor made her knees ache. Her brain was half-numb with the effort of painstakingly deconstructing the psychobomb. Part of her wanted to snuggle up in an empty chamber of my heart like a squirrel in a tree and make a permanent home there, forget who she was, forget the outside world. No amount of closeness had ever felt like enough.

She saw what I saw.

"Ah," I heard Wist utter. She sounded almost regretful. She pulled away from me.

She was exceedingly gentle. It still hurt to feel her go.

I hunched all the way over, my forehead almost to the cave floor, tearing up for no real reason. After a few seconds of this, Wist's hand reached out and started petting my back. This time without cleaving to my flesh.

"Sometimes," Wist said, "sometimes—that's how it feels when you reach in and touch my magic. When you heal me."

I raised my head a fraction. "You're kidding."

"I didn't say it was a bad sensation. Profound, yes. Not unpleasant."

"I still feel insulted," I said. "I always thought my work was very subtle."

"It is. For the most part. But sometimes you have to heal me very deeply, don't you?"

"It's your fault for having so much magic!"

"What I'm trying to say is that I like it."

"You masochist," I spat.

Wist didn't bat an eye. She didn't deny it, either. Instead she turned back to the radiant quilt currently asphyxiating the cave floor. She plucked out stitches of the thread I'd told her to start with.

"Why was it so easy for you to envision the ideal workflow?" she asked.

"Beats me," I said. "Thought it was obvious."

"Take any labyrinthine web or matted tangle of magic," Wist said as she worked. "You seem to be able to look at it and immediately understand how it fits together at a glance. You see the relationship between parts. What affects what. Is this what lets you figure out how to heal or hobble mages you've never met before?"

"All healers have to see things that way to some extent," I said. "It's kind of a prerequisite for doing any healing at all. I'm just extra good at it."

"It would be a very useful talent for a mage," said Wist. "Maybe you should have been born the Kraken."

"Who would heal me?"

That managed to tug a small half-smile out of her. "Good point."

She moved onto the next thread in the sequence she'd seen through my eyes. Or to her, perhaps it was a particular section of rock and dirt, a particular angle she needed to tap away at.

Whatever the case, she finally got it.

As she proceeded, the quilt started to cooperate, unpicking its own seams. Bits of colorful freed fabric rose to flap excited circles around the cavern. The fatigue riding Wist's shoulders—I imagined it as the hunched shapes of heavy gargoyles—began to erode away little by little.

Even after Wist finished, the dismantled scraps of the quilt continued swirling around aimlessly in the air, weightless.

Each was still a magic cutting, some mage's contribution to the elaborate psychobomb enchantment. Divorced from their greater whole, they posed no danger. They retained no distinct purpose. No more so, at least, than the mindless isolated parts of any other disassembled tool: a screw, a pin, a bolt, a spring.

Wist planned to regurgitate the bomb scraps—in a manner of

speaking—and hand them over to Public Security. She claimed she might get indigestion if she kept storing them inside her. I couldn't quite tell if this was her attempt at a joke.

She took my hand. Our palms buzzed when we touched, almost threatened to melt together.

That was the trouble with exploiting the bond. That was the trouble with trying to draw closer than any two people ever ought to get to each other. You might grow used to it. You might find it easier and easier each time.

You might come to like it.

In the end, we left through the dark well shaft. Wist floated us effortlessly up to the top. I thought of how she'd clawed her way up alone at the age of six.

Not only that, I realized now. Being Wist, she'd done it twice. Once without any idea of what was happening. Once with full knowledge of what her brothers were trying to do to her, and what it would feel like to be stranded at the bottom of the well.

Determined to change as little as possible, she'd still gone along with them the second time around. She'd still let them lower her in.

Day-to-day, I tried not to dwell too much on the fact that Wist had essentially relived the exact same life twice over. At least up until her mid-twenties.

I had plenty of my own thoughts about this, of course. I saved those thoughts for special occasions. It was a long and complicated story, and I knew I shared a good chunk of the blame for it.

14

I woke up in a morgue.

At least, that was the first thought that engulfed me when I opened my eyes. I found myself floating in some kind of horizontal tank. Like a bathtub with a lid. Or a glass coffin filled with transparent pink liquid. A watery grave.

After a brief but heartfelt panic, I realized I'd been breathing this liquid the whole time. It seemed to pass through my nose and lips no differently from regular air, except that it made the insides of my lungs itch as if they were growing hives.

I much preferred not needing to be aware that the insides of my lungs were capable of feeling anything at all.

Embalming liquid? I thought. Then: would I be able to breathe embalming liquid? Would they even bother to embalm me at a morgue? Or would they cut me open for an autopsy first?

Where was Wist?

The lid of my tank slid open of its own accord. I sat up in a rush, sloshing neon fluids everywhere. Plain old air felt startlingly cold in comparison to my warm pink bath.

I'd been put in some kind of skimpy wetsuit, with tubes coming out of all kinds of embarrassing places. It wasn't as uncomfortable as you might imagine. Still, I didn't want to think too hard about what exactly was going on down there.

I patted the side of my head. The shallow wound I'd staunched with Wist's towels now seemed to be thoroughly sealed.

My eyelashes were dripping. I rubbed some of the liquid off my face—not very successfully, given that my hands were just as wet—and looked around blearily.

By all appearances, I was utterly alone here.

I could sense some sort of activity at the other end of the bond. But whatever she was currently going through, Wist kept it well under wraps. Her control over herself was too airtight for me to tell what she felt. Inscrutable hints wafted over like the muted beat of low-volume music from the apartment below mine. No clear rhythm or melody.

A few other tanks—none of them occupied—lined up on either side of the one where I'd slept. It would've been a fitting layout for a bunch of beds in military barracks.

The room was very well-lit, but had industrial-size shutters rolled down to seal all its windows. Maybe that was what had given me the initial impression of being closed off in a morgue.

The other half of the room housed a menagerie of advanced life-support equipment, the sort that at first glance looked very much like creative instruments of torture. None of the equipment appeared to be in use at the moment.

Since no one had shown up to stop me, I sloshed to my feet and clambered out of the tank. Let's see how far these tubes could stretch.

I dripped pinkish splotches of liquid as I waddled along. The lower part of my wetsuit-like garment seemed to be fused with some sort of bulky mechanical diaper. The floor was almost painfully icy to the touch.

As I looked around for a door, part of the nearest wall split in two and lifted open like a beetle shell.

In came Manatree and Mori, followed by Wist in a thigh-length T-shirt (and little else).

I made brief eye contact with Mori. He barreled at me like an untrained sheepdog.

My sleepy reflexes weren't good enough to dodge this top-speed missile. I tolerated being hugged for about a millisecond before I slithered away, telling him I was going to get him all wet with mysterious fluids.

"Someone explain why I woke up by myself here," I said. "You all leave me for dead? Where is this?"

"The Kraken's tower," Manatree said.

Her eyes were astonishingly red. Not like a berserking mage. The more normal red of exhaustion or grief or (though probably not in this case) contagious disease.

"Never even knew this room existed," I said.

"It's a recent addition." Manatree's lips twisted. "You recall when the Kraken had to go on life support last year. Afterward, I strongly recommended adding proper medical facilities to the tower. In this one case, she actually listened to me. Miracles do happen."

I glanced over at Wist in her raggedy T-shirt. "Yeah, bet you barely had so much as a first-aid kit sitting around before then. Probably always figured that whatever happened, you could just fix yourself up with your own magic."

Wist didn't deny it.

I asked how much time had passed. Manatree informed me that it was late at night on the same day. I'd been out for six or seven hours, then.

"Dang," I said to her. "You should be home with your family."

Manatree glared, but it lacked something of her usual edge.

I did feel genuinely bad for keeping her away from home this late. She seemed like the type who would, when circumstances allowed, be snug in bed before ten in the evening and up and about again by five in the morning.

It turned out that various medical staff had stopped by the tower while I slept. They'd all taken their leave a little after Wist came to. No one stuck around to wait for my awakening.

"Wow," I said. "I see how it is."

Sadly, no one indulged my complaints.

Manatree told me I could hurry up and liberate myself from my wetsuit and tubing. But I was a little hesitant to just start ripping things out.

Wist drifted over to help. She didn't seem to know much more about it than I did. We ended up having to call out to the other two for verbal guidance while clumsily stripping me.

"Very—futuristic," I grunted as Wist poked and prodded me.

"Jacian technology," Manatree said shortly.

Indeed, the wetsuit and tubes were embedded with all kinds of magic cuttings.

"Fighting fire with fire?" I asked. "Because you thought one or both of us got hit by the psychobomb?"

No answer. Wist gave me a towel to dry myself, then passed me clean underwear and a long nightshirt. Unlike hers, mine actually went down to my knees. She collected all the wet devices I'd shed and deposited them in some sort of cleaning cubical.

Luckily, no one was forcing us to stay and chit-chat in this substitute intensive care unit. Or whatever it was supposed to be. Once I'd gotten decent, we retired to a familiar parlor with a fireplace, a piano, and out-of-season morning glory vines crawling all over the walls.

Mori promptly made hot tea for all four of us. What a thoughtful assistant.

"This is practically a reunion from last fall," I said between sips of tea. "All we're missing is Fanren. He's got better things to do, no doubt."

I turned to Mori. "What about you? Don't you have dissertation stuff to take care of?"

He blanched. "I heard—I thought—I thought we'd lost both of you!"

"Don't scare the poor kid," I told Manatree. Her aura of acute unamusement intensified.

I would've liked to witness Manatree's reaction to Wist waking up. I was highly dissatisfied to discover that Wist had revived over an hour before I did. "Why? How come she got to wake up first?" I asked the others repeatedly.

They suggested that perhaps at least part of my time in the tank had been regular tired sleep. In other words, I'd tuckered myself out by following Wist all over Old River earlier in the day. Maybe I needed to start taking longer daily walks.

Turtle the cat picked her way into the parlor to join us, tail held high. By now she seemed to know to give the morning glories a wide berth.

As soon as Mori sat down, she sprang up into his lap. His visits to the tower had been far less frequent these past few months. Maybe she'd missed him, in her haughty cattish way.

Wist sat backwards on the piano bench, facing the rest of us. A collection of statuesque harps strummed themselves mawkishly in a nearby corner. The grand piano, to its credit, knew when to keep quiet.

Manatree put down her teacup and began lecturing Wist about this and that.

I figured she probably had a point. I, however, was not her target audience. I tuned her out. In the meantime, I entertained myself by scooting closer to Mori and petting the cat on his knees until she hissed at me.

Mori, too, did his best to wear a poker face. Unlike Wist, he wasn't naturally inclined to keep his feelings sealed away, invisible from the outside. He also lacked her many years of dogged practice. Some of Manatree's remarks got him nodding, at least until he caught himself. Others made him flinch.

There were a few points where I too found myself inadvertently listening.

For instance, the time when Manatree rose to her feet and told Wist: "Death shouldn't be your only concern. If you were ruled legally incapacitated, the result would be the same. Do you understand what would happen?"

The harps, finally cowed, stopped trying to mediate the mood in the room with endless glissandos.

Manatree threw an arm out. "All your property would by law go to the Shien clan. Absolutely none of it would go to your bonded healer. Even if you went out of your way to name her in your will. Bonded healers are excluded from inheritance."

She pointed at me with such force that it felt like a threat. "Your— relationship—or whatever agreement you now have with each other is none of my business. Nor do I wish to make it my business. I didn't want to have to point this out to you. But I feel something of an obligation to mention it. In case you were truly oblivious."

Manatree watched Wist for her reaction. So did I. None was forthcoming. I would hardly have expected otherwise. Yet Manatree slowly folded her arms. The look she trained on Wist shifted from pure umbrage to something like pity.

"You really aren't aware, are you," Manatree said. "If you died, or vanished long enough to be declared legally dead, or became incapacitated, the Shiens would also inherit first right of refusal to your former bondmate.

"If the bond with you vanished, they could stop her from bonding any other mage. They could insist that she bond one of them instead.

"Even if your bond stayed intact—from you being incapacitated but not outright dead, for instance—they could block her from obtaining any other work, doing anything else with her life.

"Or if they felt particularly vengeful, they could accuse her of violating parole and get her thrown back in prison to complete her original sentence. Whatever they chose to do, the Shiens would have power over her for the rest of her life."

The thought made me sick. I already knew all of this, though. Bonded or otherwise, Osmanthian healers had hardly any legally enforceable rights.

Manatree, studying Wist, nodded to herself as if finally satisfied.

Wist hadn't said a word. She gripped the edge of the piano bench as if trying to break it.

All right, I thought. Enough bullying Wist. Time for a change of subject.

"I was wondering," I said to Manatree. "What would've happened if the psychobomb actually went off?"

She eyed me as if my ability to speak surprised her anew. As if the cat in Mori's lap had raised its head and started asking cheeky questions.

I suppose I ought to be thankful that she deigned to give me an answer.

"Roughly speaking," Manatree said, "it would be as if every single adult and child in the district—and then some—were simultaneously lobotomized. That's a crude analogy, but it's the closest one we have."

"Then the government ought to shower Wist with medals for stopping it."

"Plenty of others will praise her," said Manatree.

She didn't elaborate. But I suppose I could understand what she was getting at.

Wist was only a hero because her solution had worked. All of Osmanthus would curse her name if she took the risk of ingesting the psychobomb and then fell prey to it herself. Thus depriving them of their Kraken—their prestige, their power, their foolproof lever against every other country on the continent.

"What about the Extinguishers?" I asked. "Did PubSec catch them?"

"Some," Manatree said curtly. "Perhaps two-thirds of the Old River cell."

"Only two-thirds?"

"The rest received assistance from their Jacian contacts. They've already fled the country."

"So the Jacians helped some and cut others loose," I mused. "Makes sense. Never trust a Jacian agent."

I'd learned that lesson for myself years ago, and I'd learned it the hard way.

I recalled the clerk with the gun. "How about the Church? Were there any other Extinguishers embedded with them?"

"Only the one who attacked you. He's in custody. But the Church sanctum took significant damage."

Guess Wist hadn't quite perfected her technique for chucking munitions and biohazards into the safety of a vorpal hole. It must have worked well enough, though, if the damage had been strictly contained to the interior of the shrine building.

I thought pensively of Church's army of Wist statues—life-size, larger than life, half-scale, quarter-scale.

"Wish I could've rescued one of those figurines," I said. "The Church might be kind of kooky, but they've got some real works of art."

"The figures weren't all ruined," Manatree said. For the first time in a very long time, a hint of levity entered her tone. "I'm sure they would be thrilled to gift you one if you asked."

Brilliant idea. You know, moments like these were why I just couldn't dislike Manatree. No matter how poorly she thought of me.

All in all, it seemed safe to conclude that from the Extinguishers' perspective, today's operation had ended in utter failure.

Their attempts to assassinate Wist last year had met with disaster as well. Given how much they'd lost, chances seemed good that they would cease to be a problem for some time. At least within Osmanthian borders.

Wist and I stayed up the rest of the night even after bidding farewell to Manatree and Mori. One way or another, we'd both already gotten plenty of physical sleep.

Once the other two left, Wist turned to me a bit mournfully and asked if I really wanted one of those figurines so badly. I suppose the implication was that I shouldn't need one when I had the real Wist right here with me.

It took me a while to stop laughing. I decided that I absolutely needed a Wist figurine of my own, if only to see her getting jealous of it. Perhaps one of the relatively compact eighth-scale models. I could make adequate room for it somewhere on my apartment shelves.

Some days later, Wist took me back to the tower planetarium. She showed me the starry sky over Osmanthus City. It was much darker and clearer than anything you could see in person from a city rooftop.

She showed me the stars over the island nation of Jace, over Osmanthus

Bay, over every other country on the continent. All of this was much closer than the swathe of sky that contained the Eye of the Devil, which lay all the way on the other side of the world. These views she revealed now were ones I might someday—someday—be able to see for myself.

The parole thread around my ankle suggested otherwise. But as long as we stayed alive, it wasn't completely impossible.

This time we laid down a tarp to keep the sand at bay. The ground beneath the tarp felt almost exactly like the floor bed in my city apartment. I wasn't sure if that meant the sand was extraordinarily soft, or my usual bed was extraordinarily hard.

I rolled onto my belly and looked at Wist lying on her back, one arm thrown up behind her head.

"What'd you say?" I asked.

She'd muttered something too quiet to make out.

"Just talking to myself."

"No," I said, "you weren't. What? Was it something embarrassing? Were you cooing to yourself about how much you adore me?"

Wist focused on the stars—so many of them, a glittering bourgeois excess—instead of on me. I curled my leg around hers, leaned my weight on her. I liked cuddling up in a pile like two wanton animals.

I peered into her face. Wist was making an extraordinary effort to avoid eye contact.

"If you don't tell me," I said, "I'll just start guessing."

"I was wondering...."

"Wondering what?"

"If we should get married," Wist said stiffly.

She glanced quickly at me, then looked away again. She hurried on before I could interrupt. "I don't think I'm immortal. If anything happens, or if I die—that's the only way to make sure you get something."

"I don't care about inheriting the tower," I said. "Seems like it would be a real pain to maintain without you. And what about the land taxes? No, thank you."

"I know that much," Wist shot back. "But it would save you from being inherited by the Shiens."

She had a point there. Ironic, wasn't it? Spouses had a great deal more protection than healer bondmates.

If we were lawfully married, as Wist's widow I'd gain—through a bit of legal trickery—a chance at essentially inheriting the rights to myself as a bereaved healer. Rather than being automatically passed down to the Shien clan.

"You really get me," I said. "Nothing more romantic than getting married specifically to spite your family. I love it. Then again, it's not exactly a legal trump card. Marriage could be said to confer some rights, but it doesn't stop me from being a healer.

"So how about this," I suggested. "Let's get married if the Healers' Bill of Rights passes."

"Isn't that what you used to say about bonding?"

I elected to neither confirm nor deny. "Anyway, if you really want to protect me or whatever, the most surefire way is to stay alive. And stay of sound mind, I guess. Hey, the previous Kraken lived for centuries."

"Or so they say," Wist muttered.

"If she could do it, so can you. And you don't even have to live for centuries, really. All you have to is outlive me. You've done it once before."

I felt Wist jerk as if I'd stabbed her. She made a valiant effort to suppress herself. It would've been unnoticeable if I hadn't been all but lying on top of her.

"Oh," I said, all innocence. "Too soon?"

At last she let out a sigh. "You," she said, as if that one syllable were a complete sentence. "*You*—you."

"Yes, honey?"

Of all things, this succeeded in wrenching a smile out of her. A deeply rueful smile, but I'd take what I could get.

I kissed the dimpled corner of her mouth. I felt like a real sap for wanting to trick her into smiling like that, for my giddy surge of triumph, for the way the bond seemed to twist itself up inside me like a hungry living thing.

Nevertheless, I knew myself well enough to admit defeat. No point in denying it. There was no turning that feeling off. There was no ignoring that hunger. I got the urge to kick Wist just about as often as I got the urge to kiss her—but either way, I was a goner.

PART THREE

Vorpal Rabies

15

I SPENT THE NEXT few months begging Manatree to get me a passport. No luck so far. But I refused to stop trying.

Wist hadn't done any international travel for the entire second half of last year. Which meant that by now, every other country on the continent was rather desperate for her services.

Just like Osmanthus, they too had vorpal holes that needed closing. And until I got a passport, I wouldn't be allowed to go with her.

I told Wist—half in jest—that she ought to just pull rank and take me anyway. As I'd expected, though, she insisted on doing things by the book.

Personally I thought she was a bit paranoid about the possibility of accidentally screwing up international relations. Even so, I guess I couldn't blame her for wanting to be overly careful.

As a result, I tragically remained stuck on the sidelines in Osmanthus City while Wist hopped from country to country in April and May.

Truth be told, Wist's episode with the psychobomb had fundamentally changed my outlook. I'd always thought that between the two of us, she was inherently more inclined to be cautious. Overprotective, even.

In her defense, she did her best to keep a lid on it. As a general rule, she tried to err on the side of not saying or doing anything to stifle me. If I stopped visiting the tower, stopped uttering a word to her, I bet weeks or entire months might pass before she'd break down and reach out to me.

Now I could see all too clearly that Wist held herself to a different standard. She'd fret like a grandmother over my safety—though she strove not to vocalize it—yet seemingly cared little for her own.

That made it high time for a role reversal, I thought. Time for me to become the overprotective one.

Unfortunately, I couldn't do jack without a passport.

By June, Wist's travel schedule had started to calm down a bit, though she still flitted in and out of the country every couple of days or so. Sensing my restlessness, she told me I could get a dog and keep it in the tower. If I still wanted one.

"You accusing me of being lonely without you?" I demanded.

"Having a reason to go on long walks might do you some good," Wist said, watching me pace around like a horse. "You need it more than the dog would."

I did want a dog, now more than ever. I was getting a little tired of Wist's cat looking down her nose at me. I'd even come around to the idea of deigning to take care of the dog myself, poop and all.

But I still didn't get one. What if my request for a passport went through? Hey, one day it might actually happen.

If I got a passport, I'd take full advantage of it. I might not spend very much time at all lurking back in old Osmanthus. It didn't seem right to welcome a dog home and then go gallivanting off without it.

This was, of course, a purely hypothetical dilemma. But it concerned me just enough to stop me from bringing a dog of my own to the tower.

June also marked the beginning of the Osmanthian rainy season. Temperatures cooled, but in exchange the air grew stiflingly humid. I hardly ever saw a hint of blue sky. It was all clouds, all the time.

That said, the rainy season didn't mean constant rain. If anything, I welcomed the rain when it did come, so long as it didn't catch me outside. It hit harder and faster than at any other time of year, pouring down like a stream from a hose, too dense to make out individual droplets.

On jaunts to the corner store by my apartment, I wore purple rain boots and carried a comically wide umbrella. Passing other pedestrians was always a tricky business. Our umbrellas had wingspans far too great to fit side-by-side.

Virtually all the houses and apartments in my neighborhood spilled over with lush irises and heavy-flowering hydrangeas in every color from white to shocking pink to moody blue. In the city, the rainy season might feel like an inconvenience, but it had plenty of charm. Even the Old River district seemed likely to survive summer unscathed.

Things were far more dire out in the country. I saw reports of historical flooding, evacuations, mudslides. Geography wasn't my strong suit, but I quickly learned how to interpret the flood warnings. I found myself checking again and again to make sure that Sweet Olive had been spared.

Here in Osmanthus City, such news was quickly buried by furious rumors of an epidemic of berserking mages.

Most people hadn't encountered one in person, but they were starting to hear stories from friends of friends. Random mages—who'd exhibited no past warning signs, and who had dutifully gone to get healed right on schedule—snapped at seemingly random times.

Only recently had Public Security acknowledged that these incidents were actually happening. Last month they'd announced the formation of a special task force dedicated to investigating and stopping the rash of berserking.

Since then? Crickets. Meanwhile, berserking outbreaks continued to hit the news on a near-daily basis. Grocery stores, shoe repair shops, universities, government offices, house parties: nowhere was safe.

I myself had already glimpsed a few signs of this earlier in the year. That man on the street not far from my apartment. Berserking damage sufficient to close off an entire train platform in Anthum Station.

I wished I could see actual data about the latest incidents. How much had they increased compared to the usual (extremely low) baseline rate of mages going berserk? Was the increase starting to accelerate? Were there truly no connections, no commonalities between any of the affected mages?

No one would pay me to wonder about these things, though. Nor was I the only person consumed by curiosity. My neighbors spoke of little else. I hobbled detained mages when the government formally requested it, and I kept my speculation to myself.

It was a mid-June evening when Manatree showed up at my apartment. Rain pounded down like a mountain waterfall outside.

I hadn't seen Manatree in person since the Extinguishers threatened Old River. Months ago, in other words. Occasionally she reached out to give me work assignments, but most of her messages to me came from her subordinates.

She gave me little warning. Woozy with humidity, I'd been hanging out in an undershirt. I had just enough time to pull on more clothes before answering the door.

Rather than materialize right outside my unit, she must've ported herself to the bank of mailboxes at the bottom of the apartment's concrete outdoor staircase. The rain was fierce enough to have lashed her even during the thirty-second walk up to my floor.

I handed Manatree a towel. She delicately patted her shoulders and face and thick elbow-length locs. Once finished, she returned the towel to me and removed her shoes. She stepped from the apartment entrance into the main area, with my kitchen and meager table.

Her eyes alighted on the figurine dominating half the table. It left me little space to store my papers or lay out a proper place setting to eat.

"I see you took my advice," she said.

"And wonderful advice it was. I asked for a one-eighth scale figure, but the Church gave me a one-fourth scale. Know what that means?"

"No," replied Manatree. "I can't say I have any interest."

"It's one-fourth as tall as the real Wist. Stack four of these on top of each other, and you make a full Wist."

I gestured to emphasize the figure's height. "That's why it's so big and heavy. Isn't the craftsmanship incredible? Apparently it's worth quite a lot. But they were so grateful for Wist's visit that they gave it away for free."

"Little did they realize it would end up haunting your home rather than Kraken's," Manatree said sardonically. "Are you going to start collecting these?"

"Does it look like I have that kind of space?"

I eyed my one and only one-fourth scale statue with, I'll confess, a measure of regret. If only I had room to collect more of them.

The paintwork on the mage robes was really quite incredible—subtly shaded to enhance the intricate sculpt. They'd used semi-translucent material for parts of the fabric and for certain tendrils of hair. It lent the figure an almost heavenly glow.

"I'm sure the Kraken is thrilled to have you ogling this all day," Manatree sniped.

"The Kraken," I said huffily, "is busy aiding the less fortunate in other countries. She has better things to do than criticize my decor."

"Please quit your moping."

"I wasn't—"

"I'm a busy woman, too. I have a job for you, Magebreaker."

Manatree always exuded an air of exasperation. I think it was simply the natural set of her face. Besides, I was accustomed to seeing her in stressful situations.

Even so, right now she looked noticeably ground down. Her uniform seemed less relentlessly starchy than usual, and not just because of the humidity and rain.

"I'll take a guess," I said. "I do love guessing. Did you get put on the berserker task force?"

"This isn't about that. We need you to examine and hobble nine mages. They aren't berserkers."

"Oh. More of the usual magebreaking, then." I paused. "Right now? Isn't this after official working hours for most of you bureaucrats?"

"I'm a busy woman," Manatree repeated. "You, on the other hand, seem to have nothing better to do than to sit around alone in your poorly lit apartment and admire a frivolous statue of your absent lover. I do hope you haven't touched it in inappropriate places."

"Of course not!" I protested. "Where's the fun in that? It's hard as rock. Even the chest."

I realized belatedly that I may have incriminated myself.

Oh, well. I couldn't be too torn up about it. Manatree already regarded me with a healthy dose of derision. At this point, there wasn't much I could do to make her opinion of me even worse.

After I finished getting ready to leave, Manatree ported me to a facility I'd never seen before. I'd never even heard of it, for that matter.

The rain here fell more lightly than in the street outside my apartment.

Judging by the view from the water-speckled windows, it appeared to be somewhere on the city fringes. Near the coast. Perhaps part of the NHRI fortress complex.

I wondered if there was any chance of running into Mori or Pine.

Normally, my PubSec escort—be it Manatee herself or one of her colleagues—would accompany me into the room where I hobbled mages. Both for my own safety and, I suppose, to make sure I didn't get up to any treasonous hijinks.

This time, however, Manatree hung back in the reception lobby and sent me off alone.

Like a shy child departing for their first day of school, I kept glancing over my shoulder at her. She made shooing motions, telling me to get on with it.

Was this some kind of test? Should I refuse to enter without her?

When I looked closer, I realized that all the staff of this—prison? Laboratory?—were subliminals or healers. No actual full-fledged mages among them. Not even a single Class 1.

My inquisitiveness got the better of me. Leaving Manatree behind, I followed my unnamed subliminal guide to an entranceway that looked as if it led to a bank vault. Several different interlocking magic cuttings had been grafted to the dull metal door for extra protection.

"I'm supposed to go in alone?" I asked.

The room, they said, had a panic button. They explained how to find it.

I really didn't like the sound of this.

"Just to be clear—there's a mage inside? I have to apply a two-year hobble? That's it?"

"Nothing to fear," my guide said crisply. "You'll be under observation."

Great. Hopefully I wasn't about to go in and face a starving cannibal. Hopefully they didn't mean that they would observe me and take diligent notes while their pet mage—or whatever it was—tore me to bits.

The room beyond the vault door appeared to be empty. How anticlimactic.

I stood facing a hall lined with numerous additional doors. The grim decor (or lack thereof) immediately reminded me of my old cell. I had no idea what I was supposed to do next.

Paranoia welled up in my veins. Was the government taking advantage of Wist's absence to trick me back into prison?

The vault entrance ground shut behind me. A disembodied voice instructed me to approach a door labeled with a certain number, and to perform a rather tedious series of actions to open it.

The door closed and auto-locked the instant I slipped through to the other side. If I'd been any slower, it would've bitten a solid chunk out of my heel.

Inside I found a Class 8 mage rhythmically ramming his bed into the wall. It made quite a racket, but I hadn't heard a peep from the other side of the door. His only signs of progress were a couple of feeble dents.

"You might want to stop that," I said.

No response seemed forthcoming.

I raised my voice. "If nothing else, you've got time to think," I told him. Advice from a former prisoner. "Settle down. Collect yourself. Contemplate a different escape route. Keep this up, and they'll just bolt down your bed."

"Nice to meet you," said the mage.

It was hard to hear him over the bang-bang-bang of him using his bed as a battering ram. He hadn't paused for a second. He sounded amiable enough, though. Not even out of breath.

Most mages the government asked me to hobble were restrained, their faces anonymized, their voices processed so heavily that they sounded like machines talking. If they were even allowed to speak to me at all. I'd never been asked to visit someone whiling away the time in their own private cell.

Class 8 was fairly prestigious. If I had to guess, I'd say that he'd probably been a high-level government official before getting arrested. An assistant secretary to a Board member, for instance. Though paunchy and perhaps a few decades older than me, he looked like someone with access to expensive barbers and skin care.

One thing he had in common with the captive mages I typically saw was his uniform. It was the same off-white hue as a standard-issue prison jumpsuit, but with a large chunk missing from the lower half of his shirt. He wore a thick fabric belt fastened around the exposed small of his back. The belt crackled with magic cuttings.

While these sorts of belts weren't perfect, they had much the same end effect as my hobbling. They plugged up their wearer's magic— twisted it shut like a bottle cap.

The magic cuttings needed to complete a single belt were extremely complex, and prone to occasional failure. The more mages I hobbled, the more the government could afford to skimp out on manufacturing new magic plugs.

It might free up at least a few talented mages to learn different magic skills, to contribute to society in other ways. Rather than doggedly churn out more and more of the same magic cuttings to make more and more prisoners' belts.

That, in essence, was why the government valued my services.

I sure was glad to see mages safely belted when I first showed up to hobble them, though.

"Seriously," I said to the rich-looking Class 8. "How long have you been going at this? Give the bed a rest."

He still didn't stop. Manatree had better compensate me if this damaged my hearing.

I crept up behind him and poked a finger in the back of his belt. He remained utterly focused on beating up the wall with his bed. The wall appeared undaunted.

It was my first time hobbling someone who stayed in motion the entire time, and who didn't even acknowledge me doing it.

At least he didn't try to stop me. I flicked at his eight magic branches. They coiled up into an elegant knot. He kept slamming his bed back and forth the whole time.

The next seven mages were no less perplexing. None resisted being hobbled. None seemed particularly interested in who I was or why I'd shown up all of a sudden.

Some carried on entire conversations with me, fluidly discussing the weather despite their lack of access to any windows. Yet the words they spoke bore little or no connection to their physical actions. Some dug at the walls with bandaged bare hands. Some tried to grind away at the floor.

At first I was perplexed about why none of them targeted their cell doors. Eventually I noticed that each door had a Disappearance cutting embedded in it.

The cuttings were far too weak (perhaps deliberately so) to affect someone like me, conscious of having just stepped into the cell through that very door. It appeared, however, that the magic worked well enough on the single-minded prisoners. They seemed incapable of realizing there was a door they could attempt to break through.

The imprisoned mages fell into Class 1, Class 6, Class 2—all over the place, really, with equally varied ages and genders. No one famous. The only common traits I could detect was that all were adults, and none seemed to be bonded.

The ninth and final mage was the only one I found restrained.

He looked to be around my age or a little younger. A fit man with one arm and both legs in a cast. Grotesque bruises bloomed on nearly every inch of visible skin.

His eyes followed me as I approached. He didn't say a word. Instead he opened and closed his mouth over and over, as if in an automated simulation of speech. No sound emerged. His tongue looked intact, but he had very few teeth left.

Before I was permitted to leave the vault and go find Manatree, a bespectacled woman came and studied me from the top of my head to the tips of my fingers and toes.

Her glasses looked like the type meant to aid magical perception, not physical sight. Curiouser and curiouser. I did a little spin and curtsy for her benefit. It failed to elicit a laugh. Not even a wan chuckle.

Manatree rejoined me in a barren meeting room that looked out on a dark and turbulent sea. This mysterious facility must be housed in a particularly remote wing of the fortress.

"Not that anyone asked my opinion," I said, "but that was weird. Extremely weird."

"Did you notice anything unusual about the prisoners?"

"It'd be quicker to explain what seemed normal about them. Not much, frankly."

"Answer seriously."

Okay, fine. I could be professional about this.

"They were all totally dedicated to trying to escape. They went at it like automatons. But they chose very inefficient methods. It'd take them hundreds of years to actually get anywhere."

I sipped from the cold can of spica she'd brought me. Thanks, Manatree.

"The act of hobbling didn't feel any different. No more difficult than usual, and no less. The one thing I can't explain is that they were all littered with magic shrapnel. Didn't stop me from hobbling them, though."

"Shrapnel?"

"Fragments of magic cuttings," I said. "Foreign objects. Not their own magic. Someone else's. Broken fragments embedded deep inside them at random."

"Vorpal rabies," Manatree said abruptly.

"Vorpal what now?"

"Our working theory is that it's a disease from another world. From the other side of a vorpal hole. A disease like rabies. Magical prions."

"Prions?" I echoed. "What is that, some kind of bacteria?"

"Were you ever required to study biology?"

"Basic stuff, sure," I said. "I learned how babies get made, if that's what you're asking."

Manatree's look informed me that this was very much not what she had been asking, and also that she found my attempts at humor downright excruciating.

I shrugged. "You'll have to forgive my ignorance here, but I've never heard of prions. Magical or otherwise. I barely know how rabies works. What's it do, make you foam at the mouth and bite people like a dog?"

Manatree appeared to restrain herself from sighing. "Never mind. It's just one point of comparison." She gazed out the window at the roiling sea as she spoke. "You may have noticed that one of the mages you hobbled was in far worse shape than the rest."

"The very last one," I affirmed. "Looked like someone beat him up."

"That's the oldest case. We took him into custody around the beginning of the year."

"Six months ago," I said. "And you only decided to have me hobble him now?"

"No one has ever seen anything like this ... this disease he has. The researchers thought hobbling might interfere with their ability to analyze how those fragments—what they call prions, and what you call shrapnel—affect him."

"Was beating him senseless part of your research, too?"

"He did that to himself," Manatree said. "At first he was still capable of making small talk. He tried to dig holes in the floor and walls, but not to the point of harming himself.

"Over time, he began using his body more and more violently. By now it's clear that he'll kill himself trying to escape. Unless he stays under permanent restraint."

"How about the other eight?" I asked. "How far along are they?"

"The remaining cases are much fresher. All from the past few weeks. But we can already tell that they're beginning to deteriorate. They never sleep—they never close their eyes for longer than a blink. It's difficult to get them to drink or eat.

"Every few days, they shut down for a few hours. They stop moving, sit down or lie down, stare into space. They show no other signs of wanting or needing rest."

"This is all quite fascinating," I told her, "but is there a reason you haven't sent me home yet? Was hobbling them the end of my work here? Or was it the beginning?"

"Public Security is drastically overworked right now," said Manatree.

"With all the randomly berserking mages? I bet you are. So what is it you want me to do for you?"

"Investigate this disease." Her lips puckered inward as if it pained her to ask me a favor. "This so-called vorpal rabies. How are they being infected? Is the disease contagious—can it be spread from mage to mage? Is it curable? What is it, exactly?"

"In case you somehow forgot," I reminded her, "I'm really not a detective. I'm also not an expert on diseases. Not even the magical kind. If such a thing even exists. I'm still skeptical."

Manatree fixed me with a look of cold triumph. I braced myself.

"You can charge twice your usual hourly rate," she said.

I sucked my teeth. "Fine. You win this one."

Ever since I was a child, my nightly dreams had always been of dying. Far from a rollicking good time, but at least there were no plot twists. I knew exactly what to expect every time I went to sleep.

That changed for the first time late last year, when I learned why those dreams had followed me all my life.

Now I still dreamed of dying every once in a while—but I also got to experience the kinds of jarring, nonsensical, intrinsically meaningless dreams that just about everyone else enjoyed during REM sleep. Or so I'd been told.

The night after I hobbled the nine captive mages with vorpal rabies, I dreamt of Wist trapped on stage in a column of magical light.

Her mouth mechanically opened and closed without sound, without any coherent syllables to lip-read. Her teeth lay scattered on the wooden stage floor. She was swollen with bruises almost to the point of being unrecognizable. Alien magic fragments wiggled deep in her flesh, little maggoty parasites.

I woke up with a headache and nausea. I groped for the bond inside me just to make sure I could still sense Wist at the other end of it.

She was there, but physically so distant it felt like another world. Way on the other side of the continent. Closing vorpal holes in a minuscule city-state whose name I couldn't recall off the top of my head. Maybe I'd remember if someone showed it to me on a map.

16

AT FIRST I COULDN'T understand why they called the disease vorpal rabies. Why not mage rabies? Magic rabies? Mage dementia?

It started to make sense once Manatree explained more about the first ten known cases.

Left to their own devices, the victims were inexorably drawn to vorpal holes. As soon as they encountered a vorpal hole, they would attempt to fling themselves inside.

If no convenient vorpal holes awaited close by, they would go wandering in search of one. If held captive, they would mindlessly strive to break free.

They showed no indication of impatience, desperation, longing. They devoted themselves to seeking out vorpal holes like animals driven solely by biological instinct.

I'd hobbled nine captive mages. The tenth had already succeeded in throwing herself down a vorpal hole before anyone could stop her.

On top of that, every single victim had apparently been bitten by a vorpal beast at some point before they started showing symptoms. Hence the *rabies*.

To be frank, I found this flat-out unbelievable. I'm far from the most educated person in Osmanthus. But even I knew that there was no historical precedent for new diseases sneaking in through vorpal holes.

Vorpal beasts might wreak havoc, and they might devour you, but would they pass on viruses or parasites? Or magical prions, as Manatree had called them?

I'd never heard of such a thing. The very notion felt ridiculous.

All the victims had apparently been bitten in the greater metropolitan area. That seemed even more implausible. Thankfully, Osmanthus City was not teeming with vorpal beasts. I couldn't recall having ever glimpsed one running loose.

Ten regular civilians encountering dangerous vorpal beasts right here in the city—in the space of half a year—was a little hard to swallow.

At the same time, it wasn't as if PubSec had pulled this whole story out of their collective asses. They'd interviewed witnesses and retraced the victims' steps, using magic as well as standard forensics. They'd compiled their findings into an extremely well-organized dossier.

Manatree wouldn't let me take the dossier out of the secret research prison (or wherever it was that they kept those poor mages). But she let me stay as long as it took for me to read the binder from cover to cover.

Afterward, I told her I wanted to speak with the healer who had referred the very first case to the government.

"If you must," Manatree said, gruff as ever. "Get an introduction from Mori."

Though only twenty-three, a full ten years younger than me, Mori had a surprisingly varied social circle. Now that I thought about it, he'd become my most reliable source of private clients. Maybe I ought to pay him a referral fee.

The morning after I first heard the words *vorpal rabies*, I caught Mori busy at work in Wist's tower. He was down on his knees, feet neatly tucked beneath him, loose pink-tinged braid falling gently over his left shoulder, an off-tune song on his lips.

To be precise: he was packing Wist a suitcase.

I stood there at the entrance to Wist's bedroom and gaped as Mori dutifully folded undershirts and rolled up pairs of leggings.

Wist herself was nowhere to be seen. As far as I could tell from the bond, she remained miles and miles and miles away in one of those countries up north.

"She's the Kraken," I said once I'd regained my voice. "She can port back home if she wants new underwear so badly."

"The Kraken is the only person in the world who can close vorpal holes."

"That doesn't mean she can't learn to pack her own suitcase."

Mori spoke as if he fancied himself the voice of reason. "The northern nations are absolutely riddled with vorpal holes right now. It makes more sense for her to stay there and focus on sealing up as many as possible, as quickly as possible. It might save more lives than if she wasted energy hopping back now."

"How're you going to get those to her, anyway?"

"A mage courier service."

"Sounds expensive. You can't just go yourself?"

He shook his head. "Not this time. Visa issues."

Mori sometimes accompanied Wist abroad. Not that I was jealous or anything. I mean, it made sense. Mori was her assistant, and boy, did she ever need assistance. The almighty Kraken seemingly lacked the organizational skills to pack for herself or stick to a strict schedule without prompting.

"You just earned your doctorate," I said. "Should you really be spending time on this?"

He stopped folding.

"Would you like to take over?" he asked expectantly.

"Heavens, no."

"It's really quite satisfying work. You could even call it fun."

I did admire Mori's ability to view everything in such a positive light. All I could see was a smart young lad wasting his time on manual labor for a grown woman who ought to be perfectly capable of taking care of herself. But Mori seemed happy with it. Good for him, I guess.

Once Mori reached a good stopping point, I urged him over to the nearest dining room. With a dramatic flourish, I showed him the box of pastries I'd brought from my neighborhood bakery. His eyes lit up. Even more so than usual, anyhow.

We sat there nibbling tiny egg tarts while he told me about the healer named Larkspur.

She was in her forties, he said. She'd been one of his professors in undergrad. Not a full-time professor. More like a special lecturer.

She ran her own private mage healing practice, which was how she'd encountered the first person to come down with vorpal rabies. The victim's family had taken him to her as a patient.

"I thought your undergrad professors were all terrible," I said. "They wouldn't recommend you for a job. They were going to let you get bonded by any powerful mage that would have you. Even if you wanted a career of your own."

"Well—that's true." He wiped his fingers on a napkin. "She was the only one who showed me any sympathy. It would have been hard for any of them to openly defy the mages who'd decided to court me. It could've gotten them fired. It could've lost the school money. It's not that I couldn't understand their position."

"All right," I conceded. "So this Larkspur put on the nicest face. Did she actually do anything to help you, though? Or was she just better at staying likable while refusing to put her own neck out a single millimeter?"

"Oh, no, no, no," Mori said hastily. "It's really not like that. She couldn't recommend me openly, but I'm sure she tried to help behind the scenes.

"Actually—way later, I found out that she's worked with Wist a few times in the past. She might've been the one who pushed Wist to find me and hire me. And save me from bonding in the process."

"Hmmm. If you say so." I took a moment to savor the last few bits of my egg tart. "I look forward to meeting this lady. Don't you worry—I'll be perfectly courteous."

After hearing from Mori, the healer called Larkspur invited me to pay her a visit that very afternoon.

Larkspur ran her private practice out of a three-story house located halfway between my toad-brown apartment and the Old River district.

The first floor held her office and waiting room and such. The higher floors, which were closed to patients, appeared to be her living quarters.

Two huge hydrangea bushes framed her front door, their head-sized clouds of flowers just beginning to deepen from that first fresh blue to rich royal purple. Dew glistened on spiderwebs stretching from branch to branch, but I couldn't spot any spiders. Lustrous purple-pink ground orchids sprouted abundantly at the base of the bushes, their leaves and stems too heavy to stand up straight.

I folded up my umbrella and tested the door. It was locked. The doorbell played a broken melody like wind chimes.

My hair was damp from all the ambient mist, but lately I'd been keeping it short enough that I didn't need to worry much about styling it. Always best to have a puppy cut in summer. I rocked idly on the heels of my rain boots as I waited for Larkspur to let me in.

The door was an uncomfortably large step up from the stoop. Seemed like a great way to stub your toe.

The mistress of the house opened the door and looked down at me. Mostly because of the step. Without it, we'd have been similar in height.

The instant I saw her, I felt out of place in my own skin.

Allow me to elaborate. I thought I looked dashing enough. I was back in my suspenders. Figured I'd dress up and try to make a good impression.

Larkspur, in contrast, wore healer robes. The old-fashioned kind.

I hadn't seen anyone wearing healer robes in years. They were inarguably more practical than mage robes, with fewer layers and less feverish colors. They were meant to reach near your ankles; they didn't drag on the floor like a train.

Older healers might wear traditional garb in their everyday lives, out of simple preference. Particularly stuffy or controlling mages might demand that their bondmates wear it for show.

It was still rather startling to see a woman answer her own door in full healer robes.

The fabric was very dark, close to black, with a somber pattern of enormous white chrysanthemums. She had gray hair tucked back in a low chignon. She smiled and invited me in with an elegant tilt of her hand. I strove not to trip on the step up to the door as I followed her.

Now that we stood on the same level, I began to think that perhaps I was a tad taller than her—even after removing my rain boots. That would be a novel experience.

I introduced myself as my cover identity, Asa Lantana, and passed her a business card labeled *A. L. Consulting*.

Larkspur examined the card with an air of profound fascination, holding it up to the light with flawlessly painted taupe nails. She certainly knew how to put on a good show for the sake of politeness.

After tucking my business card away, she led me to her office. A dark leather-topped desk faced a windowsill crowded with potted calla lilies and amaryllis. The amaryllis stalks were in full bloom, with flowers so huge that they needed to be tied to a stake to keep from collapsing under their own weight.

She offered me the usual array of drinks. I requested coffee.

I eyed the artwork on the walls as I waited for her to finish making it. It was an array of relatively small pieces: pastel chalk drawings in simple black frames, ranging from the size of a postcard to the size of a pillow.

"Do you like it?" Larkspur asked from behind me.

The drawings were intensely colored depictions of … I had no idea what, actually. I'd spy disparate details like an upside-down staircase, a heap of jewels, a human figure. But the more I tried to piece them together, the more each picture broke apart into incoherence.

"Very sophisticated," I said, as if I had any idea what I was talking about. "All the same artist?"

Larkspur laughed. "My late husband. Art was his hobby. He was always too shy to tell anyone. Quite a shame. But now he's no longer around to stop me from showing off his work." Her smile turned mischievous. "I'm afraid none of it's for sale."

"Of course," I said. "Seems to be right where it belongs."

A whistle pierced the air. I jerked as if my skeleton were trying to escape its fleshly prison.

"That'll be the kettle," Larkspur said breezily. "Excuse me."

I wandered to the other side of her office and waited for my heart to stop hammering.

Once the ringing left my ears, I could again hear the steady tick of an unseen clock. Kettle aside, the house—the whole neighborhood—seemed hushed.

Her antique-looking desk was empty of papers. It did hold a variety of whimsically shaped paperweights, along with a letter opener shaped like a miniature replica of a sword from a thousand years ago. Plus a single stem of perfect white chrysanthemum in a slender crystal vase.

The artifacts were all enchanted. Each had a solitary magic cutting embedded neatly within it.

But as far as I could discern at a glance, the magic was frivolous. Borderline meaningless. A cutting to keep dust from collecting on a little bronze tortoise. A cutting to make a realistic model ladybug change color for each day of the week. Other cuttings seemed to do nothing at all.

"Those are from mages I've treated in the past," said Larkspur. "Sometimes I ask for a little memento as extra payment."

"Are they valuable?" I tried not to sound doubtful.

"Some might be, depending on the mage who made them. Although these aren't for sale, either."

She handed me a cup of coffee and a matching saucer. "There are more over in the cabinet. Do you recognize anyone?"

The cabinet by the desk was a mix of black lacquer and shining mother-of-pearl inlay. Its glass-fronted shelves bore a chaotic array of gew-gaws, some standard and some downright disturbing.

For example: a long brown lock of hair. A half-eaten fruit sandwich. A ventriloquist's dummy with an unholy glint in its eye.

I paused in front of a colorful gilded goblet that looked more expensive than everything else in the office put together. Assuming it was real blown glass, of course.

I couldn't tell what the cutting wound around the goblet was supposed to do. It might just be a broken-off branch imprinted with a magic skill incapable of functioning independently. Only certain magic skills were suited for practical use as cuttings, separated from the mage who'd grown and honed those pruned branches.

Yet I recognized this curled length of magic. It was like identifying a person based on their fingerprint or gait.

"Shien Miyu," I said.

"You know Shien Miyu?"

"I've done occasional work for the Shiens," I explained. Hey, it wasn't an outright lie. "Surprising, I know. Don't look the part, do I?"

I made a self-deprecating gesture at myself. Even dressed up from toe to chin, I wouldn't be a very good candidate for going undercover in high society.

"You treated her before she bonded?" I asked.

"Occasionally." Larkspur sipped her own coffee beside me. "She was very reluctant to let me have this memento. She insisted that I keep it a secret. But she did give it to me anyway, in the end."

I couldn't see our faces reflected in the cabinet. Guess Larkspur must've invested in museum-quality glass.

"I knew Luka," she said quietly. "Terrible shame. Seems that Ms. Shien has had quite the fall from grace lately. Perhaps her behavior finally caught up with her."

"Maybe," I said. "What about all those other mages who get away with treating their healers just the same as her?"

Her eyebrows went up. "Oh? You're a bold one."

I laughed. It came out sounding a bit weak. "Well, you know. I get a lot of work from the government. We're real buddy-buddy. It's like ribbing a sibling. Sometimes I just can't help myself."

I pivoted to examine her desk again. My eyes stopped on the lone white chrysanthemum. The magic cutting entwined with it would ensure it stayed fresh at the height of its bloom for all of eternity. Or at least until the mage who'd made the cutting perished.

"Wi—" I caught myself just in time. "The Kraken," I said, pointing at the chrysanthemum. "That one's from the Kraken."

"Well done!" Larkspur sounded delighted. "Mori did mention that you're acquainted with the Kraken. I'm so impressed you knew her magic on sight."

"Guess I have a good memory for this sort of thing."

"I saw the Kraken for a few years—starting six, maybe seven years ago. Very interesting woman."

She motioned for me to take a seat on the couch.

"I was never able to ease the Kraken's deepest pain," she mused. "They say that the greater the magical power, the greater the need for healing.

"So the greater the power, the greater the inherent suffering. Perhaps her talent isn't her endless magic—it's her ability to suffer for it."

"That sounds terrible," I said.

Larkspur curled a smile at me, close-lipped but warm. Her gray hair and conservative bun gave off the impression of a benevolent grandparent. Her old-fashioned garment covered every bit of skin from the bottom of her neck to the tops of her wrists and ankles.

On the other hand, Mori had said she wasn't that many years over forty. Her face had few lines, and her eyes were a young clear amber. It was all quite perturbing.

I know that's a rude way to describe someone whose only sin was having odd taste in memorabilia. She was otherwise so refined and put-together that it made me question if I even knew the correct way to perch my butt on a couch cushion. But I can't help how I felt.

Upon request, Larkspur told me in detail about how she'd come across the first victim of vorpal rabies.

He was an unbonded mage. She'd treated him once or twice in the past. This time, his worried family dragged him in. They thought his peculiar behavior might be a sign that he was about to go berserk.

Yet his magic wasn't particularly tangled, and healing it didn't seem to make a difference.

Troubled by his lack of improvement and compulsive wandering, she'd reached out to her contacts at the National Healing Research Institute. They in turn suggested that this mysterious condition might be a matter for Public Security.

"So he never actually told anyone about getting attacked by a vorpal beast," I said. "And no one saw it happen. But you were that confident of it, based solely on the bite marks? What if it was just a rabid raccoon?"

"I'm not the only one who examined his bite marks," Larkspur replied, unoffended.

This was true. I'd seen a bunch of notes from PubSec medical staff in Manatree's dossier. All agreed with Larkspur.

It was extremely strange that the vorpal beast in question had attacked this one man—in the middle of Osmanthus City, no less!—then faded away without hurting anyone else. Without ever getting caught.

Moreover, he'd only gotten a little roughed up. You couldn't even call it a full mauling.

One might theorize that the same vorpal beast had been responsible for at least some of the later victims. But then how did it manage to lurk unnoticed for months in between? And if it were aggressive enough to attack people unprovoked, why would it wait around for so long and do nothing?

"That's my problem," I said. "I keep getting stuck on this one point. Since when has it been so easy to run into vorpal beasts? Are we in the middle of some kind of massive infestation? If that were the case, *more* people should be seeing them. More people should be getting hurt."

Larkspur tapped her lip, her gaze fixed on a far point at the other side of the room. The gray window above her desk, perhaps, or the single white chrysanthemum that Wist had gifted her.

She leaned a little toward me—without turning her head to look at me—and said softly, "May I make a suggestion?"

"Please," I said. "Investigating isn't my strong point. I'm starved for ideas."

"Here's another way to think about it," she continued. "Yes—it's almost unheard of to encounter a vorpal beast running wild right here in the city.

"But that doesn't mean no one ever sees any vorpal beasts at all. There are some situations where their presence would be considered quite ordinary. Expected, even."

It took me a moment to understand what she was getting at. "MvB magesports," I said. "Mage versus beast. Right—that's an entire game mode."

"Yes. Where else?"

"Rich people?" I guessed.

Larkspur nodded.

I pictured the stereotypical king or queen of ye olden times. A long scepter in their manicured hands, and magic-tamed vorpal beasts hulking at their feet. Even nowadays—especially nowadays—the nouveau riche often collected vorpal beasts as a kind of status symbol.

But I didn't think the Shien clan had vorpal beasts. They probably considered themselves to be above such tawdry displays of wealth and power.

Wist kept a few back at the tower, come to think of it: docile creatures that shared aquarium space with a few species of ordinary fish. Although Wist's beasts clearly weren't for show. The only reason I even knew she had them was because I liked to poke around and stick my nose in things.

The average Osmanthian couldn't simply walk up to a pet store and buy a vorpal beast. The vorpal beast trade was highly restricted—and mostly illegal. But all those rich folks and magesports organizers had to be getting their vorpal beasts from somewhere. Legally or otherwise.

Hmm. I guess the fact that the first victim had gotten away with just a few non-lethal bites might make more sense if the vorpal beast in question were partly tame, or partly restrained.

I would assume that PubSec had already taken a look at possible connections to the vorpal beast trade. Then again, must be a whole lot of money sloshing around in there. Perhaps they felt limited by political constraints.

I'd heard enough to decide on my next step, but I stuck around a little longer to be polite.

Larkspur brought out shortbread cookies, which I gladly accepted. She looked so thrilled that I had a feeling she'd just wanted to nibble on some herself. Couldn't blame her.

On a purely selfish level, I was also curious to hear more about how she ran her private practice. My own consultancy had been in business for far less than a year, after all. I could probably stand to learn a thing or two from someone more experienced.

Her work varied from training other healers to treating unbonded mage clients. They came to her regularly for healing and check-ups, as one might visit a dentist for teeth-cleaning.

She sounded most enthusiastic when speaking about her volunteer work: providing pro bono healing for low-income mages. I praised her spirit of charity (and I wasn't even being sarcastic). Larkspur chuckled and told me that the government did provide plenty of incentives.

Still, it wasn't as if it had ever occurred to me to devote even a smidgen of my time—even a fraction of my considerable talent—to helping others for free. More specifically, to helping *mages* in need. I'd never have thought of it on my own.

So whatever Larkspur's motivation to help heal less fortunate mages, she was miles ahead of me in the morality races.

On my way out, I spotted a charcoal sketch of an unsmiling man hanging in the hallway.

"Your husband?" I asked.

"Yes," said Larkspur. She stopped beside me. "His only self-portrait."

"He looks—" I scrambled for adjectives. "Uh, hardworking."

"He certainly was." Her face softened. "He was Class 9. Part of the Osmanthian delegation to VorDef."

"Wow. That's a big deal."

"But you know, we never bonded," she confided. "He did so much international travel. He needed someone capable of being on call at all times to heal him.

"Me, I wanted to have a career. So I was the one holding him back. He could've risen so much higher if he had a proper bondmate. He sacrificed his own career progression to honor my wishes."

"Not many mages would do that," I said. "Sounds like a great guy."

"I can't believe it's already been twelve years since he passed."

Larkspur touched the frame of the portrait, adjusting it this way and that on the wall. To my eyes, it already looked perfectly straight.

"Now that I'm older, sometimes I think maybe—in some ways, perhaps it was for the best. If he'd lived, the pressure to bond me would only have grown greater and greater over time. We may not have been able to hold out forever."

She let go of the frame. "Or maybe—maybe we shouldn't have tried to defy such norms in the first place. He never would have pushed me to bond. But I know it would have made him so happy. And still I chose myself, my own independence. What was it all for, I wonder?"

It wasn't the tone of someone seeking an answer. Besides, I knew better than to try to make up an answer where none existed. At least none that I could see. My own bond felt hot and awkward inside me.

17

WIST WAS STILL making the rounds of the northern territories. No monsoon there. Late at night, as we spoke through my ear cuff, I asked if she could hear the rain hitting the street outside my apartment.

The ear cuff wasn't made for that, she said. All she could hear was my voice.

She sighed a little as I reached across the bond to heal her. She'd been using intense skills without breaks for day after day after day. As a result, she'd needed treatment nearly every night. There were moments when the creaking and aching in her magic started to leak over to me.

Sometimes Wist stayed at hotels. But on this trip, they'd decided to put her up at the local Osmanthian consulate.

I imagined her curled up on a fluffy bed in an unlit room with toile pattern wallpaper, staring dead-eyed into the shadows. She'd mentioned that sealing vorpal holes all day long—having to look at vorpal holes all day long—gave her a headache.

I asked offhand about where she'd gotten her vorpal beasts, the ones she kept at the tower.

Sounding sleepy, Wist told me she'd picked them up by accident. It happened back when she was deep into experimenting with things like vorpal hole scrying and vorpal hole travel.

Back when she'd been frantically inventing new magic skills that she alone could use, and that no one else knew were even possible.

"Why didn't you just chuck them back where they came from?" I asked.

"They seemed to like it in the tower. I felt bad."

"You're such a softy." I yawned. "All right, we both better get some sleep, so—"

"Clematis."

"What?"

"I'm almost done here. I'll be back in Osmanthus next week at the latest."

"Oh yeah? Congratulations."

"Try not to do anything too dangerous before I come back."

"What makes you think I would?" I said sweetly. "I mean, life is dangerous. But I'm not that much of a thrill-seeker."

Luckily, Wist seemed too tired to press the issue. I distracted her by slipping the ear cuff off and giving it a noisy smack of a kiss. I cackled when I felt her wince through the bond. Poor exhausted Wist. She really did need more sleep.

Maybe my sudden curiosity about vorpal beasts had gotten her worried. Well, my dear Wist had nothing to fear. I did plan to go take a closer look at some real-life vorpal beasts, but it would be in a perfectly controlled environment. Couldn't be safer. Cross my heart.

That weekend, I went to Anthum Coliseum for the first time in my life.

Anthum Coliseum was the largest magesports stadium in the entire metropolitan area. It took on the shape of an ancient royal crown, tall and glittering, with spikes that dwarfed every other building for miles around. No matter which direction you approached from, it appeared to coronate the brow of the earth.

Today, under ragged gray skies, the coliseum looked duller than it would on bright midsummer evenings. If I didn't already know the building's purpose, I might have assumed it was a dictator's citadel. Or perhaps a showy prison, one designed to intimidate the plebes.

Inside the coliseum, a seemingly impossible number of cushy seats peered down on a round field. The field resembled a slice of a nature preserve, broken up by massive heaps of lichen-covered boulders. On one side lay a half-rotted fallen tree. Its trunk diameter must've been at least three times Wist's height.

The match I'd come to watch would be starting in just a few minutes.

Everyone around me—no, nearly everyone already seated, for as far as I could see—wore black cloth blindfolds. They leaned back against their headrests as they chatted with their neighbors, eyes covered.

My own magic-infused blindfold, which I'd picked up at the ticket office, waited patiently in my jacket pocket. I took it out once I saw my friend Fanren walk onto the field below.

He was an ant-sized speck, just barely recognizable. An eager murmur flowed up through the crowd like a wave rolling toward shore.

A smooth-voiced announcer said: "And now, making his way onto the field, we see Ouro Fanren, twenty-seven, Class 8-5, an Osmanthus City native, and the defending MvM Continental Champion.

"Tonight marks a rare chance to see an elite MvM duelist face off against a formidable vorpal beast. Ouro looks relaxed and ready. Too relaxed? Only time will tell. His opponent's specs are, of course, a closely guarded secret...."

I put the soft blindfold over my eyes and tied it tight. The darkness only lasted a second. Immediately afterward, my vision opened. It didn't show me the view from my seat high up near the stadium walls. It put me right down on the field next to Fanren.

These blindfolds were a primary reason fans paid to come to the stadium. Remote viewers were forced to watch from a far more distant vantage point.

Fanren had taken out most of his piercings. Guess they were considered a hazard in competition. Nor did he have on the glasses he normally wore to enhance magic perception, though I'd seen him compete in them before.

His clothing was all simple athletic gear sprinkled with a few discreet sponsor logos. He'd fit in just fine with any weekend runner jogging suburban trails.

As the announcer had proclaimed, Fanren was most famed for his prowess as an MvM (mage versus mage) duelist. But today's match would be MvB—mage versus beast. Fanren was stepping in to replace a different duelist, someone who'd been forced to drop off the schedule for health reasons. Supposedly.

Now Fanren waited next to a slanted boulder, hands in his pockets. The jungle-green grass around his ankles sparkled with drops of evening dew.

The announcer kept prattling on, explaining the match's time limit—thirty minutes—and reading off all sorts of gambling odds.

In the interest of full disclosure, I should mention that I'd arrived at the coliseum early enough to place a few judicious bets. Specifically, I bet that Fanren would win, and that he'd do so within twenty minutes.

The chances for both of these were extremely high, which meant I'd be looking at a low payout. But even if it was just a token amount, I figured I'd give Fanren my winnings to thank him for the free ticket.

Magesports weren't just a simple matter of time limits and winning or losing, of course. All of the various rulesets revolved around giving competitors a numerical score. The faster your victory, and the fewer unique magic skills you deployed in a match, the higher your final numbers.

The core intention behind this was to even things out a bit for lower-class mages. A Class 2 might only have two unique magic skills. On the flip side, if they could actually win a match with just those two skills, they were almost guaranteed a very high score.

Higher-ranked mages needed to make more complex calculations to decide on an appropriate strategy. For instance, they might receive the same score for using three skills to win in three minutes as they'd get for using one skill to win in thirty minutes.

Don't take my word for it, anyway. The numbers could get pretty complicated. Which was why I'd avoided placing any score-related bets.

Wist got plenty of invitations to participate in exhibition matches, though she always turned them down. I couldn't blame them for trying. Anything involving the Kraken would be the match of the millennium.

Most people thought Wist declined in order to avoid crushing the morale of ordinary duelists. Surely the Kraken would destroy every competitor who so much as glanced at her.

I suspected that her real reason for declining—other than a simple lack of time and interest—was quite the opposite.

As the Kraken, Wist's strength was her unparalleled number and variety of unique magic skills.

Conversely, duelists like Fanren spent thousands of hours practicing the same skills over and over, and strove to rely on as few skills as possible during competition.

Wist could certainly overwhelm them by using dozens of skills at once. But even if she emerged the winner, she'd come out of it with a disappointingly low score.

People thought the Kraken could do anything, and most of the population was most familiar with magic through magesports. They'd lose at least some faith in her if they saw her fail to excel in the area of magical strength that they understood best.

This wouldn't deal much of a blow to Wist's ego. On a personal, emotional level, I think she'd long since stopped caring what anyone really thought of the Kraken. But part of her had bought into the government's insistence that people needed to believe she could protect them—from vorpal holes, terrorists, imaginary foreign enemies, everything.

Music swelled through the stadium, those well-known notes all of us had grown up with, hearing other children hum them on the playground before we even understood what the music meant. *Let the games begin.*

An enormous spiral rock materialized on the field as if it had been there all along. Not of its own accord, of course. Support mages must have ported it in.

Fanren tilted his head back to look up at it. My view pulled away from him and glided through the air above the rock like a bird circling.

"Yes," said the announcer, a vibrato of excitement in his voice, "you see here one of the largest vorpal beasts to ever grace Anthum Coliseum. That snail-like shell is approximately the height of a ten-story building."

I suppose it did resemble a snail shell, although the sheer size made me want to see it as a hulking piece of sculpted stone.

The shell, thankfully, didn't budge. I wondered what Fanren would've done if it started rolling at him like a bulldozer, crashing with all its force into the clear magic walls between the field and the blindfolded crowd.

A thick shimmering liquid started to gush out of the snail shell, glowing the ghostly blue of bioluminescent water. It formed a pond on the coliseum field, made the long grass ripple like seaweed.

I expected Fanren to lift himself to safety with Zero Gravity. Instead he remained standing in place, closed up inside a transparent cube of magic—a construct rather similar to the walls protecting his audience.

Soon the space inside Fanren's Barrier was the only dry spot left on the whole field.

The glimmering slime rolled over piled-up boulders and crushed them to dust as easily as if they were brittle bones left over after cremation. It dissolved and swallowed up the hulking fallen tree in the same way. It climbed the barriers all around Fanren as if hunting for a way to drown him.

Fanren laced his fingers together in a gesture of prayer. Probably a mental trick to help him concentrate. A second cube-shaped barrier appeared around the snail shell—a gossamer box far larger than my four-story apartment.

Sweat stood out on Fanren's temple. The magic walls around the snail shell started shrinking.

Huh. That was one way to do it.

For a mage to win an MvB match, they needed to destroy the vorpal beast's core within a stipulated time limit. But vorpal beast cores weren't nearly as easy to find as a human mage's magical core. Their shape and location varied greatly. Some had little or no aura of detectable magic.

They were creatures from other worlds, after all. Their magic differed from mages' magic in ways that no one could claim to truly understand. Their very existence was mystical, yet they had no discernible magic branches.

In short, Fanren was trying to brute-force his way to victory. Crush the entire shell and everything inside it with his shrinking Barrier, and he wouldn't have to bother pinpointing the core's exact location.

Not too exciting to watch for someone like me. I was far from a magesports fanatic. The crowd would be terribly impressed if he could pull it off, though.

Cracks shaped like lightning bolts lanced through the colossal shell as Fanren's Barrier squeezed it. A bellow with the resonance of whale song rose from the vorpal beast's lake of glowing ooze.

The shell started to collapse in on itself. The announcer was speaking so fast that his words ran past my untrained ears like finely enunciated gibberish.

The crowd cried out. The walls protecting Fanren himself—pressured on all sides by gooey blue fluid—had crumpled and vanished. Yet the fluid curved away from him mid-air, just before touching him. As if he frightened it. As if he repelled it.

This too, I realized, was a twisted use of the skill called Zero Gravity. It made the name start to seem a little inaccurate. Or at least as limiting as lumping everything I myself did under the general umbrella of mage healing. Then again, Barrier wasn't originally meant to be used for compressing things to death, either.

Fanren's Barrier slowly crushed the snail shell. Surges of radiant blue liquid writhed in agony all around him, desperate to touch him, yet never able to get quite close enough. The whale song built to a desperate roar.

Eleven minutes into the match, Fanren's Barrier had compacted the ten-story snail shell to a shining cube the size of an apple. His Barrier shrank inward another agonizing millimeter.

A crack resounded throughout the arena. The beast's crying instantly ceased. The luminescent blue liquid vaporized all at once, puffing up to fill the air above the field like dry ice.

Physically speaking, Fanren had hardly budged an inch from start to finish.

A deafening cheer pressed in on my ears. I wondered if vorpal beasts felt pain.

Once I'd collected my meager winnings, Fanren let me into a lounge designated for the exclusive use of competitors and their guests. Large windows looked down on the coliseum. Some duelists slouched in deep armchairs with blindfolds on, observing ongoing matches.

Fanren, apparently, was already done for the evening. He was back in his piercings, glasses, and dark jeans. He brought over drinks from the bar—plain iced coffee for me, a bitter-looking amber cocktail for him.

We'd taken a booth way at the back, out of earshot of any other duelists loitering here between matches. There I passed him the grand total of my attempt at sports gambling. It probably wasn't even enough to pay for both of our drinks.

Hey, at least I hadn't lost money.

"You had a pretty close call there," I commented.

"When my shield broke?" Fanren grimaced. "Still kicking myself over that. I should've been able to one-skill that match."

"What would've happened if the slime caught you?"

"Hopefully the refs would have extracted me before it killed me."

He clinked his glass against mine and took a sip. Despite what he'd said about kicking himself, Fanren didn't appear too torn up about ending it as a two-skill match.

He was always very quick to move on after making a mistake. I could imagine that unruffled attitude driving his human rivals mad with resentment.

The lounge had the plush decor of a swanky nightclub, but the mood was quiet and rather intense. More people seemed to be imbibing tea or spica than hard liquor. Competitors hunched across heavy tables to mutter furiously with people who looked like trainers and managers.

As Fanren crossed the room with our drinks, some of the duelists sitting alone had raised their crystal glasses his way with tight, envious smiles.

Maybe the real partying would start after the last match of the night came to an end. I planned to be out of here long before then.

I took a swig of my iced coffee. "We're friends, right?"

Fanren gave me a knowing look. "Sounds like you want something."

"Information," I said. "MvB magesports must need a whole lot of vorpal beasts. Where do they come from? How can they be sure of a reliable supply?"

"That's quite a leading question." Fanren picked the orange peel out of his cocktail and popped it into his mouth.

"Don't think you're supposed to eat that," I said.

He shrugged and swallowed.

"Look," I continued. "I know there's gotta be a black market. I don't care where they hold their secret vorpal beast auctions or whatever. I don't care who's been bribed to overlook it. I just want to know about the source of the goods. Vorpal beasts don't pop into being out of thin air."

"They kind of do, if you think about it."

I rolled my eyes. "Yeah, yeah. But they still need a vorpal hole to emerge from."

There must be one or more very large vorpal holes—in or near the city, even—being deliberately left open in order to serve as a reliable source of vorpal beasts.

Some locations might be officially registered and licensed, under government control. The ten-story beast Fanren had fought seemed a bit too large to have been casually smuggled in.

But at least some of the holes used for vorpal beast sourcing were, I suspected, off the books. Someone had paid government officials to overlook them, to let them stay open.

"I can see where you're going with this," said Fanren. "I won't ask why. But allow me to offer a suggestion. Why not wait till the Kraken gets back?"

"What makes you think I won't?"

He raised a pierced eyebrow. I held out for a few awkward seconds before dropping my gaze into my coffee. It had come in what appeared to be a thick glass beer stein, handle and all.

"So," I said. Time for a change of subject. "What happened to the guy who you came in to replace today?"

"He went berserk. Happened a little under a week ago."

"Really. No warning signs?"

"Nothing." Fanren pushed at the base of his slender glass, turning it in tiny circles. "If you really can't afford to wait for the Kraken, take me with you. I'll be your bodyguard again."

"Wouldn't want to make Wist jealous."

I was joking, of course. Fanren let out a begrudging snort. "That's never stopped you before."

"Let me offer a counterproposal," I said. "You don't need to come with me. But maybe you can lend me a weapon. Just in case."

"The last time I gave you a knife, you used it to stab yourself," Fanren said coldly.

"We've been over this," I admonished. "It was for a good cause."

"I would've appreciated some kind of advance warning."

"Oh, don't worry. This time I'll definitely make sure to stab other people. Or vorpal beasts. Whatever comes up."

"That doesn't make me feel any better." Fanren was starting to slump in his seat like a human-shaped pudding.

"What are weapons for?" I didn't wait for an answer. "I know, I know. Trust me, I'm not trying to get into trouble. I'll lie low. I'm just trying to check a few things."

"You have no magic," Fanren told me.

"I'm a healer."

"You have zero combat training."

"Did I ever claim otherwise?"

Fanren slowly leaned forward until his forehead made gentle contact with the table between us.

People often claimed he looked like Wist's twin brother. Most of the time, I didn't buy it. But this sort of reaction did remind me a little of what Wist might do when I drove her to fresh depths of exasperation.

Still slumped over on the table, Fanren turned his face sideways to eye me.

"I can give you something for self-defense," he said reluctantly. "I can point you where you want to go. I've heard rumors about the source holes, anyway. But please don't get caught. Bearing weapons would definitely count as a parole violation."

"That would be bad," I agreed.

"Not just for you," said Fanren. "Spare a thought for your friend here. The Kraken would kill me."

"Wist is really something of a pacifist at heart," I said. "You just need to get to know her better."

Fanren cast his eyes heavenward. Then he sat right back up and started planning how to arm me.

I would've felt safer with Fanren or Wist around, of course. I wasn't exactly pumped about the prospect of going on my own to scout out a giant vorpal hole teeming with vorpal beasts. Especially not one that had been subject to an illegal cover-up, and that the local MPs probably knew to avoid at all costs.

The reason I didn't want either of them to come with me was quite simple. I don't care much for most mages. But I guess I did sort of care about these two.

Vorpal rabies had no cure. To date, all the victims were mages. Not even subliminal mages. All true mages, ranked Class 1 or higher. Yet such mages—mages with an official classification—made up an extremely small proportion of the overall population.

To me this implied that either the disease-carriers exclusively targeted ranked mages, or that the disease itself couldn't infect anyone else.

I'm not saying I'd come to believe the notion that this sickness was, in fact, a type of magical rabies spread by vorpal beasts. Rather, I was hoping to eliminate that possibility from consideration.

Yet until I knew for sure, I didn't want to risk taking Wist or Fanren anywhere that might increase their chances of getting infected. Even if the chances were vanishingly small to begin with.

18

I MADE A QUICK STOP at Fanren's high-rise condo. He insisted on outfitting me in a flak jacket. I protested that it was too big, too unfamiliar. It might limit my movement. And it would definitely stand out.

Fanren showed little sympathy for my perfectly legitimate concerns. He cinched the straps tighter and told me to wear a rain jacket over it if I felt so self-conscious.

Next, he turned to dig around in a drawer. He emerged with what appeared to be a metal business card holder, the type you could slide open one-handed. He took a single card out and passed it to me to examine.

The card was made of standard cream-colored stock. It was printed with the following: a cutesy cartoon porcupine, the number *20*, and an expiration date about four years in the future. How enigmatic. Multiple redundant magic cuttings appeared to be grafted to the paper surface.

There were laws about how much redundancy you needed to build into commercial magical objects in order to claim certain good-till dates. If a mage died, after all, their cuttings would immediately stop working. The idea was that if several different mages all contributed the same branch skill, the product would still work even if one cutting failed due to its creator's untimely death.

Of course, the risk was never zero. A comet might strike and wipe out all the contributors at once. I suppose that's what business insurance was for.

I flipped the card over. The back had a series of twee icons explaining how to use it.

The first illustration showed a fist crushing the card up into a ball. The second illustration showed the fist tossing the crushed card away. The third illustration showed stick figures being pierced by porcupine-like needles of magical pain.

"It'll hit anyone within twenty feet of you," said Fanren.

"It won't hit me, will it?"

"Let's hope not."

"Oh boy," I muttered. "Where'd you get these, anyway? Doesn't seem like something you'd use in dueling."

"Free sample," said Fanren.

"What, like from the supermarket?"

"From a weapons manufacturer," he said. "A start-up. The product was never actually authorized. Not sure if the company is still around."

"So these cards are illegal," I concluded. "Better and better. Well, they seem easy enough for me to use."

"That's the idea."

Once I had Fanren's flak jacket fastened on properly and his pain grenade cards stashed in my pocket, I made him tell me where to go next.

Along the way, I stopped by a convenience store to pick up a plain grey rain poncho. It was huge and puffy and made me feel much less awkward about strolling around wearing body armor underneath.

I took the subway to the Bayside district, over in the western part of the city. Bayside Station was ferociously crowded as usual. Even well after sundown, and even with rain drizzling dolefully from a bleak starless sky. A good third of the district was devoted to a massive complex of seaside amusement parks. Hence all the train traffic.

I hadn't come here to ride merry-go-rounds, of course. I pushed my way over to wait for a tram that would carry me in the opposite direction, deep into Bayside's industrial zone. Warehouses, warehouses, and more warehouses.

I was the only one who got off at the tram stop Fanren had told me about. There were probably far more workers using the tram to commute in the early morning and early evening.

Rain spattered my shoulders as the tram lurched away on its path without me. I turned around slowly to get my bearings.

I stood at a corner where the tram line passed a quieter side street. Across the way lurked a two-story boarded-up building. Some kind of defunct cafeteria.

The buildings looming further down the side street were all far larger: full-size warehouses with few visible windows. They hulked there, dark and dormant, as I walked past.

No traffic. No voices. Few streetlights. Just my own wet footsteps and the incessant rain on my poncho.

The further I went, the more spaced-out the warehouses got, and the quieter it felt. Maybe everyone had already finished work for the day. Or maybe the buildings here were all vacant.

After some minutes of steady walking, I started to glimpse a scattering of magic cuttings welded to the empty street and equally empty sidewalk.

I stopped and crouched to take a closer look. The cuttings were haphazardly distributed and came from a variety of different mages. They lay strewn all over the place like earthworms fleeing a downpour.

I took an experimental step past, trying not to tread directly on the cuttings. Their magic still seeped up into me like water up a wick. My head throbbed.

The magic wanted me to turn around, to leave, to forget I'd come here.

It wasn't impossible to resist, now that I knew it was there. But moving forward felt like wading through old crystallized honey. I dug my nails into my palms. I hunched my shoulders and kept going.

Surely this meant I was close.

The final warehouse stood well apart from the rest, well beyond the minefield of *you-don't-want-to-be-here* magic.

I had to pause and catch my breath once I broke through. The rainy air seemed to loop in and out of the tops of my lungs without ever going deep enough to satisfy.

I slipped a few business cards out of Fanren's smooth metal case and let them bounce around loose in my poncho pocket. In case I needed them in a hurry. Hopefully it wouldn't come to that.

Just so you know, I wasn't planning on trying to enter the building. I'm not that foolhardy. For starters, I simply wanted to survey it from outside. I wanted to make sure I wasn't missing anything.

According to duelist rumors (or so Fanren had told me), this warehouse was a primary source of illicit vorpal beasts.

At some point—possibly years ago—it must've been built up around what at the time had been a newly formed vorpal hole. The roof line swelled and slanted strangely, as if to accommodate the irregular shape of the maw within.

Even here there were street lamps, though their spacing didn't seem quite up to code. I stood across the street from the warehouse, in one of the darkest spots I could find. Without moving a muscle, I studied the silhouette of the building from top to bottom.

Something abstract flickered at my senses. It was reminiscent of the sort of clear floater that might drift across your eyes on a cloudless day. But my eyes weren't the problem here. I closed them and focused all my attention on my magic perception.

Long white hairs. Clumps of spider silk.

That was what my magic perception showed me. Titanic cobwebs snagged all over the outside of the warehouse building, as if they'd gotten caught there while riding the wind to distant lands. Silver-white threads far greater in length than the full height of the five-story building waved their slender ends tenderly in an imperceptible breeze.

If the threads weren't so tangled and orderless, I might almost think the warehouse was wearing a humongous wig.

These massive skeins of spider silk were invisible to the naked eye, but they had nothing to do with human magic.

The silver hairs were a vorpal beast. Either one huge vorpal beast, or perhaps a colony of kindred.

For a bewildered instant, I wondered if vorpal beasts were running the place. But they were beasts in every sense of the word, far more so than earthly animals. No matter how they looked from the outside, they had no brain. They had nothing we would recognize as any type of coherent physical organ. Even if they had thoughts, it seemed the height of arrogance to assume their thoughts would resemble ours.

And yet for all that, I had the distinct sense that the spider silk covering the building knew I was here. It had no eyes. But I could feel it looking down at me here in the shadows. Almost as if it were being used as some kind of surveillance system.

Ridiculous. Or was it? I had a sudden urge to get the hell out of here.

This time I'm pretty sure the thought came solely from my own head.

I pivoted to slink my way back down the street. I didn't make it a single step before porting magic flared around me like little bursts of ball lightning.

One—two—three people. Three mages.

All within maybe ten feet of me.

My eyes were long since accustomed to the dark, but I still couldn't pick up many details. Black clothes. Masked faces. Glowing magic cores and magic branches.

One was a Class 3. One was a Class 4. One was a Class 7. My breath felt very high in my chest.

"Nice night," I squeaked. "G-gotta love those long walks in the rain."

My right hand crushed one of the cards in my pocket.

They said nothing. They hadn't moved yet. They must be scanning to see if I were a mage, or if I bore any obvious weapons.

The moment they decided they had nothing to lose by striking first, I'd be done for. Metaphorically or literally. I wasn't interested in finding out which.

I flicked the crumpled card out of my pocket. It didn't go far. It tumbled into the wet street noiselessly, a bunted ball.

The instant it started falling, long porcupine needles flew rapid-fire into all three mages. The needles were ephemeral; they wouldn't deal any physical damage. Just pure burning pain.

The mages grunted and staggered. I moved faster than I would've given myself credit for. I reached out both arms and lunged for the nearest two, slapping at their magic.

I'd never hobbled two people at once before. It was a crude vicious shove I gave their magic, like smacking a wet clay sculpture down into a miserable pancake of mud. I had no idea how long the hobble would last.

I kept barreling forward; I never stopped moving. I body-slammed the third mage, delivering an even rougher stunning blow to their magic core. I reached back as I scrambled past them, belatedly twisting their branches to form more of a proper hobble.

No time to turn and check my work. I fumbled for another business card. I crumpled it and flung it back at the mages. Then another and another, until I couldn't throw far enough to reach them.

Somewhere in the midst of all this, I thought I glimpsed the mages on their knees, clutching their chests as if in the throes of a heart attack. I thought I heard screaming.

Then I ran full tilt.

Thank god the magic cuttings further down the sidewalk did nothing to stop me. Guess they really were just there to deter innocent visitors from wandering too close.

My rain boots weren't the best running shoes—my toes seared worse than my lungs—but at least they had decent traction. The cheap poncho crackled around me as I galloped.

Something slammed me in the back, almost knocking me off my feet. I better remember to thank Fanren for his flak jacket.

I tried to zig-zag. Another impact. I tripped, smacked the sidewalk with raw palms.

I was up again in an instant. But the street felt impossibly long. Even once I reached the corner, there was still a little ways to go before the tram stop.

How often did the tram run at night? Twice an hour? Once an hour?

My left leg buckled. Had to catch myself with my hands again. I stagger-hopped forward. I was almost at the abandoned restaurant. No—I was there already, leaning on the boarded-up windows for support.

Why wasn't my leg working?

I looked behind me and saw blood. Or did I? Maybe I was imagining it. How could you see blood on wet asphalt late in the evening, anyway?

My left boot felt disgustingly squishy, sodden with rain on the inside. My wheezing sounded comically loud.

I crumpled up another business card with shaking hands and hurled it in the direction I'd fled from. It didn't go far.

I couldn't see anyone yet. But surely they were coming. The needles of pain wouldn't last forever. I'd hobbled their magic, not their legs.

At some point I'd stopped moving. I sank to the ground with my back to the boarded-up cafeteria building, stuck in the dim yellow shallows of the nearest street lamp's pool of light. Here it was just bright enough to say that, yes, I could most definitely see blood.

I should call Wist, I thought dimly. I should call Wist. I should call Wist.

I really should call Wist.

My brain had gone so dull and smooth that touching the bond felt like pulling at a long slack rope. Like watching endless strings of colorful flags come streaming out of a street illusionist's mouth. No matter how much I tugged and tugged, it never seemed like enough to reach her.

The guard mages started to limp around the corner. They moved like ninety-year-olds. They didn't look well.

My hobbles held true, at least for now—the mages couldn't use magic of their own. But they'd hit me with something as I ran. Clearly they had other weapons. And they were still coming.

I pulled helplessly at the bond. I shook it. I felt so weak, inside and out. I made a half-hearted effort to ball up another business card, but my hand wouldn't listen to me anymore. It took countless tries.

At last I extracted the partially folded card from my pocket. I let it fall from my fingers.

Nothing happened. Either I hadn't crumpled it hard enough, or the mages were still just a hair out of range. I would've laughed if I had the energy. My head conked back against the wall behind me.

My hand dropped to join the failed porcupine card, now dirty and wet on the ground. But someone caught at my fingertips, lifted my powerless hand again. A shadow fell over me.

I raised my eyes.

Wist stooped over me, silhouetted by the streetlight.

I couldn't make out her face.

Magic rippled away from her like a soundless shock wave. The mages stopped inching closer. The rain stopped falling. Drops hung weightless and immobile in the air. I thought I glimpsed a seagull poised frozen in the sky overhead.

"All you had to do was wait a day," Wist said. There was zero emotion in her voice. She released my hand.

More magic flowed from her, this time a bright warmth unfurling down through my useless left leg. I flexed my fingers. Now they obeyed me. I bent and straightened my left knee. No problem. Not even a tinge of soreness.

My thoughts started to coalesce. I should've been relieved, grateful. The Kraken had arrived to save the day. And somewhere beneath it all, I was indeed immensely relieved—but my heart kept racing at a nauseating pace. Worse than before, even.

Wist looked around. Her gaze landed on the folded business card beside me. "Is that yours?"

I nodded. She glanced down the dark side street, past the trio of immobile mages facing us. Surely the rest of my card-litter was too far away for Wist to see from here.

Even as I thought that, more and more crumpled business cards came soaring through the air like snowballs. Every single one I'd thrown or dropped. The lone failure next to me rose up to join them.

They swirled in a tight orbit next to Wist's shoulder, snatching quivering raindrops out of the motionless air. A moment later, the used cards vanished in a burst of hot white flame.

Wist eyed the pavement. "Your blood?" she asked.

I nodded again. No point in denying it.

Her magic snaked along down the sidewalk and street asphalt, retracing my steps, licking up and erasing every last trace of lost blood.

"All right," she said, calm as ever. "You were never here."

She picked me up—dripping poncho and flak jacket and rain boots and all. She took a step toward the frozen mages.

"Wait." I pushed at her shoulder. "I can walk. Just leave them. It's fine."

"They saw you."

"They don't know who I am. They won't stalk me all the way across the city. Wist—"

"What do you think I'm about to do?" She sounded almost curious. "Kill them? Would you prefer that?"

"No! I'm telling you, it's fine. Let's just get out of here."

A will-o-the-wisp streak of magic shot toward them, touching each mage on the head before vanishing. My stomach seized up.

A second later, Wist released her world-stopping skill. The rain resumed falling. The seagull overhead let out an indignant squawk and wheeled away into darkness. The mages slowly and gently crumpled over on the ground.

"No memory of the past week," Wist said. "No consciousness. They'll wake up in a few days. Good enough for you?"

"Right," I said weakly. "That'll do."

She still held me up. I wondered if she could feel my heart hammering sickly. Pressed this close together, even the body armor didn't seem quite thick enough to fully block it.

19

WIST PORTED US straight into her blandly decorated bedroom at the tower. The sky outside the window-wall was pitch black.

I glanced from Wist to the bed and cracked an inappropriate joke. Wist looked at me without so much as a flicker of change in expression. I withered.

"Sorry," I said. "That was uncalled for—whoa!"

She'd opened her arms and dumped me unceremoniously on the bed. I leapt up as if the covers had bitten my bum. "Oh, come on. I'm still in my rain gear here."

I gingerly stripped off the poncho, which was now more or less in shreds, with gaping holes ripped through the back of it. I deposited its carcass in the bathroom, together with my rain boots.

Upon jumping down from the bed, I'd left a nasty pair of footprints on the beige carpet. I made a few cautious attempts to rub the wetness and dirt out with a washcloth.

Wist asked me to take my clothes off. Not in an alluring way. More in the brisk tones of a doctor—or perhaps a veterinarian. She reached over to help me with the flak jacket straps.

"Was this from Fanren?" she asked.

I contemplated obfuscating, but decided against it. "How'd you know?"

"There aren't many people you would borrow body armor from."

"Is that a nice way of saying I don't have a lot of close friends?"

"Your words," Wist said. "Not mine."

"You're not exactly swimming in friends yourself, my love."

"Never claimed I was."

Once I was down to my skivvies, Wist made me show her the back of my left leg. I twisted around to see it too.

A large swathe of taut bluish scar tissue cut down from my thigh to the back of my knee to my upper calf. That blue tint was an occasional side effect of magic used to restore a wound too hastily.

Wist's brows knitted together. She touched the thickened skin with light fingers. It tickled; I wriggled away.

"Wait," she ordered. "Show me your back."

I pulled up my undershirt. Wist made an indecipherable noise.

"What?" I said.

"Terrible bruises."

"Oh, yeah. I think they tried to shoot me."

"I'm surprised you haven't been more vocal about it."

"Surprised not to hear me whining, you mean? Must be the adrenaline."

Magic sank from her hands into my back muscles. Only then did, as the pain melted, did I realize that the sites of impact had actually hurt quite a bit.

I sagged. I was chilly in my underwear, but I wanted to faceplant forward into the bed and go to sleep right then and there.

Instead I twisted around to look Wist in the eye. "Don't pick on Fanren. He tried his best to stop me."

"He's a grown man," Wist said. "He doesn't need you to defend him."

"Yeah, and you're the Kraken. Don't punch down." I swallowed. I was going about this in all the wrong order. "Look—what I mean is, thanks for saving my butt."

"My pleasure."

It was her usual low monotone, but I felt fairly confident in interpreting this as sarcasm.

"In my defense," I said, "I didn't think they'd be so nearly gung-ho about accosting a harmless-looking passer-by. It's an illegal operation. Thought they'd try harder to keep a low profile."

"Presumably you weren't supposed to escape. They could have tossed you in their vorpal hole to erase you. Then no one would be the wiser."

Wist went over to her chest of drawers and offered me a pair of pajamas. I had my own stashed elsewhere in the tower, but I suppose she just wanted me to put on something warm and dry for the time being.

"They might be on edge for other reasons," Wist added. "Rival organizations. Turf wars. Treacherous clients or partners.

"Or maybe they've suffered from random mages going berserk at random times. Must be just as much of a problem for those in the criminal underworld as it is for the rest of us."

"Huh," I said. "Your imagination really has improved over the years. Didn't know you had it in you."

"I learn from the best."

"Hah. Thanks."

I rolled up the too-long hems of Wist's pajamas. They were soft and cozy and smelled just like her bedsheets. I decided then and there that I wanted to steal them for myself.

"So," I said. "You're mad at me. When's the lecture?"

"Do I look mad?"

"I know better than to judge by how your face looks."

Wist shrugged one shoulder. "You already know what I want to say. Let's skip the part where I waste my breath spelling it out in detail."

I'll admit that made me feel a more-than-microscopic pang of guilt. She was getting a little too good at this. I apologized again for making her come all the way down from the northern territories.

"I was already close to the border," Wist said.

"Doing what?"

"Paying visits. Having dinner with an ambassador."

"Oh," I said. "Oh?"

Only then, incredibly, did I fully absorb the fact that Wist had been wearing a high-necked black evening gown the entire time. Ever since she materialized before my eyes in the warehouse district. My game of tag with the guard mages must've done quite a number on my powers of observation.

"Oh," I repeated, with typical eloquence. "Uh, is it okay for you not to go back there?"

"We were almost done with dessert. The rest of the delegation can figure out an excuse."

"I guess no one would be offended if you claimed to have left on urgent Kraken business."

Still, it sounded like Wist had better at least say a word or two to the hosts she'd abandoned. I went to take a nice hot bath in the meantime.

One of the tower's bathing rooms was as large as any respectable public bath, with steam-filled air and a vast marble pool where I could soak right up to my neck. I loved the sound of water stirring and condensation dripping in absolute solitude.

After emerging suitably boiled, I changed back into Wist's pajamas.

I found her wearing a matching pair, doing long-limbed stretches over by her gloomy bedroom window.

"Look at us," I said. "What a cute couple." Then: "Wait, did you put back your left—?"

I motioned at her chest. I'd assumed she'd padded her left breast to fit in the evening gown. But both sides still looked more or less the same even now that she'd changed into sleepwear.

"I see those fingers twitching," Wist said.

I wiggled my fingers at her harder.

She made an ironic gesture of invitation. "If you're so curious, feel for yourself."

Don't mind if I do. I gave her left breast a good squeeze through the cherry-blossom-pattern fabric. Then the right. Then both at once. The left side still seemed a tad smaller, but that had always been the case. She had more than enough to go around regardless.

Wist tolerated my groping with an air of—well, I hope it was closer to amusement than chagrin.

I threw my arms around her waist. I snuggled my head up in the perfect warm cushiony spot between the side of her chest and her armpit, right where it naturally fit. Heaven. I wasn't one to believe in higher deities, but I would gladly praise the gods or ancestors or whoever it was who'd made me stop growing at the perfect height.

"This is nice," I said. "But why now?"

Her left arm curled down around my ribs, locking me in place. "Had to make a lot of public appearances in the north. Pleas for peace, mostly."

"I hear their skirmishing has gotten worse lately."

"The diplomats all but begged me to pad myself. They didn't want anything to distract from the message. I grew tired of wearing a prosthetic or stuffing the left side. Or strapping down the right."

I suppose I could understand. You'd think people would be too awed by the Kraken's glorious presence to notice she was missing an entire breast. But if she didn't go out of her way to hide it, someone would notice eventually.

And they'd wonder: had the invincible Kraken suffered from illness? Had she been wounded in battle? Was she perhaps less invulnerable than everyone imagined?

Wist herself might not be troubled by such rumors. The potential impact on international relations was quite another matter. The Kraken couldn't afford to make decisions for herself based solely on personal preference or ideals of personal freedom.

Even so—

"You surprised me," I said, still snuggled in my happy spot.

"By reconstructing my breast?"

"Not that. You were so quick to erase their memory."

"Ah," said Wist. "The Bayside mages. What's so surprising?"

"You know."

"I do?"

I just looked at her.

"If I let them remember you, they might try to track you down," she said, as if that explained everything.

"Not that I'm in a position to complain." I hedged my words. "But memory manipulation *is* illegal. Technically speaking."

Wist pulled away a bit to look me in the eye.

"What are you going to do about it?" she inquired, perfectly straight-faced. "Report me?"

I was nearly overcome by the urge to tickle her sides like a pianist. Unfortunately, Wist wasn't particularly ticklish.

"You're starting to sound a lot like me," I said darkly.

"Or maybe you're starting to sound more like me," Wist suggested.

Loath though I was to admit it, I suppose it could go both ways.

We'd known each other on and off for two decades, after all. And in Wist's case, you could say it was nearly twice that.

The international Mage Conventions—established nearly a century ago—outlawed all forms of magical brainwashing.

Broadly interpreted, this might bring into question any magic skill that solely affected the mind, senses, or nervous system. It was likely why the porcupine pain-needle business cards had failed to get approval for mass production.

One could just as easily argue that Wist's Disappearance, which worked by making it nigh-impossible for people to notice her, was also very much a form of illegal mental manipulation. There existed a whole spectrum of gray-area skills that could still be legally deployed in some contexts (therapeutic use, for instance), given prior approval by the government.

But memory erasure wasn't simply restricted magic. It was flat-out illegal in every country on the continent. And while I could see the Osmanthian government secretly making all sorts of exceptions for Wist, I suspected she hadn't gone out of her way to request permission.

Who would be able to catch her breaking the law, anyway? Who would dare attempt to decide on a punishment for the Kraken?

I looked up at Wist's shadowed eyes. I thought to myself that the world was very lucky she hadn't turned out to be the ambitious sort.

Breasts, illegal magic, and other such distractions aside, the long bath had woken me up and gotten my mind whirling. I was also quite peckish—and envious to hear of Wist's multi-course meal, complete with dessert. My quick flatbread dinner before Fanren's match felt like an event of the distant past.

I nipped into the kitchen to pick up a cup of nutty ice cream. Turtle the cat watched me come and go with an expression that, in human speech, would clearly translate to: *You again?*

I'd told Wist I wanted another look at her vorpal beasts. We wandered through the first-floor aquarium, which felt worlds apart from the tower's barn-like entrance hall.

The ice cream made me shiver, but I kept digging in till nothing remained but a creamy residue at the bottom of the cold ceramic cup in my hands.

The aquarium tanks were huge enough that I—an amateur, of course—thought Wist could have gotten away with humanely keeping sharks. Most of her normal fish were small and shy. Fleet little streaks of silver.

The vorpal beasts dwarfed them. Lamp-like jellyfish creatures with long transparent angel wings slowly stroking the water. Eels or snakes spanning well over twenty feet in length, curling in corkscrew shapes, shimmering every color of the rainbow with patterns that changed faster than a kaleidoscope. Schools of living iridescent bubbles that split into a million microscopic bits of foam or swam together and merged into one huge bobbing bubble. Then did it all over again.

The thing I'd thought was coral was probably a vorpal beast, too, as was the slowly shifting silt on the aquarium floor.

"They don't need water," said Wist. "Not in the same way as the fish. But they seem to appreciate it."

When people used the word *tame* to describe vorpal beasts, it usually meant something like the ones in Wist's aquarium. Vorpal beasts that posed little or no threat to any humans around them. They might be inherently passive in nature. Or they might have undergone the magical equivalent of being cruelly declawed or having their wings clipped.

Sometimes tame vorpal beasts could be taught to do minor tricks. As far as I knew, it was mostly just for show. Turn a pretty color. Change a small cup of water to a smaller cup of rather bad-tasting port. Do a little jiggly dance.

In general, any practical magic you could convince a vorpal beast to perform on your behalf could be accomplished far more quickly and easily by a human mage, who understood human language.

"Back at the warehouse," I said. "There was a vorpal beast on the building. I'm not sure how, but they used it for surveillance. They came after me because the beast saw me lurking there."

I gave Wist my empty cup to hold. I could think better with my hands free. "Vorpal beasts helping people—isn't that the stuff of fairy tales?"

"A downtrodden subliminal," Wist said slowly, as if feeling her way through old memories. "Nothing to her name but kindness. Scorned by mages and healers alike. Cast aside for dead, then saved by vorpal beasts. The vorpal beasts see her loving spirit, and they reward her. They lift her up, grant her riches with their alien magic. Something like that?"

"Exactly," I said. "Lots of stories follow that pattern. But they're just stories. In real life, vorpal beasts don't think the way we do. They might eat you. They might ignore you. But they're no more likely to shower wealth on you than, say, a grizzly bear would be."

"But they can be used as a tool," said Wist.

"They can?"

"You said so yourself. The mobsters guarding that vorpal hole inside the warehouse—they used a beast for surveillance."

"Dunno about that," I said. "Maybe I didn't understand what I was looking at. Maybe I read the scene wrong."

"I trust your instincts."

"Easy for you to say," I grumbled. I gnawed on my thumb.

"All right," I said. "Supposedly the vorpal hole in there is a massive source of vorpal beasts. Maybe this one slunk out and glued itself to the building like a barnacle. Rather than go to the hassle of prying it off, they decided they might as well put it to good use. If magic can be used to declaw vorpal beasts, I guess it can also be used to force them to act as a surveillance tower."

Wist watched me pace. So did the opalescent vorpal beasts floating enigmatically in the tanks that soared far, far overhead.

How many thousand tons of water did this part of the tower hold? It seemed at least as expansive as a decent-size city aquarium. Ethereal ripples of endless reflected light played across the wide cold floor, my irritated hands, Wist's ever-impassive face.

"Something still bothers you," Wist said matter-of-factly.

I began to tell her more about vorpal rabies. About the nine still-living victims and their symptoms. About meeting the healer named Larkspur.

At first Wist didn't seem to remember Larkspur. She showed a spark of recognition once I mentioned the eternal white chrysanthemum.

"I'm just stuck on the idea that vorpal beasts are spreading this," I said. "I'm having trouble accepting the basic premise of the whole thing.

"Let's say anyone with the right connections can buy or sell a vorpal beast. And let's say that at least some vorpal beasts spring out of vorpal holes with the disease naturally dripping from their fangs.

"Who seems most likely to get infected? People nearby. Like those guards that came out and chased me down the street. Or people who have a lot of contact with vorpal beasts in general. So why haven't any rich collectors or MvB duelists gotten infected?"

"None of the victims had any connection with the black market?" Wist asked.

I curled my lip. "Believe me, I've asked. Manatree can't even confirm or deny that there's a black market for vorpal beasts in the first place. But I can read between the lines of what she tells me. They're all clear. No connection whatsoever."

"Sounds like you have a theory," Wist said. "So why are you frustrated?"

"Are you reading my mind?" I demanded.

She raised her hands in a gesture of innocence. I glowered for a moment. "Yeah. I think I know what's happening with this so-called vorpal rabies. But I have no idea who's doing it. That's what's pissing me off."

Wist waited. I shot a look at the schools of slender fish gliding carefree circles around—and sometimes through—the ghostly vorpal beasts.

Must be nice to be a fish. Probably didn't take much to make you happy. No gathering storm of thoughts to clap your brain awake like thunder late at night.

"I can accept that all of the victims got bitten by a vorpal beast," I said. "At first I was confused because I kept trying to think in terms of vorpal beasts' natural behavior. How they act in the wild.

"Then that surveillance beast got me thinking harder. When they bite, who they bite—maybe it isn't natural at all."

"You think—?"

"I think there's no such thing as vorpal rabies in the wild," I said. "This isn't a true disease. The things Manatree called prions—those little bits of magic—they look strange and misshapen, sure. But they're really just a type of magic cutting. They didn't spontaneously evolve out of nothing.

"They seem strange because they're cut in peculiar ways. Unintuitive ways. But I bet you could prune your branches the same way, if you tried. It's just very inefficient. There'd be no reason for anyone to prune their magic like that unless they were trying to be misleading. To make their cuttings appear unnatural. Unfamiliar. Inhuman.

"I think someone was trying to do exactly that. A mage produced them that way on purpose. A mage used vorpal beasts as a carrier. And the beasts they've been using are just a distraction, honestly.

"If Public Security wants to stop vorpal rabies from spreading any further, hunting down a couple bite-happy vorpal beasts won't do any good. They need to find the mage who created the disease in the first place."

Wist massaged the edge of her jaw with two fingers as she thought, eyes scaling the high aquarium walls.

"A mage with an unregistered magic skill," she said. "No—multiple unregistered magic skills. A mage with adequate money and free time, and a talent for invention."

"And it's not anyone I've ever met in my life," I said. "Unfortunately. Otherwise I might've had a chance of recognizing them from some little quirk in their cuttings."

I rubbed my head furiously. My hair was quite dry by now. One of the many benefits of keeping it short and bristly.

"You know me," I said. "I'm absolutely confident that I'm right about this. But to Manatree, it's just going to sound like a deranged made-up theory. Ughhhh."

Wist suggested that I tell Manatree anyway. I did, of course. I told her vorpal rabies wasn't a disease at all. I told her that the best chance of finding a cure was to track down the mage who'd invented it and unleashed it on the city.

Manatree reacted exactly as I'd suspected. But truth be told, I was stuck. Public Security had a much better chance of tracking down this anonymous rogue mage than little old me. If they chose not to heed my advice from here on out—that was their problem, frankly.

As for whether the alleged disease was contagious—I recommended that they try to extract some of the magic cuttings they called prions. Then pass those prions to a top forensics teams for another analysis.

You might not believe me, I said, but humor me a little. Just pretend they're regular magic cuttings. Analyze them as if you're analyzing any normal pruned branch. That might give you more of a hint about what sort of skills are embedded inside them.

It might not be any skills you recognize. It might be a set of totally new skills, never before recorded. But they'll still be human-developed magic skills.

In studying them, you might come to understand if they're equipped with any sort of built-in contagion, if they can be passed on again and again. Or if they only work for a one-time transfer, from a vorpal beast to a single unfortunate mage.

"You aren't being paid to go on flights of fancy," Manatree said in answer through my ear cuff.

It was the day after Wist came rushing back from up north. Manatree sounded like I was giving her a terrible migraine.

"It's an angle no one else has suggested," I offered. "Right? At least give me credit for being creative."

"Allow me to rephrase," said Manatree. "I assume this is your way of conceding defeat. You wish to be taken off the case?"

"Sure, if you want to put it that way. Actually, I was thinking I could help more with something else."

"What?" she asked in tones of pure dread. If I had a thinner skin, I'd be most insulted.

"All the mages berserking lately," I said. "For no reason. That's keeping you up at night, too, isn't it?"

A long pause. Then: "It's quite unusual for you to offer your services without being asked."

"I've been in business for half a year now. I'm getting better at sales."

"It's highly classified," Manatree said. "I can't guarantee I'll be able to get permission to pass you any information you haven't already gleaned."

"Hey, my whole identity is highly classified," I shot back. "But that's fine. If you can't tell me anything new, I'll just wait for the next time you need me to hobble mages. Or maybe I'll take a quick vacation."

"Please attempt not to cause any trouble," Manatree said by way of farewell.

I didn't make any promises.

Later that day I helped Wist finish unpacking. I'd been wondering where all her luggage was. Turned out that she'd abandoned it up north when she felt me calling to her from Osmanthus City. Her bags reached the tower by courier in the afternoon.

The clothes inside bore a curious scent. An aroma of foreign lands. Or perhaps just a different type of detergent.

Midway through, I felt Wist watching me. "What?" I said.

"You folded those legging three times already."

"Oh." I shoved them sheepishly in one of her drawers.

"What's on your mind?"

"Vorpal rabies and mages berserking when they shouldn't," I said, moving on to her undershirts. "Vorpal rabies is caused by prion-like magic cuttings. By a mage, in other words. I reckon the berserking incidents are the opposite. They're being caused by a healer."

"Like you," said Wist. "Like how you made Miyu go berserk."

She picked up a now-empty suitcase and heaved it into the left side of her closet.

"Like me," I said. "Exactly. In fact, I can't think of a single healer other than myself who would be even remotely capable of doing anything similar. Maybe Mori, if I had to pick someone based on purely on talent and brains. But I can't imagine he has it in him to make random mages go berserk just for kicks."

"Mm." Wist kept shuffling jackets around in her closet, her back turned to me.

"Wait a second." I felt a surge of tell-tale indignation. "Am I already under suspicion?"

"What do you think?" Wist asked vaguely.

"Turn around and look me in the eye when you say that."

Wist obeyed. Her face revealed nothing. Damn it. But I had to be right. If anything, I must've been incredibly slow to catch on.

"So I've been PubSec's number one suspect," I said. "Do they still think it might be me? Or did I inadvertently clear my name at some point? They must've told you, at least. O great and mighty Kraken—please do enlighten me."

Wist sighed. "PubSec followed your movements for months after Miyu snapped."

"What an honor."

"Out of all the berserking incidents this year, you only had direct contact with two affected mages."

"One, the guy on the street by my apartment," I interjected. "Two, your sister."

"After some time, PubSec conceded that it would have been physically impossible for you to be involved in most of the other cases."

"Gee," I said. "Thanks for letting me know."

"I thought you might act more suspicious if you knew they were watching you."

"What, just to toy with them? Or did you think I'd be pricked by the claws of my guilty conscience? I have no regrets about your sister."

"Sorry," Wist said. "I'll tell you sooner next time."

"You better." I got up and stretched my back, groaning. "I guess you and me are the only two people in the world who know for sure that there's at least one healer out there capable of making mages go berserk. Don't think I feel like incriminating myself just yet, though."

"I won't report you, either."

"There's a first." I favored Wist with a thoroughly unapologetic grin. She could take a jab or two as payment for me helping sort out her travel gear.

About a week later, Manatree came through with more details about each of the mages who'd gone berserk for no clear reason. Most of the information was too anonymized to be of much use to me.

Just one phrase stuck out.

"What's that?" I said, cupping a hand over my ear cuff. "Some kind of mage welfare service?"

"Subsidized healing for low-income mages," Manatree repeated testily. "There are several different programs. Eighteen percent of the berserkers had some kind of history with one or more of them."

I asked her if she could get me a map of all the unusual berserking incidents. After some hemming and hawing, Manatree agreed—but she sent it to the tower rather than to my apartment. I suppose she had more faith in Wist's security capabilities than in mine.

Wist peered over my shoulder as I spread the map out on a dining table. It showed the whole nation. Indeed, there were incidents marked all over Osmanthus. Yet the concentration grew thickest in and around Osmanthus City.

Nearly twenty-five percent of the Osmanthian population lived in the capital's greater metropolitan area. The cluster of berserking mages in Osmanthus City far exceeded that percentage, though. Based on eyeballing the map, I'd say it was closer to seventy percent of the total. Maybe more. Guess that must've given PubSec yet another reason to suspect me.

"Wist," I said. "How busy are you this week?"

She rested her chin on my head. "I can make time," I felt her reply.

"I want to do something risky," I told her. "Come with me."

Wist put her arms around me from behind. Her chest squished into my back. "That's one of the most loving things you've ever said to me."

Heat flared in me, so sudden that it felt almost savage. I was glad I had the stupid map to stare down at.

I liked the reassuring weight of her leaning down on me. I liked the addictive scent of her light sweat, the promise of a June afternoon with rain squalling outside and no obligations left for the rest of the day.

Wist already knew that perfectly well. She didn't need me telling her again and again. There were plenty of times when the traitorous bond let bits of me slip through to her before I had a chance to catch them, to pull them back to me and cup them deep inside me and hide them away.

This was one of those times. I felt her smiling in my hair. She all but thrummed with satisfaction against me.

Fine. I'd already gotten my fill of squinting down at Manatree's map. I curled my clammy fingers around her forearm and made a weak-sounding noise that could've meant anything. Wist would know. Wist would know what I meant.

20

A FEW DAYS LATER, Wist and I stood on the empty street outside Larkspur's house.

It was the middle of the day, right around noon, but with a sky so shuttered and brooding that it already felt like time for bed. Rain thrashed down as if it sought to give us a beating. Rivulets of water coursed along the curb.

None of it touched us. The water in the street veered away from our feet. The water in the air dodged in all sorts of crazy directions to avoid our skin and clothes and hair. Wist's magic—a skill called Drysuit—repelled wetness like a magnet, leaving us spotless in the downpour even without umbrellas or rain jackets or my trusty purple boots.

Drysuit wasn't the only skill she had active at the moment, either. This time she'd used Disappearance on both of us. If anyone in the surrounding houses happened to peer out at the rain pelting the street, they could stare straight at us and still not notice a thing.

I pointed at Larkspur's house. The hydrangea bushes looming on either side of the front door were still in perfect full bloom, the heavy round flower heads just beginning to take on a deeper reddish-violet tint.

"Look familiar?" I asked.

Wist shook her head. "I doubt I came here before. Even if I did, it would have been years ago."

That made sense. Being the Kraken, Wist was no doubt accustomed to having healers scramble to come see her at her own convenience. I suppose it would seem a little odd if the exalted Kraken popped up to politely wait her turn in the lobby of a local private practice.

Regardless, Larkspur had definitely healed her at some point in the past. Perhaps she'd gone to visit the tower, or had treated Wist at NHRI or university facilities.

We trod the rain-darkened stone walkway up to the front door. Shocking green moss furred the ground of Larkspur's small strip of garden. The moss grew so thick that it bunched up like rolls of luxuriant fat against the flagstones, the inside of the dingy garden wall.

As we reached the stoop, Wist released a flash of magic as brief and all-consuming as summer heat lightning. It covered the entire three-story house. Then the brightness was gone, in less than the time it took to blink.

"A lot of strong security magic," Wist said.

"Anything unusual?"

"Just standard off-the-shelf packages. She must be making good money to afford all these."

"All right." I rubbed my hands together. "Time for some breaking and entering."

"Wait." Wist put an arm out to block me. "I only scanned for security measures. You don't want a scan for people?"

"No need," I said. "Larkspur lives alone, and she's out right now."

The only other people we could possibly encounter inside would be cat burglars. Which would be awkward, yes. But I figured we could handle it.

I knew for a fact that Larkspur wasn't home. I knew this because I'd specifically asked Mori to take her to lunch. Preferably somewhere far away from here, like the NHRI fortress. And whatever you do, I warned him, don't mention that I'd been the one to suggest it.

I'd left most of Mori's many questions unanswered for the moment. I trusted him to play along anyway.

Wist slipped us inside Larkspur's house without a hitch. One of her magic branches spun itself into the shape of a little sparrow-sized firebird. It perched on her shoulder to light our way. The interior would otherwise have been as dim as a cave.

"I already saw most of the first floor last time I came here," I said. "Her office. Her library. Nothing too out of the ordinary. Let's try upstairs."

On the second floor we found Larkspur's kitchen and laundry. Tray upon tray of green herbs competed for space by the windows.

Right now, of course, the light from outside was dismal. Gusts of wind slapped rain sideways into the glass. Heavy carpet soaked up our footsteps in a small dining room with an imposing antique table.

"Look at that," I said. "She's got a poster of Fanren."

A tastefully framed one, to boot. Very classy.

Wist pointed at the lower right-hand corner of the poster, covered with an illegible flourish of gold pen. "Is that his autograph?"

"Sure looks like it. Wonder how much she paid for this."

I peered more closely at the rest of the pictures hung gallery-style all around the dining room. Something had begun to nag at the depths of my head, a sensation very much like tinnitus.

Some of the framed images were commercial posters. The one depicting Fanren appeared to have been printed in commemoration of his first championship. Others were magazine covers or carefully cut-out articles. New Year's greeting cards with family portraits on the front. Glossy individual headshots.

I recognized quite a few minor celebrities, but I'd have been hard-pressed to name them.

"You know what this reminds me of," I said to Wist. "It's like those old restaurants with a row of pictures showing all the famous people who ever stopped to eat there."

I wondered if Larkspur took her meals alone here, with a single impeccable place setting at the head of the table. Instrumental music playing softly in the background. Candlelight reflected in the glass-fronted frames protecting her crowded collection of faces.

Nothing wrong with that, of course. By way of contrast, consider everyone's beloved Kraken, the greatest star in Osmanthus. Left to her own devices, Wist would crouch alone on the floor of some random room in the tower and eat tuna straight out of the can.

Wist had stopped dead in front of one of the headshots. I leaned around her and found myself staring at Shien Miyu in her full Ministry of Justice regalia.

Larkspur had mentioned treating Wist's sister in the past. If so, this might be a gallery of noteworthy patients.

Once I knew what to look for, it was easy to spot Wist. She appeared in a poster as large as Fanren's. A print of a painting, perhaps, with her head turned away from the viewer. Magic branches sprouted from her spine in a shape like angel wings, or a thousand slender golden chains.

"If you ever release an album, there's your cover," I told her. Wist was cringing.

I thought of the white chrysanthemum on Larkspur's desk downstairs—plus the trophy case filled with peculiar mementos of her patients. She had no artifact from Fanren; I was sure of it. Yet here Fanren hung together with Wist and Shien Miyu, who had most definitely received healing from Larkspur at some point in the past.

Might as well check with Fanren directly. I touched my ear cuff to reach him.

I asked if he could recall ever visiting a healer named Larkspur. I described her to him as best I could, including the fact that she seemed to like wearing healer robes.

"Could've been years ago," I said. "Before you started competing. Before your stint in prison, even."

"My memory isn't *that* good, chief," Fanren said ruefully. A pause. "By the way, were you ever planning on returning my flak jacket?"

"Want Wist to bring it over? I can send her any time."

"Maybe I'll pass on that." He made a thinking noise in the back of his throat. "If we're really talking years ago—back before I snapped, I worked as a security contractor for my uncle on the Board. The Palace of Magi administration would offer these free healing clinics for unbonded staff. That's where I got all my healing at the time.

"If you want to know whether or not there's a chance this person healed me, you could try to find out if she ever got called in for the Palace clinics."

I had a feeling I already knew the answer.

This was why I'd make a terrible private investigator. I kept wanting to take shortcuts. I'd double-check my hunch sometime later. But I wouldn't ask Manatree—not about this one. Didn't want to make a big deal of it. Didn't want to risk her catching on.

At any rate, now I understood why Larkspur had requested special memorabilia from Wist and Shien Miyu, but not from Fanren. He wouldn't have been a noteworthy figure back when she was likely to have made contact with him. At the time, he hadn't competed in a single magesports match.

Besides, it would come off as extremely weird if Larkspur asked patients at a government-hosted healing clinic to provide her with a souvenir to commemorate their (presumably very brief) time together.

I sensed Wist studying me as I finished talking to Fanren. I gestured for her to go ahead and speak her mind. The incandescent firebird we'd been using for light flapped an agitated circle through the dining room before settling back down on the crown of her head.

"What sort of evidence are you looking for?" Wist asked.

"Sure wish I knew," I said. "That'd make it a lot easier."

"What do you suspect her of, then?"

I was in summer overalls. Nice comfortable clothes for sneaking around uninvited in the house of a dignified widow who had never done me any personal harm. I pulled at the front straps as if they were ropes.

"I don't have a complete answer to that," I admitted. "Just a couple of hunches. If you need one example—where do you think the name *vorpal rabies* came from?"

"Public Security? Researchers?"

"That's what they claim," I acknowledged. "But I kept bugging Manatree about it. I combed through all their patient records.

"The more I looked, the more and more sure I became that Larkspur was the first person to bring up all this nonsense comparing it to prion diseases. Larkspur was the first person to ever say *vorpal* and *rabies* in the same breath."

Though Wist's face didn't shift a millimeter, I could all but see the gears in her head turning and turning and going absolutely nowhere. Couldn't blame her.

"Is that incriminating?" she asked.

"In itself? Of course not. That said, the things Larkspur hinted at when she reported the first case ended up setting the tone for how PubSec approached every case thereafter.

"And personally, I think it made PubSec venture off down the wrong path. This isn't an innocent tragedy, a mindlessly replicating virus. It's a couple of poisonous seeds deliberately sown by some anonymous mage. It's an act of malice."

"By a mage," Wist repeated. "But this woman is a healer."

"Which is why half my suspicions don't make any sense right now."

"What about the other half?"

I beckoned Wist to follow me to what I assumed was Larkspur's bedroom—the only part of the second floor we had yet to finish exploring. I paused my step at the modest white-painted door.

"Would you say that I'm full of myself?" I asked Wist.

She seemed to be at a genuine loss for words.

"Answer truthfully," I added.

"In some areas, yes."

"Such as?"

"...Your estimation of your abilities as a healer."

"There you go." I tested the door. It came open easily. The master bedroom beyond the door bore no obvious signs of scandal or intrigue.

"Yeah, I think very highly of myself as a healer. Then again, I *am* pretty great. You can testify to that. I've never seen evidence of anyone else being able to reverse heal like me—hobble mages and such. So yes, I'm full of myself. And I'm fully justified in being full of myself."

I ducked to look under the bed, but failed to make any exciting discoveries. I popped back up.

The bed was simply and neatly made, with a pale summer coverlet and two plain pillows for sleeping. No purely decorative pillows here. It had to be a king-sized bed: too large for the room's proportions, and clearly meant for more than one person. Heck, three of me could sleep here without fighting over space.

"Were you going somewhere with that?" Wist asked.

"With what?"

"Talking about what an incredible healer you are."

"Ah, right. It's hard for me to imagine having a rival. But like I said the other day, I feel like there's a healer somewhere behind all these berserking incidents. And based on the info I squeezed out of Manatree, a lot of the mages who went berserk had some kind of past connection with Larkspur."

Wist had been looking in one of the room's two closets as she listened. "Did Public Security reach the same conclusion?"

"I sure hope not. I didn't let them. At least—I made sure not to name her. It's all circumstantial evidence, anyway. That man who went berserk right down the street from my apartment? He got his healing through a mage welfare center where she's volunteered for years."

Other mages had gone to her private practice for a consultation or two. A few of them hadn't even received any actual healing; she'd referred them to other healers. But they'd met her, at least. Some were past patients of hers from years and years ago. Some had stopped by public healing clinics at the university where she taught part-time.

The connections were tangential but numerous, a delicate web. Perhaps it was damning. Or perhaps it was the fantastical product of an overactive imagination.

Speaking of which: the moment I'd spotted Fanren's poster on her wall, I began wondering. Fanren had gone berserk once. Quite a few years ago, of course. And he'd been born with a quirk in his magic that made him predisposed to getting dangerously tangled. Far more so than other mages, anyhow.

So in retrospect there was nothing shocking, really, about the fact that Fanren had snapped. But if Larkspur were—like me—capable of pushing mages over the edge, Fanren would have made an ideal test subject.

The hypothetical timeline worked out, too. He'd been a contractor at the Palace of Magi. He'd periodically gotten healed at the clinics hosted there. Larkspur had always done a bunch of government-sponsored work. Somewhere along the way, perhaps he ran into her.

And then, sometime in his early twenties, he went berserk. He killed a child. He lost his job. In prison, he met yours truly. I noticed and fixed the birth defect in his magic without suspecting for a single second that there might be another reason he'd snapped.

Nor had I thought to question whether the quirk I'd assumed was a birth defect was, in fact, entirely natural.

If Larkspur had anything to do with Fanren snapping, she might've given an existing flaw in his magic one gentle inexorable push toward the edge. Or perhaps—perhaps she'd crafted a fatal flaw where none previously existed.

"You came here to look for proof," Wist said slowly. "But if you find something, how will you explain it to PubSec? We don't have a warrant."

I got up, dusting off my knees. Nothing peculiar to report in the nightstand cabinets. "If need be, I'm sure I can figure out some kind of pretext to nudge them along in the right direction.

"On the other hand, if we don't find anything even remotely incriminating, we can just forget this whole thing ever happened. Leave the detective work to the detectives."

We moved on to the third floor, where sliding glass doors opened onto a outdoor balcony packed with potted plants of every shape and size. I couldn't imagine how Larkspur tended to them. There was hardly any space left to walk between them. Wist drifted over like a dog smelling a treat.

I had to tug at her elbow to haul her back to reality.

"Listen," I said. "If Larkspur is innocent, I'll arrange a nice little meet-up where you can pump her for information about her gardening techniques. If she's some kind of psychopath who gets off on making mages go berserk, you probably don't want to take her advice on houseplant care anyway."

The indoor part of the third floor looked as if it had originally been meant as a space to throw parties. I poked around behind a clean but depressingly empty wet bar.

The open area beyond the bar seemed to now be devoted to storage. Full-length mirrors leaned up against the wall as if there had been nowhere else to put them. Worn-looking chairs sat stacked atop each other, flanked by empty standalone bookshelves and buckets of gardening implements. Seasonal wreaths and bundles of dry flowers hung from sagging clotheslines like laundry.

Only one door remained. It wasn't tall, thick, or imposing. Nor did it attempt to disguise itself as part of the wall, or hide its presence behind a hanging tapestry. It looked no different from any other door in the three-story house.

I tested the knob.

"It's locked," I said.

Wist pulled me back by my overalls, made me retreat a step or two behind her. One of her magic branches flicked out like a lizard's tongue tasting the air. It dipped briefly into the doorknob's keyhole, a slender whiplash of light.

The knob clicked.

Another one of Wist's magic branches stretched into a shape like a convenient third arm, a ghostly hand. Her magic pushed the door inward. The door creaked faintly, as if to resist her, but kept swinging till it stood all the way open.

From behind Wist, I glimpsed windows with a tightly closed layer of dark blinds. An old-fashioned dresser, as if from a great-grandmother's bedroom.

Atop the dresser rested a modest tank of tiny silver guppies. Far too many guppies for a tank of that size, though the water looked clear enough. A few fat water snails had glued themselves to the glass.

Wist stepped into the room, taking up a position right next to the crowded tank of guppies. Her diaphanous bird flapped up toward the ceiling, shedding a glow that trembled like firelight faced with a breeze.

It was quite a small room. Between the dresser below the covered windows, and the cot-sized bed placed up against the wall to the right of the door, there was hardly any open floor left to maneuver.

A faint stench stained the stale air, stomach-turning even in the smallest of whiffs. It didn't seem to come from a specific direction. Rather, it permeated the entire claustrophobic space.

A mummy sat upright in the bed.

I was gripping Wist's shirt. She glanced down at me. She must've felt my hand spasm.

I pretended nothing had happened. I took a silent breath and warned myself to keep my wits about me.

The man in the bed was not, in fact, a mummy. He wasn't even dead. There was simply some quality of absolute dessicated stillness to the way he rested there—an atrophied thinness that immediately brought to mind the sort of mummy one might discover air-dried in a high mountain cave.

His eyes were open. Brown-black eyes almost as dark as Wist's. They gazed emptily across the room into the constant motion whirling inside the fish tank on the dresser.

Wist's Disappearance still covered both of us. No need to worry about him seeing or hearing or smelling us here in the room with him.

And somehow it felt as if he wouldn't notice us even if she stripped off the veil of magic. Even so, I lapsed into a whisper when I spoke. The room was already so hushed that it felt wrong to talk at a normal pitch. Like holding an irreverent conversation in a graveyard.

"Wist," I said. "He's a mage."

"I noticed."

"Class 9-9," I said. "If I had to guess. A hair below S-Class. Would be very impressive if he weren't a vegetable."

I found myself clutching at Wist's arm. My voice rasped out unnaturally high. "I think—I think he's her husband."

Wist studied the motionless mage on the cramped bed. "You said her husband was dead."

"I was just going by what Larkspur told me."

His face was older and far more gaunt than the charcoal self-portrait that hung down in the first-floor hallway. But the bones looked the same.

A foreign sensation crept through me, a slow-moving horror like earthworms laboriously crawling their way backwards up my veins. "She claimed he died—what was it, ten years ago? Eleven? Twelve? Definitely over a decade ago."

I couldn't remember if she'd said anything about what had supposedly killed him. Had he simply vanished? Been declared dead in lieu of a body? Had Larkspur been keeping him here the entire time?

For over a decade?

Wist moved closer to the bed. I stuck right next to her. I pressed my face to her shoulder when I breathed in, but the ambient necrotic funk of the room still managed to find me.

"He's got the look of a psychobomb survivor," I said, muffled by Wist's shirt. "Doesn't he remind you of that old man we met in Philomena?"

Wist's magic finished scanning the male mage.

"The effect may appear similar," Wist acknowledged, "but the cause is very different. There's a specific magic skill being used to impair him." The set of her jaw seemed a fraction tenser than usual. "One of his own branch skills," she said. "He's doing it to himself."

I drew myself up. "Hold that thought," I told her. "Let me get some stuff from the first floor. Be right back."

I flew down the stairs. My feet pounded the hardwood. Rain pounded the roof. I scrabbled through drawer after drawer in Larkspur's office, seeking a pad of paper and a working pen.

Once I'd found them, I took another quick look through her trophy cabinet of mage mementos. Nothing from Fanren, just as I'd thought. Satisfied, I plucked the single white chrysanthemum from the crystal vase on Larkspur's desk. The one with a cutting from Wist's magic twined around it.

I couldn't imagine what Larkspur might do with the chrysanthemum, other than sit around with her legs elegantly crossed and meditate on the magic of its eternal beauty.

But I didn't like her having it. That seemed like a good enough reason to take it for myself.

My prizes in hand, I pelted back up to the third floor. Wist hovered at the top of the stairs with an air of abandonment.

"Sorry, sorry," I said breathlessly. "Give me a second to get organized."

I hunkered down at the bar counter to scribble on the creamy pad of lined paper.

Hi, I wrote. *I've borrowed your husband. Let's chat about it.*

Time: 6 pm this Saturday.

Place: the Church of the Kraken (the Old River building).

Hope to see you there.

"Wait," said Wist. She must've been reading over my shoulder. Good.

At least that meant my handwriting was legible. "You—what? Why? But—"

I ducked back into the tiny bedroom with the lightless windows and the dead-animal odor. I put the notepad with my scrawled message on top of the dresser, next to the busy fish tank.

"First we take him to the tower," I told Wist, inclining my head at the mage on the bed. "Surely you can agree with getting him out of here. For … for humanitarian reasons. Obviously. Then we can argue about the implications."

Wist pointed at the message on the dresser. "Explain that."

"I'll explain back at the tower."

We stared at each other. All right, time for a different tack.

"Do you trust me?" I asked.

Silence. We stared at each other some more.

"Wow," I said. "That was supposed to be easy to answer. I bind myself to you for life, and this is what I get?"

"It's a very broad question," Wist said evenly.

I tapped my note with a finger. "Don't misunderstand," I warned. "I get that Larkspur is dangerous. Even if she has nothing to do with vorpal rabies or all those mages berserking—whatever's been going on in this room with her husband is already plenty disturbing.

"But," I added, "she's also probably a lot like me. Me, if I were less harmlessly irritating and more of an actual full-blown serial killer. I've got some ideas about what she's been up to. I've got some ideas about our next steps.

"Before that, I would really, really, really like to get the hell out of here. Mori can't keep having lunch with Larkspur forever. And this house gives me the creeps."

"You'll tell me your plan," Wist said.

"It's not fully formed enough to be called a plan," I corrected, "but

I'll tell you my thought process. Everything. I promise. Till you're sick of hearing me talk."

I took her hands. "Please," I said. "I just don't want to do it all here."

At first her hands were cool and limp, almost resistant to being held. Then, after a few reluctant moments, her fingers curled tight around mine.

The man on the bed stared hollowly through us without seeing a thing. Thick dust coated the blinds over the windows, as though they hadn't been opened in years.

Wist's firebird landed on my shoulder, a warm and weightless tuft of magic. Wist raised my hands to her cheek. She tilted her face against them as if listening for whispered words, as if the skin-to-skin contact would tell her something my voice couldn't.

The unabating rain, invisible on the other side of the blocked-off windows, sounded like a storm happening in another world.

I felt Wist nod to herself. Or maybe she was just nuzzling my hand as she pondered her options.

She let go and straightened up to look around the small room—at me, at the tank of guppies, at the unseeing male mage. Her porting magic embraced all of us.

Part Four
Healer Versus Healer

21

I KNEW THIS ROOM. Wist's porting magic had landed us in the tower's newfangled medical facilities. The same place where I'd woken up after our near-miss with the Old River psychobomb.

It was an octagonal—decagonal?—space with immense windows, all covered in heavy shutters. Wist and I stood in our socks on the shining floor.

Larkspur's husband floated in the air beside us, borne up by some form of Zero Gravity. His eyes remained open, but he showed no outward response to the change in scenery.

I turned about and took stock of what we'd brought home with us.

Ourselves. Larkspur's husband. Our shoes, which we'd stashed down at the first floor entrance of Larkspur's house (props to Wist—I'd completely forgotten about them). The stem of white chrysanthemum peeking out of my pocket. The tank of guppies, for some reason. And a vague stink of rotting flesh.

"You didn't have to bring the smell all the way here," I said.

"It's him." Wist indicated the mage in the air. "It's his bedsores."

"Oh." I surveyed the tanks of mysterious liquid, the life-support devices that resembled eager mechanical octopi. "Uh, do you have any idea how to use these?"

First, Wist combined a few branch skills to treat the older man's bedsores—to make sure they weren't left completely raw and open. Next, we joined forces to remove his clothes. We squeezed him into the wetsuit-style equipment needed to safely stash him in one of the stasis tanks.

Doing so was more difficult than you might imagine. He didn't twitch a single muscle in resistance, but that also meant he didn't make the least effort to cooperate. I was relieved to find that the most complex parts of the garment seemed to snap on and adjust to fit of their own accord.

Wist laid him in a horizontal tank. The glass lid slid shut. Pinkish liquid churned in, submerging him, rising and rising until it covered the tip of his nose, then rising all the way up to the top of the glass. A few weak air bubbles filtered from the corner of his mouth.

For the first time since we'd broken into his bedroom prison, his eyes closed.

"He does look malnourished," I said. "Some time in here ought to help with that. Right?"

Wist made a noncommittal noise.

"It's also a convenient place to store him while we decide our next move," I admitted. "Before that—what's with the guppies?"

The swarming tank of guppies that Wist had pilfered from Larkspur's house still rested on the floor behind us, guarded on either side by our smartly lined-up shoes.

"What about them?" Wist asked.

"I don't remember telling you to take them with us."

"The tank is too small," she said.

"So you're their new owner? What're you going to do, add them to your aquarium with all the vorpal beasts? Won't the other fish just eat them?"

"I felt sorry for them," Wist answered, unruffled. "A lot of them are pregnant."

"*What?*" I squatted to squint more closely at the guppies. Granted, some did look tremendously swollen.

"You're pulling my leg," I said. "Fish lay eggs. They don't birth live young."

Or did they? I felt myself rapidly losing confidence in my knowledge of biology, which had never been outstanding to begin with.

Between the two of us, Wist definitely knew more fish facts. If only because she loved eating them so much. I wondered if she ever took her dinner straight from the tanks on the first floor. We might be bonded for life, but I had a feeling some things were better left a mystery.

I told Wist to figure out what to do with the guppies, since she'd decided to make them—and their unborn descendants, and their tank-cleaning snails—her responsibility. Meanwhile, I went to put our shoes away and grab myself a snack. Nothing fishy.

Wist found me up in one of the tower sunrooms, licking my fingers as I polished off a stack of plain crackers. Sometimes these bland, dry, cardboard-colored squares really hit the spot.

The rain fell a touch more softly than it had back in the city. I liked seeing it go streaming down the glass walls.

As I wiped my hands on my overalls, I caught Wist casting a rueful eye across her assembly of potted plants. They were a lot less perky than Larkspur's. They looked alive (for the most part, anyway) but didn't seem terribly excited about it.

She could've turned to horticultural magic to spur their growth and infuse them with vigor. But even assuming she possessed relevant branch skills, I doubted she would ever use them.

To Wist the Kraken, magic was a form of labor. An inescapable obligation. A wellspring of bottomless chronic pain. Of course she'd prefer not to mix magic with her hobbies.

It probably didn't help that she'd spent so much time out of the country these past few months. Mori sometimes came by to care for the houseplants in her absence. Me? I didn't lift a finger. What if, unlike Wist, I turned out to be a naturally gifted gardener? Wouldn't want to accidentally outshine her. That's my excuse, and I'm sticking to it.

Wist sat next to me on the white wicker couch. "I took another look at his branch skills." She paused. "We don't even know his name, do we?"

"No clue. What'd you learn?"

"The majority of his skills are illegal types of mind control. Including some I've never seen before. I can guess at what they're meant to do. But the skills themselves have no official name."

"Because they're not supposed to exist." I rubbed my fingers over the bumpy wicker weave of the couch as I thought. "Larkspur claimed he was a diplomat. Maybe that was just his cover story. Maybe he worked in intelligence. Or the military. Somewhere secretive."

"Officially, he's dead."

"Yeah, wish I knew how to explain that part," I said. "Those skills of his—if he produced bundles of random-looking branch cuttings, could they be combined to make people act like the victims of vorpal rabies?"

Wist tilted her head back, eyes heavy-lidded. I kept my mouth shut to give her sufficient time to ponder it.

"In isolation, each individual skill would be much more subtle," she said eventually. "I think."

"Gimme an example."

"There's one that would compel you to throw yourself into the nearest vorpal hole."

I straightened up. "That's damning, isn't it? That's just the same as vorpal rabies."

"But this skill wouldn't activate unless you actually came in sight of a vorpal hole big enough to swallow you whole. You could have a dormant cutting stuck in you for years, never noticing anything wrong."

"Until you happened to pass right by a vorpal hole," I said. "Then it'd be goodbye, fair world. Not the worst way to pull off an untraceable assassination.

"So what if you combined it with his other skills? Would that result in something closer to what they've been calling vorpal rabies?"

"It might. Theoretically."

I turned toward Wist. "Can I do an experiment on you?"

"Will it hurt?"

"Might be a little uncomfortable."

Wist offered me a cautious nod.

She was in a long-sleeved top, loose and floppy but made of material far thinner than a sweatshirt. I poked her until she twisted around to show me her back.

"Healers can't use magic," I said, as much to myself as to Wist.

Viewed with my magic perception, the core buried deep in her back glowed the color of a setting sun. I pulled up her shirt, along with the fraying undershirt beneath it, and touched warm skin near the base of her spine.

Wist jumped a little. My fingers must've felt startlingly cold to her.

"Healers can't use magic," I said again. "But we can twist it. Untangle it, or make it tangle worse than before. Ease mages' pain. Or hobble them. Or drive them berserk. Some of us can, anyway."

Saying *healers* could do this might be a bit of an exaggeration. I only knew of two people who had actually pushed the boundaries of reverse healing. Me, for one. And now Larkspur. As proven by—by whatever it was that she'd done to her husband.

Based on her age, Larkspur might've been doing it longer than me. And she might have gone much further. For years, I'd limited myself to hobbling. Only in the case of Shien Miyu had it occurred to me to deliberately make a mage go berserk.

I'd never before attempted what I was about to do to Wist. I'd never even dreamed of it. If it worked—if this turned out to be the same technique Larkspur had used on her husband to turn his own magic against him—it must mean I was sorely lacking in imagination.

I'd always prided myself on being so much more innovative than other healers, so much more daring. Blessed with the spark of genius that made it possible to pull off indescribably complex maneuvers like mage hobbling.

I was the only one, I fancied, who possessed the maverick thought process and colossal brains needed to defy all the norms of our society, the standard roles assigned to healers and mages, the accepted limits on what healers were capable of.

Yet perhaps I was just as much of a fool as the rest of them. Perhaps I'd still been limited by the baseless assumptions frozen in place in my own mind, the assumptions that were such a common-sense part of life in Osmanthus that I didn't even realize they were there, invisible barricades boxing me in.

Healers had no magic core. Healers had no magic branches. Healers could never learn any magic skills. Healers couldn't use any magic of their own. That, of course, was no assumption. It was an indelible fact.

But did this mean that healers couldn't use magic, period?

No. There were other ways.

A slight shudder went through Wist as I brushed past her core. It might have been an expression of either pleasure or discomfort.

I nudged at one of her many, many magic branches. I made sure to select one imprinted with a relatively weak skill, a skill that wouldn't have any drastic side effects.

I tugged my chosen magic branch. I stretched it like a rubber band. Wist shifted her weight from side to side on the couch. Nothing else happened.

Wist asked if I was done yet.

"Hold on," I said. "I'm still thinking through how to do this."

Finally I pinched the slender tendril of magic as if gripping the reins of a horse. I flicked at the tendril—again, much as if flicking a pair of reins.

Not to knot it up. Not to smooth out its tangles. To force Wist to unleash the skill I was touching. Regardless of her own intentions.

A ghostly hand spurted out of Wist's chest. It rocketed halfway across the sunroom, knocking houseplants from their perches. Ceramic pots shattered noisily on the tile floor.

Wist and I both flinched. The magical hand vanished. My own right hand, glued to the bare skin of Wist's lower back, felt suddenly feverish with sweat. I released her. I tugged her shirt back down, furtively wiping the clammy bits. Wist's mouth hung half-open, wordless.

"Well," I said, with all the equanimity I could muster, "healers can't use magic. But I can make you use *your* magic. That's something."

"My plants," Wist said forlornly.

We took a few minutes to clean up. Wist used a different magic skill—this time of her own accord—to repair the fallen pots. She seemed distracted, though. I had to leap over to intervene before she merged the shattered pieces of two different vessels, one plain terracotta and the other a glazed green ceramic.

I asked Wist if I could try using her magic again. Just to make sure it wasn't a fluke. She eyed me warily. Please, I said.

This time Wist selected a branch for me. It curled out of her body to lay weightlessly in my hands, an ephemeral golden vine.

I pulled it. I flicked it. I twitched it as if it were the handle of a long, long whip. For quite a while, nothing worked.

Perhaps twenty tries later, a firebird the size of a firefly flew up and away from us, veering straight for the highest point in the room. It seemed frightened, skittish. But I'd made it manifest out of nothing.

Rather—I'd forced Wist to produce it.

"Can't claim I've got the hang of it," I said. "It's doable, though."

I patted Wist on the shoulder to let her know I was done. She released a tense sigh and relaxed into the back of the couch. The minute firebird overhead puffed out of sight like a snuffed candle.

"It's like hijacking a train," I said.

"And I'm the train engine?"

"Uh, sort of. Or maybe I'm the equivalent of a doctor testing your reflexes. Hammer to the knee."

"That's it," said Wist. "It's my magic. But I'm not the one who made the decision to use it. It came out of me before I could stop it."

"Here's my hypothesis," I said. "I think this mage hijacking is how Larkspur got her husband to cooperate."

Wist pulled her legs up to her chest, arms around her knees. She slowly tilted sideways, leaning her weight on me. "It took you a lot of tries before the skill activated."

"True," I acknowledged. "If you wanted to stop me, you could've just bashed me over the head with one of your potted plants. Maybe Larkspur nailed it on her first try. Unlike me. Or maybe she drugged him to keep him from fighting back. I don't think he willingly turned himself into the equivalent of a psychobomb victim, at any rate."

"Probably not."

"Can you tell how long he's been tied up by his own magic?" I asked. "Whatever he's used on himself to make himself a vegetable, I mean."

"Years," Wist said immediately. "He's been locked in that state for years. Continuously. But his mind is still whole."

I stared at her. "What do you mean?"

"A psychobomb essentially kills the person you used to be. This isn't like that. He's still himself." Wist spoke in the same steady tone as always, her voice utterly blank of condemnation, of horror, of disgust.

"He knows what's going on," she continued. "But he's helpless. He's been trapped inside himself for however long you said it's been since he was supposed to have died. Ten years. Twelve years."

My hand covered my mouth. "I wonder if she knows," I said. "I wonder if she realizes or cares that he's still in there. She made him turn his own magic on himself. Magic to turn him into a doll. Did she really mean for his mind to stay intact the whole time?"

"Allegedly," Wist said. "I can't offer absolute proof she made him do it."

"Allegedly. But what're the chances of this all being a big misunderstanding?"

"Almost zero."

Right. So then—allegedly—she used her husband as a factory to churn out weirdly chopped-up magic cuttings, various mutant combinations of his illegal skills. He became a machine to manufacture the bits of magic they called prions. The raw material of vorpal rabies.

If I could make Wist use specific magic skills against her will, it would just be a few steps further to make her snap off the ends of a magic branch. To produce a magic cutting that could be grafted to objects or passed to other people for use at their convenience.

If I wanted Wist to produce more cuttings of the same skill, all I'd need to do was wait a little while for her broken branch to grow back in full. Then I could force her to snap off more fragmented pieces. I could sing a cheerful farmer's song to myself as I reaped a rich harvest of her magic.

"Larkspur's husband looked asleep," I said. "After you put him to rest in the tank. Is he actually sleeping now? Not just trapped awake in his body that's trapped inside the locked tank?"

"He should be asleep now. Truly asleep."

A brief respite from his decade-long nightmare, then. Although I suppose we couldn't be held accountable for any dreams he might experience while suspended in the thick pink soup of his stasis tank.

I pressed my knuckles to my chin as I thought. "Would you be able to take the magic off him?"

"To free him?" Wist asked. "I could try. PubSec experts could do it faster."

"How come? You're the Kraken."

"I'm too used to doing things my own way." Wist gestured with her fingers as if forming a cat's cradle. "The best way to safely remove a piece of magic like the one imprisoning his mind is to reverse-engineer it. To develop a new skill specifically designed to unwind it. A custom antidote."

"You couldn't do that?"

"I could make an effort. But there are people who specialize in that sort of thing. Who have a lot more training in it."

She rose from the couch and looked down at me. "Clematis. What are you planning to do with him?"

I rubbed the bristly back of my head. Wist had waited long enough for me to follow through on my promise. I owed her more details.

But. There was a non-zero chance that she'd oppose me. Don't think I'd forgotten the reason I spent seven years of my life in prison. My own foolish mistakes? Yes. That was certainly part of it. As was Wist's decision to surrender me to Public Security.

When she made up her mind about something—when she believed she was making the correct choice, the only possible choice under the circumstances—nothing would sway her. My cries hadn't fallen on deaf ears when PubSec came to drag me away. Wist had heard me, and maybe my voice had cut a scar into her that would never leave her. But it had still failed to sufficiently move her.

I'm the same way, I guess. In my mind, there was only one right way to handle Larkspur and her husband. I couldn't imagine backing down. I couldn't imagine any other course of action. Not even if my own bondmate disagreed with me.

That was what made me reluctant to speak up. As long as I kept my thoughts to myself, there was no risk of us finding ourselves diametrically opposed.

I'd promised to tell her everything, though. A tightness squeezed my throat like an unseen hand.

I raised my head. "There are two halves to this problem," I said.

"Vorpal rabies and berserking mages?"

"No," I told Wist. "I'm lumping those together. Half of the problem is just as you've said—Larkspur spreading around malicious magic cuttings from her husband and pretending it's a disease called vorpal rabies. Larkspur making random mages go berserk at random times. People have already been hurt by both these things. People have already died from them."

"All the evidence is circumstantial," Wist said.

"Agreed. Good thing we aren't MPs or lawyers. For the sake of argument, let's assume Larkspur is in fact the perpetrator.

"So if it's her, we better stop her," I continued. "Right? How? Report her to PubSec? Sure, that'd get the job done. She seems like a crafty one, and she might be capable of doing some real tricksy things to mages, but she's still just one human being. The second half of the problem is what happens after they catch her."

I could tell Wist wasn't computing. Restless, I rose from the wicker couch. The rough tile floor felt cold as an ice rink underfoot.

"I've gotten away with everyone thinking I'm a singular freak of nature," I said. "The only healer who can break all the rules of what healers can do.

"What happens once the government gets proof that another healer is capable of far worse? You think they'll be satisfied to put Larkspur on trial and call it case closed? Of course not."

I threw my arm out, as if the mopey plants arranged on pedestals and tables all around us were an audience waiting to weigh the merits of our arguments. Judging by their grim ambiance, they seemed to already understand where I was going with this. Unlike Wist.

"One is a fluke. Two will start to seem more like a pattern. The Board of Magi may have been content to call me the one and only Magebreaker. But if they find out what Larkspur's been getting up to—if it's really her—they'll start considering all healers as potentially dangerous. A potential threat to all mages.

"Then what happens? They'll use it as an excuse to crack down on healers as never before. You know how I used to push for the Healers' Bill of Rights? Yeah. That never passed.

"This'll be like—like the reverse of that. Not that we have any real legal rights in the first place. But whatever rights we do have will go backwards. It'll get worse than ever before. Not just for me. Not just for Larkspur. For every healer in Osmanthus."

At last I stopped to breathe.

"Maybe I've never succeeded at doing anything to truly help other healers in my life," I said. "Maybe I've long since given up on all that world-changing crap. I tried to take shortcuts and got my hands dirty. I made stupid choices. All I ever got good at was looking after myself, and no one else. Other healers wouldn't cry a single tear if I vanished from the country."

"Mori might prove you wrong about that," Wist said mildly.

"My point is, I failed spectacularly in my past attempts to improve the lives of fellow healers. All it got me was a prison sentence and a hatred for the legislative process. Even so—I certainly don't want to be responsible for making their lives exponentially *worse*.

"Which is exactly what will happen if Public Security realizes what Larkspur has been doing. Allegedly doing, anyway. According to you and me. Which is why I've got to stop her for good. Without letting anyone else find out that she's the culprit. The alleged culprit."

Wist appeared to be watching my chest heave.

"I think you need oxygen," she stated.

She spoke with such infuriating rationality that it made me want to launch myself at her like a blood-frenzied monkey. I managed to refrain, albeit just barely.

Wist put a hand on my head. "Question," she said.

I snapped at her to spit it out. She obliged. "Larkspur may have kept her husband prisoner for over a decade. But the first case of vorpal rabies dates back to less than a year ago. Same goes for the unusual spike in berserking mages. All quite recent. Why now?"

An abrupt calm came over me as Wist's words started to sink in.

"She must've started testing her limits ages ago," I said. I thought of Fanren. His berserking episode had taken place at least a good six years ago. "In the past, she must've done it infrequently enough that no one would notice anything unusual."

"Too infrequently to change the overall percentage of berserking mages," Wist echoed.

I nodded. "And if she inflicted vorpal rabies on anyone back then—or recruited vorpal beasts to do it for her—maybe it was a subtler variant. Maybe they acted normal right up until they took a dive down the nearest vorpal hole."

"Then it would become a standard missing person case. Nothing abnormal."

"As long as there weren't too many of them in a short period of time," I finished for Wist.

I ducked away from the hand she'd left resting on my head. The gentle weight had felt like a wordless reminder to keep my cool. Much to my chagrin, it worked.

"I see what you're getting at," I told her. "All of a sudden, Larkspur decided to escalate. She started taking much bigger risks this year. If we knew why, maybe it would help us figure out how to stop her.

"But I'm not convinced there's some kind of deeper reason. At least not a reason that would be meaningful for us. Making mages go berserk without any warning or protection for those around them, infecting mages with vorpal rabies—she really is basically a serial killer once removed. And look what she's done to her husband.

"I mean, you've got a point. There must be something driving her to go further than ever before. I just don't think there's any way to figure out what that is without talking to her.

"Even she might not know the real answer. And us knowing it might not be terribly helpful in the first place. Maybe she's got imaginary gods in her head telling her that certain mages are the devil incarnate."

Wist folded her arms. Her oversized shirt was black, with a sharp white printed pattern that bore a vague resemblance to ancient runes.

I'd asked her once if the runes meant anything. She told me it was gibberish. Just some artist's idea of a cool design.

"How do you plan to stop her?" Wist asked.

"I'll be happiest if I'm wrong. I hope it turns out to be some kind of freak accident. A bunch of coincidences that just so happened to point at her."

"What if it really is all her doing?"

"The non-violent approach would be to convince her to leave the country," I said. "Tell her the jig is up. Give her just enough warning to flee. She's a smart lady, probably. She could get herself someplace without an extradition treaty."

"She might cause the same sorts of problems in her new home."

"As long as Osmanthus never connects the dots, Osmanthian healers won't have to suffer for it."

Wist studied my face without saying anything.

"That's my only goal," I said. "If I've learned anything over the years, it's to avoid aiming too high."

We walked together through row after row of plants, doing one final check to make sure they were all back in place. Their heavy drooping leaves seemed to have taken on a faintly accusatory air.

Wist reached out to adjust the position of a few misaligned pots. "What if she refuses to stop or leave the country?"

"What do you think?" I asked.

Wist's arms stilled. "Please don't kill her," she said.

"Don't get caught, you mean."

"I won't be able to keep you out of prison if you become a murder suspect while still on parole."

"Don't worry," I said in my best imitation of Wist's standard deadpan tone. "You can help me erase the evidence. Or if I must get caught, I'll make sure I can plausibly claim self-defense."

Wist rubbed her forehead.

"Headache?" I asked brightly.

She waved a resigned hand at me as if to say: *No, no, carry on.*

"My note instructed Larkspur to meet me on Saturday," I said. "Four days from now. Between now and then, I want to cut off more of her resources. We've already got her husband. But maybe she's got spare bundles of his magic cuttings—his so-called prions—stashed in a safe somewhere.

"I want to make it harder for her to use vorpal beasts as an intermediary. If she's going to try to infect anyone, she'll have to go throw the magic cuttings at them in person. So first we've got to—"

"I already closed the vorpal hole back at the warehouse."

It took me a second to understand what Wist was saying. "You did? The one in Bayside?"

She cast the same expressionless look at me as always, and yet this time something about it struck me as being ever so slightly tinted with smugness.

"Of course," she said. "Not long after the day you called me there. Made a quick trip back by myself and sealed the hole in the building. It was nearly two stories high. Very dangerous to leave wide open."

"It must have been heavily guarded."

"I suppose it was," Wist said politely. "I hardly noticed."

"You didn't—"

"I reported them to the local MPs."

"You didn't ... hurt anyone?"

A protracted silence.

Then: "I can hardly claim to have clean hands. My actions have harmed far, far more people than the likes of Larkspur or the mafia running that warehouse. Far more than they could ever hope to harm in their entire lives."

Her lip curled. Just a tiny bit. It would've been easy to miss if I weren't watching her so closely.

"But you know," Wist said, "those Extinguishers that attacked the tower last year—they were the first people I ever murdered face-to-face. Right in the same room as them."

"You were berserk," I said. "They were trying their damnedest to kill you. They shot you three times in the forehead. And that wasn't even the worst of it."

"I was berserk," she agreed. "But the more time passes, the more clearly I remember doing it. I dismantled their bodies like a plumber. I sucked the life out of them like a vampire. They were half-mad with terror, but they felt every second of it."

Wist turned to me, her horde of morose houseplants arrayed watchfully behind her.

"You looked frightened of me, too," she said flatly. "That night I found you in Bayside. What did you fear I was going to do to those guards? Did you think I would—"

"I don't know!" My voice echoed harshly off the glass walls of the sunroom.

I took a short breath and forced myself to speak more quietly. "You're the Kraken, Wist. You have the ability to carry out just about any passing thought, any passing whim. I know that doesn't mean you'll actually do it.

"Just—take any other mage or healer or subliminal in the world. They might have moments when they get irritated. They might have moments when they want to punch someone. If they're a mage, they might even have the ability to throw stones with magic in a fit of pique, or slap someone to the ground with a gust of wind. And for the most part, they control themselves. Just like you.

"The difference with you is that you could make someone have a heart attack just by looking at them. You could make a hole appear in the ground and swallow them. You could make a piano fall from the sky and crush them. Other mages have far more limits.

"I know you won't actually do it! It's just a tad more intimidating when you're the one facing off with someone. There's more weight to the possible consequences when you're the one looking at someone like you want to choke them."

Wist ran a finger down one of the long-eared leaves poking out beside her. As if testing its green-black surface for dust.

"Is that how I looked at those guards?" she asked, face pointed at the leaves.

"Not exactly," I said. "You were very, very calm. But I could tell you were also very, very angry. That's all."

Best not to dwell on this. I asked her for more details about what happened when she closed the vorpal hole hidden inside that Bayside warehouse.

The warehouse personnel had become extremely talkative once they realized she was the Kraken. From them she learned the location of several other black-market vorpal holes scattered around the perimeter of the city. She visited them one by one and sealed them all in a single night.

It still wouldn't be completely impossible for a civilian with the right connections to circumvent official channels. But for a time, at least, the city's underground vorpal beast trade would suffer from an extremely restricted supply.

"Must be some Ministry of Justice bureaucrats sweating bullets right now," I remarked. "Wish I could see their faces."

For places like that Bayside warehouse to have operated unmolested for years on end, there must be quite a few high-ranking officials getting some kind of kickback. Among them might be people who outranked Manatree in the hierarchy of Public Security. It could even go as high as the Board of Magi.

None of my business, honestly, although it was fun to imagine their consternation. I could just picture Wist breezily reporting that she'd discovered and promptly closed all these unreported vorpal holes. Who could fault her?

We were still left with the question of what to do with Larkspur's husband. But first I wanted to get Larkspur herself out of the way. Preferably by chasing her out of the country.

Then we could devote more energy to cleaning up her loose ends. Hopefully without alerting the government to the fact that an allegedly widowed healer living in a modest suburban neighborhood had been single-handedly responsible for all their biggest headaches of the year to date.

I ended up storing Wist's eternal stem of white chrysanthemum (her one-time gift to Larkspur) in the sunroom. I scrounged up an appropriately sized vase. I cleared a little space for it on one of the tables covered in lackluster houseplants and slow-growing trimmings. Perhaps the enchanted chrysanthemum—so white that it nearly glowed—would inspire its brethren to regain a smidgen of their lost zest for life.

22

FRIDAY FOUND US back in the tower's medical bay. We peered down at the tank housing Larkspur's husband—the only occupied tank in the room.

Her husband looked a tiny bit better-fed than before. Although it might have been an optical illusion. I suspected the thick pink liquid in the tank of lending a ruddier cast to his sunken complexion. I hoped his dreams—if he had any—were peaceful. Or at least cathartic.

Larkspur hadn't made any obvious moves in the days since we stole him away. Not that I'd expected her to report his kidnapping to the authorities. The man was supposed to be dead.

I couldn't claim to have any idea what drove her, or what she was really thinking. I'd only met her once.

By all appearances, she'd held her husband captive for over a decade. She'd driven mages berserk for no particular reason I could discern. No grand revenge plot; no financial gain; no cry for revolution.

So there was a risk, in theory, that her reaction to the loss of her husband might be just as unpredictable. She might throw caution to the wind and go on a wild mage-snapping rampage. She might call up Public Security and try to turn herself in.

I'd gambled that she wouldn't, though. I'd gambled that she'd lie low till our meeting. Maybe she'd be sincerely interested in hearing me out, in bargaining. Or maybe she had something she wanted to say to me in turn.

Anyway, with one day remaining till our little appointment, Larkspur seemed content to stay quiet. So far, so good.

Mori mentioned that she'd reached out later and thanked him profusely for the lovely lunch outing. I wondered if it was before or after she'd discovered her husband missing.

Maybe she'd spoken to Mori through an earring while standing in the empty shell of her husband's third-floor prison. Soaking up the aftermath of his bedsore stench. Eyes fixed to the empty bedspread. Or perhaps to the rectangular mark atop the wooden dresser showing where the stolen tank of guppies had rested.

"Oh, yeah," I said to Wist. "How're those guppies?"

She suddenly showed an inordinate interest in the health of Larkspur's husband, despite having already studied him for a good long minute.

"Don't tell me you brought them all the way here just to have your other fish eat them. Can't say I didn't warn you."

Wist didn't quite meet my eye. "Not all of them."

"What a tragedy," I uttered.

The slumped line of her shoulders suggested that she was legitimately broken up over it.

I patted her on the arm. "Well, it's not so bad. Considering how crowded they were in their original tank, they must've already been used to eating each other. At least you gave them more room to swim around in."

Wist made a gruff noise in response. She didn't sound very comforted.

I stood back, giving her space to finish doing her daily inspection of the stasis tank. Afterward, she asked me how early we ought to show up at the Church tomorrow.

"We? Hm, didn't I already tell you?" I asked, although I knew very well I hadn't. "You aren't coming with me."

Wist slowly straightened up. Her hands left the curved surface of the coffin-like glass tank and drifted back to her sides, holding nothing. She looked down at me with lightless eyes and asked, with so little intonation that it hardly sounded like a question at all: "Why not?"

I refused to be cowed. I tapped my temple. "Wist," I said. "Use your brain. Larkspur's a healer who held a Class 9-9 mage captive for years. She's a healer who—unless I've read this whole situation hopelessly wrong—is uniquely talented at making mages go berserk out of nowhere. I don't want you anywhere near her."

Wist's gaze dropped to the lid of the silent tank. She might've been scrutinizing the sleeping face of Larkspur's shriveled husband, or she might have been looking blankly down at her own reflection.

"But we're bonded," she said.

"What's that got to do with anything?"

"A bonded mage can only be healed by their bondmate."

"And?"

"Won't that afford me some protection?"

"Guess who else has a bondmate," I countered. "Your favorite sister Miyu. Didn't stop me from giving her the little extra shove she needed to tip over the edge and go berserk. And the government's had me hobble plenty of bonded mages in the past.

"Being bonded stops other healers from *healing* you, yes. Doesn't seem to stop us from doing the opposite of regular healing. Inconvenient? Yes. But that's how it is. Neutralizing you out of berserk mode was hard enough last year. I really don't want to have to do it again."

I let Wist sit with this thought for a while. She was stewing, all right—she hardly said a word the rest of the evening. She kept bumping into walls. During dinner, she absentmindedly transformed her soup spoon into a yellow arms-length string of overcooked spaghetti.

I took pity on her and stayed at the tower that night. Once we'd washed up, I stretched out on my stomach, picking bits of brown-black cat hair off the sheets.

I'd never actually managed to catch Turtle in Wist's bed, but the bedding seemed to suck up a constant supply of freshly shed fur. It wouldn't surprise me if Wist one day confessed that the tower was in fact occupied by several dozen more lookalike cats.

Animal hair aside, my only other complaint about her bed was that she made it far too cushy, with heaps of spongy foam padding out the mattress. Always gave me a bit of a backache the morning after.

Thanks to my years in prison, I'd grown too accustomed to sleeping on thin bedding laid out over hard surfaces. Even my floor bed back at the apartment was scarcely any thicker than a workout mat. By now my body seemed incapable of adapting to anything softer.

A row of Wist's miniature firebirds perched along the headboard above us, glowing sweetly. Their creator, in contrast, stared up at the shadowed ceiling as if it were her mortal enemy.

"Tell me one thing," she said abruptly. "Why the Church?"

I stopped collecting cat fur. I groped for the nightstand until I found my apartment key. I dangled it in front of Wist's face.

The key hung from the cheap Church of the Kraken logo keychain I'd bought back in—when was it, March? Three or four months ago, at any rate.

"Remember this?" I asked.

Wist's eyes followed the keychain. "What about it?"

"I felt it in my pocket. When I was thinking about what to say in my note to Larkspur."

"Surely that's not why you told her to meet you at the Church."

I grinned. "I mean, it's not the only reason. But it did give me inspiration."

I dropped my key back on the nightstand and thew myself down on my side, level with Wist.

"It was process of elimination," I said. "The reason I picked the Church. I didn't want to invite her right into your domain. Much less mine. So not here, and not my apartment. And not government property, either. The whole point is to keep them from realizing what a danger she poses.

"Try to meet her in a public place, like a restaurant or park? That's no good, either. Might be all kinds of innocent bystanders wandering around nearby. Mages among them."

"How is the Church any safer?" Wist asked.

"For whatever reason, they seem to think I'm your secretary or something. All I have to do is drop your name, and they'll rush to do me any number of favors. Clear the building? Keep out all visitors except for Larkspur? No problem. I already spoke to them and made arrangements for tomorrow.

"Plus," I added, "if nothing else, we can absolutely trust the Church to be discreet about it. They're your Church, after all."

"They are *not* my Church," Wist said at once.

"They might claim otherwise. Anyway, if they ever had to choose between loyalty to you and loyalty to, say, the Board of Magi—I'm sure they'd pick you. Simple as that."

Wist seemed less than thrilled by my reasoning, but she didn't nitpick.

I felt her relax a touch when I snuggled up against her back. It was still cool enough most nights to fall asleep holding each other—usually with me as the big spoon, despite being quite a bit smaller than her.

Sometimes, when I had to sleep alone in my apartment, I'd hug a spare pillow I'd pilfered from the tower. Not that I would ever tell Wist. It was her fault I'd gotten so used to drifting off with something secure in my arms.

Let it be noted, however, that we hadn't spent the entire week lazing around and cuddling. Far from it.

Wist, for her part, had numerous local requests to catch up with now that she was finally back in the country. She kept vanishing to go seal recently reported vorpal holes, attend Board hearings, and take care of various other missions from the government.

On the whole, I had far more free time. But when PubSec asked me to hobble a fresh cohort of newly sentenced mages, I decided I'd better report for duty. Didn't want to make a show of acting too busy. Didn't want anyone wondering what I was getting up to instead.

In the rare moments when I did manage to get a hold of Wist, I practiced hijacking her magic again. Not because I wanted or expected to get better at it. I wanted Wist to try resisting me.

She kept saying she couldn't. It wasn't a matter of willpower or strength, really. She simply couldn't—no more than she or any other mage could resist the ordinary type of healing.

Come to think of it, I'd never encountered a mage who could do anything to fight back when I reached out to hobble them, either.

Mages were incredibly vulnerable to healers. It was just that the vast majority of healers—as far as the government knew, every last one of them except for yours truly—couldn't do mages any actual harm.

The way they saw it, the worst possible thing a healer could to do a mage was to deny them healing.

And sure, the opposite scenario wasn't completely impossible. An eccentric healer might theoretically decide to leap at some random unbonded mage in a restaurant and heal them right on the spot, without their consent. But at most, the mage would walk away with less tangled magic and less chronic pain. Hardly an outcome to dread.

Besides, I'd almost never heard of such a thing happening. The healer wouldn't get anything out of it unless they were some kind of stalker or obsessive fan.

Mages believed—the mageocracy believed—that the only healer they truly needed to fear was the one called the Magebreaker. And she, whether due to incompetence or cowardice or plain old fatigue, had long since resigned herself to living under government control for the rest of her life.

Which meant that mages didn't really have any reason to fear any healers at all.

I wanted so badly for Wist to be able to resist hijacking. She was the Kraken, after all, as different from other mages as Larkspur and I seemed to be from other healers. Even if no other mages could resist, Wist might at least have a chance.

Yet our practice sessions gave me little reason to hope.

In a weird way, it felt like the opposite of wrestling Wist in bed. If she made the least bit of actual effort to pin me, I could never escape. It felt downright impossible. Conversely, if I seriously attempted to hijack her magic, I barely even noticed her straining to stop me. A complete role reversal from our usual play-fighting.

And it didn't seem like a muscle she could strengthen much through repetition, at least not in the short term. Perhaps months or years of training might make a difference. If only we had that much time to work with.

Besides, Wist had plenty of other pressing business to attend to.

So did I, for that matter.

Earlier on Friday, before meeting Wist at the tower, I went back to the National Healing Research Institute fortress with Manatree. She seemed determined to pay me for my time spent working on the vorpal rabies investigation, despite my attempts to proclaim failure and call the whole thing off. I figured I owed her some sort of follow-up report.

The nine living victims were still kept in isolation, without any unaffected mages allowed anywhere near them.

I took another quick look at each of them. Their hobbles held firm. Their behavior remained unchanged. They worked diligently to dig away at unyielding cell walls, yearning for unseen vorpal holes that surely lay far outside the fortress complex.

Were they like psychobomb survivors, their minds permanently altered? Or were they like Larkspur's husband, sane yet trapped in their own bodies, incapable of communicating their true thoughts?

Afterward, I beckoned Manatree outside. We took a walk along the high stone walls, still guarded by their original parapets.

Sunlight shafted sideways through breaks in the clouds, forming shapes like long golden staircases stretching down to the opaque surface of the sea. A steady wind helped blow away the latent humidity. Luckily, between Manatree with her long locs tied back and me with my extra-short pixie cut, neither of us had to fight to keep hair out of our face.

Just as I'd hoped, there was no one else in sight. These outermost walls were purely a historical artifact. NHRI staffers had little reason to come here. Nor was it the type of place where tourists could stroll up unannounced.

"Genuine question," I said to Manatree. "You haven't seen any of the vorpal rabies cases in person, have you?"

She shook her head.

"Would you be allowed to examine them in person if you asked? If you begged for permission?"

Sour lines deepened around the sides of her mouth. "No," she said. "There remains a fear of mage-to-mage contagion."

"Who fears it?" I pressed. "Not you, surely."

Manatree didn't answer. Then again, I hadn't expected her to. I went on. "I don't think anyone's listening right now, so I'll be straight with you. Stop me if you don't want to hear it."

I waited a moment. She didn't blink.

"All right," I said. "The fear of contagion is clearly just a front. Someone above you—maybe many someones—made the decision to cage the victims like animals. To keep other mages from looking too closely at them. To let them deteriorate rather than make the choice to try and help them."

Manatree seemed about to interrupt.

I held up a hand. "Realistically, if these people were in any way contagious, they would've already infected plenty of other mages before getting rounded up by PubSec.

"Even if contagion were a real worry, you could still try plenty of measures to prevent it. Protective gear, shielding magic, all that good stuff. If the victims weren't being cooperative, you could sedate them in order to make the process of examining them safer. I'm sure it's been suggested. But no one's tested any of that, have they?"

Wind gusted between us. Manatree waited for it to ease before speaking. "You seem to have a thesis in mind. State it clearly, then, if you're so sure of yourself."

"I couldn't solve the case for you," I said. "But here's what I think. The people suffering from vorpal rabies aren't contagious. They don't have any kind of special disease, supernatural or otherwise. Those things you call prions are just plain old human-made magic cuttings."

"The reports specifically stated that the prions resemble nothing we've ever seen before."

"Reports by who?" I asked. "How many people have been allowed to see the victims in person? Not many, huh? Not even you."

"And yet they let you in quite easily," said Manatree. "How do your conspiracy theories account for that?"

"Yeah, I get why they let me in. Even if some healer saw too much, I bet they didn't think a mere healer would understand what they were looking at. Even if a healer raised concerns, their words wouldn't carry any weight."

She didn't attempt to counter this. Satisfied, I sallied forth to my next point. "I bet you'd know exactly what I meant if you walked into one of their cells. Almost no one has actually contemplated these so-called prions in person, with their own magic perception, and without bringing in any preconceived notions.

"If they did—if you did—you'd come to the same conclusion as me. These prions are normal human magic cuttings, strangely pruned and slashed up as a crude sort of disguise. Seems like your higher-ups prefer to pretend the victims are truly sick, though.

"Why?" I mimed confusion. "I can take a couple of guesses. If it's magic, it's magic that flouts the Mage Conventions. It takes total control of the victims.

"Maybe the skills found in those cuttings look a little too familiar to some of your bosses. Maybe they're skills originally developed in secret by Osmanthian intelligence agencies. Or maybe it's a form of magic they can identify as being from an enemy of the state.

"Maybe they want to leave the vorpal rabies cases untreated—infected, as it were—to make it easier to hunt down and identify the culprit. Or maybe they just want to take this opportunity to watch and see exactly what happens to the affected mages over time. Not the type of experiment they could get away with organizing internally, but since these victims conveniently popped up out of nowhere...."

I raised both hands in a gesture of surrender. "Even if this were all true, what can you or I do about it? Nothing, really. You know, I think you came to me because you genuinely wanted to help those nine mages locked in solitary. But what kind of miracle did you expect from me? That's the part I just don't understand. Even now."

Manatree touched the crumbling edge of the ancient stone wall. The stone was the color of ash, pale and chalky beneath her deep brown hand.

"You've performed seemingly impossible feats in the past," she said, her voice only a fraction louder than the incessant shushing of the wind. "You're the one and only Magebreaker. Last year you brought back the Kraken's lost magic. You received a life sentence for treason, yet only had to serve seven years of it."

That last one was more thanks to Manatree herself than anything I'd done. But I didn't bother trying to correct her.

"Sorry it didn't work out this time," I said. "Guess I'm not always a good-luck charm."

Manatree was not amused. To tell you the truth, I felt a little bad leaving her there.

But if I were right about Larkspur (and if I succeeded in stopping her) at least there wouldn't be any new cases of vorpal rabies cropping up again in the future. Not here in Osmanthus, anyhow.

As for the nine infected mages trapped alone without anyone making the least effort to actually cure them—well, maybe someday Manatree would succeed in convincing her bosses to send help.

In the meantime, I had to take care of Larkspur without anyone noticing. Then Wist and I would carry out our plan to release her husband. One step at a time.

Try to save everyone at once, and you risk failing to save anyone at all. Like it or not, that's the way of the world.

Sometimes, in spare moments, I tried to imagine being Larkspur. Me living genteelly in that trophy-filled house. Wist trapped upstairs, voiceless, slowly atrophying, but still very much alive. Still brimming with magic.

I tried to imagine sitting down to enjoy a slow-cooked meal bathed in candlelight, surrounded by newspaper clippings and posters of celebrities like Fanren. Soothing music flowing from a melodium. Chewing my food without a care in the world while Wist's motionless weight lay suffocating in the tiny bedroom right overhead.

I tried to imagine repeating that day after peaceful day, for years on end.

I couldn't. I couldn't get my mind around it. Even at the absolute nadir of the greatest rage I'd ever felt at Wist, I couldn't conceive of lasting more than a day or two with her sitting helpless like a mannequin on the bed, blank eyes watching the fish tank on the dresser—knowing she was still right there in her body. Still human. Still my Wist.

But what if it were someone completely different?

What if it were, say, Shien Miyu?

If I were Miyu's healer, how far would I go to get her voice out of my head?

I didn't have a good answer for that. I didn't think I ever would.

The rainy season would officially continue for another couple of weeks. Yet Saturday, the day of my scheduled meeting with Larkspur, turned out to be one of those rare days without any precipitation whatsoever. It felt like a sneak preview of the full-blown summer heat that lay in wait perhaps a month from now. When I left the tower to stretch my legs around mid-day, unseen insects hummed busily all over the prairie of sleek blue grass.

I still hadn't returned Fanren's flak jacket. When it came time for me to get ready to leave, Wist helped me put it on and tighten the straps.

"Shouldn't you replace this?" she asked. "It's already been hit multiple times."

"What, these things aren't reusable?"

"There's visible damage."

I twisted around in an effort to see what she was talking about.

"Well," I said, "it's got to be better than absolutely nothing. Right? Right?"

"Don't ask me," Wist said grimly. "No, wait. Hold your arms up."

I stood obediently in place while one of her magic branches encircled my torso like an invisible anaconda. If I looked down with my magic perception, I could just barely detect a scale-like shimmering. The branch snaked to cover every inch of the flak jacket.

After a few more moments of breathless squeezing, Wist's magic released me. "Fixed it," she said.

"Really? How sweet of you."

Underneath the repaired flak jacket I wore a short-sleeved top, a pair of cut-offs, and athletic shoes. Just in case I ended up needing to make a run for it.

I'd selected the cut-offs because of their generous pockets. I slipped in the pack of sample business cards Fanren had lent me. Again, just in case. I hadn't touched them since that night outside the Bayside warehouse. There were still quite a few left unused.

I realized belatedly that Wist had been trying to say something while I fussed with the porcupine-print business cards.

I glanced up and found her watching me with her mouth set in a line. Which was essentially how she always looked. I thought I detected a tiny hint of extra tension, but it might have just been my eyes playing tricks on me.

She seemed resigned to repeating herself. "Clematis," she said again.

"What?"

"Promise you'll call me if you need me."

"Sure," I said. "As long as it won't put both of us in greater danger."

"Don't overthink it."

"Me? Overwork this little brain of mine? Never."

She pulled me in close, flak jacket and all. I had to turn my face sideways to keep from getting smothered in her chest.

Her heartbeat felt inhumanly slow. Not that I'm a medical expert or anything. But there was an almost fearful tightness to the way she held me.

23

As I'd requested, Wist stayed behind at the tower. When the time came, she ported me straight to Old River, depositing me alone—like an abandoned package—in the shadow of the Church building.

It was a touch cooler than earlier in the day, but still very bright out, the atmosphere rife with leftover heat. It felt like strolling about in the dense overcooked air of a recently used oven. Syrupy amber light painted rococo shadows across the shrine's frivolously carved facade.

I took a breath. It was less than refreshing. The rainy season wasn't even over yet, and I already missed it.

I could sense Wist at the other end of the bond deep in my body, quivering like a hyperactive dog on a leash. Or maybe that was just my own nascent anxiety. At least one of us needed to calm down, but I wasn't sure which.

The Church staff left the building at half after five, as I'd requested. One of them passed me the keys and instructions on how to lock up.

I wedged the double doors open to let in fresh air. I stood in the shadow of the gift shop window to wait for Larkspur.

The numerous statues and figurines of Wist watched over me in solemn silence. They appeared to be in impeccable shape, although they must've gotten quite battered back when Wist defended Old River from the Extinguishers.

I guess enough time had passed by now—three, almost four months later—for the Church to finish making any needed repairs. I suspected Wist of anonymously contributing to their renovation fund, although I doubted she'd ever admit it to me. Much less to them.

The vorpal hole at the back of the room remained intact as well. The Church members seemed to like having it there. Perhaps for mysterious religious reasons beyond the understanding of us common folk. Since it was stable in size and had yet to spit out any dangerous vorpal beasts, the city government and Wist must've agreed to continue to let it slide.

A frisson went through me when I caught sight of Larkspur. She strolled across the street at what must have been a perfectly normal, leisurely pace for a woman of her size.

To me, waiting and watching from inside the shrine building, her approach felt obnoxiously slow. I took my last chance to drink in a few noisy chest-filling breaths.

I couldn't see any magic cuttings on her. She'd be able to spot some on me, though. Before we parted, Wist had insisted on weaving additional reinforcement into my vest. Perhaps the extra functionality might help make up for the fact that it was taking me such a long time to return it to Fanren.

Larkspur wore healer robes again, as genteel as the first time we'd met, albeit now with little lace-up ankle boots on beneath. The boots sent a soft clip-clopping echo through the shrine as she crossed the threshold to join me.

She stood just inside the wedged-open double doors, her small shadow stretching across the shrine floor, holding in front of her a short-handled purse with a single demure twist lock.

Her hands were gloved. For fashion purposes, presumably, rather than to stay warm. She'd bound her hair up at the nape of her neck again, this time with two plain wooden hair sticks poking out of the gray braided knot.

Her face was utterly serene. Almost smiling. It was enough to make me wonder if I'd dreamed the whole thing—her hollow-cheeked husband, his stinking bedsores, those poor crowded guppies.

We were alone in the building, and she had her back to the street. Absolutely nothing about her demeanor seemed any different from the first time we'd met.

I swallowed to cleanse the apprehension clogging my throat. "Let me get those doors," I said.

Larkspur stepped aside, polite as ever, to give me room to close the double doors. I hesitated there for a moment afterward, undecided, then went ahead and locked them.

I glanced at Larkspur from the corner of my eye as I turned the lock. She remained disturbingly unruffled.

"I like your vest," she told me.

I patted the flak jacket. "That's me, all right. Always on the cutting edge of—of street style."

"It looks very safe."

"You never know who might be packing heat," I added.

She laughed with what sounded like genuine amusement and hoisted her petite purse in both hands. "Oh, dear. Are you worried I might have a gun in here? Believe me, I've never touched a gun in my life. I wouldn't even know how to hold one."

"What a coincidence," I said. "That makes two of us. Then again, who's to say you won't stab me with those hair sticks? You'll have to forgive my paranoia."

Her smile lingered. "I have no intention of harming you."

"Thanks. Very reassuring."

"Between the two of us, don't I have rather more reason to worry?" she inquired. "You chose the time and location of our meeting. And it seems that you arrived here quite early."

"What can I say?" I threw up my hands. "I work too hard. That's what everyone tells me. I didn't pack the Church with traps, though. Might've been a good idea, now that you mention it."

"No need to thank me," Larkspur said modestly.

"You know what's funny?" I asked.

"Not at all. Please tell me."

"You don't seem even the slightest bit surprised to see me. I may have left a note for you, but I'm pretty sure I didn't sign it."

"Yes," said Larkspur. "I was quite touched. I can't even remember the last time I received a handwritten letter. A love note from my husband, perhaps?"

"That would definitely have been years and years ago."

Her eyes crinkled. "Indeed. How nostalgic."

"So how'd you know it was me?"

Instead of answering, Larkspur walked forward to gaze up at the host of elaborate Wist statues. The clip-clop of her boots sounded like the slow ticking of some huge hidden clock.

"These are incredible." She sounded like she meant it.

"Right. Your husband was something of an amateur artist, wasn't he? Would you consider yourself a connoisseur?"

"Hardly," she said. "But I can certainly appreciate this level of devotion."

"It's kind of like your house, isn't it," I pointed out. "Except your collection pays homage to all sorts of different mages."

She half-turned to look back at me.

The last amber light of day poured down from the glass ceiling to wash over all of us down here in the shrine: me, Larkspur, hundreds of different iterations of Wist.

Only now did I realize that Larkspur's healer robes bore a different pattern from the first time we'd met. Pink-tipped water lilies, far larger than life, on a background of fabric as dark as night.

No—not water lilies, not the type that appear to float right on the surface. My mistake. They were tall-stemmed lotus flowers, the kind that would sprout up high above the water.

"So," I said again. "How'd you know it was me?"

She just kept smiling.

"You expected me?" I guessed. "You wanted to get caught? You were waiting for me to—"

"I've been so curious." She had the gentle tone of a long-time teacher, the sort of teacher everyone loved. "Won't you tell me your real name?"

"Aren't you a bit young to be getting forgetful?"

"Wait till you pass forty," she said wryly. "I have no idea what your name is, but I'm quite certain it isn't Asa Lantana."

"Believe what you like," I retorted. "I think it's a perfectly lovely name. Lantana for the flower, the little colorful one. You seem like a gardener. You must know it."

She inclined her head in agreement.

"An unusual name?" I went on. "Sure. But my parents picked it out themselves. Even if you suspect otherwise."

"No matter," said Larkspur. "Let's agree to disagree. I suppose your real name matters little."

She raised a hand to shield her eyes from the concentrated golden dregs of the dying sun.

"Many healers have heard rumors of the Magebreaker," she said. Still soft-spoken. Still conversational. "Nowadays, that title rarely appears in state broadcasts, in any sort of official media. But stories get passed along anyway. Some likely true. Some likely false. A loose collection of urban legends."

"Fascinating." I sounded almost as deadpan as Wist. My stomach ached. I wondered how Larkspur would react if I told her I needed a bathroom break.

"Look," I said. Time to regain control here. "Who cares about the Magebreaker?"

"I do."

"Whatever you say about that person, I can neither confirm nor deny it. So no point in asking. More importantly—aren't you wondering at all about your husband?"

Larkspur scanned the collection of Wist statues as if expecting to spot her husband crouching among them like a child playing hide-and-seek.

"I assume he's in good hands."

I waited for her to continue. She didn't.

The problem with approaching this like a hostage negotiation was that I had no idea what Larkspur wanted. To get her husband back? To receive assurance that I wouldn't inform on her?

I'd expected her to approach me with some kind of plea or demand. Instead she kept watching me with that signature small smile of hers that didn't show any teeth.

Wist was tough to read because she rarely let anything resembling a real expression slip onto her face. Larkspur, in contrast, smiled with both her eyes and her mouth. But I still had no idea what any of it meant.

"Let me clarify a few things." The huge arching inner space of the shrine lent my voice a disquieting resonance. "For some reason I keep having to tell people this, but I'm not a private investigator. I'm not a detective. And I'm not with the government, either."

She put a hand to her cheek. "How curious. I could swear that Mori told me you were working for PubSec."

"As a private contractor," I said. "Just a consultant. Point is, it isn't my job to make arrests. I don't want to turn you in to the authorities. And I really don't need to know your whole big story."

I thumped the part of the flak jacket right over my breastbone. "Me, I'm just interested in reaching an agreeable outcome."

"Very businesslike."

"I *am* an entrepreneur of sorts, come to think of it. A small business owner, even."

I took a few steps closer. Though I was careful not to get too close. I had no idea what Larkspur kept in that bag of hers. Best to stay well out of stabbing range.

"Leave the country," I said. "That's my only request."

"A foreign vacation?" Larkspur beamed. "What a thoughtful suggestion. How long of a trip do you recommend?"

"Forever," I answered. "Leave Osmanthus, and never come back."

She put a gloved hand to her heart. "Oh, I couldn't possibly leave forever. I'd be much too worried about my garden."

I didn't like this. Her easy manner, her mild jokes—I didn't like any of it.

"I hear Jace is pretty nice this time of year," I said. "Start a new garden in Jace, why don't you. Whatever you've done, wherever you go, I'll make sure no one ever finds out it was you."

"And my husband?"

"Like you said, he'll be in good hands."

"That's really all it would take to satisfy you?" Larkspur inquired. "All you wish for me to do is flee abroad? No questions asked?"

"A generous deal, isn't it? A much better deal than you deserve, frankly. Not to be judgmental."

She slowly shook her head. "Magebreaker, do you have a purpose in life?"

It was a struggle to keep from snapping. I forced myself to respond in measured tones. "One, I have no idea who you think you're talking to. There's no Magebreaker here. Two, what kind of question is that? None of your business."

Simply put, if I were willing to answer her, my answer would have been *no*. Life is complicated enough without trying to make it fit some kind of mission statement.

Anyway, the difference between me and Larkspur (and just about everyone else alive today) was that this was my second crack at life. Not my first. However unintentionally, Wist had sacrificed an entire world to bring me back.

And I'd already screwed up plenty of times in this second life of mine. My clumsy past attempts to reform Osmanthus had backfired spectacularly. Meanwhile, I'd grown old enough to admit that I lacked both the brain and the stomach for a true bloody revolution.

Now that I knew I was in overtime, the least I could do was to avoid making things worse.

Magebreaker or not, I was ultimately just one stubby little human being. Just one city-born Osmanthian healer in her thirties. I hadn't existed a hundred years in the past, and a hundred years from now I'd be gone forever.

In short, the world as a whole wouldn't really notice whether I was dead or alive, except insofar as my death might affect Wist. I had to figure I was doing fine as long as my presence didn't cause any more damage than my potential absence.

"I understand," Larkspur said. "Most people don't have a single purpose. Fanatics like the Extinguishers, yes. The same might be said for the owners of this building. The people you pass by when grocery shopping? Perhaps not. Perhaps they're simply living their lives."

Better not let her steer me off course. "If you need help leaving the country quietly, I'll see what I can do," I said. "Wouldn't you rather live abroad than live in jail, or worse? Let's just say that I know a thing or two about life behind bars."

We'd reached that point in the evening when the sinking sun suddenly accelerates its fall. For a few moments a swampy dimness sank into the shrine, shadowing Larkspur's face.

Then the skylights filling the ceiling began to brighten again. A new deluge of light poured forth like time reversing course. Even from down here I could glimpse hints of magic cuttings embedded in the window-glass, a lace of tiny golden cracks. The skill called Suncatcher, perhaps.

"I myself have always been skeptical of people who claim to have a purpose," said Larkspur.

"I thought we were already done talking about the meaning of life."

"But I do believe," she continued, "that everyone needs a hobby. It's good for the soul."

This conversation wasn't coming together at all. I rubbed my temples.

"A hobby," I repeated. "A hobby? What would that be for you? Gardening? Collecting memorabilia from celebrities? Driving mages berserk? Infecting them with mind-jacking magic snatched from your husband? Why couldn't you just stick to grooming your front yard? It already outshines all your neighbors."

Larkspur beamed. "Why, thank you."

"Please listen." I was on the verge of begging. "Don't take this the wrong way, but I don't care about your hobbies. I mean, I think you could've chosen much better ones. Gardening aside. But I didn't come here to interrogate you. I definitely didn't come to get a confession."

"What about the reason I came here?" she asked innocently. "What if *I* want to tell you about my story, my hobbies? What if I *want* to confess?"

I stared at her. In her graceful healer robes, Larkspur fit much better with all the colorfully clad statues of Wist than I ever would.

"Why?"

I knew as soon as I said it that—even if I had no idea where this was going—I was playing into her hands.

She gave me a curious look. "If we were the only two women on the continent, or the only two healers, or the only two human beings left alive, wouldn't it only be natural to wish to meet?"

"Maybe," I said. "But we aren't."

"Aren't we? Are we not two of a kind? Hmm—could it be that the Magebreaker finds herself reluctant to acknowledge the existence of a competitor?"

"I'm not the—" I heaved a breath. "For the sake of your argument, let's pretend I'm the Magebreaker. Even if that were the case, it wouldn't change anything. I'd still ask you to leave Osmanthus. It's really not a bad offer, compared to becoming a prisoner and going on trial."

"...I suppose it's understandable for you to feel that way," Larkspur said softly. "You must have thought you were the only person in the world capable of full-spectrum healing."

"Full-what healing?"

"Do you call it something different? The name matters little, of course. You had no idea I existed. But it's different for me. I've heard rumors of the Magebreaker for years."

A sick feeling festered in my belly. The golden glow of Suncatcher submerged the whole sanctum in undying light. There was a merciless quality to it, a refusal to let shadows eke out a meager existence even when night fell outside the building.

"You knew the Magebreaker was in prison," I said.

"So the stories went."

"Then you heard new stories," I went on. "This year? Late last year? You heard whispered hints that I—that the Magebreaker had gotten released."

"Indeed."

"Only then did you—accelerate your activities. Dive deeper into your so-called hobbies. Drive more and more mages berserk. Spread magic cuttings from your husband, the ones you like to call vorpal rabies. All of a sudden you went wild, years and years after your husband's supposed death. After over a decade of living happily unsuspected."

Larkspur faced me with that saintly close-lipped smile. She said nothing.

"And you're claiming you did this because you felt some kind of kinship with the Magebreaker," I said tautly. "Because you wanted to meet your counterpart.

"You call me the Magebreaker. So you're saying every mage you drove berserk this year, every bystander they maimed or killed, every mage locked up with vorpal rabies—you're saying it's all because of me."

"Why, I said nothing of the sort," Larkspur replied, gentle as ever. "Of course, you're free to think as you like. All I did was reach out to the Magebreaker in a special language only the two of us could understand."

"A special language," I echoed dumbly.

"Surely there's a reason you're the first person to cast doubt on me. You alone understand what full-spectrum healers are truly capable of."

When she spoke she peered into my eyes as if she were praising me, as if she were striving to build up a timid student's self-esteem.

"All I cared about was if my message reached you," she said. "It didn't need to be understood by anyone else. And it worked, didn't it? You suspected me. You found me."

"...All right." At least my voice still came out steady. "Satisfy yourself. Say your piece. Then leave Osmanthus. Can we agree on that?"

I had to remind myself not to rush things. We could chit-chat all night if needed.

It already felt like I'd been talking to her forever, standing here in the Church like a dolt. Objectively speaking, though, it must've been far less than half an hour. Under fifteen minutes, even. Only just long enough for the sun outside to slink down into its grave.

The problem wasn't a lack of time. It was my own lack of patience, and my absolute disinterest in prolonging this verbal fencing match for so much as another second.

Maybe Larkspur could tell how badly I wanted to end this. If she were a sadist at heart, maybe she'd enjoy dragging it out.

I fingered the pack of business cards in my pocket. It would be quicker, of course, to fling a few balled-up cards at her. The cards would floor her, at least temporarily. They'd flood her nervous system with incomprehensible amounts of pain.

Reverse healing—what she seemed to call full-spectrum healing—required concentration. I certainly couldn't do it while being tortured. I doubted Larkspur could, either.

Which meant that if I wanted to summon Wist's help, if I wanted to abduct Larkspur and forcibly deport her to distant lands, all I had to do was crumple one of these cards and drop it on the shining shrine floor.

Larkspur would be no threat to Wist—or any other mage, for that matter—while lying collapsed in agony. Wist could then use magic to steal her consciousness, to ship her off to some faraway continent.

But for now I needed to hold firm and hear Larkspur out. I needed to resist temptation. Punting her out of Osmanthus would be the easy part. If she didn't depart the country of her own free will, she might very well find a way to come back. For my own peace of mind, I wanted her to *want* to leave.

Which meant I was trapped here, a captive audience, until Larkspur had satisfied her desire for a tête-à-tête with the Magebreaker.

She glided over to the chairs lined up along the wall. I watched without moving as she sat down neatly, legs together, and put her little handbag on the seat to her left.

She patted the seat to her right as if inviting a dog to jump up on it. Guess that meant me.

I took her invitation. I plopped myself down beside her, but I left an open chair between us. It was still plenty close enough to hear each other.

These seats offered a side view of the massed statues—some towering, some just about life-size, some tiny. From here, the replica Wists with their long snaking braids and extravagant sleeves seemed to have something of a pensive air.

"I will say," Larkspur uttered, looking straight ahead at the colorful figures, "it came as a bit of a shock to realize that you're bonded."

I wasn't afraid of her. I swear to you I wasn't afraid of her. I wouldn't request a one-on-one meeting with someone I had a legitimate reason to fear. Those words jolted me with something very much like a heave of nausea. Surely not terror. And yet—

"Don't believe everything you hear," I said lightly.

She tapped the corner of her eye. "No, no," she assured me. "I have very highly rated magic perception. I couldn't help but see the bond in you. I can't see who it leads to, of course, but it's certainly there."

Ankles crossed primly, she turned in her seat to gaze at me. "You yourself have very good magic perception as well, don't you? Maybe that's a prerequisite for being able to do more than just regular by-the-book healing."

"Perhaps," I said, channeling Wist. No emotion.

"Why don't you wear a bond thread?"

"Because I'm a delicate little flower," I said, still wooden. "Very private in nature. Very shy."

"Oh, silly me," said Larkspur. "I thought perhaps the Magebreaker might be ashamed to be bonded. Humiliated, even. I'm so glad to hear that's not the case."

In the moments when neither of us spoke, the shrine was utterly devoid of sound.

"Are you trying to pick a fight with me?" I inquired. "I honestly can't tell."

"I didn't realize the Magebreaker would be almost a decade younger than me," she said thoughtfully.

"I've got an old soul."

"It just goes to show that one ought not to cling to preconceptions."

"No kidding," I said. "When I saw your husband's art all over your walls, I figured it was because you genuinely mourned him. Foolish of me."

"Did I tell you he never pushed me to bond?" Larkspur asked. "That's true, in a sense. Publicly, he certainly made a show of not pushing me to bond. Of martyring his career for my freedom. In private, it was rather different."

"You never told me his name."

"That man has no name anymore."

For a confused instant, I thought I smelled something like the stink of his bedsores.

"If you've seen his branch skills, you must have guessed that he wasn't merely a diplomat," she continued. "That was his cover job. In reality, he worked for an agency you've probably never even heard the name of. He was a spy, you could say colloquially. A saboteur.

"Not that I knew any of this when I married him. Most of his branch skills are illegal. Completely against the Mage Conventions. But the Osmanthian government secretly authorized him to acquire those skills, to strategically deploy them on foreign soil.

"They're all quite subtle, of course. By the time they caused a target any actual harm, my husband might long since have returned to Osmanthus. Or his delegation might have traveled to another country altogether."

"That's strange. The creation you call vorpal rabies isn't subtle at all," I said baldly.

"I made him shed cuttings of his various branch skills." Was it pride that I now heard in her voice? "Bundled together in all sorts of combinations, his skills turned out to have some rather fascinating interactions. One might think of it as a sort of magical chemistry. As healer, I can't learn any skills of my own, but I do seem to have something of a knack for remixing my husband's cuttings."

"Great," I said. "Brilliant. Is this what you wanted? Recognition of your genius? Some kind of acknowledgment from your only true peer? I can clap all night if you wish. Applause costs me nothing."

You might call me foolish for trying to bait her. But I wasn't, not really. Larkspur certainly didn't seem like she would be so easily baited, anyway.

She took her purse from the seat beside her and placed it on her lap again. Her gloved hands rested softly atop it as if to soothe a frightened pet rabbit.

"I'm not quite sure of the details," she said, "but it seems my husband was some sort of double agent. Or he feared being cut loose by his own agency, even if he hadn't yet betrayed them. Whatever the reason, he faked his death on foreign soil. I received a formal notification of his passing. I had no reason not to believe it. I shed a few tears, I think."

"You think?"

"A month or two later, my supposedly deceased husband appeared in front of me again. He begged me to run away with him. Call me cold, but I wasn't thrilled about the idea of giving up my home, my life—my citizenship—for the sake of a dead man.

"When I hesitated, he tried to bring me by force. Not physical force."

"He still had all the same branch skills," I said, understanding.

"He used his most powerful mind-control magic. He could have made me do anything. He could have forced me to consent to bonding."

Larkspur turned the twist lock of her purse, as if about to open it, then snapped the lock back into place. Twist, twist. It only gave off the faintest of clicks.

"I had never done anything other than perfectly standard healing in my life," she said. "I had never even dreamed of it.

"I felt that magic branch of his writhing inside me like a tapeworm. He put his hand on me and injected that magic in me as if he had every right to do it. As if I owed it to him.

"I sensed parts of me—my mind, my self, my horror, my rage—dissolving into a kind of primordial ooze. I sensed parts of me being lost forever. It was like watching your own body decompose before your eyes. But I was very calm. He'd already robbed me of any ability to panic.

"And somehow, in my calmness, I realized I could take hold of that tapeworm. Even as my consciousness disintegrated around it. It was his magic, after all. It was still part of him. I could take it and twist it. Not like I normally did to heal mages. Not simply to smooth out the knots. I could snap his magic like a pair of reins.

"I could do to him what he was doing to me. I could puppeteer him. I could win."

She stopped twisting at the lock. "You can imagine the rest, I'm sure.

He was already officially dead. No need to worry about anyone missing him."

"Why'd you leave him alive?" I asked. "Don't try to pretend sparing his life was an act of mercy."

"Why?" She seemed almost puzzled. "Why not leave him alive? I'm not a crime lord. I don't know anything about how to safely dispose of a body."

"Yet somehow you figured out how to get access to vorpal beasts."

"That came much later." Larkspur pressed together the tips of her gloved fingers. "I'm afraid I was never quite the same after he used his magic on me. Although that might not necessarily be a bad thing.

"I can't recall what it was like to experience anything resembling fear, guilt, apprehension, envy, regret. I've felt extraordinarily peaceful ever since. No matter how he looked at me. No matter how the light left his eyes.

"I don't really see people when I look at mages now. I see intricate puzzle boxes. A series of fascinating mechanisms—something akin to a mechanical clock."

She gestured at me as if calling on a pupil. "What do you see, Magebreaker?"

"Some people would pay good money for a sensation of eternal peace," I said.

Larkspur chuckled. "Ah, if only I could sell it."

"It'll be harder to maintain perfect tranquility if you get a death sentence," I warned her. "All the more reason to make a quiet exit from Osmanthus."

"I'm curious," said Larkspur. "Have you ever tasted an all-consuming loneliness?"

"I was in prison for seven years," I retorted.

But even as I said it, I realized the memories felt bizarrely distant.

Like something from another life. Like those constant dreams I used to have of dying.

"I felt something almost like that whenever I heard stories of the Magebreaker," Larkspur continued. "It intrigued me. It was the only real thing I felt in all those years."

"Not sure I can do much to help you with looming solitude."

"No," Larkspur agreed. "You can't. I was drawn to the idea of a kindred spirit. I was drawn to the idea of the Magebreaker."

Her smile turned apologetic. "But when I look at you now, all I see is another type of puzzle box. And I'm terribly sorry to have to tell you this, but I'm afraid I've already solved it."

I swallowed my overwhelming desire to flee. I didn't believe her. I had no reason to believe her. "Do tell," I said.

She caressed the handles of her bag as if checking it for wounds. Or perhaps for ticks. This purse of hers was starting to remind me of something, but I couldn't begin to articulate what.

Well, it wasn't like she could be hiding something like a psychobomb in there. My magic perception would've picked up on it ages ago, the light of the cuttings piercing straight through the fabric lining and the fine leather surface.

"You made one specific fatal mistake." Larkspur sounded like a professor again. "The second time you visited my house. You took something of mine you shouldn't have."

"Your husband?" I guessed. "The guppies?"

This only seemed to amuse her. "No, no. Do you recall the first time we met? We spoke briefly of the Kraken."

I kept my eyes fixed on the silent army of Wist statues. I could feel Larkspur studying the side of my face. I had to order my jaw not to jump in place, my throat not to swallow.

"Did we?" I said at last, non-committal. "I don't quite remember."

"I knew you were acquainted with the Kraken. But I wouldn't have thought you were particularly close to her. It seems counterintuitive, after all. A Kraken-class mage and the Magebreaker."

"Exactly." At this point in the conversation, I'd long since given up on outright denying being the Magebreaker. "I know her through my business."

"Oh my," said Larkspur. "Such a professional."

"Are you being sarcastic?"

"Yet out of all my souvenirs, you took only the one she gifted me. My white chrysanthemum."

I nearly swung my head to look around for it. Yet I knew for sure it was safe in the tower, resting in a little vase in Wist's favorite sunroom.

Wist was probably there right now, curled up in one of her white wicker chairs, staring glumly at the perfect chrysanthemum surrounded by all her imperfect attempts at houseplant cultivation.

"Yeah, that flower is mine now," I said. "Too bad."

For some reason, my hand was in my pocket, touching the porcupine-print business cards.

For some reason, Larkspur had resumed toying with the twist lock on the front of her purse.

Maybe she'd been lying about not packing heat. Maybe she had a gun in her purse. Or a kitchen knife. Surely not anything magical. She knew how good my magic perception was. She must've realized she wouldn't be able to get away with smuggling in any magic-embedded artifacts.

For some reason, I thought of the district right outside the Church building. Old River. Luxury apartments, green parks, tiny sooty restaurants in decaying old shopping districts. The half-dried river itself.

Wist had sought to shield the entire district rather than attempt to hunt down and defuse the psychobomb. Why? Why do things the hard way—no, the hardest way possible?

Why?

Because there was no point in searching, no point in scanning, when the Extinguishers could've simply used a Jacian briefcase to conceal the bomb's magic.

My gaze became glued to the soft pinkish leather of Larkspur's handbag. Her gloved fingers twisted the lock open, then shut again. Open. Shut.

A Jacian briefcase could camouflage even the strongest of magic cuttings. What about a Jacian purse?

24

In the end, mere physical gestures decided our fate. Not borrowed magic or healing prowess or brains.

Maybe I should've listened to Wist and gotten in the habit of exercising. Sharp, breathless exercise, not my usual leisurely strolls around the neighborhood. Maybe then my reflexes would've been fast enough to make a difference.

Which is not to say that I reacted slowly.

The moment I saw Larkspur start to open her bag—this time for real, not another feint with the outer twist lock—my fist crushed one of the business cards in my pocket.

All I had to do was flick it away from me. That's all it would take to activate its magical spikes of pain.

I didn't hesitate.

Crumpled paper hit the shrine's hard glistening floor.

Larkspur made a choking noise, as if she'd sucked in a breath to scream but couldn't finish. One gloved hand gripped at her chest, right over the V-shaped fold of her elegiac healer robes.

I realized belatedly that the mouth of her handbag gaped wide open. Something had already come shooting out of it.

A dark brown cockroach clung to the bare skin of my left arm.

Larkspur whimpered. She collapsed sideways in her chair. A nigh-endless row of empty seats stretched on and on along the wall beyond her slumped form.

Her bag tumbled to the floor with an anticlimactic *whump*, tipping softly on its side. Nothing rolled out.

I stared blankly at the cockroach on my bicep. When I first saw it, I'd jerked with the impulse to slap at it. But I didn't. Wist was more of a wimp about this type of bug than me. You wouldn't know it, though, since she could just zap them with magic.

This one wasn't a real insect, anyhow. It was a cheap replica made of molded rubbery material. A toy, basically. The type you might pick up at a store specializing in gag gifts, embedded with a single cheap magic cutting meant to make it go flying out at the nearest innocent person—at anyone other than its owner.

You might wonder why I sat there like a lump, gawking at the eyeless toy cockroach latched onto my arm.

You might wonder why I no longer moved a single muscle. Not even after noticing the tangle of more dangerous magic cuttings clinging burr-like to the cockroach's back.

I recognized the crooked shape of those threads. I knew who they'd originally been chopped from. They were the same sort of broken-looking cuttings that Manatree had compared to the prions known for causing diseases like rabies.

The only reason I wasn't shuddering—the only reason I hadn't already ripped the cockroach off me—was because I couldn't.

I couldn't twitch a finger. I couldn't even attempt to strain against my invisible bindings.

My conscious brain seemed to have completely surrendered authority over my physical body.

And perhaps because of that, I couldn't fully panic. There was no rushing in my blood, no frantic heart skipping steps in its haste to sprint full-tilt ahead. No aching stomach. No tight-twisted chest. No hollow swallowing of extra spit down an awkwardly convulsing throat.

I just kept existing, limbs at ease, right there in the same chair as moments before.

The clump of magic cuttings carried by the toy cockroach had already lanced deep inside me. It felt like sitting there and watching parasitic worms bore into my flesh.

My stupid flesh, of course, offered zero resistance.

I had a vague sense that my understanding of the passage of time was beginning to warp. Slowing? Speeding up? I couldn't tell which.

I had a vague sense that Wist was going to be unfathomably angry once she found out about this.

Angry at who? Quite possibly me.

From a few seats to my left, Larkspur coughed violently. Somehow she sounded much further away than she really was. Maybe because of how her coughing echoed around and around the sanctuary.

How long would that one business card keep torturing her? The warehouse guards I'd attacked with multiple cards had recovered far too quickly for comfort, although presumably they possessed more combat training than a refined lady like Larkspur.

I had my answer soon enough. I saw Larkspur start to push herself up with difficulty. She bent—slowly, achingly—to retrieve her purse. She took out a small floral handkerchief and patted her brow. She breathed in and out with great care and deliberation.

Then, as if nothing had happened, she turned to me.

"Let me get that for you," she said, hoarser than before.

She plucked the cockroach from my left bicep. Its payload of magic cuttings had penetrated almost as deep as the bond in the deepest part of me.

I wanted to laugh. I wanted to laugh loud and bitterly. Not that I could. As far as I knew, she'd only ever used this particular cocktail of cuttings from her husband—the concoction she called vorpal rabies—on mages.

It genuinely hadn't occurred to me that she might use it on me.

But why not? It wasn't actually a mystical vorpal illness. There was no rule to say it could only consume mages. She could use it on anyone she pleased. As long as she didn't care about the consequences. As long as she still had a few secret stashes of the necessary cuttings in stock.

Larkspur wrapped the toy cockroach in her handkerchief. She secreted the flowery little packet back inside her bag.

"Crude, I know," she said apologetically. "Vorpal beasts have become very difficult to come by lately. Tremendous turmoil in the marketplace. I wonder why?"

She sounded as if she already knew the answer. She scooted over into the one empty seat I'd left between us. Her hair sticks had gone askew. Her low gray bun slumped to one side.

She leaned forward to scrutinize my face.

"You are somewhat resistant, aren't you?" she said. "More so than any of the infected mages to date." Amber eyes searched me. "I wonder if it's because you're a healer? Or perhaps it's because you're a very special sort of healer. Perhaps it's because you're the Magebreaker."

Without preamble, my body rose uncertainly to its feet. My ears were listening to her. I didn't have any choice but to listen, for that matter.

I lacked the ability to scream and drown her out. I lacked the ability to will myself to cover my ears.

Yet my body turned away from her. It shifted foot to foot, restless. It didn't seem to care much for whatever Larkspur had to say.

Not that Larkspur minded. She circled around in front of me. She put a well-mannered gloved hand to her face.

"Now I regret not experimenting with infecting healers or subliminals." She imbued her voice with an exaggerated air of sorrow. "But please don't be mistaken," she added. "I didn't spare them out of a sense of, shall we say, obligation. Protect the weak and all that.

"I was simply interested in how Public Security might react if my rabies were framed as an affliction exclusive to mages. I do think that made them take notice quicker, and treat it more seriously. Don't you agree?"

As she spoke, I'd begun to walk amongst the myriad statues of Wist. Some only came up to my waist. Some were far taller than the real-life Wist. They neither moved nor breathed nor watched me go as I passed.

None said a word. None reached out to catch me, to stop me. I couldn't stop myself, either.

The statues wore elaborate collarbone-length earrings, the sort that would hang unbearably heavy in real life unless they came treated with magic cuttings to lighten the burden. These figures incorporated no magic. But through deft tricks of craftsmanship, the jeweled strands of their earrings seemed to float all the same, fanning out like long hair gone weightless underwater.

When was the last time I'd seen Wist wearing earrings? All that came to mind was a pair of melancholy black studs. Months and months ago, then, when we got all dressed up to visit the Shiens. Weaving through the staggered rows of effigies gave me much the same sense of impending doom as standing outside the Shien family gate.

I had no control where my feet took me. And no idea, at first, why I'd started moving.

Then I recalled that the mixture of magic called vorpal rabies was what moved me.

I recalled that a convenient vorpal hole lay right at the back of the shrine.

I opened my mouth to speak. It took tremendous effort.

"Good day," I said blandly.

I couldn't quite remember what I'd been about to say. It definitely hadn't been that.

Somewhere behind me came the sound of Larkspur laughing. It was a musical, likable laugh, the kind that might help set just the right mood if you heard it tinkling in the background of an upscale party. Not that I go to many parties nowadays.

My brain seemed profoundly reluctant to summon any sense of true urgency. But with another step or two, I'd come in full sight of the vorpal hole. I'd come close enough to make a running leap for it, probably.

Somehow that seemed like a bad idea.

I turned ever so slightly left and careened full speed into the nearest statue.

The statue was life-size but startlingly lightweight. It rocked, then toppled sideways into its neighbor—which fortunately seemed to be made of much sturdier material.

Just as I'd been able to open my mouth—though I'd proven incapable of articulating anything meaningful—I'd been able to adjust my trajectory by perhaps a fraction of a degree. Just enough to cause this traffic accident.

My face smarted from the collision. My body remained still, staring haplessly down at the diagonally-tipped figure of Wist. Broken bits of the most delicate components—her floating earrings, fine strands from the very end of her long undulating braid—lay scattered on the slick floor. The shrapnel looked like evidence at a crime scene.

"That reminds me," said Larkspur, coming up beside me.

She slipped a gloved hand in my pocket and extracted the remaining business cards. She fanned them in her fingers as if inviting me to play a game with her.

"Cute," she said, indicating the cartoon porcupine icon on the cards. "Extremely effective, however. I haven't felt anything like that since childbirth."

She saw the look on my face and smiled broader. "Just pulling your leg. I've never had children."

She tapped the cards into a clean stack, then removed the top one and studied it diligently, front and back. "Oh, I see. Very user-friendly."

She tucked the pack of cards away in her bag. My body had started shifting from foot to foot again.

Larkspur and I had, in a way, fallen prey to the same logical fallacy. We'd both assumed we were fundamentally the same type of creature.

In her case, that had led to her mistakenly believing she might be able to derive some sort of profound meaning out of the mere act of meeting me.

In my case, I'd figured that Larkspur could be reasoned with. Even if she saw the world very differently than I did. I'd figured she'd be motivated to avoid getting caught by the government. To avoid losing her freedom. To avoid tangling with me as an enemy.

She didn't seem to care very much about any of that, really.

Which meant Larkspur was a completely different type from me. Much more difficult to predict. Thinking I could reason with her just because we were both unconventional healers was ultimately as foolish as thinking you could reason with a serial killer simply because you happened to share the same birthday. Or, say, a passion for calligraphy.

My body lurched off to the right, slipped between the last few rows of statues. I couldn't course-correct fast enough to cause another crash landing.

The Church's vorpal hole hid inside an imposing cage of prismatic glass. The cage was at least the size of a small solarium. The outer ridges on the glass blurred the appearance of the hole within.

The previous version of this cage had shattered ignominiously when Wist ported a bunch of Extinguisher bombs right to the rim of the vorpal hole within. Now it was rebuilt to perfection, its only door thoroughly locked.

I slammed a hand into the ridged glass. It hurt like hell. I did it again anyway. Couldn't even seem to slow the swing of my arm.

Larkspur emerged from the forest of statues to watch over me.

My hand kept banging the glass. The glass hardly even shuddered in response. Magic shimmered like oil on its corrugated surface. Hopefully a cutting strong enough to keep me from shattering it.

Repetition made the pain recede, as if each *bang* chased it further from my senses. At last I had to strain to feel it there, like listening in dead silence for the faintest beginnings of tinnitus.

Something caught at my right arm. Larkspur.

"You'll break your hand," she admonished.

The ensuing struggle suggested that neither of us was particularly fit. Larkspur didn't seem like the type of gentlewoman who would see value in spending a whole lot of time at the gym.

"Even if you're mildly resistant," she said breathlessly, holding me back with what seemed like all her strength, "I'm sure you can see there's no way to escape this on your own. I regret to say that I'm not strong enough to restrain you forever, either. Such a shame."

"Nice evening," I choked out. "Every moon has a dark side. Every cloud has a diamond lining."

Remarkable, really, how the magic wriggling around inside me managed to translate every thwarted attempt at speech into small talk and platitudes.

At least I'd tried.

"Indeed," Larkspur agreed.

She was clutching my right wrist with both hands. My arm all but vibrated as it fought to rip free. Her arms shook, too, as she hung onto me.

Luckily, my body wasn't clever enough to immediately start pounding away with my left hand. Or switch to kicking the glass wall down instead. Hopefully my thinking that wouldn't give it any bright ideas.

"I can recommend two courses of action." Larkspur's voice was still unsteady from the sheer effort it took to stop me.

"One—you could try to puppeteer the mage who originated those cuttings inside you. My husband. You could make him go berserk, or use his own magic on him. Force him to kill himself.

"His death would nullify every cutting he's ever made. Including the ones inside you. It would save all the other victims of vorpal rabies, to boot.

"But have you ever puppeteered a mage before?" Larkspur asked. "Might you need help getting started? Here's a small hint. Did you realize you can do it through a cutting, not merely through a still-connected magic branch?

"The cutting dies when its mage dies, after all—no matter how much time has passed since it was originally pruned. Even after being broken off, it still resonates with its creator.

"So it's certainly possible for you to play puppet-master with my husband. How kind of me to teach you that. I imagine you've stashed him quite a distance from here, though. That'll make it incredibly difficult. Especially if you have little or no past experience. I myself struggle to puppeteer any mage more than a scant few rooms away from me."

Technically possible? Sure. Maybe so.

Could I figure it out before the glass cage shattered, or my body shattered while attempting to break it?

No. I knew my limits. Larkspur was taunting me.

I knew what she was about to say next. I wanted to vomit.

"Your other choice," Larkspur said, "is to call over a mage capable of counteracting the cuttings inside you on short notice. Without metaphysically blowing your brains out."

She pursed her lips. "Hm—I can only think of one mage in the world who might have a chance at it."

I shook my head. I actually shook my head. From the outside it must've looked like some kind of involuntary spasm.

"I wonder—how well do you know her?" Larkspur asked slyly. "I wonder if she'll come when you call her?"

A buzzing like cicadas filled my ears. Judging by Larkspur's lack of reaction, I was the only one who could hear it.

I wondered if I could will myself into fainting. I wondered if that would solve it. Or would my unconscious body pick itself right off the ground and start ramming the glass cage again?

"I really must commend you for having the mental fortitude to bond with anyone." Larkspur's voice sounded very close now.

"I couldn't bring myself to be bound by a mage. Not even by my husband. Not even when I believed I loved him. The thought of bonding made me sick, somehow. On a visceral level. Really put me off my dinner.

"But I suppose we all have our little phobias. Truthfully, that sense of horror feels like an ancient memory now. Something that happened to another person. A character in a faraway fairy tale."

Eloquent though she was, she'd grown increasingly short of breath. Without warning, she let go of my arm.

My hand hovered uncertainly in the air for a moment. Then it recalled its purpose. It crashed into the prism-ridged glass. Pain called out to me dully, distant as the crack and whistling bloom of fireworks going off on the opposite bank of a river.

Larkspur put her hand in my other pocket. She withdrew the ring of Church keys and dangled them in front of me.

"Oh, what a relief," she said. "This should speed things up."

She knelt to test various keys in the lock fixed to the bottom of the glass door, right by the floor.

Kick her, I told my body. She's in my way. Kick the damn woman as hard as you can. Break her ribs.

My body didn't listen. It hammered away at the thick glass with both fists now. I had to make an effort not to look too closely at what had become of my hands.

"You think this is bad?" Larkspur asked, kneeling below me.

Unhurried, she switched calmly from one key to the next. There were only so many left on the ring to test.

"The urge to reach that vorpal hole will only increase over time. Even if I tried to keep holding you back, you'd drag me right in the hole with you.

"Can you feel it? Your body will react as soon as this door comes open. As soon as the barrier vanishes. There isn't much time left to decide."

She wanted me to call Wist. Which meant I shouldn't. Anything but that.

There was no definitive proof as to what became of people who fell through vorpal holes. If you simply stuck your arm in one, without stepping all the way through—your arm would vanish as if it had never existed. As if it'd been vaporized.

But who's to say the severed arm didn't carry on in another form, in another world?

Other worlds awaited on the far side of vorpal holes. That I knew for sure. Who's to say I'd stop existing if my body decided to fling itself down the vorpal hole on the other side of that glass?

No matter what kind of world I ended up in, Wist would come find me.

As long as I actually ended up somewhere. As long as I didn't instantly die.

Promise you'll call me.

Calling on her would play right into Larkspur's hands. Not that I understood Larkspur's plans. Or her full capabilities as a reverse healer.

Overall it was surely much safer for Wist to go world-hopping to come get me. I just had to gamble that diving in a vorpal hole wouldn't flat-out kill me.

Would Wist ever forgive me for taking that gamble?

Something clicked.

Larkspur straightened up, dusting off the lotus-pattern knees of her healer robes. She stood to one side of the glass door and pushed it in just a millimeter, as poised as a fancy theater usher.

The hinges whined as if the door had never been opened before. As if no one were meant to actually open it.

Fear swelled like a balloon in my chest, thin-stretched to the point of exploding. My body lurched into the door, shouldered its way through. I caught a glimpse of the impossible nauseating nothingness inside the vorpal hole.

The hole was twice my height and much wider than the doorway. No way to miss it just by making my body veer off too far to one side or another. At best, I'd still lose an arm and a leg.

Better to go in all the way, all at once. Better to go all the way through.

I couldn't hear what Larkspur was saying. I couldn't feel myself breathing. I couldn't feel my heart beating.

All I felt was the tender thread of the bond and the invasive magic cuttings swimming stomach-churning circles around it.

I was the one moving, yet because I had no control over myself, I was consumed by a sensation of stillness, of helplessness. I was the one hurtling toward the vorpal hole. But it felt instead as if the mouth of the vorpal hole had come to life, as if it were hurtling forward to devour me.

I realized far too late that I was already crying out with my whole being for Wist.

Stop, I told myself. Stop that. You already decided you wouldn't. Stop!

It came out as *Wist*. No sound or air or hope. The vorpal hole loomed close enough for my breath to pass through it, for my desperate breath to be swallowed up by hidden worlds on the other side. I couldn't stop my body. I couldn't even stop the pathetic keening voice inside me.

Wist. Wist. Please. Wist—

Wist—!

25

The Church of the Kraken saw Wist as something greater than human. A living deity, even.

Honestly, I couldn't fault them for it. In terms of raw potential world-changing power, Wist was objectively more qualified for godhood than anyone else since, well, the previous Kraken.

But she was far from invulnerable. Last year I'd seen her bereft of her magic. After she regained it, I'd seen her—from very close up—in berserk mode.

And then there was everything that had happened in our previous lives. Wist hadn't been able to stop me from dying. Nor had she anticipated the full consequences of bringing me back.

Yeah, I'd promised to call Wist if I needed her. That didn't mean it was necessarily the right thing to do.

The right thing to do would've been to turn the entire Church building into a perfect trap. To plan from the start on immediately killing or vanishing Larkspur. Instead, I'd let our similarities fool me into thinking I could talk my way into some kind of peaceful compromise.

I disgusted myself. Either I went way too far—like in the incident that got me sent to prison all those years ago. Or I didn't go nearly far enough. Like today.

Worse, faced with the unbearable yawning void of a vorpal hole right in front of my eyes, I didn't even have the guts to choke down the consequences of my own errors in judgment.

I didn't call Wist because I had made her a promise. I didn't call Wist because I had a clever plan for how to protect her from Larkspur, who clearly required more physical proximity to exercise her full skills in mage hijacking. If she were capable of doing anything to Wist across great distances, no need to waste all this time playing around with me.

She needed me to deliver Wist up to her for devouring.

I did exactly what she wanted. I called Wist because I couldn't stop myself. Because I was too weak to confront the kaleidoscopic emptiness within that vorpal hole all by myself. Because I was terrified, crumbling like a sand sculpture on the inside with Larkspur's rabies digging holes in my mind.

All excuses. There was no good reason.

I'd dreamt countless times of dying, but it had never felt like this. I was going to disappear forever inside that hole. I knew it all the way down to the root of the bond that burned like a fever inside me.

That hole was going to eat me and never let me go.

All I wanted in my overwhelmingly selfish last moment was Wist.

So I wasn't surprised when, rather than topple forward into the vorpal hole, I toppled into Wist. She'd appeared out of nowhere.

I'd known she would be there. I hadn't thought for a second that she might not come when I called.

She stood rigid. She was the sole physical obstacle between me and the hole my body still strained for. I felt her breathing quick and high in her chest.

A whisper of a sound came from behind us. A noise like balled-up paper kissing the floor.

If I had control over my body, I would've braced myself for pain. It would've been too late to make any real difference, of course.

But the porcupine quills never came.

My eyes still insisted on drilling down into the vorpal hole behind Wist. The bleary periphery of my magic perception just barely detected the needle-like magic that had come shooting out of Fanren's fallen business card.

Those countless long needles hung poised in the air around us. Frozen in place, they trembled like muscles vibrating in the effort to lift a weight too great to bear.

"Commendable reflexes," Larkspur said from the other side of the open door.

Wist didn't answer. She took a few dragging steps forward, pushing me further from the vorpal hole. The thwarted needles in the air swooped up and away to make room for us. They moved with the glinting precision of dragonflies.

My arms stretched past Wist, clawing feebly for the receding hole at her back.

Finally I managed to beat my thoughts into a pretense of cohesion. Into something resembling actual words.

Wist, I said through the bond. *Get us out of here. Port as far as you can.*

She was shaking her head. My body pressed up against hers as if it thought it had the strength to bulldoze both of us straight back into the vorpal hole.

Wist?

I can't, she said.

Wist didn't port anywhere. She threw me over her shoulder and stalked through the open door of the prismatic glass cage. Past Larkspur. Through the assembly of figurines with the very same dark-eyed face as her.

Wist's plain, soundless answer repeated itself dully in my head. I can't. I can't. I can't.

You can't flee? I finally managed to ask. *Did she already—*

My stupid body started kicking, twisting, flailing, as if every step away only served to aggravate its yearning for the oblivion of the vorpal hole. My wrists and ankles smacked passing statues.

There was something deeply wrong with my hands, already purple-red and contused and swollen. Hammering on the glass cage had only served to hammer my hands themselves into unrecognizable shapes.

The pain flowed past somewhere far below my consciousness: dirty water streaming through the darkness of hidden city sewers.

Larkspur strolled behind us, mingling with the crowd of statues, dropping crumpled business cards to her left and right as she went. Her gestures gave the impression of an attendant strewing flowers at some kind of overblown ceremony. A religious function for Wist, perhaps. Or a truly twisted wedding.

The porcupine needles should've been far too fast for Wist to block. I saw Larkspur tossing about her stolen cards. I never saw the needles coming.

Yet Wist stopped them every time. They popped into being at point-blank distance, golden and trembling with frustration, millimeters away from injecting us with debilitating pain.

Although I had to wonder what, if anything, they would succeed in making me feel in my current state.

Wist carried me to the open area beyond the forest of statues. Then she stopped. She stood like a general with her feet planted apart, her motionless copies lined up behind her, both arms needed to keep my uncooperative body from hurling itself headfirst at the nearest hard surface.

With effort, Wist lowered me to the floor.

It could've been a touching tableau, the way she cradled me, but it turned out more like a lopsided wrestling match. My limbs resisted with such blind fury that I may as well have been trying to fight off the reaper.

My field of vision was all over the place. Behind Wist, I glimpsed Larkspur counting her business cards. Not many left. She gave a small shrug and tucked the remainder back in her purse.

Glimmering needles filled the air thicker than a sky full of snowflakes, parting silently for Larkspur as she approached us.

Sorry, Wist said. *I can't do this gently.*

A jolt of her magic fried me.

I've never been struck by lightning, but I have to think it must be something like this.

The air evaporated from my lungs. My body locked in place, hard as a corpse, then relaxed. White spots ate at my vision. A sensation of fire devoured my broken hands, surging from elbows all the way down to spasming fingertips.

The worm-like cuttings from Larkspur's husband—the raw ingredients of vorpal rabies—rushed out of my flesh. A panicked exodus of little ghosts. They writhed as if prostrating themselves on the floor before Wist. They twisted up in desperate knots. They dissolved into soft sneeze-like puffs of dust.

I realized slowly that I'd turned my head to watch. I'd moved all on my own.

I could uncurl my fingers, too. They'd shrunk to their original size and color. No more distant drumbeat of swollen throbbing. I felt extraordinarily light. The lightness of getting a big haircut, of throwing off all your clothes, of life-threatening wounds being sealed by magic.

I sat up. I tried to tug at Wist. We had to get out of here.

"Tired already?" Larkspur said from behind Wist. "I recall you having more stamina in the past."

She had one hand tucked in her purse.

Wist still said nothing. There was a look on her face I hardly recognized. Not the standard blank neutrality. Wiped of emotion, yes, but locked instead in an attitude of utter concentration.

The whispery fabric of her long summer jacket pooled on the floor around her, shushing as she twisted to glare at Larkspur.

"You let me do that," Wist said.

"Do what?" Larkspur asked.

"You let me purge the rabies. You let me fix her hands."

Larkspur's smile deepened. "I was curious to see how you would handle it. It's been a while, Magus Shien."

"I'm not on the Board of Magi anymore." A puzzled pause. "I'd already left the Board by the time you treated me."

"My mistake," Larkspur said graciously. "Shall I call you the Kraken, then?"

As they spoke, illuminated by the warm false glow falling from the skylights, I crept away backwards on wavering legs.

There was no way Larkspur wouldn't notice me moving. Just had to hope she wouldn't read too much into it.

Here in this shrine, it seemed Wist was now physically close enough for Larkspur to do—something—to throttle her magic use.

I had no idea how she was doing it. She wasn't touching any of Wist's magic branches. She hadn't tried to touch Wist at all, period.

Regardless, it had to be something much more severe and restrictive than simply blocking off Wist's porting abilities. If not, Wist could've already put Larkspur to sleep or stopped her time or made her forget why she was here or erased us from her awareness. Or any number of other solutions.

I wondered if our practice was paying off. Was Wist's resistance to being hijacked partly working, in some faint subtle fashion? Were her attempts at resistance perhaps more effective with a healer not bonded to her, a healer who knew her magic less intimately? Or was Larkspur so confident in her superiority that she could afford to take her time, to toy with us?

They were still talking. It mostly sounded like Larkspur reminiscing. Wist's voice came out low and uninflected.

I inched all the way over to the wall, stopping only when I bumped up against the long empty row of fiddle-back wooden chairs.

I straightened up without making a sound.

"As I recall," Larkspur said to Wist—I had to strain to hear everything—"you have extraordinarily high pain tolerance. I remember being very impressed."

"Could you have done this to me back then?" Wist gestured at herself.

"Taken control of your magic? But of course."

"Why didn't you?"

"What a peculiar question," Larkspur said. "Why would I? At the time, I had no reason to annex you."

This silenced Wist for a good long second. Then she said the exact thing I was screaming on the inside. "Not to brag, but there are countless people—organizations—nations—all over the world who would do anything for a chance to control me."

"Indeed they would."

"You simply weren't interested?"

"Not back then," Larkspur said. "No disrespect meant."

"None taken," Wist said dryly. "What's changed?"

As Wist spoke, as Larkspur focused on Wist alone, I grabbed the carved wooden back of the nearest antique-style chair. I bounded two, three huge steps across the room with it before hurling it at Larkspur's head.

She ducked just in time. The chair crashed spectacularly into an unfortunate statue.

I grabbed Wist's hand and pulled her as hard as I could toward the double doors at the front of the building.

Harsh breaths rasped in and out of my chest, too fast to catch. Only now that we were sprinting did I realize Wist had arrived completely barefoot. But if Wist couldn't port, if she couldn't get us out of here with any kind of magic, then what choice did we have but to run like hell?

Wist stumbled. She almost yanked me down with her. We were so close to the doors—the doors I'd stooped to lock myself.

Now Larkspur had the keys. I wished I could grab another one of those mahogany chairs and beat my past self over the head with it.

I tugged at Wist anyway. Perhaps we could hurl ourselves hard enough to break the lock. Perhaps we could reroute toward the nearest window.

Wist faltered. Then came to a complete stop, pulling me up short.

She remained rooted in place, one knee back on the floor. Her fingers would've slipped through mine if I hadn't caught at them harder. Her palm had suddenly gone slick and clammy.

"About that pain tolerance," Larkspur called from back by the statues, utterly unhurried.

Now I saw it. No more golden needles of magic glittering suspended like frozen confetti. The needles were all in Wist now. A dozen or more cards' worth of torture all at once.

Her head was bent. I couldn't see her face.

For a long moment she didn't make a sound. But only because she wasn't breathing. I realized it gradually, then all at once, as she sucked in air for the first time in many seconds. Her bowed back quivered. The sound of that breath made my own lungs cringe up inside me.

I had no idea what she was experiencing. I couldn't even imagine it.

"I suspect the Kraken won't be able to speak for some time," Larkspur said to me.

She took her time approaching, as if strolling about to admire her garden. She stopped a few feet from me and Wist. She smoothed the modest sleeves of her healer robes.

Wist's breathing sounded like something getting cut open by a serrated knife. Sometimes her hand went limp in mine. Sometimes it gripped my hand as if trying to wring blood from it. I too hung onto Wist for dear life. I didn't know what else to do.

Any pretense I'd had at clever stratagems hung ruined in my head, spiderwebs slashed apart by a quick swipe of a hiker's stick. I couldn't think of how to reconstruct them. I couldn't think, period.

Wist was in agony, and here I stood, a helpless fool, hobbled by my own arrogance.

Wist was in agony.

The cards were supposed to torture everyone within a twenty-foot radius. Everyone except the person who'd dropped them.

So why not me?

Why only Wist?

"It seems that the Kraken's pain tolerance remains as world-class as her magic," Larkspur remarked. "I let her pause those needles. Until I didn't."

She reached back to adjust her sagging bun. "I must tell you, I was quite surprised she found a way to make sure all the needles hit her and her alone. You didn't feel so much as a twinge of pain, did you? Astonishing."

Larkspur eyed me sideways as she kept fiddling idly with the angle of her hair sticks.

"I suppose the Kraken felt she had no choice but to spare you," she said thoughtfully. "She must have been sure you couldn't take it. She must see you as weak and frail, a flower in need of protection. Very chivalrous."

"I doubt it." I sounded like a dullard. I sounded like I'd already accepted defeat.

Larkspur continued. I may as well have been a lifeless scarecrow. Clearly she'd say what she wanted to say regardless.

"There's one thing I've always found terribly fascinating about the Kraken." She leaned in closer to me and lowered her voice as if confiding a secret.

Not that it would stop Wist from hearing us, if Wist were capable of processing speech right now.

"When government officials introduced me to her, they said most healers weren't capable of making much of a dent in her pain. Her magic was too complex, too easily tangled. The effects of most healers' work would vanish far too fast.

"Or so they said. I saw it with my own eyes, of course. I could smooth out her magic branches in a superficial sort of way, but I couldn't bring her anything resembling true, deep relief. Nor did she seem to expect it.

"That's all very well. But I found myself extremely puzzled. True, none of the healers the government brought to her could render her utterly pain-free. But she still seemed to resist every effort to make her life easier. She came in for healing only when she absolutely needed it. Not just for pain relief, but to stave off the risk of going berserk.

"If she wanted her pain eased, she could have demanded to be healed every day. Every hour, even. The mageocracy wouldn't have hesitated to help supply her with plenty of healers.

"Yes, some of her suffering lay in a place none of us healers seemed able to touch. But the rest of it—frankly, she chose it. She brought it on herself. She delayed healing, skipped appointments. As if she wanted to suffer as much as she possibly could.

"It looked to me as if she were forcing herself to do penance. Punishing herself somehow."

Larkspur's voice came very close to my ear now. "Perhaps you know what I mean?"

"—"

Wist had mumbled something, or tried to. We both looked at her. Her damp hand convulsed in mine again, then tightened.

"Step—back," Wist said from her spot on the floor below us.

Larkspur laughed. "Jealous? No need to be. I can certainly promise you that." She made a show of shifting a short distance away.

Her eyes lingered curiously on Wist, but when no more words seemed forthcoming, she turned to me again.

"Ah, yes," she said. "I neglected to tell you about your other mistake."

"My other mistake," I repeated slowly. "Pretty sure I've made way more than just two."

All I could smell was my own rank sweat, sour with sublimated panic. Larkspur gave a light, polite laugh.

Whatever I'd said—milliseconds later, I'd already clean forgotten—I hadn't meant it as a joke. Even if I had, I was pretty sure it hadn't been particularly funny. Perhaps this entire situation was a bit of a joke to her.

"Your other mistake," Larkspur said serenely, "was in thinking that the Kraken only gave me one of these."

The clasp of her handbag was already turned open, her right hand resting inside it as if tucked in a warm winter muff.

I had no idea what she meant until she took out a flawless chrysanthemum, blinding white and so perfect in form that it looked downright fake. Despite having been stashed at the bottom of her purse all this time.

"She gave me two," Larkspur explained. "One to thank me for my services. One in memory of my husband, though she'd never met him in person. So very thoughtful.

"I remember her telling me—in a clumsy sort of way—that she knew what it was like. To lose the love of your life. To be rent apart from someone whose loss made it feel as if you yourself were dying.

"I remember wondering what in the world she was talking about. I've heard that sort of thing plenty of times since my husband was presumed dead, of course. Always quite difficult to relate to."

Somewhere far disconnected from my brain, I felt my legs fold up beneath me. I found myself sitting limply next to Wist.

She knelt there rigid, her fingers twisted in mine. Stray drops of sweat from her face gleamed cold and still on the merciless floor.

Larkspur gazed down at us with the air of an underwhelmed schoolteacher. I stared at her gloved fingers holding the light green stem of the many-petaled chrysanthemum.

I hadn't taken the other white flower out of her house because I understood exactly what she could do with it. I reckoned she must've wanted it for a reason. But for all I knew, that reason was to fill up a lonely spot on her desk or in her trophy cabinet.

I just didn't like the idea of her having it.

Nor could I blame Wist for forgetting she'd given Larkspur two chrysanthemums, not one. A minor bit of preservation magic, a gift sent years ago to someone she'd met a handful of times at most—I'd have been more surprised if Wist remembered it in detail.

Have you ever puppeteered a mage before? Larkspur had asked me as my body fought to pound at the glass cage around the vorpal hole. *Did you realize you can do it through a cutting?*

Now she lifted the chrysanthemum to her nose, pretending to smell it. In reality, I doubted it had much of a fragrance. The old cutting of Wist's magic curled around the stem like a ghostly tendril from a parasitic vine.

Larkspur twirled the stem between her forefinger and thumb. A tiny, tiny tremor flowed through the curlicue cutting.

An answering tremor flowed through the innumerable magic branches seething inside Wist.

The golden needles piercing her were starting to fade and gutter. But each time Larkspur twirled the chrysanthemum stem, Wist's body clenched inward as if she'd been lanced in the gut.

Without even thinking about it, I reached out to heal her.

Wist's magic branches fled me like a pack of startled snakes.

I put a hand on her lower back. Her core couldn't writhe and dodge like her branches, but it cringed as far as it could from me. Even if I managed to brush at a thread of her magic, it would curl itself up into a completely different shape right afterward. Almost the opposite of what I'd been intending.

"Feels rather like a game of tag, doesn't it?" said Larkspur.

I looked up. She was still smiling. She raised her chrysanthemum like a glass of wine.

Wist made a muffled teeth-crunching noise next to me. She ground her knuckles into her forehead, as if to keep the pain from overflowing. I could almost envision it gushing out through her helpless fingers. A few long sparkling needles still impaled her back, her skull, her neck. They stuttered erratically in and out of sight.

Wist, I said through the bond. *How bad is it? Can you move?*

....

Wist?

I can move. Wist sounded strained even inside my mind, even without actually speaking.

You sure?

She's tied up my magic. Not my body.

I locked eyes with Larkspur as I spoke to Wist. Larkspur's control over Wist didn't seem to extend to the bond, at least.

Either she couldn't listen in on us, or she was a phenomenal actress.

"How do you do it?" I asked in all sincerity.

"Trade secret," Larkspur said blithely. "Although one would think the Magebreaker could tell simply from looking."

"Sure," I said, "but it's been a rough day. Maybe slow down a little?"

When I say now, I told Wist, *knock her down. Hard as you can. I'll go for the flower.*

"If you were quicker on the uptake, you could already have launched a counterattack," Larkspur said.

I gave her half a shrug. "Sorry for being slow-witted. I'm new to this whole mage hijacking gig."

She opened her mouth to answer.

NOW!

Wist slammed into Larkspur's knees like a wrestler going for a takedown, a wild hog on the attack.

I dove for the chrysanthemum before Larkspur even hit the ground. For a second the wide whites of her eyes pierced my sight. My fingers scrabbled at her dark prim robes, her arm—

Something crashed into me harder than Wist tackling Larkspur.

I felt myself briefly in the air, bewildered. I hit the ground or maybe the wall. I was too disoriented to tell.

For a few seconds the impact squelched out my senses. My eyes were packed full of gray-white fog. My magic perception became littered with nonexistent phantom sparks. They winked in and out like the stars you hallucinate when blood pressure drops hard. No sounds reached me but incoherent voices, garbled as if passing through water, and a distant ringing in my ears.

Eventually my sloshing consciousness settled back into my body. My cranium ached like hell. I blinked as I began to regain my sight.

I was slumped at the base of the largest statue. One well over twice the height of the real Wist.

Larkspur and Wist were both on their feet again. Larkspur's silver bun had unraveled halfway down her back. She didn't otherwise look much worse off than before we'd assaulted her. She'd moved further away from Wist. To what she now judged to be a safer distance, perhaps.

She still held the enchanted chrysanthemum.

Wist stood frozen, her eyes fixed on—I couldn't tell what, actually. Maybe the floor beneath me. A single transparent magic branch lashed at her feet in the manner of a long muscular tail, then coiled itself up like a hose and vanished inside her. She had her right hand pressed to her mouth.

I touched my own lip and felt blood on it. Hot puffy skin. I ran my tongue over my teeth. Didn't seem to be any missing yet.

Something had definitely hit me in the torso, too. A lot harder than on my face. Maybe the magic on my flak jacket had dulled the blow. Or maybe I was just feeling the aftermath of crash-landing into the largest statue in the room.

"You shouldn't have done that."

Wist spoke with, if anything, even less emotion than usual. Without lifting her gaze. But something about the sound of her voice made me want to crawl up under the statue's long mage robes, hide there in the dark like a field mouse quaking in the hollow of a tree.

"I might say the same to you," Larkspur replied, unfazed. "Physical violence? That's a remarkably crass tactic, coming from the Kraken and the Magebreaker."

"You shouldn't have done that," Wist repeated.

"Me?" Larkspur said. "I did nothing. I tweaked your magic just a fraction. Only in self-defense, of course. I'm afraid I'm not terribly well-versed in hand-to-hand combat."

"You shouldn't have done that."

"I didn't lay a finger on her." Larkspur reached back with her free hand and plucked out her hair sticks, tucked them at an angle in her handbag. "*Your* magic hit your healer. Your magic sent her flying."

She glanced between Wist and me with interest. "Don't tell me you've never hit her before?"

I swallowed a sticky welling mix of saliva and blood. Didn't seem right to spit on the Church floor. We'd already gotten the room plenty messed up.

Wist's hand dropped to her side.

"You shouldn't have done that," she said, her voice almost vanishing, only audible because there were no other sources of sound in the entire shrine except the three of us.

Perhaps Larkspur thought Wist was trying to snarl some kind of warning. To me it seemed obvious that Wist was talking to herself, and only herself.

Our eyes met.

Wist was—

Wist was terrified.

My chest constricted.

She made a half-turn toward Larkspur, ready to lunge at her.

Chains of Wist's own magic sprouted from her spine—shot down into the floor—leashed her in place.

Larkspur, well out of reach, rotated the chrysanthemum this way and that as if to inspect it for blemishes.

Wist strained for a moment longer. Then she stopped. The soundless chains sagged. She looked at me again. Something unidentifiable passed through her face.

I'm sorry, she said without moving. *Please come find me.*

Her body folded itself up with a surprising gentleness. The magical chains piled limp on the floor around her, unneeded.

Her lips were still parted, as though snagged on the syllables of an unfinished thought. Half-closed black eyes stared out at the lavishly robed legs of all the statues carved in her image.

Larkspur watched for a few cautious moments. Then she walked right up to Wist with small neat steps. She stood with her little boots lined up right next to each other.

"I see," she said. "A strategic retreat. Yet the only place she can flee is inside herself. Not quite a successful escape."

"Why're you doing this?" My voice had gone gravelly. "Because I took your husband—your favorite toy? Because I took your fish?"

"Hardly," said Larkspur. "I can abide by the principle of finders keepers."

She stooped to prod at Wist's core. An iridescent film of Wist's magic streamed out to coat the building, melting into every surface and corner of the walls, windows, ceiling, floor. A magical skill for soundproofing. For privacy. For hiding things.

Larkspur frowned. "Not quite what I was looking for."

"Why," I said through my teeth, "are you doing this?"

She paused to glance back at me, as if only now remembering my question. "Yes," she said, "I wanted to meet the Magebreaker. But you don't really live up to the name, now do you?"

"What, so you think you have to punish me for it?"

"Don't think I have any hard feelings toward you personally. The solution to a puzzle—a mystery, a riddle—the solution always brings the puzzle to an end, doesn't it? I was intrigued by you. Now I'm solving you. Using only the tools you yourself provided."

Larkspur kept poking at the thicket of branches coming out of Wist's magic core.

"I'll admit this is highly inconvenient," she said. "It was much easier to locate specific skills before she decided to go unconscious. Now it feels rather like flipping through a disordered dictionary in search of one single tiny word.

"She has so many empty branches, too. Far more than I recall seeing the last time I treated her. It's a bit shocking to look at, to be candid. Such a waste of potential. I was so sure the Kraken would have a much fuller skill set at this stage in her life."

I pushed myself heavily to my feet. Couldn't seem to do it quietly.

Apropos of nothing, woody wisteria vines unfurled from the base of the statues. They wound upward in creaking spirals, dangled soft purple cascades of hanging flowers, grew delicate stems of matching leaflets. Larkspur clicked her tongue.

"You're a gardener," I said. "You ought to appreciate this sort of magic."

"Oh, but it's really not the same as growing them yourself."

I limped closer to her and Wist.

"What are you planning to do this time?" Larkspur asked conversationally.

"Take a guess."

"Hmm. Strangle me, perhaps? Do you have the strength?"

"I'll find the strength somewhere," I said. "Trust me."

I reached my arms out. She had a slender neck, the skin a bit tired but not quite sagging yet.

My fingers closed on empty space.

"There we go," Larkspur said from behind me.

I turned. She and Wist had ported back among the statues. She knelt and plucked at Wist's magic branches as if they were harp strings.

The shrine roof vanished, taking with it the light-shedding panes of glass. Evening darkness filled the building, so total and sudden that I could see almost nothing.

"Let's put that back," Larkspur said.

The ceiling returned instantly, together with the Suncatcher skylights. Confused bright splotches played across my dazzled field of sight, then fuzzed away.

I took another few steps toward Larkspur. What was left for me to do but chase her?

A black lance materialized in the air high above Wist. Piercer. Larkspur made a delighted noise.

I don't know why I thought she was about to plunge the lance straight down into Wist. I truly don't know why I thought that. The image of it happening rocked me as if the lance were already falling, already nailing Wist to the sanctuary floor.

I hurled myself forward as if I thought I could leap up and catch the damn thing with my bare hands.

Instead—of course—the lance shot at me like a bullet. I ran straight into it.

I stopped.

I looked down, expecting to see myself impaled like lunch meat on a toothpick, my torso torn open.

But there was no blood, no organs, no shock. The flak jacket remained intact, as if nothing had touched it.

The lance hung in the air, perpendicular to the floor, its deadliest point kissing a spot right over my breastbone.

Then it burst apart into a cloud of mystified black flies.

What could stop Wist's magic? More of her own magic. The new cuttings she'd added to upgrade Fanren's vest. They hadn't been able to offer any protection against something as intangible as vorpal rabies. But a direct attack with a stabbing weapon? No problem. I let out a long shuddering breath.

"My," Larkspur said. "That's annoying."

I cleared my throat. "I know what your deal is."

"Do you?"

"You're like a lone predator. A leopard or something. One of those animals that can't bear to share territory with another of its kind. That's why you felt compelled to spread vorpal rabies, drive mages berserk. That's why you thought I'd get your message. *This is my city*. Same as a leopard peeing to leave its scent, or scratching up tree trunks."

"I'm not sure I agree," she said. "You make it sound awfully primitive."

She'd straightened up to meet my stare. Yet she still nudged Wist's magic with the toe of her boot. It looked like a pianist pumping pedals.

A long sword pushed up out of Wist's chest. Larkspur took the newborn hilt in both hands, lifted it with some difficulty. The tip of the blade emerged bloodlessly, leaving Wist's black shirt intact as it passed.

Larkspur shook her head. She laid the sword down with a gentle thunk beside her.

"Not quite for me," she said.

She reached in her bag.

I didn't know how to use a sword, either, but I threw myself at it anyway.

At the same time, Larkspur tossed something in the air. Two somethings. Small and dark, they veered toward me, buoyed forward by Wist's magic. Zero Gravity.

The dark things swooped at me like bats. I ducked. My hand closed around the hilt of the sword.

Those flying shapes were blunt-ended hair sticks, I realized, a split-second before both of them plunged into my eye.

26

Because I'm a moron, I kept trying to lift the sword Wist had birthed. It jerked down out of my fingers. That's how it felt, anyway, as if the hilt were actively struggling to slip away from me. In reality it was probably just that my grip had gone weak.

I heard the sword hit the floor again. Couldn't see very well. It looked as if it immediately melted into a puddle of useless water. Thanks, Larkspur.

You might wonder why I wasn't screaming. I may very well have been, but I was a bit too preoccupied to take note of it. Time was very slow, and my thoughts were very fast.

I'd never experienced adrenaline like this. It came in like a riptide, strong enough to knock me off my feet. Almost strong enough to disconnect me from my body. It flooded away any burgeoning hints of pain.

I took a single staggering step closer to Larkspur and Wist before recalling that I had two hair sticks impaling my right eye. More to the point, I had no real plan for what to do next.

"Here you—here you were—"

"I know little of you," Larkspur said, "yet this seems so unlike you. Are you finding it difficult to speak?"

"You were—you called—" The words made sense in my head, but they would only leave my mouth in retching fits and starts.

"—called my tactics crude." I gestured at my face. "What's this?"

"Blame the Kraken," said Larkspur. "Her little game of playing dead. It's become too much of a hassle to access high-level skills."

Well, that explained why Larkspur hadn't jumped straight to stopping my heart in my chest, or transmuting my brain into a hunk of cold marble, or porting me into a trench at the bottom of the ocean.

I kept reaching spasmodically for the sticks in my eye. Then I'd think better of attempting to yank them out. My right eyelid had squinched as far shut as it could get. My left eye kept trying to clench shut, too, as if in sympathy.

It definitely felt far more difficult to parse the look on Larkspur's face now. But I was in no position to judge the precise visual effects of getting one of my eyes skewered. As opposed to the overall effects of sheer physical shock.

Thankfully, magic perception has no reliance on the eyes as a sensory organ. I understood what Larkspur meant once I focused on the body curled at her feet. Wist had rolled up her magic branches into a tight ball of yarn, an armored vault to shelter her buried self.

"If she was trying to make it more difficult for me, she succeeded," Larkspur told me. "Then again, I wonder what she thought would happen next. Surely she understood that this was only delaying the inevitable.

"What do you think, Magebreaker? Perhaps she had no grand strategy in mind. Perhaps she simply couldn't bear to stand there and watch herself hurt you."

I gripped my hands together to stop them from twitching up toward my face.

"Let me help you with that," Larkspur said.

I recoiled from her, but not nearly fast enough. Wist's Zero Gravity—wielded by Larkspur—wrenched out the hair sticks.

I made a witless noise from somewhere deep in my belly. Hot liquid cascaded from my right eye socket. More than just blood. There were all kinds of precious liquids in the eye, weren't there? I doubled over as if I thought I could catch the discharge and stuff it back inside.

"You look like something out of a horror story," Larkspur said. "Or one of the crueler fairy tales, perhaps. An urban legend."

I knew without her saying it that she would go for my left eye next. I knew before it happened that this tide of adrenaline could only carry me so far.

I knew without being a prophet that Wist would survive even if I didn't. She always did, somehow. And I couldn't let her wake up to find me with both my eyes gouged out. I couldn't. I couldn't.

The hair sticks were still floating and bobbing before me, borne up by Wist's magic, their matte wood surface now dark and wet and slick. They pulled back little by little, the string of a bow being drawn. Readying their shot.

I clutched at my chest as if I were having a heart attack. At the flak jacket Fanren had lent me. At the cuttings Wist had woven through the fabric to further strengthen it.

The flying hair sticks stopped so close to my left eye that I couldn't see them clearly. Just massive blobs, blunt and thick. The sticks oscillated in the air. They never quite managed to touch me.

There was no artistry in how I'd touched the cuttings Wist had left in my vest. It was like banging with both fists on a piano to interrupt the dazzling melody of a concerto. Like laying both forearms down to press as many keys as possible, solely to stymie the pianist.

I hadn't merely been lounging around like a dolt ever since Wist arrived. I'd been watching Larkspur manipulate the chrysanthemum's cutting. I'd been watching the specificity with which she touched it, how each touch resonated with the magic branches still rooted deep in Wist.

I was in no state to accomplish anything creative. The best I could come up with was a rough imitation.

"I'm impressed," said Larkspur.

"Sounds like faint praise." And I sounded like I had tuberculosis.

"You might very well be able to force a stalemate," she said.

"Already have."

"But how long will it last?" she asked tenderly. "How much blood can you afford to lose in the meantime?"

She had a point. I was getting dizzy. Sensations I very much didn't want to experience were starting to claw their way up from the dank ocean floor beneath my sea of adrenaline.

Meanwhile, Larkspur and I kept playing tug-of-war with Wist's magic.

Whether from her years of practice, or by dint of being in far better physical condition than me right now, Larkspur seemed like a much stronger hijacker.

I could just barely block the flying hair sticks from boring their way into my left eye socket. I couldn't seem to block her from toying with other skills at the same time.

Past the blur of the still-threatening sticks, past the sensation of horrible wetness all down the right side of my face and neck—soaking the top of my shirt beneath the protective vest—I saw sparrow-sized firebirds rocket off in every direction. They slammed into the Church walls and vanished. Larkspur hummed to herself.

I saw Wist's hair grow out like black water flowing across the floor, longer and longer, until it was even longer than the hair on the statues. It braided itself from top to bottom with inhuman efficiency.

"Now she looks the part," Larkspur said approvingly.

I kept pressing on Wist's cuttings in the flak jacket. Larkspur's hair sticks refused to relent. They made stabbing feints at my ear holes as well as at my one good eye. It was getting difficult to hold them at bay without holding my breath.

Wist's thick black braid zigzagged across the floor, traveling much further than the full length of her body, further than it should have been able to stretch. As if it were still growing. As if it could unspool unto infinity.

Her braid touched my ankle. It coiled up to touch my knee. It climbed higher.

I shifted my death grip on the cuttings in the vest. The hair sticks over my left eye quivered closer, touching my cornea, sticking there even when I yanked my head back.

The hair sticks followed me as I attempted to retreat. Wist's braid wound its way up to my shoulders, my neck. It curled around and around my throat like a scarf. It pulled tighter.

No need to worry about holding my breath now. I couldn't breathe at all.

Larkspur smiled with closed lips.

She'd questioned why Wist had fled to the well at the bottom of her own soul. Now—without air, with graying sight, with dammed-up pain pounding angrily on all my doors—I thought I knew.

Wist hadn't abandoned me. She hadn't succumbed to fear of what Larkspur was about to make her do to me.

She was making space for me. She was inviting me in.

What difference was there, after all, between me and Larkspur? Aside from being born a decade apart. Aside from one of us being much more of a sociopath than the other.

Wist and I were bonded.

What was the use of a bond, really?

Some mages found that it gave them a power boost. Some healers found that it gave them greater job security. For others, it was hell. Imagine being bonded to Shien Miyu.

A bonded mage could only be healed by their bondmate. And bonding greatly facilitated the healing process, even across great distances. Too bad it didn't seem to offer any protection from reverse healing, from hijacking.

On the other hand, perhaps it could facilitate that too. Perhaps, if I used the bond, I could hijack Wist better than anyone.

I already knew how to enter her. I'd done it the last time she collapsed like this, when she took hold of the Old River psychobomb. This time I'd have to use the bond in a different way—to take over her, to take control of her.

I didn't want to.

But the ends of the hair sticks ground harder against the surface of my eye. Wist's winding braid locked my legs in place, steadily constricted my throat.

Larkspur had been reduced to a smudge of dark robes in the background. My head felt like a balloon swelling past the snapping point. My heart stammered in my chest as if drumming out a slurred plea for mercy.

Inside myself, I touched the bond.

I fled my stifled bleeding body. I fled all the way into Wist. I assumed the empty throne she'd left behind.

A spectral hand erupted from Wist. It rammed Larkspur headfirst into the nearest statue. Then it rammed her again. Before she had a chance to plea with me. Before she had a chance to make a sound.

Larkspur had been right. With Wist all balled up inside herself to make room for me, the plainest, most rudimentary skills seemed the easiest to locate.

I was more in Wist's body than in my own now, but I could sense the braid loosen around my neck. Something light clattered to the floor. The hair sticks, perhaps.

The hand that had shot out of Wist was a thing of pure magic, colorless, formed of fluctuating ripples like light coming through water. And it was all me. Me, pulling the strings. Me making it ram Larkspur's skull into the giant majestic statue of Wist herself.

I'd always envied mages. I'd always resented the fact that they could do anything—anything!—if they really tried. If they were smart enough. Most of them weren't, of course. But look at me, look at what I could do as a healer. I was peerless (or so I'd believed, before meeting Larkspur). Just imagine how much more I could have done as a mage.

Of course I wanted magic. All my life I'd longed for magic. All my life I'd wished I were born as a mage. Even if I were far too proud to have ever said it out loud.

But like this?

The phantom hand dissipated. I felt my body—*my* body—gasping and coughing uncontrollably.

Larkspur hit the floor. She wasn't moving. Yet fear brimmed in me, almost worse than before. Think of killing a bug. Hit them once, twice, three times, and sometimes they still twitch back into movement.

This wasn't enough. I pictured Fanren in the arena, crushing that enormous vorpal beast with his Barrier. I groped for Wist's Barrier branch but couldn't find it. Instead I found myself holding Zero Gravity.

It was right there, after all. Larkspur had been using it to buoy up her hair sticks mere seconds ago.

Bury her, I thought.

Bury her so there's no chance she'll ever come back.

Erase her.

I cast Wist's Zero Gravity out like a fishing line. I cast it over every single statue in the sanctuary. Towering sculpts, life-size replicas, fragile figurines only as high as my knees. They rose as one, hovering as if borne up in flight by their many-layered carved robes.

They fell as one, rushing down toward Larkspur's body, crashing in the shape of a mountain, breaking each other in their heavy eagerness to crush her.

Stone smashed into wood. Undulating hair and sleeves and beautiful long fingers snapped off with a crack like tree boughs breaking. Some vanished in the pile. Some tumbled down and rolled away across the room.

The building shook beneath me when the statues plummeted. But the subtle luster of soundproofing magic lining the walls held true all the while.

I tumbled fully back into my own body, no longer bridging myself and Wist. Everything ached. My right eye saw nothing. My left eye was increasingly reluctant to open further than the narrowest of slits.

I still hung on to Wist's Zero Gravity branch through the bond. I flicked it to make statues pick themselves up out of the mountain and tumble away, head over heels, toss themselves aside. One at a time. As if searching through rubble after an earthquake.

The fallen statues were rife with the lush wisteria vines that Larkspur had grown while testing Wist's magic. Some clusters of flowers hung full and untouched. Some were flattened and covered in dust.

It took several minutes of searching to find the white chrysanthemum.

A colorful marble rendition of Wist had belly-flopped right on top of it. Yet it wasn't even the slightest bit crushed. Not a hint of dirt glazed the petals.

Blood crept toward the chrysanthemum along the shiny-smooth floor. My blood or Larkspur's? Maybe both. The trickle changed direction just before touching the dense cluster of white petals, curving away as if repulsed.

I forced Wist's magic to push aside more statues. The whole colossal heap shifted, groaned, seemed to threaten to come down right on top of my head.

Larkspur would've liked that.

Finally I glimpsed her hand and forearm, a scrap of a lotus-patterned sleeve. I crouched to take her pulse.

Of course she had none. Could've guessed that merely by observing the state of her hand, how it stuck out from beneath the ceiling-high stack of painted figures. Still, I couldn't say for sure if I'd really confirmed anything. My fingertips might be insensate. At this point, in fact, I'd bet on it.

I turned about and stumbled back over to Wist. I used her magic to heave us all the way over to the double doors, as far as possible from the piled statues. Just in case they got out of balance and decided to collapse in a landslide.

Wist's braid dragged across the entire floor of the shrine, impossibly long. A pitch-black tether stretching back toward her broken avatars, the faultless chrysanthemum, the macerated body of the woman I'd just murdered with her magic.

I didn't even feel sick. Not because of the brutal way I'd killed Larkspur, anyhow.

If I felt sick, it was because the area that had been my right eye had started to sear as if it cradled embers rather than remnants of an eyeball.

If I felt sick, it was because I wouldn't be able to hide any of this from Wist.

I slid down to sit next to her, my back to the locked doors. I'd buried the Church keys with Larkspur. At the moment, however, we had more pressing worries.

"Sorry, Wist," I said. Both in my head and with my voice, which sounded horrendous. Like me ninety years in the future. Like a completely different person.

I put a hand on her side. I could feel her breathing, slow and quiet. "Sorry," I rasped again. "You'll have to come find me this time."

I couldn't focus enough to keep clutching the bond, to keep twitching the reins of her magic. I leaned my head on the door. I called to Wist without any real strength.

Sure, I needed her. I needed her badly. But in my gut I didn't want her to see me like this.

Time settled around us like amber. Eventually I couldn't bear to sit up anymore. I slumped over on Wist.

My skull pounded. My neck throbbed. It took much, much longer than I'd expected to pass out. Or perhaps it only felt that way. In total, perhaps it was just a couple more brittle thin-stretched minutes. All I knew was that once we got out of here, I never wanted to set foot inside this accursed building again.

27

You can wake someone by shaking them, calling their name, ripping open their bedroom curtains, setting an analog alarm clock.

Alternatively, you can wake them with magic.

Being roused by magic is the best way, really. It never fails. It never leaves you groping around half-drowned in a sleepy stupor. I've seen luxury magical alarm clocks in department stores, but I've never owned one. My only experiences with being woken by magic come from Wist.

The vast majority of mages have a limited number of magic branches—one or two, or perhaps a handful—and so they have to choose their skill set very carefully. Especially if they use magic for a living.

The vast majority of mages could hardly afford to allocate an entire branch to a skill as relatively frivolous as being able to give someone a pleasant awakening.

My Wist, of course, had no such worries.

Her magic steered me awake so smoothly that I almost forgot I'd been sleeping. Passed out, rather.

I seemed to be curled up on a heap of blankets. Some sort of makeshift floor bed. I rolled onto my back and found Wist kneeling beside me.

I sat up. We were in the tower. The medical bay? I spotted the shadows of the life-support tanks. All but one were presumably still empty.

The commercial shutters normally used to cover the angular walls had fully retracted for the first time. They revealed a wan pre-dawn sky, a full 360-degree view of the horizon. Endless dark forest, mirage-like blueish mountains.

I wasn't blind. But nothing looked quite the way it should.

I reached up to touch my right eye. Wist caught my wrist.

"What?" I said. "I know it's gone. I mean, I can tell my sight's not the same."

"Just a reflex," she said after a moment.

Wist released me. My fingers touched something cottony. A medical eyepatch, probably. The puffy kind. Felt as if it were stuck on with surgical tape.

No pain whatsoever. Guess I had Wist to thank for that. But the absolute absence of pain heightened the nibbling sensation that something was lost from me. Something was missing.

I pushed that sensation aside.

"What'd you do with the body?" I asked.

"Put it in the vorpal hole at the back of the Church."

"Wow," I said. "You read my mind. What about the keys?"

"Locked them in the mailbox."

"Perfect." I twisted in my nest of blankets to face Wist head-on. "You were able to restore everything in the Church back to normal, then?"

"Took me the rest of the night," she said. "It's almost morning now."

I let out a deep breath.

It felt like the first time in a long time that my lungs had been able to fully deflate.

If Wist said she'd done it, that meant not even the sharpest-eyed Church staff would be able to tell anything had happened. No decapitated statues, naturally. No wild wisteria vines. No congealed puddles of blood. No evidence of murder.

I looked Wist in the eye. It was harder to focus than before.

Wist met my gaze—tolerated it—without uttering a sound. No outward signs that she'd gnashed her teeth or torn at her hair or cursed without anyone to hear her while I slept.

On the inside, her magic was a hideous mess.

"You need healing," I said. "You need healing right now."

"You're in no shape to—"

"How much magic did it take to fix the Church? All those statues? How are you even capable of staying upright?"

"I'm not—"

"Don't try to lie to me," I snarled. "I can tell from the look of your damn branches. I can feel it through the bond. You're in worse pain than—you might as well be stabbed full of those porcupine quills again."

I pushed at her, feebly, until she shifted to give me access to the small of her back. I closed my left eye. I rested my forehead on her spine as I pressed the tangles out of her branches, handful after handful of them, such a dizzying amount.

I lacked the energy to speak as I worked. But I could at least give her the bare minimum of necessary healing.

When I finished and raised my head, I saw her furtively reaching up to wipe at her face.

Wist, you utter imbecile. How long had she planned to keep enduring the agony in silence?

I gave her a few moments to get it together. "You okay?" I asked afterward.

"Me?"

"Who else?"

"You already healed my magic," she replied. "And I haven't lost any body parts. Not this time."

"I was fighting Larkspur for control of you," I said. "We were tussling over you for our lives, basically. Hard to believe you wouldn't still feel any of that."

Wist touched the side of her head. Her hair was back to its previous length. I wondered if she'd lobbed that long black braid down the Church vorpal hole after Larkspur.

"...It's like a hangover," she said. "I'll live."

"Going to turn me in?" I asked.

Wist stared.

"Just kidding. Hey, I thought it was funny."

She didn't so much as blink. I squirmed on the inside.

"Maybe you did lose something," I tried. A beat passed. "Your sense of humor?"

I'm not quite sure why, but for a second there I thought she wanted to slap me with both hands like a house fly. Instead she pulled me into her arms without a word, squashing the breath out of me. With the left side of my face crushed into her chest, I couldn't see a damn thing.

"I never thought—"

"Wist," I gasped, "you're suffocating me."

Only when she eased up a little did I realize she was shaking. "I never thought I would be the one to hurt you like this."

It wasn't much different from her standard colorless voice. But right now, somehow, she didn't sound merely empty of emotion. She sounded stripped bare of it, flayed raw with nothing left.

Because I'm chronically incapable of knowing when to hold my tongue, I said, "Frankly, it hurt more when you sent me to prison. And that was all you.

"This"—I pulled back to gesture at the right half of my face—"this was just Larkspur picking up your magic and using it as a handy tool. It's my eye she popped like a balloon. You better not mope about it more than I do."

For a long, long moment, Wist just sat there and examined my expression.

All she said in the end was: "You seem more upbeat than I would have expected."

"Yeah, bet you expected me to moan and groan and whimper my head off."

"I expect most people would," she said. "In the same situation."

"Don't worry. I'll do plenty of that later. It's difficult to wallow in a good solid whining session when we've still got business to take care of."

The aftermath of Larkspur's disappearance, for instance.

With all due respect, Larkspur wasn't anyone the government would consider important. A widowed middle-aged healer. At some point in the future, somebody would report her missing. Perhaps a private client, or perhaps an acquaintance from one of her teaching gigs. It might even end up being Mori.

"Trying to think of loose ends," I said. "Can you do a sweep of Larkspur's house? I want to get rid of my note. Wouldn't have left that if I were planning on killing her from the start. Also better hide any leftovers that might point to her husband being alive."

"Already done. But she brought the note to the Church. Kept it in her purse."

"You've been busy." I found myself grudgingly impressed. "Osmanthus is lucky you've never been very interested in using your powers for crime."

If Wist had already double-checked the house, there'd be little reason to worry about the Mage Police tracing Larkspur's absence back to the two of us.

At most, they might do a cursory search. They'd probably conclude she'd wandered off to die alone somewhere. People had a hard time imagining an unbonded, self-employed healer being happy. Especially one who used to have a high-status partner.

I breathed in all the way to the bottom of my lungs to ground myself.

"Then we've just got two issues left to deal with," I concluded. "One, how to explain my missing eye. Two, Larkspur's husband. We can put my eye off till later—for now I'll just pretend I have an infection. Or something. The real question is what to do about him."

I started to get up. Dizziness hit me with such sudden totality that it felt like being cut off at the knees.

I didn't quite understand what had happened until I came to realize that Wist's arm around me was the only thing keeping me on my feet.

She didn't utter a word. She knew how much I hated feeling weak.

We went over to peer down at the nameless man's tank. The sky outside grew steadily brighter. If we lingered here much longer, we'd need to put down the eastern shutters to keep the morning sun from scorching us. No sign of rain today, either.

"Technically speaking," I said as an aside, "this is all his fault. That's one way to look at it, anyhow."

"What did he do?"

Wist hadn't been there to hear most of my chit-chat with Larkspur.

"Tried to use some kind of brainwashing magic to force her to consent to bonding. She turned it around on him and broke him instead. She claimed she was never the same afterward.

"Maybe it's too neat of an excuse," I said. "I guess most attempts at bonding don't involve directly messing with someone's mind. Then again, other types of forced bonding happen all the time.

"There are mages no healer would feel comfortable saying no to. There are healers who have to take any mage they can get, just to survive. Financial distress, societal pressure—people bond for all kinds of reasons.

"Mori only got out of it because you intervened on his behalf. And me—if we'd never met, right now I'd probably be bonded to someone like your sister."

"Then I'm glad I'm the Kraken," Wist said quietly.

I couldn't look at her. I gazed dazedly down at the grizzled face of Larkspur's husband, his features warped by the pink fluid filling his coffin-tank.

I'd never heard Wist say that before. Not once. Not even when we were teenagers. Not even when the government first certified her.

Being the Kraken had brought her nothing but a gravity of responsibility that no single person could realistically bear. Being the Kraken had brought her nothing but a terror of messing up, of making things worse. Only the Kraken could look at the vorpal hole that had swallowed an elementary school and wonder if maybe there was something she could've done to prevent it.

What had she gotten in exchange? Unfathomable guilt and two lifetimes chained to me. I mean, look, I like myself way more than I deserve. Parts of life would've been downright unendurable if I didn't love myself to pieces, underneath it all.

Still, I'm not nearly so foolish as to think that I'm enough to make up for the burden of being the Kraken. If Wist had ever felt that—even for a second—she was deluded. A madwoman.

I leaned sideways against her shoulder, arms tight around her middle. The backs of my eyes burned, the right side no less than the left.

Finally I managed to mutter: "I should be the one saying that. I should be the one telling you I'm glad you're the Kraken. But I'm not glad it's made you suffer."

She put a hand up around my head, fingers digging idle furrows through my short tufty hair. "We've both suffered," she said. "The suffering balances out in the end."

28

I DEVELOPED A multi-step plan for taking care of Larkspur's husband.

First, Wist barged in on the NHRI facility housing all the remaining victims of vorpal rabies. She didn't ask for permission. She just showed up there and purged them of the prion-like cuttings, the same way as she'd figured out how to purge me in the Church of the Kraken.

I'd only had vorpal rabies for a few minutes. Well under half an hour in total. The others had remained in its grip for weeks or months on end. It would take them far, far longer to feel comfortable leading normal lives. (Whatever a normal life is.) But at least the government no longer had a handy excuse to keep them trapped in isolation.

Meanwhile, I hovered over Larkspur's husband day in and day out, hour after hour, striving to erase his skill set.

Nearly every single one of his skills were illegal. Incriminating. We couldn't safely release him unless we succeeded in blanking out each of his branches. So he couldn't use any of his old magic skills, not even by accident, and no one could tell which skills he used to possess in the first place.

It was a tedious, exhausting, and highly technical process. No instruction manual for how to do it. No guarantee that it was even possible.

I supposed I had Larkspur to thank for making me wonder about what other feats I might be capable of as a healer.

If I were in peak condition, perhaps I could've done it faster. My one good eye felt constantly strained, like a pulled muscle never given a chance to heal. I kept getting strange cricks in my neck. Sometimes my missing eye showed me phantom shapes. Ghostly blots of color. Nothing with any meaning. Less formless than a dream.

Anyway—it felt like it took forever, but I figured out how to strip out the skills imprinted on each and every one of his branches. I did it. I turned the man's magic into a blank canvas.

Next I asked Wist to erase his memory of his identity—of his whole life from childhood—as thoroughly as she could.

We weren't planning to adopt him. And barring that, it was unrealistic to think his identity would forever remain a mystery.

Someday, somebody would figure out who he was. Someday, somebody from his former agency would track him down.

My hope was that when the time came, they'd realize he was devoid of the secret skills they'd once assigned him. Devoid of any memory of having ever worked for them.

There'd be no way for them to determine why he'd suddenly turned up alive or where he'd been all this time. If he was lucky, they'd decide there was nothing to be gained from keeping him in custody.

We made sure all the bedsores were cleanly healed over. We gave him an amateur haircut and a fresh outfit. Wist's magic kept him from waking, from ever seeing us.

In the end, Wist ported him to the street outside that one little cafe in the city of Philomena. She placed him sleeping by the door just before opening hours.

We watched from a distance, over by the train station, as the cafe owner came out and stooped to look closer at him. Beside me, Wist silently released the magic locking the man deep in unconsciousness.

Perhaps the owner would deliver this mystery visitor to the local MPs. Perhaps he'd consult with his regulars. The one woman who worked as a psychobomb survivor's caretaker, for instance. Or perhaps the owner would first take him straight to a hospital.

I wondered if he would ever again have the urge to make art like the shattered-looking sketches I'd seen on Larkspur's walls.

I wondered if he'd expected to succeed in hijacking Larkspur's mind, in forcing her to bond. What had he fancied would happen next? A romantic escape to distant lands? A happy ending?

Summer passed in a haze after we turned our backs on Larkspur's husband. The rainy season lifted. Cicadas screeched all day and seemingly all night.

Mori mentioned to me once, in passing, that he couldn't seem to get in touch with Larkspur. He told me later that he was getting worried about her. He told me later still that she'd been declared missing.

"That's so strange," I said. "Hope she's safe. Hope they find her."

Mori asked—very tentatively—if there was a reason I'd wanted him to take Larkspur out to lunch that one time.

"Oh, that? You have to admit she's eccentric." I described the trophies she'd collected from mages like Wist and her sister Miyu. "Made me want to check into her background a little. Didn't turn up anything suspicious, though."

I'd meant to end the topic there. Instead I heard myself saying: "I only met her that one time. But I do get why you've got so much respect for her. She's got her quirks. But I can see her—I can see her being a great teacher."

Mori made a sniffling noise. Heaven help me.

I wondered if Larkspur's students had meant anything at all to her. I wondered if she'd been capable of caring about them. Or if she'd wanted to, but couldn't. Or if she hadn't even been able to want it.

She'd gone through years with a smile on her face, her husband locked inside his own body, and the equivalent of a vorpal hole gaping open deep within her. A hole he himself had torn in her, whether accidentally or on purpose. A hole that swallowed everything equally, guilt and despair and fear and compassion alike.

I pictured the hydrangea bushes in front of Larkspur's house growing wild without anyone to cut them back. The heavy flower heads would age from resplendent purple to a murky wine-red, then wither away to hoary brown without ever falling.

The dead dry flowers would hold their shape all winter. They might even last untouched till next spring.

Wist studied top-of-the-line magical prosthetic eyes until she could replicate one for me. It would do far more to improve my appearance than to improve my vision, though it was better than nothing. No magic skills in existence could fully replace human eyesight.

Given enough opportunities to experiment, Wist could invent an appropriate skill from scratch. She kept telling me that. She kept telling me to let her do it.

I shook my head. Sure, she could try. But the effort might eat up months or entire years of her time. The Kraken's time. She still had thousands more old lost branch skills that she needed to work on relearning first, in my opinion.

I didn't care so much about being able to see perfectly. Not for the time being.

I could live like this. Just didn't want anyone in PubSec to notice my eye was gone, or to wonder what had happened.

I needed to be extra careful when pouring myself a tall glass of water, when browning sausages over the stove or walking down staircases. The world seemed to shift around me like a trickster, sometimes dancing too close—I knocked over a lot of bottles and shampoo pouches in the shower—and sometimes hovering just a fraction further out of reach than my vision suggested.

I knew I could get used to this. All I needed was time and a healthy dose of caution.

Yet even after Wist gave me a prosthetic that looked convincing enough (from the outside, anyway) for me to stop wearing an eyepatch, I found myself utterly devoid of motivation to leave the tower.

At the height of midsummer, I'd lie in the shade of one of the rooftop gardens. I'd feel hot air—hardly pleasant enough to call a breeze—pass over my motionless skin.

Sometimes Turtle the cat would stop by to watch me suspiciously. Sometimes I instead retreated to the coolness of the tower's sandy planetarium.

I could spend hours that way, Wist's perfect false eye rooted firmly in my face, zero thoughts in my head.

I couldn't even remember the last time I'd stepped in my city apartment. My rent and all the bills would get deducted automatically anyway. Wasn't like I had a pet there to take care of.

"Manatree's been asking after you," Wist said once.

"Tell her I'm having a midlife crisis."

I wasn't sure if Wist obliged. I knew I'd have to get back to hobbling mages eventually, though. And I did. I performed my job perfectly. Manatree didn't suspect a thing, if I do say so myself.

Even if she did harbor suspicions, she had nothing to base them on.

By the end of summer, PubSec decided to dissolve their new task force. You know—the one they'd created to investigate the recent mini-epidemic of berserking mages. Without anyone understanding why, new cases had dropped back to normal levels.

Larkspur was dead. No one remained to vouch for her, to vet my memory of the things she'd said to me.

She'd asked me if I had a purpose in life. I didn't think she'd ever actually spoken the words *What good is the Magebreaker?* or *What is the Magebreaker for?*

Those, however, were the words I kept hearing in my distorted memory of her forever-gone voice.

What good was I? What was the point of me? What was I for?

I could counter that easily. What was anyone for? You didn't need a higher purpose to justify the mere act of existing, of eating your greens and blowing your nose and generally trying not to cause more trouble to the world than you're worth.

No. Larkspur's death, gruesome though it may have been, weighed little on my conscience.

Instead I found myself thinking of Shien Miyu, who had already finished serving her piddling three-month sentence. Of her bonded healer, still nameless to me.

Miyu's healer had seemed quite young. Almost certainly in the first half of her twenties. Maybe even as young as the likes of Mori. I flinched to guess at how many more years she'd have to keep suffering Miyu's bond in her body, Miyu's voice and thoughts piercing her mind. And there was absolutely nothing anyone could do about it.

I suppose I could throw a fit and demand that Wist, as a preeminent member of the family, somehow insist that Miyu and her healer be separated. But physical distance would mean little in the face of their unbreakable bond.

I could learn, like Larkspur, to adroitly manipulate and torment mages. It might turn out to save my ass in times of crisis.

Could it save even one single bonded healer from a lifetime of misery? The answer was no. Not in the slightest. Not unless I committed to becoming a murderer of bonded mages.

One day Wist brought home a sack of baby watermelons, each only a tad larger than a good-sized grapefruit. I sawed one in half and hunkered down in a kitchen chair to pick out the seeds. I was much more interested in the act of dissecting the melon than in actually eating it.

Wist put something down on the center of the kitchen table. I didn't spare it a glance until she pushed it closer to me.

"Your passport," she said.

It took me several long seconds to comprehend what I was looking at. I wiped my fingers on a towel. But I still didn't reach out to touch it.

Right. Wist knew how much I wanted a passport. I'd asked Manatree to help me get one. I hadn't expected the request to go through for ages, though. Maybe not even for years.

"You helped with this?" I asked.

"I threw my weight around a little."

I eyed the uneaten watermelon, my neat pile of black seeds. "Have I been that pathetic lately?"

"Clem—"

"I already told you, I'm not depressed or anything," I said. "Just—unmotivated. You know."

"You seem sick of Osmanthus. Or at least of Osmanthus City." Wist stopped speaking for a moment. "Even if you weren't, I'd like you to come with me. If you want to. Only if you want to."

"Where?"

"A lot of places. Everywhere. I have another international tour this fall. Less than a month from now."

I picked the passport up by its corners. Didn't want to leave sugary fingerprints all over the cover.

After a moment I opened it and perused the (mostly blank) pages. Parts of it were printed with a faded version of the Osmanthian flag: black, red, and purple. Here the black came off as more of a sickly gray.

I closed the passport. My passport. I looked up across the table. Wist wore an old holey top—about as sturdy as a sheet of cobwebs—over a burly sports bra. She waited for me to respond with that infuriating patience of hers.

I thought of Larkspur's determination to make a home in the capital city. To have her own life and career rather than follow her husband everywhere and dedicate herself to healing him.

I'd never dreamt of being anyone's loyal healer. Nor did I aspire to root myself more firmly in the city, to introduce myself to more neighbors with my false name, to cultivate houseplants on my apartment balcony.

My whole adult life, I'd spent more time in prison than in any one apartment or home. Virtually all of my personal possessions were less than a year old.

I wouldn't feel much if you told me my apartment had burned to a crisp overnight. Just about the only thing I'd miss would be the one-fourth scale figure of Wist I'd been gifted by the Church of the Kraken.

I might not even spare much of a thought for all the thrift-store art I'd collected. After a relatively short absence, the only piece I could clearly picture in my head was that one garish painting of giraffes kissing. The rest were all but forgotten.

Then again, I hadn't felt much of anything lately. No regret over killing Larkspur. What else was there to be done? No regret over abandoning my private consulting work. I wouldn't starve without it;

still had plenty of mages to hobble for cash. No rage at the mageocracy. Rage was exhausting.

"If we both leave," I said, "who'll take care of your cat?"

"Mori can help."

I tapped the passport on the edge of the table. "You probably had to go up to the highest levels of government to make this happen. You probably had to drop a hint of a threat or two."

Wist made a small sound in her throat. It could've meant acknowledgment, or denial, or something altogether different.

"You never do that. You never make them feel in their bones the fact that you possess the power to do *anything you want*. Anything, truly. It's just a matter of whether you're willing to abuse that power or not. And you aren't. You've always gone out of your way to make sure no one has to be afraid of you. Even if they should be."

"That's the most you've spoken in weeks," Wist said.

I gave a slow blink. "You're accusing me of being untalkative? Too stoic? That's a new one."

"No one's accusing anyone of anything."

Wist got up. She moved to the chair right next to me. She nudged the plate of uneaten watermelon out of the way. She leaned forward to look me in the face.

A fruit fly tried to follow her over. She flicked it out the nearest window with a puff of magic, precise as a sniper.

"I didn't want to force you to come everywhere with me," she said. "Thought Osmanthus would be safer. And yes, generally I make a rule of not pressuring the government to get my way."

I put the passport down. "So what's changed?"

"Nowhere in the world is truly safe."

"Well, yeah," I scoffed. "That's not exactly breaking news. A vorpal hole could open right here in this kitchen. It could manifest in your bedroom and swallow us in our sleep. I could trip and fall down the stairs and crack my head open while you're snoozing in the bath. Or someday the Extinguishers might even get the best of you."

I felt her gaze on my right eye, the replacement.

"I phrased that wrong," she said after a thick pause.

"What were you trying to say, then?"

"We've already spent more than enough time apart."

"Have we?"

"Osmanthus is just one country. The continent is full of places so different, you wouldn't even recognize them as being part of the same world. And there are other worlds out there, beyond vorpal holes.

"You don't have to be trapped here. If you don't want to, you don't—you don't have to grow to fit the shape of Osmanthus. There are other ways to live."

"In other words," I said, "the great Kraken gets too lonely without me."

"That's not what I—"

I ducked in closer to get a good sniff of her raggedy shirt. Sometimes I wondered how it was possible to love the smell of someone's skin so much. Wist twitched in her seat as if I'd given her a chill.

"The bond isn't enough for you?" I said into her neck. "You can feel me all the time. Even from five countries away. Hell, I've learned how to go right inside your skin."

"...That's different," she muttered.

"You mean you're just too overcome by your lust for my body. Understandable."

Wist ignored my witty repartee. "Is the bond enough for you?" she asked.

Earlier in the year I would've said it was too much for me—that unbearable sensation of always being touched and seen with zero distance, zero armor. A hermit crab ripped out of its shell. A turtle stranded on its back.

Then again, the bond was the only reason I hadn't lost to Larkspur. The bond was the only reason I'd found Wist at the bottom of her well, patiently unraveling the Extinguishers' psychobomb. The bond was what I unintentionally seized at when terror closed over my head like winter lake water, when I lurched milliseconds away from toppling into a vorpal hole, when mobster mages shot at me on a deserted Bayside street.

The feeling of souls interlacing could be a bit bizarre. Distressingly umbilical. Vexingly like a two-way leash. It could also be comforting.

But it was no replacement for this—for being able to nuzzle at the warmth behind her ear. For the scent of her hair.

What is the Magebreaker for?

"I can go anywhere now," I said to Wist. I brandished my passport.

"It won't be quite that easy. But yes. More or less."

"I can use magic now, if I really want to. Your magic, anyhow."

I felt her wince. "Please warn me first. If you can."

"I can drive mages berserk. Given enough time to work on it, I can even erase their branch skills. Not that I plan on doing more of that. But if I were to make a resume, and I didn't mind people finding out about it, I could include all that stuff with confidence. Hobbling, too."

Wist craned her neck to get a better look at my face. "Planning to apply for a job somewhere?"

"There's an idea. Maybe I'll go corporate."

I could all but hear her struggling with how to convey to me that this might not be the brightest notion I'd ever had.

"I'm joking," I said. "My point is, healers aren't supposed to be able to do anything like what I do. Larkspur, too. We've both accomplished all kinds of things that all the theories say are impossible."

I slid back a bit so I could look Wist in the eye. Focusing on her had once been effortless. Now, with my vision incomplete, it always took extra strain. Of course, the strain was worth it.

"I'm starting to wonder why I've been so rock-solid convinced that bonds are unbreakable."

A very lengthy moment passed before Wist spoke in return. When she did speak, her voice came out startlingly small.

"You want to break our bond?"

"What? No! You think *that's* what I was building up to? You—"

I clamped my mouth shut before I started calling her a bunch of names she'd done nothing to deserve. Deep breaths.

Okay, maybe I'd never shown much open enthusiasm for being bonded. Maybe her reaction was perfectly understandable.

Maybe I ought to be more surprised at myself—at how the thought of removing our bond hadn't crossed my mind for a second. Even if it did turn out to be possible. But I wasn't surprised at all, somehow. The bond was as much a part of me now as my most heartfelt convictions and desires and aching.

"Wist," I said, "rest assured that you're stuck with me. I'm thinking of—remember Pine and Luka? Remember your sister's healer?"

Wist gave a tiny nod.

"I'll give Larkspur this," I said. "She was a lot more creative than me. We turned our backs on your sister's healer. We figured there was nothing more that could realistically be done for her. Larkspur—if an impossible puzzle caught her interest, she'd simply stop and figure out how to solve it. Or break it.

"What kind of Magebreaker am I if I can't work out a way to break the one spindly thread of a mage-healer bond? I don't need proof that it can be done. I don't need any historical precedents. Larkspur had none of that when she started pushing mages over the brink into berserking—when she took her husband and tied him up with his own magic."

Wist's eyes grew wider as she listened. I charged onward.

"I might take forever. I might fail. That's still better than what I've been doing to date. Sulking. Brooding in circles. Accepting the premise that some healers in Osmanthus are going to suffer for the rest of their lives because they had the ill luck to get picked by the worst kind of mage. And little old me, ready to coast for the rest of my own life on being one of the few lucky healers out there. The luckiest, really."

"If you succeed," Wist said, "you might earn a new title."

"What, something like Bondbreaker?"

"Sounds heroic."

I snorted. "You mean villainous? We'll see about that. Anyway, you can relax. It's not our bond I'll be targeting. Far from it. If I go abroad with you, we'll be spending so much time together that you just might get sick of me."

"Try me."

"Oh, I will. Besides, you need a bodyguard."

Wist cocked her head. "I do?"

"Who knows? There might be another savant healer somewhere out there who's figured out how to hijack. Puppeteer. Annex. Whatever they want to call it."

Wist pulled me into her lap. The kitchen chairs weren't exactly built for two, but I suppose we had to make do.

"Then I trust you'll protect me," she said in all seriousness.

In early fall, before I left Osmanthus for the first time in my life, Wist convinced me to peek in on my parents in the tiny town of Sweet Olive.

The glazed tile roof gleamed azure, vibrant as ever. Raucous stems of lantana grew wild around the garden gate. Clematis vines in full flower climbed a gray-weathered wooden trellis.

A small brown-white dog ran with frantic joy from one end of the garden to the other. They definitely hadn't had a dog the last time we spied on them. I fixed Wist with a look of the utmost suspicion. "Did you...?"

She shook her head. "I had no idea. I would have told you about it if I'd known. Would've made it easier to get you to come here."

True. I took her hand as we watched the dog exhaust itself. Then, startled, I raised her hand so I could look at it closer.

A Church of the Kraken keychain dangled from the blue bond thread around her wrist.

"What's this?" I asked, incredulous.

"You gave it to me."

"To annoy you," I said. "I wasn't going to force you to flaunt it in public."

"I wear it with pride," said Wist. "I think of it as a kind of engagement ring. You've got a matching keychain, don't you?"

I was momentarily rendered speechless. The little dog stopped in its tracks as if it could smell my bafflement from across the street.

The fields all around us were now rich with tall rice, midway through its transformation from summer green to pure autumn gold. Cumulus clouds stacked up all the way to the top of the sky above. Sweat stuck my shirt to my back. Wist wove her fingers through mine.

I hadn't been nearly this nervous when we visited the Shien estate.

Nowhere is truly safe.

"Fine," I said. "I give up. You win. Let's see if they're in."

Wist looked at me askance. "You want to meet their dog?"

"Not just because of the dog!"

I dragged Wist across the street before cowardice could get the best of me. The top of the wooden garden gate only came up to around Wist's nose. She'd have to duck to get in.

The brown-white dog started yapping furiously, long ears flopping like wings. Voices echoed from inside the house. I hadn't meant to squeeze Wist's hand nearly this hard. But once I started, I couldn't stop.

The door started to come open. My heart threatened to implode on the spot.

There was something a bit ridiculous about all this. Wist faithfully wearing her Church keychain, no matter how it embarrassed her. My parents' long-haired dog going absolutely mad with the thrill of seeing us apparent strangers standing there. Or maybe it was just overexcited from catching the scent of Wist's cat on our clothes.

And then there was me—the one-eyed remorseless killer, the half-hearted Magebreaker, the would-be breaker of lifelong sacred bonds—secretly hoping to faint from anxiety before my parents caught sight of me.

I'd smashed a woman to death with hundreds of statues, and still I couldn't bear the thought of how my parents might look when they saw me for the first time in eight years.

Look how much you can still feel, I thought. I wanted to laugh. Oh, how I wanted to laugh.

Wist squeezed my hand in response, even though by now I'd probably cut off her circulation. She bent to murmur something by my ear. I was too far gone to comprehend actual words, but I got the gist of what she'd meant. Even if it had nothing to do with what she'd actually said.

No matter what my parents thought of their prodigal daughter, there was a whole continent out there full of people who weren't Shiens, who weren't Asas, who weren't bound by the strictures of the Osmanthian mageocracy.

I inhaled the heavy humid air of early September. I raised my head. Stood up straight. Reminded myself not to squint.

I knew what it felt like, now, to use magic. I wasn't particularly eager to channel that power again. But I knew how it felt now, even if it wasn't my own. I could cross borders now. I could go anywhere Wist went.

Wherever we traveled, two eternal white chrysanthemums would be waiting back at the tower for our return. Even if all her other houseplants died from neglect, even if we ignored them for decades, the chrysanthemums would always be there for us.

I didn't have to fall in love with any one town or city or condo or mansion. I didn't have to belong here in Osmanthus. I didn't have to belong in any one place. Home was this hand entwined with mine. It was the miracle of having met again and again.

She'd do almost anything to avoid saying it out loud, but apparently she'd be lonesome without me. Poor Wist. Not even the constant magical entwinement of our bond was enough to satisfy her.

Guess I'd better make sure I was still there when she needed me. Guess I'd better keep sticking close by her side. Just like how we were here right now, together, hand in sweaty hand, confronting my parents' big-mouthed little dog and their dinky garden gate. Just like this.

A Note from the Author

THANK YOU SO MUCH for reading! No matter how you felt about it, please know that I truly appreciate every single rating and review.

When I published the previous book in this series (*The Lowest Healer and the Highest Mage*), I already knew I wanted to write more related novels. What I didn't know at the time was how profoundly humbling and motivating it would be to see real people—people I've never met before!—reading my work. People like you.

I've written for fun and personal satisfaction all my life, and yet I've never been so incredibly excited to write before. That excitement stayed with me the entire time I worked on *The Reverse Healer Case Files*. And I'm already bubbling over with ideas for future entries in the series.

It's all thanks to every one of you who gave Clem and Wist's story a chance. I'm so grateful to every reader who has taken the time to step into their world.

Although I'm not the fastest writer ever, I'm now alight with a whole new kind of motivation. More books will most certainly be forthcoming!

Follow my Author Page for future updates if you'd like to see more: **amazon.com/author/hiyodori**

Hope to see you again next time!

– Hiyodori

Novels by Hiyodori

The Clem & Wist Series

Book 1: The Lowest Healer and the Highest Mage

Book 2: The Reverse Healer Case Files

Prequel: No One Else Could Heal Her

Set in the World of Clem & Wist

The First and Last Demon (Standalone)